ii

INTRODUCTION

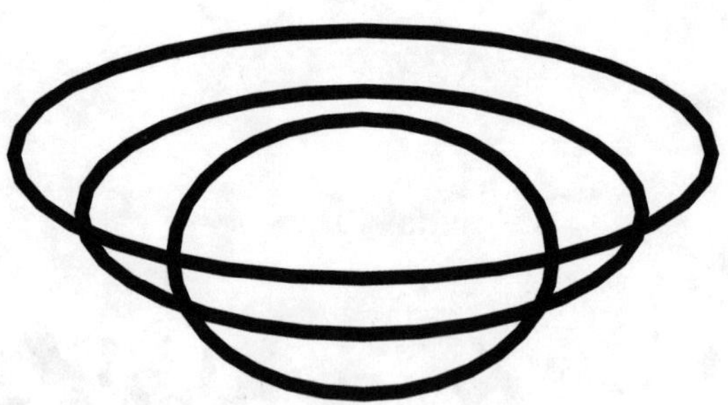

DANTE'S

Edited by
PETER CROWTHER
and
EDWARD E. KRAMER

Original Fiction by:

MICHAEL BISHOP

HARLAN ELLISON

STORM CONSTANTINE

GENE WOLFE

MAX ALLAN COLLINS

and twenty-one others

Introduction by James O'Barr

Cover Illustrations and Design By Michael Scott Cohen

Borealis is an imprint of White Wolf Publishing.

White Wolf Publishing
780 Park North Blvd.
Suite 100
Clarkston, GA 30021

DANTE'S DISCIPLES

Edited by Peter Crowther and Edward E. Kramer

Scholarly Marauders

An Introduction by James O'Barr

Dante's Disciples...When I was asked to write the introduction to this fine volume inspired by the "Inferno" cantos of Dante's *Divine Comedy* you are now holding in your hands, the title jumped out at me, forcing me think about it. It also made me wonder what the ghost of Dante Alighieri himself thought of it.

The first thing that came to mind, of all things, was Dante's Disciples as a motorcycle club. Can you imagine the terror and despair a band of leather-clad marauders in mirrorshades on Harleys roaring down a highway would cause unsuspecting vacationers or journeying salesmen plying their wares? Especially with colors on their backs flying in the wind with grim purpose? The design would be perhaps a spiral of fire heading straight up from the bottom with a ruined cityscape fanning out on both sides. Unnerving, to say the least.

Then too, I thought of a group of scholarly types reflecting on Dante's considerable achievement in the academy, writing papers, debating the finer points of obscure stanzas, obsessing endlessly over arcane fourteenth-century Italian grammar.

Both scenarios are humorous, and I even thought to draw them out, letting their images hang above my writing table as I read these many submissions. And while they are fictional in the literal sense, there is a grain of truth in them both, and our editors have done a worthy job of commissioning and gathering a group of "scholarly marauders" together under a wonderfully devilish theme.

Editors Peter Crowther and Edward E. Kramer decided to ask a number of our best known and most innovative writers in science fiction, fantasy and horror to write stories inspired by Dante's "Inferno," in other words, to use Dante as a muse in this waning, sputtering, terrifying century of ours, nearly seven hundred years after he walked the earth and committed his monumentally influential meditation on Hell, Purgatory (good Catholic that he was) and Heaven to paper.

Specifically Crowther and Kramer fixated themselves and their requests on cities which serve as "demonic gateways to the Netherworld." This too, is an achievement, because physical space, or terrain, was extremely important to Dante. He located his "Inferno" concentrically just below Jerusalem, and extended it toward the center of the earth, with various stages, or "circles" representing different gateways into the unknown as either sins or challenges. It is a mammoth allegory on the failings of humanity and atonement for sins, peopled not only with characters from Greek mythology and saints, but with Dante's contemporaries as well. It has inspired liturgical and secular literature since it was completed and issued in 1304.

Ironically, the other two parts of the *Divine Comedy*, "Purgatorio" and "Paradiso," which represent the going through the earth and coming out on its other "lighter" side, were written decades earlier, and served perhaps as a reminder that Dante himself grew more cynical as he aged.

All right, all right… I can already hear you saying, "So… who cares? What does that have to do with this anthology?" Be patient. What our editors have done so expertly is link Dante's allegory with the urban, suburban, rural and post-urban terrain we dwell and conduct our lives upon. They have asked these many contributors to concentrate on these locales that "serve as demonic gateways to the Netherworld."

To say that they have succeeded is one thing, and I'm not asking you to take my word for it. What I'm asking you to do is first and foremost read the stories contained within, and then, if you are so inclined—and I can only hope that you will be—hit the public library and check out a copy of Dante's original masterpiece and see how they did.

This is not to say that one volume depends on the other. Each of the pieces collected here stands on its own as a work of not only high originality and keen and startling vision, but also as a complementary reading of an enduring classic. The stories collected here by these scholarly marauders actually extend Dante's text and give it a contemporary context. This is no small achievement.

Just a look at the table of contents will hip you to what you will be dealing with here in terms of thought, skill and creative juice. What does it tell you? You already know the answer.

In Gene Wolfe's "Bed & Breakfast" we get the most curious read of Dante. In his particular Midwestern language, Wolfe begins amiably enough by relating his tale with the sentence: "I knew an old couple who live near Hell." He doesn't mean the small town in my state of Michigan either. His tale catches readers off guard with its informality before carrying them over the edge with his imagination, introducing demons the way one would a familiar acquaintance. He humanizes his characters—mortal or not—making them all part of a comfortable world where the supernatural and the natural blend and shapeshift, converging informally on the road to who really knows where. The story is unsettling and funny, but it unearths some profound truths.

Far from Wolfe's Midwestern heart lies Storm Constantine's Gothic punk one. Her "Return To Gehenna" is full of flash and fire. It's over the top in a way that only Constantine can be. Her characters are all, in some way or another, desperate, living on an edge of normalcy or excitement with only uncertainty as a common bond. Her tale is horror in its classic sense, drawing us in with her edgy language and gorgeous descriptions. Its sense of place is hellishly visual, and I can see myself illustrating her landscape if I close my eyes.

And then of course, there's Ellison. About his "Chatting With Annubis" there's not much to say except that it is elegant, learned and brilliant in a way that only Harlan can be. His knowledge of his subject matter, the god of the Underworld, is extensive, yet his writing, as always, is full of grace and subtlety.

The point is this: *Dante's Disciples* is a collection that when placed among the dozens of other sci-fi and horror anthologies on the shelf will reveal its achievement as not only different in an entertaining way, but in a profoundly artful way. When was the last time you heard anyone talk about either science fiction or horror as art?

When I think about it now, the images I mentioned earlier of the title *Dante's Disciples* are fitting in both cases. The authors here, led by two editors who are fine writers themselves, are truly "scholarly marauders" running rampant and challenging our notions about not only Dante's masterpiece, but about great writing as well. In an age when we regard history as merely a matter of interpretation, and the classic of literature as mere dusty remnants of a bygone age, this volume and its authors have perhaps even made history, as well as making their Muse, the sly old ghost Dante Alighieri himself, laugh and shout his approval from somewhere outside the realm of time and space, somewhere in the wind.

Perhaps I'll design the Dante's Disciples club colors myself.

—James O'Barr

August, 1995

Bed & Breakfast

by Gene Wolfe

I know an old couple who live near Hell. They have a small farm, and, to supplement the meager income it provides (and to use up its bounty of chickens, ducks, and geese, of beefsteak tomatoes, bull-nose peppers, and roastin' ears), open their spare bedrooms to paying guests. From time to time, I am one of those guests.

Dinner comes with the room if one arrives before five; and leftovers, of which there are generally enough to feed two or three more persons, will be cheerfully warmed up afterward—provided that one gets there before nine, at which hour the old woman goes to bed. After nine (and I arrived long after nine last week) guests are free to forage in the kitchen and prepare whatever they choose for themselves.

My own choices were modest: coleslaw, cold chicken, fresh bread, country butter, and buttermilk. I was just sitting down to this light repast when I heard the doorbell ring. I got up, thinking to answer it and save the old man the trouble, and heard his limping gait in the hallway. There was a murmur of voices, the old man's and someone else's; the second sounded like a deep-voiced woman's, so I remained standing.

Their conversation lasted longer than I had expected; and although I could not distinguish a single word, it seemed to me that the old man was saying no, no, no, and the woman proposing various alternatives.

At length he showed her into the kitchen; tall and tawny-haired, with a figure rather too voluptuous to be categorized as athletic, and one of those interesting faces that one calls beautiful only after at least half an hour of study; I guessed her age near thirty. The old man introduced us with rustic courtesy, told her to make herself at home, and went back to his book.

"He's very kind, isn't he?" she said. Her name was Eira something.

I concurred, calling him a very good soul indeed.

"Are you going to eat all that?" She was looking hungrily at the chicken. I assured her I would have only a piece or two. (I never sleep well after a heavy meal.) She opened the refrigerator, found the milk, and poured herself a glass that she pressed against her cheek. "I haven't any money. I might as well tell you."

That was not my affair, and I said so.

"I don't. I saw the sign, and I thought there must be a lot of work to do around such a big house, washing windows and making beds, and I'd offer to do it for food and place to sleep."

"He agreed?" I was rather surprised.

"No." She sat down and drank half her milk, seeming to pour it down her throat with no need of swallowing. "He said I could eat and stay in the empty room—they've got an empty room tonight—if nobody else comes. But if somebody does, I'll have to leave." She found a drumstick and nipped it with strong white teeth. "I'll pay them when I get the money, but naturally he didn't believe me. I don't blame him. How much is it?"

I told her, and she said it was very cheap.

"Yes," I said, "but you have to consider the situation. They're off the highway, with no way of letting people know they're here. They get a few people on their way to Hell, and a few demons going out on assignments or returning. Regulars, as they call them. Other than that," I shrugged, "eccentrics like me and passers-by like you."

"Did you say Hell?" She put down her chicken leg.

"Yes. Certainly."

"Is there a town around here called Hell?"

I shook my head. "It has been called a city, but it's a region, actually. The Infernal Empire. Hades. Gehenna, where the worm dieth not, and the fire is not quenched. You know."

She laughed, the delighted crow of a large, bored child who has been entertained at last.

I buttered a second slice of bread. The bread is always very good, but this seemed better than usual.

"Abandon hope, you who enter here. Isn't that supposed to be the sign over the door?"

"More or less," I said. "Over the gate Dante used, at any rate. It wasn't this one, so the inscription here may be quite different, if there's an inscription at all."

"You haven't been there?"

I shook my head. "Not yet."

"But you're going," she laughed again, a deep, throaty, very feminine chuckle this time, "and it's not very far."

"Three miles, I'm told, by the old county road. A little less, two perhaps, if you were to cut across the fields, which almost no one does."

"I'm not going," she said.

"Oh, but you are. So am I. Do you know what they do in Heaven?"

"Fly around playing harps?"

"There's the Celestial Choir, which sings the praises of God throughout all eternity. Everyone else beholds His face."

"That's it?" She was skeptical but amused.

"That's it. It's fine for contemplative saints. They go there, and they love it. They're the only people suited to it, and it suits them. The unbaptized go to Limbo. All the rest of us go to Hell; and for a few, this is the last stop before they arrive."

I waited for her reply, but she had a mouthful of chicken. "There are quite a number of entrances, as the ancients knew. Dodona, Ephyra, Acheron, Averno, and so forth. Dante went in through the crater of Vesuvius, or so rumor had it; to the best of my memory, he never specified the place in his poem."

"You said demons stay here."

I nodded. "If it weren't for them, the old people would have to close, I imagine."

"But you're not a demon and neither am I. Isn't it pretty dangerous for us? You certainly don't look—I don't mean to be offensive—"

"I don't look courageous." I sighed. "Nor am I. Let me concede that at once, because we need to establish it from the very beginning. I'm innately cautious, and have been accused of cowardice more than once. But don't you understand that courage has nothing to do with appearances? You must watch a great deal of television; no one would say what you did who did not. Haven't you ever seen a real hero on the news? Someone who had done something extraordinarily brave? The last one I saw looked very much like the black woman on the pancake mix used to, yet she'd run into a burning tenement to rescue three children. Not her own children, I should add."

Eira got up and poured herself a second glass of milk. "I said I didn't want to hurt your feelings, and I meant it. Just to start with, I can't afford to tick off anybody just now—I need help. I'm sorry. I really am."

"I'm not offended. I'm simply telling you the truth, that you cannot judge by appearances. One of the bravest men I've known was short and plump and inclined to be careless, not to say slovenly, about clothes and shaving and so on. A friend said that you couldn't imagine anyone less military, and he was right. Yet that fat little man had served in combat with the Navy and the Marines, and with the Israeli Army."

"But isn't it dangerous? You said you weren't brave to come here."

"In the first place, one keeps one's guard up here. There are precautions, and I take them. In the second, they're not on duty, so to speak. If they were to commit murder or set the house on fire, the old people would realize immediately who had done it and shut down; so while they are here, they're on their good behavior."

"I see." She picked up another piece of chicken. "*Nice* demons."

"Not really. But the old man tells me that they usually overpay and are, well, businesslike in their dealings. Those are the best things about evil. It generally has ready money, and doesn't expect to be trusted. There's a third reason, as well. Do you want to hear it?"

"Sure."

"Here one can discern them, and rather easily for the most part. When you've identified a demon, his ability to harm you is vastly reduced. But past this farm, identification is far more difficult; the demons vanish in the surging tide of mortal humanity that we have been taught by them to call life, and one tends to relax somewhat. Yet scarcely a week goes by in which one does not encounter a demon unaware."

"All right, what about the people on their way to Hell? They're dead, aren't they?"

"Some are, and some aren't."

"What do you mean by that?"

"Exactly what I said. Some are and some are not. It can be difficult to tell. They aren't ghosts in the conventional sense, you understand, any more than they are corpses, but the person who has left the corpse and the ghost behind."

"Would you mind if I warmed up a couple of pieces of this, and toasted some of that bread? We could share it."

I shook my head. "Not in the least, but I'm practically finished."

She rose, and I wondered whether she realized just how graceful she was. "I've got a dead brother, my brother Eric."

I said that I was sorry to hear it.

"It was a long time ago, when I was a kid. He was four, I think, and he fell off the balcony. Mother always said he was an angel now, an angel up in heaven. Do dead people really get to be angels if they're good?"

"I don't know; it's and interesting question. There's a suggestion in the book of Tobit that the Archangel Raphael is actually an ancestor of Tobit's. *Angel* means 'messenger,' as you probably know; so if God were to employ one of the blest as a messenger, he or she could be regarded as an angel, I'd think."

"Devils are fallen angels, aren't they? I mean, if they exist." She dropped three pieces of chicken into a frying pan, hesitated, and added a fourth. "So if good people really get recycled as angels, shouldn't the bad ones get to be devils or demons?"

I admitted that it seemed plausible.

She lit the stove with a kitchen match, turning the burner higher than I would have. "You sound like you come here pretty often. You must talk to them at breakfast, or whenever. You ought to know."

"Since you don't believe me, wouldn't it be logical for you to believe my admissions of ignorance?"

"No way!" She turned to face me, a forefinger upraised. "You've got to be consistent, and coming here and talking to lots of demons, you'd know."

I protested that information provided by demons could not be relied upon.

"But what do you think? What's your best guess? See, I want to find out if there's any hope for us. You said we're going to Hell, both of us, and that dude—the Italian—"

"Dante," I supplied.

"Dante says the sign over the door says don't hope. I went to a school like that for a couple years, come to think of it."

"Were they merely strict, or actually sadistic?"

"Mean. But the teachers lived better than we did—a lot better. If there's a chance of getting to be one yourself, we could always hope for that."

At that moment, we heard a knock at the front door, and her shoulders sagged. "There goes my free room. I guess I've got to be going. It was fun talking to you, it really was."

I suggested she finish her chicken first.

"Probably I should. I'll have to find another place to stay, though, and I'd like to get going before they throw me out. It's pretty late already." She hesitated. "Would you buy my wedding ring? I've got it right here." Her thumb and forefinger groped the watch pocket of her bluejeans.

I took a final bite of coleslaw and pushed back my plate. "It doesn't matter, actually, whether I want to buy your ring or not. I can't afford to. Someone in town might, perhaps."

A booming voice in the hallway drowned out the old man's; I knew that the new guest was a demon before I saw him or heard a single intelligible word.

She held up her ring, a white gold band set with two small diamonds. "I had a job, but he never let me keep anything from it and I finally caught on—if I kept waiting till I had some money or someplace to go,

I'd never get away. So I split, just walked away with nothing but the clothes I had on."

"Today?" I inquired.

"Yesterday. Last night I slept in a wrecked truck in a ditch. You probably don't believe that, but it's the truth. All night I was afraid somebody'd come to tow it away. There were furniture pads in the back, and I lay on a couple and pulled three more on top of me, and they were pretty warm."

"If you can sell your ring," I said, "there's a Holiday Inn in town. I should warn you that a great many demons stay there, just as you would expect."

The kitchen door opened. Following the old man was one of the largest I have ever seen, swag-bellied and broad-hipped; he must have stood at least six-foot-six.

"This's our kitchen." the old man told him.

"I know," the demon boomed. "I stopped off last year. Naturally you don't remember, Mr. Hopsack. But I remembered you and this wonderful place of yours. I'll scrounge around and make out all right."

The old man gave Eira a significant look and jerked his head toward the door, at which she nodded almost imperceptibly. I said, "She's going to stay with me, Len. There's plenty of room in the bed. You don't object, I trust?"

He did, of course, though he was much too diffident to say so; at last he managed, "Double's six dollars more."

I said, "Certainly," and handed him the money, at which the demon snickered.

"Just don't you let Ma find out."

When the old man had gone, the demon fished business cards from his vest pocket; I did not trouble to read the one that he handed me, knowing that nothing on it would be true. Eira read hers aloud, however, with a good simulation of admiration. "J. Gunderson Foulweather, Broker, Commodities Sales."

The demon picked up her skillet and tossed her chicken a foot into the air, catching all four pieces with remarkable dexterity. "Soap, dope, rope, or hope. If it's sold in bulk I'll buy it, and give you the best price anywhere. If it's bought in bulk, I sell it cheaper than anybody in the nation. Pleasure to meet you."

I introduced myself, pretending not to see his hand, and added, "This is Eira Mumble."

"On your way to St. Louis? Lovely city! I know it well."

I shook my head.

She said, "But you're going somewhere—home to some city—in the morning aren't you? And you've got a car. There are cars parked outside. The black Plymouth?"

My vehicle is a gray Honda Civic, and I told her so.

"If I—you know."

"Stay in my room tonight."

"Will you give me a ride in the morning? Just a ride? Let me off downtown, that's all I ask."

I do not live in St. Louis and had not intended to go there, but I said I would.

She turned to the demon. "He says this's close to Hell, and the souls of people going there stop off here, sometimes. Is that where you're going?"

His booming laugh shook the kitchen. "Not me! Davenport. Going to do a little business in feed corn if I can."

Eira looked at me as if to say, there, you see?

The demon popped the largest piece of chicken into his mouth like an hors d'oeuvre; I have never met one who did not prefer his food smoking hot. "He's giving you the straight scoop though, Eira. It is."

"How'd you do that?"

"Do what?"

"Talk around that chicken like that."

He grinned, which made him look like a portly crocodile. "Swallowed it, that's all. I'm hungry. I haven't eaten since lunch."

"Do you mind if I take the others? I was warming them up for myself, and there's more in the refrigerator."

He stood aside with a mock bow.

"You're in this together—this thing about Hell. You and him." Eira indicated me as she took the frying pan from the stove.

"We met before?" he boomed at me. I said that we had not, to the best of my memory.

"Devils—demons, are what he calls them. He says there are probably demons sleeping here right now, up on the second floor."

I put in, "I implied that, I suppose. I did not state it."

"Very likely true," the demon boomed, adding "I'm going to make coffee, if anybody wants some."

"And the—damned. They're going to Hell, but they stop off here."

He gave me a searching glance. "I've been wondering about you, to tell the truth. You seem like the type."

I declared that I was alive for the time being.

"That's the best anybody can say."

"But the cars—" Eira began.

"Some drive, some fly." He had discovered slices of ham in the refrigerator, and he slapped them into the frying pan as though he were dealing blackjack. "I used to wonder what they did with all the cars down there."

"But you don't any more." Eira was going along now, once more willing to play what she thought (or wished me to believe she thought) a rather silly game. "So you found out. What is it?"

"Nope." He pulled out one of the wooden, yellow-enameled kitchen chairs and sat down with such force I was surprised it did not break. "I quit wondering, that's all. I'll find out soon enough, or I won't. But in places this close—I guess there's others—you get four kinds of folks." He displayed thick fingers, each with a ring that looked as if it had cost a great deal more than Eira's. "There's guys that's still alive, like our friend here." He clenched one finger. "Then there's staff. You know what I mean?"

Eira looked puzzled. "Devils?"

"J. Gunderson Foulweather," the demon jerked his thumb at his vest, "doesn't call anybody racial names unless they hurt him or his, especially when there's liable to be a few eating breakfast in the morning. Staff, okay? Free angels. Some of them are business contacts of mine. They told me about this place, that's why I came the first time."

He clenched a second finger and touched third with the index finger of his free hand. "Then there's future inmates. You used a word J. Gunderson Foulweather himself wouldn't say in the presence of a lady, but since you're the only lady here, no harm done. Colonists, okay?"

"Wait a minute." Eira looked from him to me. "You both claim they stop off here."

We nodded.

"On their way to Hell. So why do they go? Why don't they just go off," she hesitated, searching for the right word, and finished weakly, "back home or something?"

The demon boomed, "You want to field this one?"

I shook my head. "Your information is superior to mine, I feel certain."

"Okay, a friend of mine was born and raised in Newark, New Jersey. You ever been to Newark?"

"No," Eira said.

"Some parts are pretty nice, but it's not, like, the hub of Creation, see? He went to France when he was twenty-two and stayed twenty years, doing jobs for American magazines around Paris. Learned to speak the language better than the natives. He's a photographer, a good one."

The demon's coffee had begun to perk. He glanced around at it, sniffed appreciatively, and turned back to us, still holding up his ring and little fingers. "Twenty years, then he goes back to Newark. J. Gunderson Foulweather doesn't stick his nose into other people's business, but I asked him the same thing you did me, how come? He said he felt like he belonged there."

Eira nodded slowly.

I said, "The staff, as you call them, might hasten the process, I imagine."

The demon appeared thoughtful. "Could be. Sometimes, anyhow." He touched the fourth and final finger. "All the first three's pretty common from what I hear. Only there's another kind you don't hardly ever see. The runaways."

Eira chewed and swallowed. "You mean people escape?"

"That's what I hear. Down at the bottom, Hell's pretty rough, you know? Higher up it's not so bad."

I put in, "That's what Dante reported, too."

"You know him? Nice guy. I never been there myself, but that's what they say. Up at the top it's not so bad, sort of like one of those country-club jails for politicians. The guys up there could jump the fence and walk out. Only they don't, because they know they'd get caught and sent down where things aren't so nice. Only every so often somebody does. So you got them, too, headed out. Anybody want coffee? I made plenty."

Long before he had reached his point, I had realized what it was; I found it difficult to speak, but managed to say that I was going up to bed and coffee would keep me awake.

"You, Eira?"

She shook her head. It was at that moment that I at last concluded that she was truly beautiful, not merely attractive in an unconventional way. "I've had all I want, really. You can have my toast for your ham."

I confess that I heaved a sigh of relief when the kitchen door swung shut behind us. As we mounted the steep, carpeted stair, the house seemed so silent that I supposed for a moment that the demon had dematerialized, or whatever it is they do. He began to whistle a hymn in the kitchen, and I looked around sharply.

She said, "He scares you, doesn't he? He scares me too. I don't know why."

I did, or believed I did, though I forbore.

"You probably thought I was going to switch—spend the night with him instead of you, but I'd rather sleep outside in your car."

I said, "Thank you," or something of the kind, and Eira took my hand; it was the first physical intimacy of any sort between us.

When we reached the top of the stair, she said, "Maybe you'd like it if I waited out here in the hall till you get undressed? I won't run away."

I shook my head. "I told you I take precautions. As long as you're in my company, those precautions protect you as well to a considerable extent. Out here alone, you'd be completely vulnerable."

I unlocked the door of my room, opened it, and switched on the light. "Come in, please. There are things in here, enough protection to keep us both safe tonight, I believe. Just don't touch them. Don't touch anything you don't understand."

"You're keeping out demons?" She was no longer laughing, I noticed.

"Unwanted guests of every sort." I endeavored to sound confident, though I have had little proof of the effectiveness of those old spells. I shut and relocked the door behind us.

"I'm going to have to go out to wash up. I'd like to take a bath."

"The Hopsacks have only two rooms with private baths, but this is one of them." I pointed. "We're old friends, you see; their son and I went to Dartmouth together, and I reserved this room in advance."

"There's one other thing. Oh, God! I don't know how to say this without sounding like a jerk."

"Your period has begun."

"I'm on the pill. It's just that I'd like to rinse out my underwear and hang it up to dry overnight, and I don't have a nightie. Would you turn off the lights in here when I'm ready to come out of the bathroom?"

"Certainly."

"If you want to look you can, but I'd rather you didn't. Maybe just that little lamp on the vanity?"

"No lights at all," I told her. "You divined very quickly that I am a man of no great courage. I wish that you exhibited equal penetration with respect to my probity. I lie only when forced to, and badly as a rule; and my word is as good as any man's. I will keep any agreement we make, whether expressed or implied, as long as you do."

"You probably want to use the bathroom too."

I told her that I would wait, and that I would undress in the bedroom while she bathed, and take my own bath afterward.

Of the many things, memories as well as speculations, that passed through my mind as I waited in our darkened bedroom for her to complete her ablutions, I shall say little here; perhaps I should say nothing. I shot the nightbolt, switched off the light and undressed. Reflecting that she might readily make away with my wallet and my watch while I bathed, I considered hiding them; but I felt certain that she would not, and to tell the truth my watch is of no great value and there was less than a hundred dollars in my wallet. Under these circumstances, it seemed wise to show I trusted her, and I resolved to do so.

In the morning I would drive her to the town in which I live or to St. Louis, as she preferred. I would give her my address and telephone number, with twenty dollars, perhaps, or even thirty. And I would tell her in a friendly fashion that if she could find no better place to stay she could stay with me whenever she chose, on tonight's terms. I speculated upon a relationship (casual and even promiscuous, if you like) that would not so much spring into being as grow by the accretion of familiarity and small kindnesses. At no time have I been the sort of man women prefer, and I am whole decades past the time in life in which love is found if it is found at all, overcautious and overintellectual, little known to the world and certainly not rich.

Yet I dreamed, alone in that dark, high-ceilinged bedroom. In men such as I, the foolish fancies of boyhood are superseded only by those of manhood, unsought visions less gaudy, perhaps, but more foolish still.

Even in these the demon's shadow fell between us; I felt certain then that she had escaped, and that he had come to take her back. I heard the flushing of the toilet, heard water run in the tub, and compelled myself to listen no more.

Though it was a cold night, the room we would share was warm. I went to the window most remote from the bathroom door, raised the shade, and stood for a time staring up at the frosty stars, then stretched myself quite naked upon the bed, thinking of many things.

I started when the bathroom door opened; I must have been half asleep.

"I'm finished," Eira said, "you can go in now." Then, "Where are you?"

My own eyes were accommodated to the darkness, as hers were not. I could make her out, white and ghostly, in the starlight; and I thrilled at the sight. "I'm here," I told her, "on the bed. It's over this way." As I left the bed and she slipped beneath its sheets and quilt, our hands touched. I recall that moment more clearly than any of the rest.

Instructed by her lack of night vision (whether real or feigned), I pulled the dangling cord of the bathroom light before I toweled myself dry. When I opened the door, half expecting to find her gone, I could see her almost as well as I had when she had emerged from the bathroom, lying upon her back, her hair a damp-darkened aureole about her head and her arms above the quilt. I circled the bed and slid in.

"Nice bath?" Then, "How do you want to do it?"

"Slowly," I said.

At which she giggled like a schoolgirl. "You're fun. You're not like him at all, are you?"

I hoped that I was not, as I told her.

"I know—do that again—who you are! You're Larry."

I was happy to hear it; I had tired of being myself a good many years ago.

"He was the smartest boy in school—in the high school that my husband and I graduated from. He was Valedictorian, and president of the chess club and the debating team and all that. Oh, my!"

"Did you go out with him?" I was curious, I confess.

"Once or twice. No, three times. Times when there was something I wanted to go to—a dance or a game—and my husband couldn't take me, or wouldn't. So I went with Larry, dropping hints, you know that I'd like to go, then saying okay when he asked. I never did this with him, though. Just with my husband, except that he wasn't my husband then. Could you sorta run your fingers inside my knees and down the backs of my legs?"

I complied. "It might be less awkward if you employed your husband's name. Use a false one if you like. Tom, Dick, or Harry would do, or even Mortimer."

"That wouldn't be him, and I don't want to say it. Aren't you going to ask if he beat me? I went to the battered women's shelter once, and they kept coming back to that. I think they wanted me to lie."

"You said that you left home yesterday, and I've seen your face. It isn't bruised."

"Now up here. He didn't. Oh, he knocked me down a couple times, but not lately. They're supposed to get drunk and beat you up."

I said that I had heard that before, though I had never understood it.

"You don't get mean when you're drunk."

"I talk too much and too loudly," I told her, "and I can't remember names, or the word I want to use. Eventually I grow ashamed and stop talking completely, and drinking as well."

"My husband used to be happy and rowdy—that was before we got married. After, it was sort of funny, because you could see him starting to get mad before he got the top off the first bottle. Isn't that funny?"

"No one can bottle emotions," I said. "We must bring them to the bottles ourselves."

"Kiss me."

We kissed. I had always thought it absurd to speak of someone enraptured by a kiss, yet I knew a happiness that I had not thought myself capable of.

"Larry was really smart, like you. Did I say that?"

I managed to nod.

"I want to lie on top of you. Just for a minute or so. Is that all right?"

I told her truthfully that I would adore it.

"You can put your hands anyplace you want, but hold me. That's good. That's nice. He was really smart, but he wasn't good at talking to people. Socially, you know? The stuff he cared about didn't matter to us, and the stuff we wanted to talk about didn't matter to him. But I let him kiss me in his dad's car, and I always danced the first and last numbers with him. Nobody cares about that now, but then they did, where we came from. Larry and my husband and I. I think if he'd kept on drinking—he'd have maybe four or five beers every night, at first—he'd have beaten me to death, and that was why he stopped. But he used to threaten. Do you know what I mean?"

I said that I might guess, but with no great confidence.

"Like he'd pick up my big knife in the kitchen, and he'd say, I could stick this right through you—in half a minute it would all be over. Or he'd talk about how you could choke somebody with a wire till she died, and while he did he'd be running the lamp cord through his fingers, back and forth. Do you like this?"

"Don't!" I said.

"I'm sorry, I thought you'd like it."

"I like it too much. Please don't. Not now."

"He'd talk about other men, how I was playing up to them. Sometimes it was men I hadn't even noticed. Like we'd go down to the pizza place, and when we got back he'd say, the big guy in the leather jacket—I saw you. He was eating it up, and you couldn't give him enough, could you? You just couldn't give him enough.

"And I wouldn't have seen anybody in a leather jacket. I'd be trying to remember who this was. But when we were in school he was never jealous of Larry, because he knew Larry was just a handy man to me. I kind of liked him the way I kind of liked the little kid next door."

"You got him to help you with your homework," I said.

"Yes, I did. How'd you know?"

"A flash of insight. I have them occasionally."

"I'd get him to help before a big quiz, too. When we were finishing up the semester, in Social Studies or whatever, I wouldn't have a clue about what she was going to ask on the test, but Larry always knew. He'd tell me half a dozen things, maybe, and five would be right there on the final. A flash of insight, like you said."

"Similar, perhaps."

"But the thing was—it was—was—"

She gulped and gasped so loudly that even I realized she was about to cry. I hugged her, perhaps the most percipient thing I have ever done.

"I wasn't going to tell you that, and I guess I'd better not or I'll bawl. I just wanted to say you're Larry, because my husband never minded him, not really, or anyhow not very much, and he'd kid around with him in those days, and sometimes Larry'd help him with his homework too."

"You're right," I told her, "I am Larry; and your name is Martha Williamson, although she was never half so beautiful as you are, and I had nearly forgotten her."

"Have you cooled down enough?"

"No. Another five minutes, possibly."

"I hope you don't get the aches. Do you really think I'm beautiful?"

I said I did, and that I could not tell her properly how lovely she was, because she would be sure I lied.

"My face is too square."

"Absolutely not! Besides, you mean rectangular, surely. It's not too rectangular, either. Any face less rectangular than yours is too square or too round."

"See? You are Larry."

"I know."

"This is what I was going to tell, if I hadn't gotten all weepy. Let me do it, and after that we'll… You know. Get together."

I nodded, and she must have sensed my nod in a movement of my shoulder, or perhaps a slight motion of the mattress. She was silent for what seemed to me half a minute, if not longer. "Kiss me, then I'll tell it."

I did.

"You remember what you said in the kitchen?"

"I said far too many things in the kitchen. I'm afraid. I tend to talk too much even when I'm sober. I'm sure I couldn't recall them all."

"It was before that awful man came in and took my room. I said the people going to Hell were dead, and you said some were and some weren't. That didn't make any sense to me till later when I thought about my husband. He was alive, but it was like something was getting a tighter hold on him all the time. Like Hell was reaching right out and grabbing him. He went on so about me looking at other men that I started really doing it. I'd see who was there, trying to figure out which one he'd say when we got home. Then he started bringing up ones that hadn't been there, people from school—this was after we were out of school and married, and I hadn't seen a lot of them in years."

I said, "I understand."

"He'd been on the football team and the softball team and run track and all that, and mostly it was those boys he'd talk about, but one time it was the shop teacher. I never even took shop."

I nodded again, I think.

"But never Larry, so Larry got to be special to me. Most of those boys, well, maybe they looked, but I never looked at them. But I'd really dated Larry, and he'd had his arms around me and even kissed me a couple of times, and I danced with him. I could remember the cologne he used to wear, and that checkered wool blazer he had. After graduation most of the boys from our school got jobs with the coal company or in the tractor plant, but Larry won a scholarship to some big school, and after that I never saw him. It was like he'd gone there and died."

"It's better now," I said, and I took her hand, just as she had taken mine going upstairs.

She misunderstood, which may have been fortunate. "It is. It really is. Having you here like this makes it better." She used my name, but I am determined not to reveal it.

"Then after we'd been married about four years, I went in the drugstore, and Larry was there waiting for a prescription for his mother. We said hi and shook hands, and talked about old times and how it was with us, and I got the stuff I'd come for and started to leave. When I got to the door, I thought Larry wouldn't be looking any more, so I stopped and looked at him.

"He was still looking at me." She gulped. "You're smart. I bet you guessed, didn't you?"

"I would have been," I said. I doubt that she heard me.

"I'll never, ever, forget that look. He wanted me so bad, just so bad it was tearing him up. My husband starved a dog to death once. His name was Ranger, and he was a blue-tick hound. They said he was good coon dog, and I guess he was. My husband had helped this man with some work, so he gave him Ranger. But my husband used to pull on Ranger's ears till he'd yelp, and finally Ranger bit his hand. He just locked Ranger up after that and wouldn't feed him any more. He'd go out in the yard and Ranger'd be in that cage hoping for him to feed him and knowing he wouldn't, and that was the way Larry looked at me in the drugstore. It brought it all back, about the dog two years before, and Larry, and lots of other things. But the thing was—thing was—"

I stroked her hand.

"He looked at me like that, and I saw it, and when I did I knew I was looking at him that very same way. That was when I decided, except that I thought I'd save up money, and write to Larry when I had enough, and see if he'd help me. Are you all right now?"

"No," I said, because at that moment I could have cut my own throat or thrown myself through the window.

"He never answered my letters, though. I talked to his mother, and he's married with two children. I like you better anyway."

Her fingers had resumed explorations. I said, "Now, if you're ready."

And we did. I felt heavy and clumsy, and it was over far too quickly; yet if I were given what no man actually is, the opportunity to experience a bit of his life a second time, I think I might well choose those moments.

"Did you like that?"

"Yes, very much indeed. Thank you."

"You're pretty old for another one, aren't you?"

"I don't know. Wait a few minutes, and we'll see."

"We could try some other way. I like you better than Larry. Have I said that?"

I said she had not, and that she had made me wonderfully happy by saying it.

"He's married, but I never wrote him. I won't lie to you much more."

"In that case, may I ask you a question?"

"Sure."

"Or two? Perhaps three?"

"Go ahead."

"You indicated that you had gone to a school, a boarding school apparently, where you were treated badly. Was it near here?"

"I don't remember about that—I don't think I said it."

"We were talking about the inscription Dante reported. I believe it ended *Lasciate ogni speranza, voi ch'entrate!* Leave all hope, you that enter!"

"I said I wouldn't lie. It's not very far, but I can't give you the name of a town you'd know, or anything like that."

"My second—"

"Don't ask anything else about the school. I won't tell you."

"All right, I won't. Someone gave your husband a hunting dog. Did your husband hunt deer? Or quail, perhaps?"

"Sometimes. I think you're right. He'd rather have had a bird dog, but the man he helped didn't raise them."

I kissed her. "You're in danger, and I think that you must know how much. I'll help you all I can. I realize how very trite this will sound, but I would give my life to save you from going back to that school, if need be."

"Kiss me again." There was a new note in her voice, I thought, and it seemed to me that it was hope.

When we parted, she asked, "Are you going to drive me to St. Louis in the morning?"

"I'll gladly take you farther. To New York or Boston or even to San Francisco. It means Saint Francis, you know."

"You think you could again?"

At her touch, I knew the answer was yes; so did she.

Afterward she asked, "What was your last question?" and I told her I had no last question.

"You said one question then it was two, then three. So what was the last one?"

"You needn't answer."

"All right, I won't. What was it?"

"I was going to ask you in what year you and your husband graduated from high school."

"You don't mind?"

I sighed. "A hundred wise men have said in various ways that love transcends the power of death; and millions of fools have supposed that they meant nothing by it. At this late hour in my life I have learned what they meant. They meant that love transcends death. They are correct."

"Did you think that salesman was really a cop? I think you did. I did, too, almost."

"No or yes, depending upon what you mean by 'cop.' But we've already talked too much about these things."

"Would you rather I'd do this?"

"Yes," I said, and meant it with every fiber of my being. "I would a thousand times rather have you do that."

After some gentle teasing about my age and inadequacies (the sort of thing that women always do, in my experience, as anticipatory vengeance for the contempt with which they expect to be treated when the sexual act is complete), we slept. In the morning, Eira wore her wedding band to breakfast, where I introduced her to the old woman as my wife, to the old man's obvious relief. The demon sat opposite me at the table, wolfing down scrambled eggs, biscuits, and home-made sausage he did not require, and from time to time winking at me in an offensive manner that I did my best to tolerate.

Outside I spoke to him in private while Eira was upstairs searching our room for the hairbrush that I had been careful to leave behind.

"If you are here to reclaim her," I told him, "I am your debtor. Thank you for waiting until morning."

He grinned like the trap he was. "Have a nice night?"

"Very."

"Swell. You folks think we don't want you to have any fun. That's not the way it is at all." He strove to stifle his native malignancy as he said this, with the result that it showed so clearly I found it difficult not to cringe. "I do you a favor, maybe you'll do me one sometime. Right?"

"Perhaps." I hedged.

He laughed. I have heard many actors try to reproduce the hollowness and cruelty of that laugh, but not one has come close. "Isn't that what keeps you coming back here? Wanting favors? You know we don't give anything away."

"I hope to learn, and to make myself a better man."

"Touching. You and Doctor Frankenstein."

I forced myself to smile. "I owed you thanks, as I said, and I do thank you. Now I'll impose upon your good nature, if I may. Two weeks. You spoke of favors, of the possibility of accommodation. I would be greatly in your debt. I am already, as I acknowledge."

Grinning, he shook his head.

"One week, then. Today is Thursday. Let us have—let me have her until next Thursday."

"Afraid not, pal."

"Three days then. I recognize that she belongs to you, but you'll have her for eternity, and she can't be an important prisoner."

"Inmate. Inmate sounds better." The demon laid his hand upon my shoulder, and I was horribly conscious of its weight and bone-crushing strength. "You think I let you jump her last night because I'm such a nice guy? You really believe that?"

"I was hoping that was the case, yes."

"Bright. Real bright. Just because I got here a little after she did, you think I was trailing her like that flea-bitten dog, and I followed her here." He sniffed, and it was precisely the sniff of a hound on the scent. The hand that held my shoulder drew me to him until I stood with the almost insuperable weight of his entire arm on my shoulders. "Listen here. I don't have to track anybody. Wherever they are, I am. See?"

"I understand."

"If I'd been after her, I'd of had her away from you as soon as I saw her. Only she's not why I came here, she's not why I'm leaving, and if I was to grab her all it would do is get me in the soup with the big boys downstairs. I don't want you either."

"I'm gratified to hear it."

"Swell. If I was to give you a promise, my solemn word of dishonor, you wouldn't think that was worth shit-paper, would you?"

"To the contrary." Although I was lying in his teeth, I persevered. "I know an angel's word is sacred, to him at least."

"Okay, then. I don't want her. You wanted a couple of weeks, and I said no deal because I'm letting you have her forever, and vice versa. You don't know what forever means, whatever you think. But I do."

"Thank you, sir," I said; and I meant it from the bottom of my soul. "Thank you very, very much."

The demon grinned and took his arm from my shoulders. "I wouldn't mess around with you or her or a single thing the two of you are going to do together, see? Word of dishonor. The boys downstairs would skin me, because you're her assignment. So be happy." He slapped me on the back so hard that he nearly knocked me down.

Still grinning, he walked around the corner of someone's camper van. I followed as quickly as I could, but he had disappeared.

Little remains to tell. I drove Eira to St. Louis, as I had promised, and she left me with a quick kiss in the parking area of the Gateway Arch; we had stopped at a McDonald's for lunch on the way, and I had scribbled my address and telephone number on a paper napkin there and watched her tuck it into a pocket of the denim shirt she wore. Since then I have had a week in which to consider my adventure, as I said on the first page of this account.

In the beginning (especially Friday night), I hoped for a telephone call or a midnight summons from my doorbell. Neither came.

On Monday I went to the library, where I perused the back issues of newspapers; and this evening, thanks to a nephew at an advertising agency, I researched the matter further, viewing twenty-five and thirty-year-old tapes of news broadcasts. The woman's name was not Eira, a name that means "snow," and the name of the husband she had slain with his own shotgun was not Tom, Dick, Harry, or even Mortimer; but

I was sure I had found her. (Fairly sure, at least.) She took her own life in jail, awaiting trial.

She had been in Hell. That, I feel, is the single solid fact, the one thing on which I can rely. But did she escape? Or was she vomited forth?

All this has been brought to a head by the card I received today in the mail. It was posted on Monday from St. Louis, and has taken a disgraceful four days to make a journey that the most cautious driver can complete in a few hours. On its front, a tall, beautiful, and astonishingly busty woman is crowding a fearful little man. The caption reads, *I want to impress one thing on you.*

Inside the card: My *body*.

Beneath that is the scrawled name *Eira*, and a telephone number. Should I call her? Dare I?

Bear in mind (as I must constantly remind myself to) that nothing the demon said can be trusted. Neither can anything that she herself said. She would have had me take her for a living woman, if she could.

Has the demon devised an excruciating torment for us both?

Or for me alone?

The telephone number is at my elbow as I write. Her card is on my desk. If I dial the number, will I be blundering into the snare, or will I have torn the snare to pieces?

Should I call her?

A final possibility remains, although I find it almost impossible to write of it.

What if I am mad?

What if Foulweather the salesman merely played up to what he assumed was an elaborate joke? What if my last conversation with him (that is to say, with the demon) was a delusion? What if Eira is in fact the living woman that almost every man in the world would take her for, save me?

She cannot have much money and may well be staying for a few days with some chance acquaintance.

Am I insane? Deluded?

Tomorrow she may be gone. One dash three one four—

Should I call?

Perhaps I may be a man of courage after all, a man who has never truly understood his own character.

Will I call her? Do I dare?

Chatting with Anubis

by Harlan Ellison

When the core drilling was halted at a depth of exactly 804.5 meters, one half mile down, Amy Guiterman and I conspired to grab Immortality by the throat and shake it till it noticed us.

My name is Wang Zicai. Ordinarily, the family name Wang—which is pronounced with the "a" in *father*, almost as if it were Wong—means "king." In my case, it means something else; it means "rushing headlong." How appropriate. Don't tell me clairvoyance doesn't run in my family... Zicai means "suicide." Half a mile down, beneath the blank Sahara, in a hidden valley that holds cupped in its eternal serenity the lake of the oasis of Siwa, I and a young woman equally as young and reckless as myself, Amy Guiterman of New York City, conspired to do a thing that would certainly cause our disgrace, if not our separate deaths.

I am writing this in Yin.

It is the lost ancestral language of the Chinese people. It was a language written between the 18th and 12th centuries before the common era. It is not only ancient, it is impossible to translate. There are only five people alive today, as I write this, who can translate this manuscript, written in the language of the Yin Dynasty that blossomed northeast along the Yellow River in a time long before the son of a carpenter is alleged to have fed multitudes with loaves and fishes, to have walked on water, to have raised the dead. I am no "rice christian." You cannot give me a meal and find me scurrying to your god. I am Buddhist, as my family has been for centuries. That I can write in Yin —which is to modern Chinese as classical Latin is to vineyard Italian —is a conundrum I choose not to answer in this document. Let he or she who one day unearths this text unscramble the oddities of chance and experience that brought me, "rushing headlong toward suicide," to this place half a mile beneath the Oasis of Siwa.

A blind thrust-fault hitherto unrecorded beneath the Mountain of the Moon had produced a cataclysmic 7.5 temblor. It had leveled villages as far away as Bir Bū Kūsā and Abu Simbel. The aerial and satellite reconnaissance from the Gulf of Sidra to the Red Sea, from the Libyan

Plateau to the Sudan, showed great fissures, herniated valleys, upthrust structures, a new world lost to human sight for thousands of years. An international team of paleoseismologists was assembled, and I was called from the Great Boneyard of the Gobi by my superiors at the Mongolian Academy of Sciences at Ulan Bator to leave my triceratops and fly to the middle of hell on earth, the great sand ocean of the Sahara, to assist in excavating and analyzing what some said would be the discovery of the age.

Some said it was the mythical Shrine of Ammon.

Some said it was the Temple of the Oracle.

Alexander the Great, at the very pinnacle of his fame, was told of the Temple, and of the all-knowing Oracle who sat there. And so he came, from the shore of Egypt down into the deep Sahara, seeking the Oracle. It is recorded: his expedition was lost, wandering hopelessly, without water and without hope. Then crows came to lead them down through the Mountain of the Moon, down to a hidden valley without name, to the lake of the Oasis of Siwa, and at its center… the temple, the Shrine of Ammon. It was so recorded. And one thing more. In a small and dark chamber roofed with palm logs, the Egyptian priests told Alexander a thing that affected him for the rest of his life. It is not recorded what he was told. And never again, we have always been led to believe, has the Shrine of Ammon been seen by civilized man or civilized woman.

Now, Amy Guiterman and I, she from the Brooklyn Museum and I an honored graduate of Beijing University, together we had followed Alexander's route from Paraetonium to Siwah to here, hundreds of kilometers beyond human thought or action, half a mile down, where the gigantic claw diggers had ceased their abrading, the two of us with simple pick and shovel, standing on the last thin layer of compacted dirt and rock that roofed whatever great shadowy structure lay beneath us, a shadow picked up by the most advanced deep-resonance-response readings, verified on-site by proton free-precession magnetometry and ground-penetrating radar brought in from the Sandia National Laboratory in Albuquerque, New Mexico, in the United States.

Something large lay just beneath our feet.

And tomorrow, at sunrise, the team would assemble to break through and share the discovery, whatever it might be.

But I had had knowledge of Amy Guiterman's body, and she was as reckless as I, rushing headlong toward suicide, and in a moment of foolishness, a moment that should have passed but did not, we sneaked out of camp and went to the site and lowered ourselves, taking with us nylon rope and crampons, powerful electric torches and small recording devices, trowel and whisk broom, cameras and carabiners. A pick and a shovel. I offer no excuse. We were young, we were reckless, we were smitten with each other, and we behaved like naughty children. What happened should not have happened.

We broke through the final alluvial layer and swept out the broken pieces. We stood atop a ceiling of fitted stones, basalt or even marble, I could not tell immediately. I knew they were not granite, that much I did know. There were seams. Using the pick, I prised loose the ancient and concretized mortar. It went much more quickly and easily than I would have thought, but then, I'm used to digging for bones, not for buildings. I managed to chock the large set-stone in place with wooden wedges, until I had guttered the perimeter fully. Then, inching the toe of the pick into the fissure, I began levering the stone up, sliding the wedges deeper to keep the huge block from slipping back. And finally, though the block was at least sixty or seventy centimeters thick, we were able to tilt it up and, bracing our backs against the opposite side of the hole we had dug at the bottom of the core pit, we were able to use our strong young legs to force it back and away, beyond the balance point; and it fell away with a crash.

A great wind escaped the aperture that had housed the stone. A great wind that twisted up from below in a dark swirl that we could actually see. Amy Guiterman gave a little sound of fear and startlement. So did I. Then she said, "They would have used great amounts of charcoal to set these limestone blocks in place," and I learned from her that they were not marble, neither were they basalt.

We showed each other our bravery by dangling our feet through the opening, sitting at the edge and leaning over to catch the wind. It smelled *sweet*. Not a smell I had ever known before. But certainly not stagnant. Not corrupt. Sweet as a washed face, sweet as chilled fruit. Then we lit our torches and swept the beams below.

We sat just above the ceiling of a great chamber. Neither pyramid nor mausoleum, it seemed to be an immense hall filled with enormous statues of pharaohs and beast-headed gods and creatures with neither animal nor human shape… and all of these statues gigantic. Perhaps one hundred times life-size.

Directly beneath us was the noble head of a time-lost ruler, wearing the *nemes* headdress and the royal ritual beard. Where our digging had dropped shards of rock, the shining yellow surface of the statue had been chipped, and a darker material showed through. "Diorite," Amy Guiterman said.

"Covered with gold. Pure gold. Lapis lazuli, turquoise, garnets, rubies—the headdress is made of thousands of gems, all precisely cut… do you see?"

But I was lowering myself. Having cinched my climbing rope around the excised block, I was already shinnying down the cord to stand on the first ledge I could manage, the empty place between the placid hands of the pharaoh that lay on the golden knees. I heard Amy Guiterman scrambling down behind and above me.

Then the wind rose again, suddenly, shrieking up and around me like a monsoon, and the rope was ripped from my hands, and my torch was blown away, and I was thrown back and something sharp caught at the back of my shirt and I wrenched forward to fall on my stomach and I felt the cold of that wind on my bare back. And everything was dark.

Then I felt cold hands on me. All over me. Reaching, touching, probing me, as if I were a cut of sliced meat lying on the counter. Above me I heard Amy Guiterman shrieking. I felt the halves of my ripped shirt torn from my body, and then my kerchief, and then my boots, and then my stockings, and then my watch and glasses.

I struggled to my feet and took a position, ready to make an empassing or killing strike. I was no cinema action hero, but whatever was there plucking at me would have to take my life despite I fought for it!

Then, from below, light began to rise. Great light, the brightest light I've ever seen, like a shimmering fog. And as it rose, I could see that the mist that filled the great chamber beneath us was trying to reach us, to touch us, to feel us with hands of ephemeral chilling ghostliness. Dead hands. Hands of beings and men who might never have been or who, having been, were denied their lives. They reached, they sought, they implored.

And rising from the mist, with a howl, Anubis.

God of the dead, jackal-headed conductor of souls. Opener of the road to the afterlife. Embalmer of Osiris, Lord of the mummy wrappings, ruler of the dark passageways, watcher at the neverending funeral. Anubis came, and we were left, suddenly, ashamed and alone, the American girl and I, who had acted rashly as do all those who flee toward their own destruction.

But he did not kill us, did not take us. How could he… am I not writing this for some never-to-be-known reader to find? He roared yet again, and the hands of the seekers drew back, reluctantly, like whipped curs into kennels, and there in the soft golden light reflected from the icon of a pharaoh dead and gone so long that no memory exists even of his name, there in the space half a mile down, the great god Anubis spoke to us.

At first, he thought we were "the great conqueror" come again. No,

I told him, not Alexander. And the great god laughed with a terrible thin laugh that brought to mind paper cuts and the slicing of eyeballs. No, of course not that one, said the great god, for did I not reveal to him the great secret? Why should he ever return? Why should he not flee as fast as his great army could carry him, and never return? And Anubis laughed.

I was young and I was foolish, and I asked the jackal-headed god to tell *me* the great secret. If I was to perish here, at least I could carry to the afterlife a great wisdom.

Anubis looked through me.

Do you know why I guard this tomb?

I said that I did not know, but that perhaps it was to protect the wisdom of the Oracle, to keep hidden the great secret of the Shrine of Ammon that had been given to Alexander.

And Anubis laughed the more. Vicious laughter that made me wish I had never grown skin or taken air into my lungs.

This is not the Shrine of Ammon, he said. Later they may have said it was, but this is what it has always been, the tomb of the Most Accursed One. The Defiler. The Nemesis. The Killer of the dream that lasted twice six thousand years. I guard this tomb to deny him entrance to the afterlife.

And I guard it to pass on the great secret.

"Then you don't plan to kill us?" I asked. Behind me I heard Amy Guiterman snort with disbelief that I, a graduate of Beijing University, could ask such an imbecile question. Anubis looked through me again, and said no, I don't have to do that. It is not my job. And then, with no prompting at all, he told me, and he told Amy Guiterman from the Brooklyn Museum, he told us the great secret that had lain beneath the sands since the days of Alexander. And then he told us whose tomb it was. And then he vanished into the mist. And then we climbed back out, hand over hand, because our ropes were gone, and my clothes were gone, and Amy Guiterman's pack and supplies were gone, but we still had our lives.

At least for the moment.

I write this now, in Yin, and I set down the great secret in its every particular. All parts of it, and the three colors, and the special names, and the pacing. It's all here, for whoever finds it, because the tomb is gone again. Temblor or jackal-god, I cannot say. But if today, as opposed to last night, you seek that shadow beneath the sand, you will find emptiness.

Now we go our separate ways, Amy Guiterman and I. She to her destiny, and I to mine. It will not be long in finding us. At the height of his power, soon after visiting the Temple of the Oracle, where he was told something that affected him for the rest of his life, Alexander the Great died of a mosquito bite. It is said. Alexander the Great died of an overdose of drink and debauchery. It is said. Alexander the Great died of murder, he was poisoned. It is said. Alexander the Great died of a prolonged, nameless fever; of pneumonia; of typhus; of septicemia; of typhoid; of eating off tin plates; of malaria. It is said. Alexander was a bold and energetic king at the peak of his powers, it is written, but during his last months in Babylon, for no reason anyone has ever been able to explain satisfactorily, he took to heavy drinking and nightly debauches… and then the fever came for him.

A mosquito. It is said.

No one will bother to say what has taken me. Or Amy Guiterman. We are insignificant. But we know the great secret.

Anubis likes to chat. The jackal-headed one has no secrets he chooses to keep. He'll tell it all. Secrecy is not his job. Revenge is his job. Anubis guards the tomb, and eon by eon makes revenge for his fellow gods.

The tomb is the final resting place of the one who killed the gods. When belief in the gods vanishes, when the worshippers of the gods turn away their faces, then the gods themselves vanish. Like the mist that climbs and implores, they go. And the one who lies encrypted there, guarded by the lord of the funeral, is the one who brought the world to forget Isis and Osiris and Horus and Anubis. He is the one who opened the sea, and the one who wandered in the desert. He is the one who went to the mountaintop, and he is the one who brought back the word of yet another god. He is Moses, and for Anubis revenge is not only sweet, it is everlasting. Moses—denied both Heaven and Hell—will never rest in the Afterlife. Revenge without pity has doomed him to eternal exclusion, buried in the sepulcher of the gods he killed.

I sink this now, in an unmarked meter of dirt, at a respectable depth; and I go my way, bearing the great secret, no longer needing to "rush headlong," as I have already committed what suicide is necessary. I go my way, for however long I have, leaving only this warning for anyone who may yet seek the lost Shrine of Ammon. In the words of Amy Guiterman of New York City, spoken to a jackal-headed deity, "I've got to tell you, Anubis, you are one *tough* grader."

The Ripening Sweetness of Late Afternoon

by Douglas Clegg

Sunland City was the last place in the world Jesus was ever going to come looking for Roy Shadiak.

He returned to his hometown in his fortieth year, after he felt he could never again sell Jesus to the rabble. Something within him had been eating him up for years. His love for life had long ago dried up, and then so had his marriage and his bitter understanding of how God operated in the world. He'd gotten off the bus out at the flats and brushed off the boredom of a long trip down infinite highways. He stood awhile beside the canals and watched the gators as they lay still as death in the muddy shallows. He'd been wearing his ice cream suit for the trip because it was what his mother liked him to wear and because it was the only suit of his that still fit him. And it fit Sunland City, with its canals and palmettos and merciless sunshine. It was a small town, the City was, and they would think him mad to arrive on the noon bus in anything other than creamy white. He would walk down Hispaniola Street and make a detour into the Flamingo for a double-shot vodka. The boys in there, they'd see him, maybe recognize him, maybe the whores would, too, and call him the King, and he'd tell them all about how he was back for good. He'd tell them that he didn't care what the hell happened to Susie and the brats and that doctor she took up with. He'd tell them he was going to open a movie theater or manage the A&P or open a boat-rental business. He'd tell them that anything you really needed, and all you could depend on in this life, you could find in your own backyard. Didn't need God. Nobody needed God.

God was like the phone company: You paid your bill, and sometimes you got cut off anyway. Sometimes, if you changed your way of thinking, you just did without a phone. Sometimes you switched companies.

Oh, but he still needed God. Within his secret self, he had to admit it. Roy Shadiak still needed to know that he could save at least one soul in the world. His feet ached in his shoes. He'd only brought one suitcase. He had just walked out on Susie. It was in his blood to walk. His father had walked, and his grandfather had walked. They probably got tired of Jesus and all the damn charity, too. Even Frankie had walked, as best he could. All leaving before they got left. Roy had blisters on the bottoms of his feet, but still he walked. He passed beneath the Lovers' Bridge, and the Bridge of Sighs with its hanging vines and parrot cages. He walked along the muddy bank of the north canal, knowing that he could close his eyes and still find his way to Hispaniola Street. All the street names were like that: Spanish, or a mix of Indian and slave, names like Occala and Gitchie and Corona del Mar. Sunland City was a many-flavored thing, but in name only; for its inhabitants would've been pale and translucent as maggots if not for the sulfurous sun. All the canals were thick with lilies, and snapping turtles lounged across the rock islets. The water was murky and stank, but beautiful pure-white swans cut across the calm surface as if to belie the muck of this life. Roy saw three men, old-timers with their fresh-rolled cigarillos and panama hats, on a punt. He waved to them, but they didn't notice him, for they were old and half-blind.

After climbing the steep steps up to the street level again, he was surprised to observe the stillness of clay-baked Sunland City. As a boy, it had always seemed to him like an Italian water town, not precisely a Venice and something less than a Naples, thrust into the Gulf Coast like a conqueror's flag.

But now it seemed as ancient as any dying European citadel: It looked as if the conqueror, having pillaged and raped, had left a wake of buildings and archways and space. It had been a lively seaport once. It was now a vacant conch. The hurricane that had torn through it the previous year had not touched a building, but it had cleaned the streets of any evidence of life. When he found the Flamingo, he kissed the first girl he set eyes on, a wench in the first degree with a beer in one hand with which to wipe off that same kiss. A teenage boy in a letterman's jacket sat two stools over. The boy turned and stared at him for a good long while before saying anything. Then suddenly, as if possessed, the boy shouted, "Holy shit, you're King!"

"And you, my friend, are underage."

The boy stood up—he was tall and gangly, with a mop of curly blond hair, a face of dimming acne and cheek of tan. He thrust his hand out. "Billy Wright. *I* swim, too."

"Oh."

"But you're like a legend. A fucking legend. The King. King Shadiak."

"Am I?"

"You beat out every team to Daytona Beach. You beat out

fucking Houston."

"Did I? Well, it was a long time before you were born."

"You ever see the display they got on you?" Billy pressed his palms flat against the air. "The glass cabinet in the front hall, near the locker room. Seven gold trophies. Seven! Pictures! Your goggles, too. Your fucking goggles, man."

"If they do all that for you at your high school, you should really be something, shouldn't you?"

Billy made a thumbs-up sign. "Fucking-A. You *are* something, man."

"I'm nothing," Roy said, downing his drink and slamming the glass on the bar for another. "No, make that: I'm fucking nothing, man."

"What you been doin' all this time, man?" Billy asked, apparently oblivious to anything short of his own cries of adoration.

"Selling Jesus."

"Who'd you sell him to?"

Roy laughed. "You're all right, boy. You are all right."

"Thanks," Billy said, then glanced at his watch. "I better get going. Curfew soon. Listen, you come by and see me if you got car trouble. I work at night at Jack Thompson's. You know him? I can fix any problem with any car. I'm not the King of anything like you, but I may be the Prince of Mechanics."

"Why would anyone around here care if his car got fixed?"

The boy laughed. "That's a good one."

When Roy arrived at his mother's house a half-hour later, he was three beers short of a dozen.

"The great King comes home." His mother's voice was flat, like the land. "You had to get drunk before you saw me. And you couldn't shave for me, could you?" Alice Shadiak asked. His mother wore khaki slacks and a white blouse. She had lost some weight over the past few years, and seemed whiter, as if the sun had bleached her bones right through her skin. A sun-visor cap protected her face. She had seen him from the kitchen window, and had come to greet him on the porch. "I suppose you need a place to stay."

"I can stay downtown."

"With your whores?"

"They all missed curfew, apparently," he attempted a light note. "Must've heard I was on my way."

His mother sighed as if a great weight had just been given her. "Some man of God you turned out to be. I just wish you'd've called ahead. I'd've had Louise fix up your old room. Lloyd's in Sherry's old room. The house is a mess. Don't act like such a foreigner, Roy, for god's sakes. Give me a hug, would you?" She moved forward. In all his life, he could count the times she'd hugged him. But he knew he needed to change, somehow. He had not hit on precisely how. He would have to listen to his own instincts and then disobey them to find out how he might change. He held his mother, smelled her saltwater hair. When he let go, she said, "Susie called. She wants to know when you're going to forgive her."

"Never," Roy said.

"What are you going to do?" Alice asked.

Roy Shadiak said, "Mama, I had a dream. It came to me one night. A voice said—"

His mother interrupted. "Was it Jesus?"

"It was just a voice. It said, 'Set your place at the table.' Something's trying to come through me. I know it. I can feel it. Like a revelation."

"It was just a dream," Alice said, sounding troubled. "What could it mean? Oh, Roy, you're vexing yourself over nothing."

"This is my table. Sunland City. I have to set my place here," Roy said. Then he began weeping. His mother held him, but not too close.

"A man as big as you shouldn't be crying."

"It's all I have left," he said, drying his tears on the cuffs of his shirt. "You live your life and make a few mistakes, but you lose everything anyway. Everything I ever had, it all came from here. Everything I ever *was*."

Alice Shadiak took a good hard look at her son and slapped him with the back of her hand. "You did it to yourself, what you are. Who you are. Don't blame me or your father or anyone else. All this big-world talk and wife-leaving and crying. Don't think just because it's been twenty-two years that you can just walk back in here and pretend none of it ever happened." She raised her fist, not at him, but at the sky, the open sky that was colored the most glorious blue with cloud striations across its curved spine. "No God who takes my boys away from me is welcome in my house."

"I told you, I don't work for God anymore," Roy said. He went past her, into the house. He found the guest bedroom cluttered, but pushed aside his mother's sewing and the stacks of magazines on the bed. He wrapped the quilt around his shoulders, and fell asleep in his suit.

In the morning, he took a milk crate down to the town center. He set it down and stood up on it just like he had in other towns when he had preached the gospel. Folks passed by on their ways to work, and barely noticed him. He spread his arms out as if measuring Sunland City and cried out, "I am King Shadiak, and I have come here to atone for the murders of my brother Frankie and his friend, Kip Renner!"

A woman turned about as she stepped; a laborer in a broad straw hat glanced up from the curb where he sat with a coffee cup; an old Ford pickup slowed as its owner rolled down the window to hear.

As Roy Shadiak spoke, others gathered around him, the older crowd, mostly, the crowd that knew him, the people who had been there when he'd drowned the two boys at the public swimming pool over on Hispaniola Street, down near the Esso station, by the railroad tracks.

"No need, Roy," one of the men called out. "We don't need your kind of atonement. We been fine all these years without it."

"That's right," several people added, and others nodded without uttering a word.

"No," Roy said, pressing the flat of his hand against the air in front of him as if it were an invisible wall. "All these years I've squandered my life in service to others. I owe Sunland City an atonement."

"You want us to crucify you, King?" Someone laughed.

Others chuckled more quietly.

"That is exactly what I want," Roy Shadiak said. "Two atonements, two murders."

A woman in the crowd shouted, "Two atonements for two murders!"

"Two atonements! Two murders!" Others began chanting.

"Frankie Shadiak!" Roy shouted. "Kip Renner!"

"Two atonements! Two murders!" The crowd became familiar now — Roy saw Ellen Mawbry from tenth grade, Willy Potter from the corner store, the entire Forster clan, the Rogers, the Sayres, the Blankenships, the Fowlers—as he chanted and as they chanted, as the day loped forward, they all gathered—labor stopped, activity ceased, schools let out for a spontaneous holiday, until the town center of Sunland City was a sea of the familiar and the new. All turned out for the returning hero, their King, who was passing among them to offer his life for their suffering.

"Two atonements!" They cried as if their voices would reach beyond that Florida sky.

It was what Roy had expected from a town that God had turned his back on twenty-three years before.

And then Helen Renner, her hair gone white, stepped out of the crowd, toward him. She wiped her hands on her apron, as if she'd just finished baking, and went and stood at the foot of the milk crate.

Roy crouched down and took her face in his hands.

"Don't do it," she said. "Roy Shadiak, don't you do it. Neither one of them was worth it. We all let it happen. We're all responsible. It may not even fix anything, Roy. There's no guarantee."

He kissed her on her forehead. "I've got to. It's something inside of me that needs room to grow, and I've been killing it all these years. I've been killing every one of you, too. Two atonements," he repeated, "for two murders."

Joe Fowler was a crackerjack carpenter. He and his assistant, Jaspar, were at the Shadiak house within an hour of Roy's leave-taking of the makeshift podium. He stood on the porch in paint-spattered overalls, his khaki hat in his hands, looking through the screen door at Roy's mother. "We got some railroad ties from out the Yard," he said. "They got pitch on 'em, but I think they gonna be just fine for the job." His voice quavered. "We'd like to offer our services, Alice."

Alice Shadiak stood like stone. "You and your kind can get off my porch. I don't mean to lose two sons in this lifetime."

Roy came up behind her, touching her gently on the shoulder. "Mama, it's got to be done."

"Where is it written? Where?"

"On my soul," he said.

"Our kind has no soul," she said, pulling away from him. "I don't need God's forgiveness on my house. I don't want sweet Jesus' tears."

"It's Jesus that keeps you here."

"He doesn't even look on us, Roy," his mother said. "He doesn't even come to our churches. What does it matter? Does anyone in Sunland really believe there's a Jesus waiting to shine his light on us?"

"That's because of me."

"It's because your brother and his sick little friend were unnatural and perverted, and God cared more for them than for decency or nature or for any of us. I don't mind burning for that, Roy. I don't mind that sacrifice."

"I do," Roy said. "I saw Jesus out in the fields up north, and in the alleys of the fallen. Nobody else did. And you know why? Because Jesus was laughing at me; he was showing me that he was not going to be mine. He was going to belong to every fool who walked this earth."

Joe Fowler nudged the screen door open and stepped inside. "He's right, Alice. We ain't had Jesus or God for all this time, only those… things." He shivered a little, as if remembering a nightmare. In a softer voice, he said, "I'm getting tired of this life."

"I would advise you to get out of the light, Joe," Alice Shadiak said, sounding like the retired schoolteacher that she was. "I heard about your little Nadine."

All of them were silent for a moment, and Roy thought for a second he heard the cry of some hawk as it located its prey.

"Your boy knows what he's doing," Joe said, spreading his hands like he could convince her with gestures. Still, he glanced briefly up at the empty sky. "We can't keep on like this." Then Joe grinned, but Roy could tell he was tense. "I'm prouder of you now, King, than I was when you won all those ribbons at the championship. Why don't we get on with this business?"

"Yes," Roy said, feeling an ache in his heart for Susie and the kids, but not wanting to retrace his steps. He glanced out on the porch, and beyond, to Joe's truck. "That's a sturdy-looking piece of wood, Joe."

"From the old Tuskegee route, before the tracks got tore up. We're going to have to balance them good. That's why I brought Jaspar here," he nodded toward his assistant who stood, mutely, on the porch. "We can get this going now, you like."

"Why wait?" Roy shrugged.

His mother retreated into the shadowy parlor. She called to him, but Roy did not respond.

Jaspar suddenly pointed to the sky and made a rasping sound in his throat.

Calmly, Joe Fowler said, "Come on in, Jasp, come on, it's okay, you'll make it."

As if too frightened to move, Jaspar stood there, sweat shining on his face. He stared up at the sky, pointing and shaking.

"Jaspar," Joe opened the screen door slightly, beckoning with his hand.

Roy shoved Joe out of the way, and ran out to the porch. He grabbed the young man by his waist.

The cry grew louder as the great bird in the sky dropped, blackening out the sun for a moment.

The smell was the worst thing, because they got it on their talons sometimes, from an earlier victim; that sweet, awful stink that overrode all other senses.

Roy hadn't slept a night without remembering that smell. He couldn't get it out of his head for the rest of the afternoon.

"Where do they take them?" Roy asked.

Joe, who was still jittery, helped himself to the vodka. "Down to the shore. There's at least a hundred out there. And the rotting seaweed, too, and the flies, all the crawling things… it turned my stomach when I had to go down there to try and find Nadine."

"That's where it has to be."

"No, King. No. I won't go down there, no matter if it's midnight or midday."

"But how can you abandon her?"

Joe turned his face toward his glass. "She ain't her. I saw her. I risked my sanity, and I saw her. It ain't her. It's a It, not a little girl. I told her not to go out between two and four. All of us know about the curfew. All of us know to stay inside. And you," Joe shook his head. He raised his glass, as if to toast Roy. "You're the luckiest son-of-a-bitch alive; you can get out, and instead, you decide to come back. You fucked up once, King, you don't need to keep on doing it."

"How many are left?"

"First, have a drink." Joe pushed the glass across the kitchen table.

Roy picked it up. Downed the remainder. Set the glass down. "How many?"

"Twenty-six in one piece. The rest in as many as they leave us in. Some morning, you take a walk down there. Only, if any of them calls your name, you just run, you hear? You don't want to know who it is, believe you me."

Roy reached across the table and pressed his hand against Joe's shoulder. "That's where we need to do it."

"I ain't never going down there again."

"You'd rather all this continued?"

"Than go down there? You're damned right."

"I'll find someone else, then."

Joe stood up, pushing his chair back. He said nothing. He stomped out of the kitchen and went to sit with Jaspar and Alice.

Roy drank some more vodka. He glanced out the bay window. On the roof, two houses over, three of them had a woman pressed against the curved Spanish tile. Their wings had folded against their bodies, and they were digging with their talons into the soft flesh of her stomach.

He was sure that one of them saw him spying, and grinned.

That night, he found the teenager working at Jack Thompson's garage on the south corner of Hattatonquee Plaza.

"Billy?" Roy asked as he stood beneath a streetlamp.

The boy dropped the wrench he was using and bounded out to the sidewalk. "Hey, it's the King. How you doin'?" He snapped his fingers several times as if he was nervous.

"I'm doing just fine. And yourself?"

"Hey, any day you get through the afternoon here's a good day. So I heard you're going to try something."

Roy nodded. "Let's go for a walk, Billy. Can you get off work?"

"Sure, let me just tell Mr. Thompson, okay?"

Several minutes later, they were walking down along Hispaniola Street towards Upper Street. Roy had been doing all the talking, ending with, "And that's where you come in. Joe'll give me the ties, but I need someone to help."

"I don't know," Billy said. "You ever see how big those suckers are?"

"Yep. But we won't be out that late. We can do this at nine or ten in the morning. Hell, if you want, we can probably do it tonight."

"I heard the beach is really a bad scene. My dad got taken down there. I heard this guy at school say that they're like cracked eggs, or they're all ripped up, only not quite dead yet. If I think about it too much I get sick."

"It must be strange."

"What's that?"

"Well, you grew up in it. You never knew what the world was like before. You don't know what the rest of the world is like."

Billy stopped walking. "I thought it happened everywhere."

Roy shook his head. "Only here. Because of what I did."

"I don't believe you."

"Other places, you can walk around any time of the day or night and those things don't attack. Honest. When I was the King here, I used to skip classes at two and take off with my friends to Edgewater to the McDonald's. Didn't anyone tell you? Not even your dad?"

Billy shook his head. "Well, if God did this, why didn't he do it just to you?"

Roy shrugged. "Who knows? It may not even have been God. I've never seen Jesus. Maybe there's just those things. The way I figured it, it's not just because of me killing those boys. It's because everybody here thought it was okay, no big deal. Nobody made a fuss."

"You loved your brother?"

"I did, but I didn't know it then. I wanted him and his friend to go to hell, back then. I was the King back then. I thought I was God, I guess."

They came to the end of Upper Street, which stopped at the slight dune overlooking the stretch of flat beach.

The full moon shone across the glassy sea. The sand itself glowed an unearthly green from the diatoms that had burst from the waves.

On the sand, the shadow of slow, pained movement as a hundred or more mangled, half-eaten Sunlanders struggled to die in a corner of the earth where there was no death.

Billy said, "I saw one of them up close. When they got my dad. She had long hair, and her eyes were silver. She had the fur, and the claws and all, and her wings, like a pterodactyl. But there was something in her face that was almost human. Even when she tore my dad's throat open, she looked kind of like a girl. Boy," he shivered. "I'm sure glad I'm up here and not down there. Down there looks like hell."

Roy said, "From down there, up here looks like hell, too. And it won't just end by itself."

Billy seemed to understand. "You swear you're not lying about what everywhere else is like?"

"I swear."

"Okay. Let's go down there. But in the morning. After the sun's up. I still can't believe it." Billy cocked his head to the side, looking from the moon to the sand to the sea to Roy. "I'm standing here with the King."

"Is that enough for you?"

"I guess. I got laid once, and that was enough. Standing here with you, that's enough." Billy pointed out someone, perhaps a woman, trying to stand up by pushing herself against a mass of writhing bodies, but she fell each time she made the attempt. "When I was little, we used to come down here and throw stones at some of them. But it's kind of sad, ain't it? Some of the guys I used to throw stones with, they're down there now. Someday I'm going to be down there, too, and if there are any girls left, they'll have babies, and they'll start throwing stones at me, too. Where does it end?"

"Now," Roy said. "In the morning. You and me and a couple of railroad ties."

"There's going to be lots of pain though, huh?"

"There's always pain. You either get it over with quick, or it takes a lifetime."

Billy rubbed his hands over his eyes. "I'm not crying or nothing."

"I know."

"I just want to get my head straight for this. I mean, we're both going to hurt, huh?"

"You don't have to. I do. I can find someone else to help."

"No. We'll do it. Then I'll be a legend, too, huh? Maybe that's enough.

We just drag those ties down there and set it up. One way or another, we all end up on that beach, anyway, huh?"

It was easier said than done. They had to borrow Joe's truck to get the railroad ties to the beach, which was the easy part. Lugging those enormous sticks across the burning sand, sliding them across the bodies, the faces… it made a mile on a Thursday morning at nine o'clock seem like forty or more. By the time they'd arrived at a clearing, Billy was too exhausted to speak. When he finally did, he pointed back at Sunland. "Look."

Roy, whose body was soaked, his ice cream suit sticking to his skin, glanced up.

There on the edge of Upper Street and Beach Boulevard was the entire town, lined up as if to watch some elegant ocean liner pass by. The chanting began later. At first the words were indistinct. Gradually, the boy and the man could hear them clearly: *Two murders, two atonements.*

"Roy?" Billy asked.

"Yes?"

"I'm scared. I'm really scared."

"It's okay. I'm here. I'll go first."

"No. I want to go first. I want you to do me first. I might run if I go last. I can't do it right if I go last—I mean, I'll fuck it up somehow."

"All right." Roy went over and put his arm across Billy's shoulder. "Don't be afraid, son. When this is over, it'll all change again. Atonement works like that."

"I wasn't even born when you did it. Why shouldn't one of them do it with you? Why me?"

"Now, Billy, don't be afraid. If they could've done it before, they would've. I think Jesus brought you and me together for this."

"I don't even know Jesus."

"You will. Come on," Roy lifted up one of the smaller spikes and placed its end against Billy's wrist. "This one'll fit. See? It's not so bad. It's just a nail. And all a nail can do is set something in place. It's so you won't fall. You don't want to fall, do you?"

"Tell me again how you'll do it?"

"Oh, well, I set this rope up around my hand so I can keep it up like this… and then I press the pointed part of the nail against my hand and pull on the rope. My hand goes back in place, see? Like this, only I have to push a little, too."

"You won't leave me, will you?"

"No, I won't. I'm the King, and you're the Prince, remember? I won't abandon you. Now why don't you just lie down on it, like that, and your hand, see? It's going to pinch a little, but just pretend it's one of those things with the claws. Just pretend you won't scream because you know they like it when someone screams. Okay? Billy, don't be afraid, don't be afraid...." Roy spoke soothingly as he drove the spikes through Billy's wrists.

By two, they'd both gotten used to the pain of the crosses. Roy tried to turn his head toward Billy to see how he was holding up, but his neck was too stiff and he could not.

"When's it going to happen?" Billy's voice seemed weak.

"Soon, I guarantee it. I had a dream from God, Billy. Something inside of me knew what to do."

Billy began weeping. "Just because of a couple of queers. What kind of God is that?"

"It's the only God."

"I don't believe it," Billy whimpered. "I don't believe that God would punish everyone just because of what you did. I don't believe that God would punish the unborn just because of what you did. It's all a lie, ain't it? We just did something stupid, building crosses and crucifying ourselves. Look at that, look up."

Roy tried to look up, but he couldn't. What he could see was the endless sea, and the shimmering sky as the sun crisped the edges of the afternoon. The smell was growing stronger from the bodies.

"I don't believe in God!" Billy cried. "Somebody! Get me down! Get me down! He's crazy! Somebody help me! Somebody get me down! Jesus!"

Roy tried to calm him with words, but Billy didn't stop screaming until an angel dropped from the sky and tore into him.

Roy remained, untouched, on the cross, amidst the writhing bodies on the shore of the damned. He waited for Jesus, he waited for God, but only night came, and the promise of a new day.

A Wreath for Marley

by Max Allan Collins

Private detective Richard Stone wasn't much for celebrations, or holidays—or holiday celebrations, for that matter.

Nonetheless, this Christmas Eve, in the year of our Lord 1942, he decided to throw a little holiday party in the modest two-room suite of offices on Wabash that he had once shared with his late partner, Jake Marley.

Present for the festivities were his sandy-tressed cutie-pie secretary, Katie Crockett, and his fresh-faced young partner, Joey Ernest. Last to arrive was his best pal (at least since Jake died), burly homicide dick Sgt. Hank Ross.

Katie had strung up some tinsel and decorated a tiny tree by her reception desk. Right now the little group was having a Yuletide toast with heavily rum-spiked eggnog. The darkly handsome Stone's spirits were good—just this morning, he'd been declared 4-F, thanks to his flat feet.

"Every flatfoot should have 'em!" he laughed.

"What'd you do?" Ross asked. "Bribe the draft board doc?"

"What's it to you?" Stone grinned. "You cops get automatic deferments!"

And the two men clinked cups. Actually, bribing the draft board doctor was exactly what Stone had done; but he saw no need to mention it.

"Hell," Joey said—and the word was quite a curse coming from this kid—"I wish I *could* go. If it wasn't for this damn perforated eardrum..."

"You and Sinatra," Stone laughed.

Katie said nothing; her eyes were on the framed picture on her desk—her young brother Ben, who was spending Christmas in the Pacific somewhere.

"I got presents for all of you," Stone said, handing envelopes around.

"What's this?" Joey asked, confused, opening his envelope to see a slip of paper with a name and address on the South Side.

"Best black-market butcher in the city," Stone said. "You and the missus and the brood can start the next year out with a coupla sirloins, on me."

"I'd feel funny about that.... It's not legal...."

"Jesus! How can you be such a square and still work for me? You're lucky there's a manpower shortage, kid."

Ross, envelope open, was thumbing through five twenty-dollar bills. "You always know just what to get me, Stoney."

"Cops are so easy to shop for," Stone said.

Katie, seeming embarrassed, whispered her thanks into Stone's ear.

"Think nothin' of it, baby," he said. "It's as much for me as for you."

He'd given her a fifty-dollar gift certificate at the lingerie counter at Marshall Field's. Not every boss would be so generous.

They all had gifts for him, too: Joey gave him a ten-dollar war bond, Katie a hand-tooled leather shoulder holster, and Hank the latest *Esquire* "Varga" calendar.

"To give this rat-trap some class," the cop said.

Joey raised his cup. "Here's to Mr. Marley," he said.

"To Mr. Marley," Katie said, her eyes suddenly moist. "Rest his soul."

"Yeah," Ross said, lifting his cup, "here's to Jake—dead a year to the day."

"To the night, actually," Stone said, and hoisted his cup. "What the hell—to my partner Jake. You were a miserable bastard, but Merry Christmas, anyway."

"You shouldn't talk that way!" Katie said.

"Even if it's the truth?" Stone asked with a smirk.

Suddenly it got quiet.

Then Ross asked, "Doesn't it bother you, Stoney? You're a detective and your partner's murder goes unsolved? Ain't it bad for business?"

"Naw. Not when you do mostly divorce work."

Ross grinned, shook his head. "Stoney, you're an example to us all," he said. He waved and ambled out.

Katie had a heartsick expression. "Doesn't Mr. Marley's death mean *anything* to you? He was your best friend!"

Stone patted his .38 under his shoulder. "Sadie here's my best friend. And, sure, Marley's death means something to me: full ownership of the business, and the only name on the door is mine."

She shook her head, slowly, sadly. "I'm so disappointed in you, Richard...."

He took her gently aside. "Then I'm not welcome at your apartment anymore?" he whispered.

"Of course you're welcome. I'm still hoping you'll come have Christmas dinner with my family and me, tomorrow."

"I'm not much for family gatherings. Ain't it enough I got you the black-market turkey?"

"Richard!" She shushed him. "Joey will hear...."

"What, and find out you're no Saint Kate?" He gave her a smack of a kiss on the forehead, then patted her fanny. "See you the day after.... We'll give that new casino on Rush Street a try."

She sighed, said, "Merry Christmas, Richard," gathered her coat and purse and went out.

Now it was just Joey and Stone. The younger man said, "You know, Katie's starting to get suspicious."

"About what?"

"About what. About you and Mrs. Marley!"

Stone snorted. "Katie just thinks I'm bein' nice to my late partner's widow."

"You being 'nice' is part of why it seems so suspicious. While you were out today, Mrs. Marley called about five times."

"The hell! Katie didn't say so."

"See what I mean?" Joey plucked his topcoat off the coat tree. "Mr. Stone—please don't expect me to keep covering for you. It makes me feel... dirty."

"Are you *sure* you were born in Chicago, kid?" Stone opened the door for him. "Go home! Have yourself a merry the hell little Christmas! Tell your kids Santa's comin', send 'em up to bed, and make the missus under the mistletoe one time for me."

"Thanks for the sentiment, Mr. Stone," he said, and was gone.

Stone—alone, now—decided to skip the eggnog and head straight for the rum. He was downing a cup when a knock called him to the door.

Two representatives of the Salvation Army stepped into his outer office, in uniform—a white-haired old gent with a charity bucket, and a pretty, shapely thing, her innocent face devoid of make-up under the Salvation Army bonnet.

"We're stopping by some of the offices to—" the old man began.

"Make a touch," Stone finished. "Sure thing. Help yourself to the eggnog, Pops." Then he cast a warm smile on the young woman. "Honey, step inside my private office…. That's where I keep the cash."

He shut himself and the little dame inside his office and got a twenty-dollar bill out of his cashbox from a desk drawer, then tucked the bill inside the swell of the girl's blouse.

Her eyes widened. "Please!"

"Baby, you don't have to say please." Stone put his hands on her waist and brought her to him. "Come on…. Give Santa a kiss."

Her slap sounded like a gunshot and stung like hell. He whisked the bill back out of her blouse.

"Some Christmas spirit *you* got," he said, and opened the door and pushed her into the outer office.

"What's the meaning of this?" the old man sputtered, and Stone wadded up the twenty, tossed it in the bucket and shoved them both out the door.

"Squares," he muttered, returning to his rum.

Before long, the door opened and a woman in black appeared there, like a curvaceous wraith. Her hair was icy blond, her thin lips blood red, like cuts in her angular, white Joan Crawford face. It had been awhile since she'd seen forty, but she was better preserved than your grandma's strawberry jam.

She fell immediately into his arms. "Merry Christmas, darling!"

"In a rat's ass," he said coldly, pushing her away.

"Darling… What's wrong…?"

"You been calling the office again! I told you not to do that. People are gonna get the wrong idea."

He'd been through this with her a million times. They were perfect suspects for Jake Marley's murder; neither of them had an alibi for the time of the killing—Stone was in his apartment, alone, and Maggie claimed she'd been alone at home, too.

But to cover for each other, they had lied to the cops about being together at Marley's penthouse, waiting for his return for a Christmas Eve supper.

"If people think we're an item," Stone told her, "we'll be prime suspects!"

"It's been a year…."

"That's not long enough."

She threw her head back and her blond hair shimmered, as did her diamond earrings. "I want to get out of black, and be on your arm, unashamed."

"Since when were you ever ashamed of anything?" He shuddered, wishing he'd never met Maggie Marley, let alone climbed in bed with her; now he was in bed with her, for God knew how long, and in every sense of the word....

She touched his face with a gloved hand. "Are we spending Christmas Eve together, Richard?"

"Can't, baby. Gotta spend it with relatives."

"Who, your uncle and aunt?" She smirked in disbelief. "I can't believe you're going back to *farm* country, to see them.... You *hate* it there!"

"Hey, wouldn't be right not seein' 'em. Christmas and all."

Her gaze seemed troubled. "I'd hoped we could talk. Richard... we may have a problem...."

"Such as?"

"...Eddie's trying to blackmail me."

"Eddie? What does that slimy little bastard want?"

Eddie was Jake Marley's brother.

"He's in over his head with the Outfit," she said.

"What, gambling losses again? He'll never learn...."

"He's trying to squeeze me for dough," she said urgently. "He's got photos of us, together. At that resort!"

"So what?" he shrugged.

"Photos of us in *our* room at that resort... and he's got the guest register."

Stone frowned. "That was just a week after Jake was killed."

"I know. You were... consoling me."

Who was she trying to kid?

Stone said, "I'll talk to him."

She moved close to him again. "He's waiting for me now, at the Blue Spot Bar.... Would you keep the appointment for me, Richard?"

And she kissed him. Nobody kissed hotter than this dame. Or colder....

Half an hour later, Stone entered the smoky Rush Street saloon, where a thrush in a gown cut to her toenails was embracing the microphone, singing "White Christmas" off-key.

He found that mustached weasel Eddie Marley sitting at the bar working on a scotch—a bald little man in a bow tie and a plaid zoot suit.

"Hey, Dickie... nice to see ya. Buy ya a snort?"

"Don't call me Dickie."

"Stoney, then."

"Grab your topcoat and let's talk in my office," Stone said, nodding toward the alley door.

A cat chasing a rat made garbage cans clatter as the two men came out into the alley. A cold Christmas rain was falling, puddling on the frozen remains of a snow-and-ice storm from a week before. Ducking into the recession of a doorway, Eddie got out a cigarette and Stone, a statue standing out in the rain, leaned in with a Zippo to light it for him.

For a moment, the world wasn't pitch dark. But only for a moment.

"I don't *like* to stick it to ya, Stoney... but if I don't cough up five G's to the Outfit, I won't live to see '43! My brother left me high and dry, ya know."

"I'm all choked up, Eddie."

Eddie was shrugging. "Jake's life insurance paid off big—double indemnity. So Maggie's sittin' pretty. And the agency partnership reverted to you—so you're in the gravy. Where's that leave Eddie?"

Stone picked him up by the throat. The little man's eyes opened wide and his cigarette tumbled from his lips to sizzle in a puddle.

"It leaves you on your ass, Eddie."

And the detective hurled the little man into the alley, onto the pavement, where he bounced up against some garbage cans.

"Ya shouldn'ta done that, ya bastid! I got the goods on ya!"

Stone's footsteps splashed toward the little man. "You got nothin', Eddie."

"I got photos! I got your handwritin' on a motel register!"

"Don't try to tell *me* the bedroom-dick business. You bring me the negatives and the register page, and I'll give you five C's. First and last payment."

The weasel's eyes went very wide. "Five C's?!? I need five G's by tomorrow—they'll break my knees if I don't pay up! Have a heart— have some Christmas charity, fer chrissakes!"

Stone pulled his trenchcoat collar up around his face. "I gave at the office, Eddie. Five C's is all you get."

"What are ya—Scrooge? Maggie's rich! And you're rolling in your own dough!"

Stone kicked Eddie in the side and the little man howled.

"The negatives and the register page, Eddie. Hit me up again and you'll take a permanent swim in the Chicago River. Agreed?"

"Agreed! Don't hurt me no more! *Agreed*!"

"Merry X-mas, moron," Stone said, and exited the alley, pausing near the street to light up his own cigarette. Christmas carols were being piped through department-store loudspeakers: *Joy to the world!*

"In a rat's ass," he muttered, and hailed a taxi. In the back seat, he sipped rum from a flask. The cabbie made holiday small talk and Stone said, "Make you a deal—skip the chatter and maybe you'll get a tip for Christmas."

Inside his Gold Coast apartment building, Stone was waiting for the elevator when he caught a strange reflection in a lobby mirror. He saw —or *thought* he saw—an imposing trenchcoated figure in a fedora standing behind him.

His late partner—Jake Marley!

Stone whirled, but… no one was there.

He blew out air, glanced at the mirror again, seeing only himself. "No more rum for you, pal."

On the seventh floor, Stone unlocked 714 and slipped inside his apartment. The *art modern* furnishings reflected his financial success; the divorce racket had made him damn near wealthy. He tossed his jacket on a half-circle white couch, loosened his tie and headed to his well-appointed bar, already changing his mind about more rum.

He'd been lying, of course, about going to see his uncle and aunt. Christmas out in the sticks—*that* was a laugh! That had just been an excuse so he didn't have to spend the night with that blood-sucking Maggie.

From the icebox he built a salami and swiss cheese on rye, smearing on hot mustard. Drifting back into the living room, where only one small lamp was on, he switched on his console radio, searching for sports or swing music or even war news, anything other than damn Christmas carols. But that maudlin muck was all he could find, and he switched it off in disgust.

Settling in a comfy overstuffed chair, still in his shoulder holster, he sat and ate and drank. Boredom crept in on him like ground fog.

Katie was busy with family tonight, and even most of the hookers he knew were taking the night off.

What the hell, he thought. *I'll just enjoy my own good company….*

Without realizing it, he drifted off to sleep; a noise woke him, and

Sadie—his trusty .38—was in his hand before his eyes had opened all the way.

"Who's there?" he said, and stood. Somebody had switched off the lamp! *Who in hell?* The room was in near darkness....

"Sorry, keed," a familiar voice said. "The light hurts my peepers."

Standing by the window was his late partner—Jake Marley.

"I must be dreamin'," Stone said rationally, after just the briefest flinch of a reaction, "'cause, pal—you're dead as a doornail."

"I'm dead, all right," Marley said. "Been dead a whole year." Red neon from the window behind him pulsed in on the tall, trenchcoated, fedora-sporting figure—a hawkishly handsome man with a grooved face and thin mustache. "But, keed—you ain't dreamin'."

"What sorta gag *is* this...?"

Stone walked over to Marley and took a close look: no make-up, no mask—it was no masquerade. And the trenchcoat had four scorched holes stitched across the front.

Bullet holes.

He put a hand on Marley's shoulder—and it passed right through.

"Jesus!" Stone stepped back. "You're not dead—I'm dead *drunk*." He turned away. "Havin' the heebie-jeebies or somethin'. When I wake up, you better be gone, or I'm callin' Ripley...."

Marley smiled a little. "Nobody can see me but you, keed. Talk about it, and they'll toss ya in the laughin' academy, and toss away the key. Mind if I siddown? Feet are killin' me."

"Your eyes hurt, your feet hurt—what kinda goddamn ghost *are* you, anyway?"

"'Zactly what you said, keed," Marley said, and he slowly moved toward the sofa, dragging himself along to the sound of metallic scraping. "The God-*damned* kind... and I'll stay that way if you don't come through for me."

Below the trenchcoat, Marley's feet were heavily shackled, like a chain-gang prisoner.

"You think *mine's* heavy," Marley said, "wait'll ya see what the boys in the metal shop are cookin' up for you."

The ghost sat heavily, his shackles clanking. Stone kept his distance.

"What do ya want from me, Jake?"

"The near-impossible, keed—I want ya to do the right thing."

"The right thing?"

"Find my murderer, ya chowderhead! Jesus!" At that last exclamation, Marley cowered, glanced upward, muttering, "No offense, Boss," and continued: "You're a detective, Stoney—when a detective's partner's killed, he's supposed to do somethin' about it. That's the code."

"That's the bunk," Stone said. "I left it to the cops. They mucked it up." He shrugged. "End of story."

"*Nooooo!*" Marley moaned, sounding like a ghost for the first time, and making the hair stand up on Stone's neck. "I was your partner, I was your only friend… your *mentor*… and you let me die in an unsolved murder while you took over my business—*and* my wife."

Stone flinched again; lighted up a Lucky. "You know about that, huh? Maggie, I mean."

"Of course I know!" Marley waved a dismissive hand. "Oh, her I don't care two cents about…. She always was a witch, with a capital *B*. Having her in your life is punishment enough for *any* crime. But, keed—you and me, we're *tied* to each other! Chained for eternity…"

Convinced he was dreaming, Stone snorted. "Really, Jake? How come?"

Marley leaned forward and his shackles clanked. "My best pal—a detective—didn't think I was worth a measly murder investigation. Where I come from, a man who can't inspire any more loyalty than *that* outa his best pal is one lost soul."

Stone shrugged. "It was nothin' personal."

"Oh, I take gettin' murdered *real* personal! And you didn't give a rat's ass *who* killed me! And that's why *you're* as good as damned."

"Baloney!" Stone touched his stomach. "…Or maybe salami…."

Marley shifted in his seat and his shackles rattled. "You *knew* I always looked after my little brother, Eddie—he's a louse and weakling, but he was the only brother I had…. And what have you done for Eddie? Tossed him in some garbage cans! Left 'im for the Boys to measure for cement overshoes!"

"He's a weasel."

"He's your dead best pal's brother! Cut him some slack!"

"I did cut him some slack! I didn't kill him when he tried to blackmail me."

"Over you sleeping with his dead brother's wife, you mean?"

Stone batted the air dismissively. "The hell with you, Marley! You're not real! You're some meat that went bad. Some mustard that didn't agree with me. I'm goin' to bed."

"You were right the first time," Marley said. "You're goin' to hell… or anyway, hell's waitin' room. Like me." Marley's voice softened into a plea. "Stoney—help me outa this, pal. Help yourself."

"How?"

"Solve my murder."

Stone blew a smoke ring. "Is that all?"

Marley stood, and a howling wind seemed to blow through the apartment, drapes waving like ghosts. "*It means something to me!*"

Now Stone was sweating; this *was* happening.

"One year ago," Marley said in a deep, rumbling voice, "they found me in the alley behind the Bismarck Hotel, my back to the wall, one bullet in the pump, two in the stomach and one in between… *remember?*"

And Marley removed the bullet-scorched trenchcoat to reveal the four wounds—beams of red neon light from the window behind him cut through Marley like swords through a magician's box.

"*Remember?*"

Stone was backing up, patting the air with his palms. "Okay, okay. Why don't you just *tell* me who bumped you off, and I'll settle up for you. Then we'll be square."

"It's not that easy. I'm not… *allowed* to tell you."

"Who *made* these goddamn rules?"

Marley raised an eyebrow, lifted a finger, pointed up. "Right again. To save us both, you gotta act like a detective…. You gotta look for clues…. And you must do this *yourself*… though you *will* be aided."

"How?"

"You're gonna have three more visitors."

"Swell! Who's first? Karloff, or Lugosi?"

Marley moved away from the couch, toward the door, shackles clanking. "Don't blow it for the both of us, keed," he said, and left through the door—*through* the door.

Stone stood staring at where his late partner had literally disappeared, and shook his head. Then he went to the bar and poured himself a drink. Soon he was questioning the reality of what had just happened; and, a drink later, he stumbled into his bedroom and flopped onto his bed, fully clothed.

He was sleeping the sound sleep of the dead-drunk when his bed was jostled.

Somebody was kicking it.

Waking to semi-darkness, Stone said, "Who in hell…"

Looming over him was a roughly handsome, Clark Gable-mustached figure in a straw hat and a white double-breasted seersucker.

Stone dove for Sadie, his .38 in its shoulder holster slung over his nightstand, but then, in an eyeblink, the guy was gone.

"Over here, boyo."

Stone turned and the guy in the jauntily cocked straw hat was standing there, picking his teeth with a toothpick.

"Save yourself the ammo," the guy said. "They already got me."

And he unbuttoned his jacket and displayed several ugly gaping exit wounds.

"In the back," the guy said, "the bastards."

He looked oddly familiar. "Who the hell are you?"

"Let's put it this way. If a bunch of trigger-happy feds are chasin' ya, don't duck down that alley by the Biograph—it's a dead-end, brother."

"John Dillinger!"

"Right—only it's a hard G, like in gun: Dillin-*ger*. Okay, sonny? Pet peeve o'mine." Dillinger was buttoning up his jacket.

"You… you must not have been killed wearing *that* suit."

"Naw—it's new. Christmas present from the Boss. I got a pretty good racket goin', here—helpin' chumps like you make good. Another five hundred years, and I get sprung."

"How exactly is a cheap crook like you gonna help *me* make good?"

Dillinger grabbed Stone by the shirt front. Stone took a swing at the ghost, but his hand passed through.

"There ain't nothin' cheap about John Dillinger! I didn't rob nobody but banks, and times was hard, then, *banks* was the bad guys… and I never shot nobody. Otherwise, I'd'a got the big heat."

"The big heat?"

Dillinger raised an eyebrow and angled a thumb downward. "Which is where you're headed, sonny, if you don't get your lousy head screwed on right. Come with me."

"Where are we goin'?"

"Into your past. Maybe that's why *I* got picked for this caper—see, I was a Midwest farm kid like you. Come on! Don't make me drag ya…."

Reluctantly, Stone followed the spirit into the next room…

…Where Stone found himself not in the living room of his apartment, but in the snowy yard out in front of a small farmhouse.

Snowflakes fell lazily upon an idyllic rural winter landscape; an eight-year-old boy was building a snowman.

"I know this place," Stone said.

"You know the *kid*, too," Dillinger said. "It's you. You live in that house."

"Why aren't I cold? It's gotta be freezing, but I feel like I'm still in my apartment."

"You're a shadow here, just like me," Dillinger said.

"Dickie!" a voice called from the porch. "Come inside—you'll catch your death!"

"Ma!" Stone said, and moved toward her. He studied her serene, beautiful face in the doorway. "Ma...."

He tried to touch her and his hand passed through.

Behind him, Dillinger said, "I told ya, boyo—you're a shadow. Just lean back and watch... maybe you'll learn somethin'."

Then eight-year-old Dickie Stone ran right through the shadow of his future self, and inside the house, closing the door behind him, leaving Stone and Dillinger on the porch.

"Now what?" Stone asked.

"Since when were you shy about breaking and entering?" Dillinger said.

And walked *through* the door....

"Look who's talking," Stone said. He took a breath and followed.

Stone found himself in the cozy farmhouse, warmed by a wood-burning stove whose heat, surprisingly, he could feel. In one corner of the modestly furnished living room stood a pine tree, almost too tall for the room to contain, decorated with tinsel and a star, wrapped gifts scattered under it. A spinet piano hugged a wall. Stone watched his eight-year-old self strip out of an aviator cap and woolen coat and boots and sit at a little table where he began working on a puzzle.

"Five hundred pieces," Stone said. "It's a picture of Tom Mix and his horse what's-his-name."

"Tony," said Dillinger.

"God, will ya smell that pine tree! And my mother's cooking! If I'm a shadow, how come I can smell her cooking?"

"Hey, pal—don't ask me. I'm just the tour guide. Maybe somebody upstairs wants your memory jogged."

Stone moved into the kitchen, where his mother was at the stove, stirring gravy.

"God, that gravy smells good.... Can you smell it?"

"No," said Dillinger.

"She's baking mincemeat pie, too.... You're *lucky* you can't smell that. Garbage! But Pa always liked it...."

"My ma made a mean plum pudding at Christmas," Dillinger said.

"Mine, too! It's bubbling on the stove! Can't you smell it?"

"No! This is *your* past, pal, not mine...."

The back door opened and a man in a blue denim coat and woolen knit cap entered, stomping the snow off his workboots.

"That mincemeat pie must be what heaven smells like," the man said. Sky-blue eyes were an incongruously gentle presence in his hard, weathered face.

"Pa," Stone said.

Taking off his jacket, the man walked right through the shadow of his grown son. "Roads are still snowed in," his father told his mother.

"Oh dear! I was so counting on Bob and Helen for Christmas supper!"

"That's my uncle and aunt," Stone told Dillinger. "Bob was Mom's brother."

"They'll be here," Pa Stone said, with a thin smile. "Davey took the horse and buggy into town after them."

"My brother Davey," Stone explained to Dillinger.

"Oh dear," his mother was saying. "He's so frail... oh how could you..."

"Send a boy to do a man's job? Sarah, Davey's sixteen. Proud as I am of the boy for his school marks, he's got to learn to be a man. Anyway, he *wanted* to do it. He *likes* to help."

Stone's ma could only say, "Oh dear," again and again.

"Now, Sarah—I'll *not* have these boys babied!"

"Well, the old S.O.B. sure didn't baby *me*," Stone said to Dillinger.

"Davey just doesn't have Dickie's spirit," said Pa. "Dickie's always getting in scrapes, and he sure don't make the grades Davey does, but the boy's got gumption and guts."

Stone had never known his pa felt that way about him.

"Then why are you so hard on the child, Jess?" his mother was asking. "Last time he got caught playing hookey from school, you gave him the waling of his life."

"How else is the boy to learn? That's how my pa taught *me* the straight and narrow path."

"Straight and narrow razor strap's more like it," Stone said.

Ma was stroking Pa's rough face. "You love both your boys. It's Christmas, Jess. Why don't you tell 'em how you feel?"

"They know," he said gruffly.

Emotions churned in Stone, and he didn't like it. "Tour guide—I've had about all of this I can take…."

"Not just yet," Dillinger said. "Let's go in the other room."

They did, but it was suddenly later, after dark, the living room filled with family members sitting on sofas and chairs and even the floor, having cider after a supper that everybody was raving about.

A pudgy, good-natured man in his forties was saying to eight-year-old Dickie, "How do you like your gift, young man?"

The boy was wearing a policeman's cap and a little tin badge; he also had a miniature nightstick, a pair of handcuffs and a traffic whistle. "It's the cat's meow, Uncle Bob!"

"Where does he get those vulgar expressions?" his mother asked disapprovingly, but not sternly.

"*Cap'n Billy's Whiz Bang*," Stone whispered to Dillinger.

"Never missed an issue myself," Dillinger said.

The boy started blowing the whistle shrilly and there was laughter, but the boy's father said, "Enough!"

And the boy obeyed.

The door opened. A boy of sixteen, but skinny and not much taller than Dickie, came in; bundled in winter clothes, he was bringing in a pile of firewood for the wood-burning stove.

"Davey," Stone said.

"Did you like your older brother?" Dillinger asked.

"He was a great guy. You could always depend on him for a smile or a helpin' hand…. But what did it get him?"

Out of his winter jacket, firewood deposited, Davey went over to his younger brother and ruffled his hair. "Gonna get the bad guys, little brother?"

"I'm gonna bop 'em," Dickie said, "then slap the cuffs on!"

"On Christmas?" Davey asked. "Even crooks got a right to celebrate the Savior's birth, don't ya think?"

"Yeah. Well, okay… day *after*, then."

Everybody was laughing as little Dickie swung his nightstick at imaginary felons.

"Dickie my lad," said Uncle Bob, "someday I'll hire you on at the station."

Stone explained to Dillinger: "He was police chief, over at DeKalb."

"Peachy," said Dillinger.

Davey said, "Ma—how about sitting down at the piano, and helping put us all in the Yuletide spirit?"

"Yeah, Ma!" said little Dickie. "Tickle the ol' ivories!"

Soon the group was singing carols, Davey leading them: *God rest ye merry gentlemen....*

"Seen enough?" Dillinger said.

"Just a second," Stone said. "Let me hear a little more. This is the last decent Christmas I can remember...."

After a while, the gaily singing people began to fade, but the room remained, and suddenly Stone saw the figure of his father, kneeling at the window, a rifle in his hands, face contorted savagely. There was no Christmas tree, although Stone knew at once that this was indeed a later Christmas Day in his family's history. His mother cowered by the piano; she seemed frightened and on the verge of tears. A fourteen-year-old Dickie was crouched beside his father near the window.

"God," said Stone. "Not *this* Christmas..."

"Son," his pa was saying to the teenaged Stone, "I want you and your mother to go on out."

"No, Pa! I want to stay beside you! Ma should go, but..."

"You're not too big to get your hide tanned, boy."

"Pa..."

A voice through a megaphone outside called: "Jess! It's Bob! Let me come in and at least talk!"

"When hell freezes over!" Pa shouted. "Now get off my property, or so help me, I'll shoot you where you stand!"

"Jess, that's my *brother*," Ma said, tears brimming. "And it's... it's not *our* property, anymore...."

"Whose is it, then? The bank's? Did the bankers work this ground for twenty years? Did the bankers put blood and sweat and years into this land?"

Dillinger elbowed Stone. "*That's* why this country *needed* guys like me. Say—where's your older brother, anyway?"

"Dead," Stone said. "He caught pneumonia the winter of '28... stayed outside for hours and hours, helping get some family's flivver out of a ditch in the wind and cold. All my folks' dreams died with him."

"Let Bob come in," Ma was saying. "Hear him out."

Pa thought it over; he looked so much older, now. Not years older—decades. Finally he said, "All right. For you, Sarah. Just 'cause he's kin of yours."

When the door opened and Bob came in, he was in full police-chief array under a fur-lined jacket; the badge on his cap gleamed.

"Jess," he said solemnly, "you're at the end of your string. I wish I could help you, but the bank's foreclosed, and the law's the law."

"Why's the law on *their* side?" teenaged Stone asked. "Isn't the law supposed to help everybody equal?"

"People with money get treated a hell of lot more equal, son," his father said bitterly.

"I worked out a deal," Bob said. "You can keep your furniture. I can come over with the paddy wagon and load 'er up with your things; we'll store 'em in my garage. There'll be no charges brought. Helen and I have room for you and Sarah and Dick—you can stay with us till you find something."

The rifle was still in Pa's hands. "*This* is my home, Robert."

"No, Jess—it's a house the bank owns. Your home is your family, and you take them with you. Let me ask you this—what would Davey want you to do?"

Stone looked away. He knew what was coming: one of two times he ever saw his father cry—the other was the night Davey had died.

A single tear running down his cheek, Pa said, "How am I supposed to support my family?"

Bob's voice was gentle: "I got friends at the barb-wire factory. Already talked to 'em about you. They'll take you on. Having a job in times like these is a blessing."

Pa nodded. He sighed, handed his rifle over. "Thank you, Robert."

"Yeah, Uncle Bob," teenaged Stone said sarcastically. "Merry Christmas! In a rat's ass..."

"Richard!" his ma said.

His father slapped him.

"You ever do that to me again, old man," teenaged Stone said, pointing a hard finger at his father, "I'll knock your damn block off!"

And as his teenaged self rushed out, Stone shook his head. "Jesus! Did I have to say that to him, right then? Poor bastard hits rock bottom, and I find a way to push him down lower...."

Pa was standing rigidly, looking downward, as Ma clung to him in a desperate embrace. Uncle Bob, looking ashamed of himself, trudged out.

"You were just a kid," Dillinger said. "What did you know?"

"Why are you puttin' me through this hell?" Stone demanded. "I can't change the past! What does any of this have to do with finding out who killed Jake Marley?!"

"Don't ask me!" Dillinger flared. "I'm just the damned help!" The bank robber's ghost stalked out, and Stone—not eager to be left in this part of his past—quickly followed.

Stone now found himself, and his ghostly companion, in the reception area of a small-town police station where officers milled and a reception desk loomed. Dillinger led Stone to a partitioned-off office where a Christmas wreath hung on a frosted glass door, which they went through without opening.

Jake Marley, Deputy Chief of Police of DeKalb, Illinois, sat leaning back in his chair at his desk, smiling as he opened Christmas cards; as he did, cool green cash dropped out of each card.

"Lot of people remembered Jake at Christmas," Stone said.

"Lot of people remember a *lot* of cops at Christmas," Dillinger sneered.

A knock at the door prompted Marley to sweep the cash into a desk drawer. "Yeah?" he called gruffly. "What?"

The uniformed police officer who peeked in was a young Dick Stone. "Deputy Chief Marley? I had word you wanted me to drop by…?"

"Come on in, keed, come on in!" The slick-mustached deputy chief gestured magnanimously to the chair opposite his desk. "Take a load off."

Young Stone sat while his future self and the ghost of a public enemy eavesdropped nearby.

Marley's smile tried a little too hard. "Yesterday was your first day on, I understand."

"Yes, sir."

"Well, I just wanted you to know I don't hold it against you, none—you gettin' this job through patronage."

"What's that supposed to mean?"

Marley shrugged. "Nothin'. A guy does what he has to, to get ahead. It's unusual, your Uncle Bob playin' that kinda game, though. He's a real straight arrow."

"Uncle Bob's kind of a square john, but he's family and I stand by him."

"Swell! Admirable, keed. Admirable. But there's things go on around here that he don't know about… and I'd like to keep it that way."

Young Stone frowned. "Such as?"

"Let me put it this way—if you got a fifty-dollar bill every month, for just lookin' the other way… if it was for something truly harmless… could you sleep at night?"

"Lookin' the other way, how?"

Marley explained that he was from Chicago—in '26, a local congressman had greased the wheels for him to land this rural deputy chief slot, so he could do some favors for the Outfit.

"Not so much goin' on now," said Marley, "not like back in dry days, when the Boys had stills out here. Couple roadhouses where people like to have some extra-legal fun…"

"Gambling and girls, you mean."

"Right. And there's a farmhouse the Boys use, when things get hot in the city, and a field where they like to do some… planting… now and then."

"I don't think I could sleep at night, knowing that's going on."

Marley's eyebrows shot up. "Oh?"

"Not for fifty a month." The young officer grinned. "Seventy-five, maybe. A C-note, and I'd be asleep when my head hit the pillow."

Marley stuck his hand across his desk. "I think this is gonna be the start of beautiful friendship."

They shook hands, but when young Stone brought his hand back, there was a C-note in it.

"Merry Christmas, Mr. Marley."

"Make it Jake. Many happy returns, keed."

Dillinger tugged Stone's arm and they walked through the office wall and were suddenly in another office: the outer office of MARLEY AND STONE: CONFIDENTIAL INVESTIGATIONS. Katie was watering the base of a Christmas tree in the corner.

"This is, what?" Dillinger asked Stone. "Five years ago?"

"Right. Christmas Eve, '37, I think…"

Marley was whispering to a five-years-younger Stone. "Nice lookin' twist you hired."

"She'll class up the front office. And remember, Jake—I saw her first."

Marley grinned. "What do I need with a kid like her, when I got a woman like Maggie? Ah! Speak of the devil…"

Maggie was entering the outer office on the arm of a blond, boyishly handsome man in a crisp business suit.

"Stoney," Marley said, "meet our biggest client: This is Larry Turner. He's the V.P. with Consolidated who's tossing all that investigating our way."

"Couldn't do this without you, Mr. Turner," Stone said.

"Make it Larry," he said. "Pleasure to do business with such a well-connected firm."

Dillinger said, "What's *this* boy scout's angle?"

Stone said, "We been kicking that boy scout back twenty percent of what his firm pays us since day one. I don't know how Jake knew him, but Consolidated was the account that let us leave DeKalb and set up shop in the Loop."

"How'd your Uncle Bob feel about you leaving the force?"

"He damn near cried. He always figured I'd step in and fill his shoes someday. Poor yokel… just didn't have a clue—all that corruption going on right under his nose."

"By his deputy chief and his nephew, you mean."

Stone said nothing, but the five-years-ago him was saying to Marley, "Look—this insurance racket is swell. But the real dough is in divorce work."

"You're right, keed. I'm ahead of you… we get the incriminating photos of the cheating spouse, then sell 'em to the highest bidder."

"Sweet! That's what they get for not love-honor-and-obeyin'."

The private eyes shared a big horse laugh. Katie looked their way and smiled, glad to see her bosses enjoying themselves on Christmas Eve.

"Come on," Dillinger said, summoning Stone with a crooked finger.

And the late bank robber walked Stone through a wall into the alley where Jake Marley lay crumpled against a brick wall between two garbage cans, holes shot in the front of him, eyes wide and empty and staring.

Sgt. Hank Ross was showing the body to Stone. "Thought you better see this, pal. Poor slob never even got his gun out. Still tucked away under his buttoned-up topcoat. Shooter musta been somebody who knew him, don't ya figure?"

Stone shrugged. "You're the homicide dick."

"Now, Stoney, I don't want you looking into this. I know he was your partner and your friend, but…"

"You talked me out of it." Stone lit up a Lucky. "I'll take care of informin' the widow."

Ross just looked at him. Then he said, "Merry goddamn

Christmas, Stoney."

"In a rat's ass," he said, turning away from his dead partner.

"Jeez!" Dillinger said. "That's cold! Couldn't ya squeeze out just one tear for your old pal?"

Stone said nothing. His year-ago self walked right through him.

"You want the truth, Dillin-*ger*? All I was thinkin' was, with all the people he jacked around, Jake was lucky to've lived *this* long. And how our partnership agreement spelled out that the business was mine, now."

"Hell! I thought *Gillis* was cold."

"Gillis?"

"Lester Gillis. Baby Face Nelson to you. Come on, sonny. You and me reached the end of the line."

And Dillinger shoved Stone, hard—right through the brick wall; and when the detective blinked again, he was alone on his bed, in his apartment.

He sat up, rubbed his eyes, scratched his head. "Meat shortage or not, that salami gets pitched...."

He flopped back on the bed, still fully dressed, and stared at the ceiling; the dream was hanging with him—thoughts, images, of his mother, father, brother, even Marley, floated in front of him, speaking to him....

Out in the other room, the doorbell rang, startling him. He checked the round bakelite clock on his nightstand: 2:00A.M. Who in hell would be calling on him at this hour?

On the other hand, he thought as he stumbled out to his door, *talking to somebody with a* pulse *would be nice for a change....*

And there on his doorstep was a crisply uniformed soldier, a freshly scrubbed young man with his overseas cap tugged down onto his forehead.

"Mr. Stone?"

"Ben? Is that *you*? Ben Crockett!" Stone's grin split his face. "Katie's little brother, back from the wars—is *she* gonna be tickled!"

The boy seemed somewhat dazed as he stepped inside.

"Uh, Ben... if you're lookin' for Katie, she's at her place tonight."

"I'm here to see *you*, Mr. Stone."

"Well, that's swell, kid... but why?"

"I'm not really sure," the boy said. "May I sit down?"

"Sure, kid, sure! You want something to drink?"

"No thanks. You'll have to excuse me, sir—I'm kinda confused. The briefing I got… it was pretty screwy."

"Briefing?"

"Yeah. This is a temporary assignment. But they said I was 'uniquely qualified' for this mission."

"What do they want you to do, kid? Haul me down for another physical?"

"That reminds me!" Private Crockett dug into a pocket and found a scrap of paper. "Does this mean anything to you? 'Tell the 4-F Mr. Stone he really *does* have flat feet, and the doctor he paid off was scamming *him*.'"

Stone's mouth dropped open; then he laughed. "Well, that's a Chicago doc for ya. So, is that the extent of your 'mission'? "

The boy tucked the scrap of paper away. "No. There's more… and it's *weird*. I'm supposed to tell you to go look in the mirror."

"Look in the mirror?"

"Yeah—that one over there, I guess."

"Kid…"

"Please, Mr. Stone. I don't think I get to go home for Christmas till I get this done."

Stone sighed, said okay, and shuffled over to the mirror near his console radio; he saw his now unshaven, slightly bleary-eyed reflection, and the boy in his trim overseas cap looking gravely over his shoulder. "Now what, kid?"

"You're supposed to look in there, is all. I was told you're gonna see tomorrow… or, actually, it's after midnight already, ain't it? Anyway, Christmas Day, 1942…"

And the mirror before Stone became a window.

Through the window, he saw Maggie Marley and Larry Turner, the insurance company V.P., toasting cocktail glasses—Maggie in a negligee, Turner in a silk smoking jacket; they were snuggled on a couch in her fancy apartment.

"What the hell's this?" Stone asked. "Maggie and that snake Turner… since when are *they* an item?"

"How much longer," Maggie was saying to Turner, "do I have to put up with him?"

"You *need* Stone," Turner said, nuzzling her neck. "He's your alibi, baby."

"But I didn't *kill* Jake!"

"Sure you didn't. Sure you didn't… Anyway, string him along a little way, then let him down easy. Right now you still need him in your pocket. He helped you get Eddie off your tail, didn't he?"

Maggie frowned. "Well… you're right about that. But his touch… it makes my skin crawl."

"Why you little," Stone began.

But the images on the mirror blurred and were replaced with another image: Eddie Marley in his sleazy little apartment, not answering his door, cowering as somebody out there was banging with a fist.

"Let us in, Eddie! We got a Christmas present for ya!"

Eddie, sweating, shaking like crazy, looked at a framed photo of his late brother Jake.

"How could you do this to me, Jake?" he whispered. "You promised you'd take care of me…."

The door splintered open and two Outfit thugs—huge, hulking, faceless creatures in topcoats and fedoras—cornered him quickly.

"Gimme another week, fellas! I can get ya five C's today, to tide us over till then!"

"Too late, Eddie," one ominous goon said. "You kept the Outfit waitin' just one time too many…."

A hand filled itself with a .45 automatic that erupted once, twice, three times. Eddie crumpled to the floor, bleeding. Dying.

"Jake… Jake… You let me down. You promised…."

The mirror blurred again. Stone looked at Private Crockett. "Is that a done deal, kid? If that's gonna happen Christmas Day, can't I still bail that little weasel out…?"

"I don't know, Mr. Stone. They didn't tell me that."

A new image began to form on the mirror: Stone's young employee, Joey Ernest, seated in his living room by a fireplace, looking glum—in fact, he seemed on the verge of tears. Nearby, his little boy of six and his little girl of four were playing with some nice new toys under a tree bright with Christmas lights.

Joey's wife Linda, a pretty blonde in a red Christmas dress, came over and slipped an arm around him.

"Why are you so blue, darling?"

"I can't help it…. I know I should be happy. It's been a great Christmas… but I feel so… so ashamed…."

"Darling…"

"Other guys my age, they're fighting on bloody beaches to preserve the honor and glory of God and country. Me, I crawl around under beds and hide in hotel closets and take dirty pictures of adulterers."

"Joey! The children!"

"I know! The children… I want to give them a good life… but do I have to do it like this? Covering up for my philandering boss, among a million other indignities? I'm quitting! I swear, I'm quitting Monday!"

She kissed his cheek. "Then I'll stand right beside you."

He gave her a hangdog look. "I shouldn't have got us so far in over our heads with all these time payments…. How are we gonna make it, Linda?"

"I'm going to take that job at the defense plant. Mom can look after the kids when one of us isn't here. It's going to be fine."

"Aw, Linda. I love you so much. Merry Christmas, baby."

"Merry Christmas, darling."

They were embracing as the image blurred.

Now the mirror filled with a tableau of homeless men in a soup kitchen. They were standing in line for soup and bread and a hot meal. Serving them was the pretty young Salvation Army worker Stone had made a pass at, at the office. In the background, voices of men at the mission were singing a carol: *God rest ye merry gentlemen.*

"We used to sing that song at home," Stone told the soldier. "My ma would play the piano. Christ! What a heel."

"Who, Mr. Stone?"

But the image on the mirror was different again: Katie Crockett and a plump older woman and a frail-looking older man…

"Hey, kid," Stone said, "it's your sister!"

"And my folks," he said quietly.

…Sitting around the Christmas tree in Katie's little apartment, opening presents and chatting happily. The doorbell rang, and Katie bounced up to answer it.

But she didn't come bouncing back.

"It's… it's a telegram from the War Department," Katie said.

"Oh no!" her mother said. "Not…"

"It's Ben, isn't it?" her father said.

They huddled together and read the telegram and tears streamed down their faces.

"Well, that's wrong, kid," Stone said to Private Crockett. "You gotta go there tomorrow, and straighten that out. It's breaking their hearts—

they think you're dead!"

"Mr. Stone," the boy said, removing his overseas cap, revealing the bullet hole in the center of his forehead, "I'm afraid they're right."

"God..."

"I have to go home now," he said. "Tell Sis I love her, would you, Mr. Stone? And the folks, too?"

The young soldier, like another image blurring in the mirror, faded away.

Alone in his bedroom again, Stone held his throbbing head in his hands. "Did somebody slip me a mickey or something?" Exhausted, he stumbled back to his bed, falling face first, and sleep, mercifully, descended.

I'll have a blue Christmas without you....

Stone's eyes popped open; his bedroom was still dark. Someone was singing, a sort of hillbilly Bing Crosby, a strange voice, an earthy, unearthly voice....

...blue Christmas, that's certain...

The little round clock said 4:00 A.M.

...decorations of white....

"What the hell is that racket? The radio?"

"It's me, sir," the same voice said. Mellow, baritone, slurry.

Stone hauled himself off the bed and beheld the strangest apparition of all: The man standing before him wore a white leather outfit with a cape, glittering with rhinestones. The (slightly overweight) man had longish jet-black hair, an insolently handsome if puffy face, and heavy-lidded eyes.

"Who the hell are you?"

"Ah don't mean to soun' immodest, sir," he said huskily, "but where Ah come from they call me the King."

"Don't tell me *you're* Jesus Christ!" Stone said, eyes popping.

"Not hardly, sir. Ah'm just a poor country boy. Right now, Ah'd be about seven years old, sir."

"If you're seven years old, I'd cut down on the Baby Ruths if I was you."

The apparition in white moved toward him, a leather ghost; his shoes were strange, too—rhinestone-studded white cowboy boots. "Ah'm afraid you don't understand, sir—Ah'm the ghost of somebody who hasn't grown up and lived yet, in your day... let alone died."

"You haven't died yet, but you're a ghost? A ghost in a white-leather zoot suit! This is the best one yet. This is my favorite so far…."

"See, Ah was a very famous person, or Ah'm goin' to be. Ah really don't mean to brag, but Ah was bigger than the Beatles."

"You're the biggest bug I ever saw, period, pal."

"Sir, Ah abused my talent, and my body, so Ah'm payin' some dues. That's how come Ah got this gig."

"Gig?"

"Ah'm here to show you a little preview of comin' attractions, sir. Somethin' that's gonna go down 'long about next Christmas… Christmas of '43…"

The apparition struck a strange pose, as if turning his entire body into a pointing arrow, and suddenly both the King and Stone were in a small chapel, bedecked rather garishly with Christmas decorations that seemed un-church-like, somehow.

"Where *are* we?"

"Welcome to *my* world, sir. We're a few years early to appreciate it, but someday, this is gonna be a real bright-light city."

"What are you *talkin'* about?"

The King grinned sideways. "We're in Vegas, man!"

Up at the front of the chapel, a man and woman faced a minister. Canned organ music was filtering in. A wedding ceremony was under way.

Stone walked up to have a look.

"I'll be damned," Stone said.

"That's what we're tryin' to prevent, sir."

"It's Maggie and that creep Larry Turner! Getting hitched! Well, good riddance to both of 'em…."

"Maybe you oughta see how *you're* spendin' next Christmas…."

And now Stone and the rhinestone ghost were in a jail cell. So was a haggard-looking, next-year's Stone—in white-and-black prison garb, seated on his cot, looking desperate. On a stool across from him was Sgt. Hank Ross.

"Hank, you *know* I'm innocent!"

"I believe you, Stoney. But the jury didn't. That eye-witness held up…."

"He was bought and paid for!"

"…And your gun turning out to be the murder weapon, well…."

"You get an anonymous phone tip to match the slugs that killed Jake with my gun, a *year* later, and you don't think that's suspicious?"

"The ballistics tests were positive."

"Some crooked cop must've switched the real bullets with some phonies shot from my gun! I told you, Hank, when I went to Miami on vacation, I left the gun in my desk drawer. Anybody coulda…"

"Old news, Stoney."

"You gotta believe me…."

"I do. But with your appeal turned down…"

"What about the governor?"

"The papers want your ass, and the governor wants votes. You know how it works."

"Yeah, Hank. I know how it works, all right."

"Stoney, better put things right between you and your Maker." Ross sighed, heavily. "'Cause tomorrow about now… you're gonna be meetin' him."

Ross patted his friend on the shoulder, called for the guard and was soon gone. Stone stood and clung onto the bars of his cell as a forlorn harmonica played "Come All Ye Faithful."

"Death row?" Stone said to the King. "Next Christmas, I'm on death row?"

"Sir, Ah'm afraid that's right. And Ah think we're gonna have to be movin' on…."

And they were back in the apartment.

"I have no idea who the hell you are," Stone said, "but I owe you. Of all the visions I've seen tonight, yours are the ones that brought it all home to me."

"Thank you vurry much," the King said.

Stone glanced away, but when he turned back, his visitor had left the building.

Almost dizzy, Stone fell back onto his bed, head whirling; sleep descended….

When he awakened, it was almost noon. He felt reborn. He showered and shaved, whistling "Joy to the World." As he got dressed, he slung on his shoulder-holstered revolver, removing the gun and checking its cylinder.

"Jeez, Sadie," Stone said. "What kinda girl *are* you? Loaded on Christmas…"

Chuckling, he tucked the gun into its holster, then frowned and had a closer look at the .38, studying its handle.

"I'll be damned," he said to himself. Then he smiled knowingly. "Or maybe not."

He slipped the gun back in its hand-tooled shoulder holster, tossed on his topcoat. Then, as an afterthought, he went to his wall safe and counted out five thousand in C-notes, and folded the wad in his pocket.

When Stone knocked at Eddie's apartment, there was no answer. Was he too late? He yelled: "Eddie—it's Stone! I got your cash. All five grand of it!"

Finally Eddie peeked out; he was a little bruised-up from the rough handling Stone had given him last night. "What is this—a gag?"

"No. Lemme in."

In the little apartment—strewn with old issues of *Racing News*, dirty clothes and take-out dinner cartons—Stone counted the cash out to a stunned Eddie.

"What is this?"

"It's a Christmas present, you little weasel."

"Why…?"

"You're my partner's brother. I had a responsibility to help you out. But this is *it*. This'll bail you out today, and don't ask me for no more bail-outs in the future, got it? When the goons come, pay 'em off. And if you wanna lose your gambling habit, I might find some legwork for you to do at the office. But otherwise, you're on your own."

"I don't get it. Why help me, after I tried to blackmail you…?"

"Oh, well, I'll break your arms if you try *that* again."

"Now, that sounds like the old Stoney."

"No—the old Stoney woulda killed you. Eddie—you said your brother promised to take care of you, if anything happened to him. You seemed real sure of that…."

Eddie nodded emphatically. "He told me I was on his insurance policy—fifty percent was supposed to go to me, but somehow that witch wound up with *all* of it!"

Before long, Stone was knocking at the penthouse apartment door of the widow Marley.

Maggie tried not to betray her discomfort at seeing Stone. "Why, Richard," she said, raising her voice, "what a lovely Christmas surpri—"

But he pushed past her before Larry Turner could find a hiding place. Turner was caught by the fireplace, where no stockings were hung.

"Merry Christmas, Larry," Stone said. "I got a present for ya…."

Stone pulled the .38 out from under his shoulder and pointed it at the trembling Turner, who wore the silk smoking jacket Stone had seen in the vision in the mirror last night.

"Actually, it's a present *you* gave *me*," Stone said. "My best friend—my best girl—is Sadie. My gun. Kind of a sad commentary, ain't it?"

"I don't know what's gotten into you, Stone… Just don't point that thing at me…."

"Funny thing is, this isn't Sadie. Imagine—me goin' around with the wrong dame for over a year, and not knowin' it!"

Maggie said, "Richard, please put that gun away—"

"Sweetheart, would you mind standin' over there by your boyfriend? I honestly don't think you were in on this, but I'm not takin' any chances."

She started to say something. Stone said, "Move!" and, with the .38, waved her over by Turner.

Stone continued: "Sometime last year, Larry… I don't know when exactly, just that it had to be before Christmas Eve… you stole my Sadie and substituted a similar gun. Trouble is, Sadie has a little chip out of the handle… tiny, but it's there, only it's *not* there on *this* gun."

"Why in hell would I do that?" Turner asked.

"Because you wanted to use *my* gun to kill Jake with. Which you did."

"Kill Jake! Why would I…"

"Because you and Maggie are an item. A secret item, but an item. You fixed her insurance policy so that *all* those double-indemnity dollars went to her, even though Jake intended his no-good brother to get half. Jake considered you a friend—that's why his hands were in his pockets, and his gun under his coat, when you got up close to him and sent him those thirty-eight caliber Christmas greetings."

"With *your* gun? If any of this were true, I'd have given that gun to the police, long ago."

"Not necessarily. You're an insurance man… using my gun was like takin' out a policy. Any time it looked like suspicion was headed your way, or even Maggie's, you could switch guns again and make a nice little anonymous call."

Maggie was watching Turner, eyes wide, horror growing. "Is this true? Did you kill Jake?"

"It's nonsense," Turner told her dismissively.

"Well, then," she said bitterly, "what was that gun you had me put in my wall safe? For my protection, you said!"

"Shut up," he said.

"Now I know what *I* want for Christmas," Stone said. "Maggie, open the safe."

She went to an oil painting of herself, removed it, and revealed the round safe, which she opened.

"Stand aside, sweetheart," Stone said, "and let *him* get the gun out."

Turner, sweating, licked his lips and reached in and grabbed the gun. He wheeled and fired, then dove behind the nearby couch. When Turner peeked around to fire again at Stone, the detective had already dropped to the floor. Stone returned fire, his slug piercing a plump couch cushion. Turner popped up again, and Stone nailed him through the shoulder.

Turner yelped and fell, his dropped gun spinning away harmlessly on the marble floor.

Stone stood over Turner, who looked up in anger and anguish, holding on to his shot-up shoulder. "You *wanted* me to try to shoot it out with you!"

"That's right."

"*Why?*"

"'Cause it was all theory till you tried to shoot me. Now it'll hold up with the cops and in court."

"You bastard, Stone.... Why don't you just do it? Why don't you just shoot me and be the hell done with it?"

"I don't think so. First of all, I like the idea of you spendin' next Christmas on death row. Second, you're not worth goin' to hell over."

Stone phoned Sgt. Ross. "Yeah, I know you're at home, Hank—but I got another present for ya—all gift-wrapped...."

He hung up, then found himself facing a slyly smiling Maggie.

"No hard feelings?" she asked.

"Naw. We were both louses. Both running around on each other."

Maggie was looking at him seductively, running a finger up and down his arm. "You were so *sexy* shooting it out like that... I don't think I was ever more attracted to you."

He just laughed, and shook his head, pushing her gently aside.

"I would rather go to hell," he said.

Later, with Turner turned over to Ross, Stone stopped at Joey Ernest's house out in the north suburbs.

"Mr. Stone—what are you…?"

"I just wanted to wish you a Merry Christmas, kid. And tell you my New Year's resolution is to dump the divorce racket."

"Really?"

"Really. There's some retail credit action we can get. It won't pay the big bucks, but we'll be able to look at ourselves in the mirror."

Joey's face lit up. "You don't know what this means to me, Mr. Stone!"

"I think maybe I do. Incidentally, Mrs. Marley and me are kaput. No more covering up for your dirty boss."

"Mr. Stone… come in and say hello to the family. We haven't sat down to dinner yet. Please join us!"

"I'd love to say hi, but I can't stay long. I have another engagement."

Finally, he knocked at the door of Katie's little apartment.

"Why… Richard!" Her beaming face told him that certain news hadn't yet reached her.

"Can a guy change his mind? And his ways? I'd love to have Christmas with you and your folks."

She slipped her arm in his and ushered him in. "Oh, they'll be so thrilled to meet you! You've made me so happy, Richard…."

"I just wanted to be with you today," he said, "and maybe sometime, before New Year's, we could drive over to DeKalb and see my Uncle Bob and Aunt Helen."

"That would be lovely!" she said as she walked him into the living room with its sparkling Christmas tree. Her mother and father rose from the couch with smiles.

It would be a blue Christmas for this family, when the doorbell rang, as it would all too soon; but when it did, Stone at least wanted to be with them.

With Katie.

And when they would eventually go to the young soldier's grave, to say a prayer and lay a wreath, Stone would do the same for his late friend and partner.

SMART GUY

by Darrell Schweitzer

George Barlow was a smart guy. He knew it. His associates knew it, and as for his friends, well, he was smart enough to know he didn't have any of those. When other people were pleasant, it was a trap. When *he* was pleasant, it was business of the sort which led to "enterprises" and "operations" and enormous cash-flows.

If just a *little* of that cash-flow got diverted, if he somehow filled a shot-glass out of the torrent from a fire-hose—in a proper world, who was to notice?

So, if he was so smart, why was he hiding out in a Motel Six on a Godforsaken stretch of highway somewhere on the outskirts of East Armpit, Idaho, desperately hoping he would *not* receive a sudden visit from his old pals Eddie "Mongo" Riemer, Luigi "Razors" Norcini, and Seymour the Flattener?

He was smart enough to know that this *isn't* a proper world, that there are screw-ups and conspiracies and nice guys not only fail to finish first, they seldom finish at all.

He was smart enough not to have acquired any absurd moniker such as his former partners proudly sported. They *enjoyed* being stereotypes. These were the kind of guys who watched old gangster movies and said, *Yeah, yeah, let's be just like that,* even if they were not clever enough to reach for the Off button before the final reel.

Not very smart at all, but effective enough for such limited purposes as their stunted imaginations could conceive.

Eddie "Death by Mongo" Riemer's introductory pleasantries usually began with kneecaps.

His colleagues had even less flair.

But George Barlow's smartness had saved him again and again, and now that mix of bluster, caution, experience and actual intelligence was doing the trick one more time.

The phone in his room rang. He picked up the receiver but said nothing, turning the mouthpiece away so the person on the other end wouldn't hear him breathing. He just listened to what he knew *he* was supposed to think was a dead line, the result of one of the innumerable switching errors that happen in the phone system every day. Ring. You pick it up. Click, click. Dead line. You listen to the empty distance for a while, repeating like an idiot, "Hello? Hello? Is anyone there?" until *they* have what they want, be it a recording of your voice or just to establish that you're where they think you are. Then, a dial tone.

Barlow called their bluff and just listened. Which established nothing, at least at first.

He listened carefully, mentally shutting out the occasional traffic noises from the highway outside and the somewhat more frequent clanking of the plumbing and even the beating of his own heart. Much more faintly than any of those came whispers from somewhere else, like what you might hear if there were two lines in the house and voices bled from one to the other accidentally.

He was certain this was no accident. He took mental notes.

The voices were searching for someone.

Where is the Light Bearer?

Servants of the Wyrm reach out to him.

To eliminate, by the liturgies of Kadath.

We'll find him.

It was fascinating, almost hypnotic. The imagery was much too exotic for a drug deal, if they'd even found out about drugs here in rural East Armpit.

Then the whisperers mentioned a name in the news, the mayor of a large Midwestern city recently indicted for a long series of very interesting, scandalous activities.

The language seemed to shift into… was it Latin? *Non… caput… occidere… nolite timere.*

He'd flunked Latin in Catholic school. Hadn't everybody? But he knew that *caput* meant "head," and those other words suggested "fear" and possibly "kill," though in what precise order, he wasn't sure.

What the fuck?—to use a technical term familiar to the likes of Seymour the Flattener. He was very, very tempted to shout, "Hey guys! I know it's you! I ain't fooled."

But none of his former partners knew even a word of Latin, not even Luigi, who had been an altar boy just long enough to get caught stealing the wine. He finally had to consider the possibility that this was a genuine electronic switchboarding glitch, and what he was hearing was *not* intended for his benefit.

While he was considering, the line went truly dead.

Dial tone.

To make sure the phone was really working, he called out for pizza. The delivery came almost on time. The pizza was cold, and the face of the kid delivering it revealed less understanding of the inner workings of the real world than might be found in the placid visages of any of the cud-chewing bovines in nearby pastures, but George tipped the kid, just enough to avoid attracting attention, and sent him away. If this town wasn't really called East Armpit, the local cuisine suggested that maybe it should be. But George hadn't eaten in the nearly forty-eight hours of his precipitous retirement from the firm of Mongo, Razors and Flattener, Inc., and so it would have to do.

The overall quality of bread, cheese and toppings landed him in the crapper for quite some time, and he had only just emerged when the phone rang again.

Once.

Fortunately he was there to snatch it, and still smart enough not to say anything or breathe into the mouthpiece.

It is done.

In the solidarity of Nyarlathotep.

Dial tone.

What was done? He sorted through the word-salad that rose to the fore of his not-entirely-focused brain, put two and two together and got three and a half; then, following a similarly erratic hunch, he turned on the motel room's TV to the evening news. It was one of those astounding coincidences of cosmic synchronicity which defy analysis by the best minds of our time, even those who have not been driving and switching a series of rented, stolen, and variously ditched cars for the last two days, who have had enough sleep and have escaped the ravages of Grease with Extra Grease Special Pizza. Even he, George Barlow, in his impaired state, recognized in this particular happenstance a sinister meaning. There, on the news, in hushed and shocked tones and precious little detail, was the report of the murder of the previously mentioned Midwestern mayor whose life had become unduly complicated due to federal indictments. The old boy had been found—and George couldn't believe it until he switched channels and heard the same story twice—*decapitated. Caput. Occidere.* Head not merely off, but missing.

Barlow snapped the TV off and sat down on the bed, amazed, exhausted and, he had to admit, just a bit frightened, muttering more technical terminology of the sort his erstwhile buddies would have appreciated for its comfortably low signal-to-noise ratio.

He just wanted to get out of here, to lie low somewhere for days and sleep, to pretend none of this had ever happened, that his whole life had been a dream ever since he'd flunked high-school Latin. But no, he couldn't do that. Smart guys *thought* their way out of tight spots, even situations like this one. (Like what? What precisely was *this one?*)

He had been dealt a wild card, something surely intended for someone else's hand, which had, accidentally but very conveniently, come fluttering down into *his*.

Now all he had to do was figure out what to do with it.

The Extra Grease Special stirred in his guts once more, and he had plenty of time to ponder the matter, sitting in the posture of Rodin's *Thinker* for at least an hour before the phone rang again.

This time he didn't quite make it in time, but still there had been only one ring, then silence. He hesitated for several seconds before picking up the receiver, expecting, maybe even hoping, that this really was a mechanical misconnection this time and he would hear nothing more than a dial tone.

But, no, whispering somewhere not very far away, coming through almost as clearly as if he'd tapped into a party line, were a whole series of voices. One, which screamed and pleaded, then blubbered and finally grew docile, repeating everything the others said no matter how absurd, was a voice he recognized from the news. It was the murdered mayor, the guy whose head had been snatched.

Presumably a headless body could say little, so this must have been just the head, at the end of an exhaustive and exhausting interrogation.

At the very last, the dead man said something which made Barlow's heart stop.

We are joined by a stranger.

Is it the Light Bearer, the one we seek?

It was as if the wild card in George Barlow's hand flashed a message: THIS CARD WILL EXPLODE IN FIVE SECONDS UNLESS YOU DO SOMETHING REALLY CLEVER.

Smart guys *thought*, and they did it quickly.

George knew he couldn't run away. They knew he was there and he knew they knew, and they knew he knew they knew… or something like that. He didn't have time to sort it out. The pain in his gut grew suddenly and sharply worse. He wondered if some weird nanotechnological atrocity had been implanted in his intestines; atom-sized computer doohickeys racing to his brain, which had already changed him, which let him hear different frequencies, enabling him to tap into the doings of the world's genuine Secret Masters. Smart guys read up on that sort of thing. Conspiracies. The Trilateral Commission. The men in black whom even the CIA feared, the ones who showed up where people had been abducted by space aliens and *abducted the aliens*. He was like an actor in a play who has been hypnotized into thinking the play is real life, all there is; only a mistake has been made, and now he could see the backstage, the guy in the pit whispering the script, and the stagehands in black suits flickering through the wings. But the show must go on at all costs, and an actor who stops and calls attention to the fake scenery must be eliminated swiftly and unobtrusively, so the rest of the cast could ad-lib around him and the audience wouldn't notice.

A smart guy, as opposed to a dead guy, is someone who can ad-lib *first*.

George Barlow whispered into the phone, "The man you are looking for is named Luigi Norcini." He gave the address of Luigi's storefront in Jersey City.

The voices at the other end paused, shocked.

Barlow went on before they could say anything. "I tell you this on higher authority, which may not be questioned. Eliminate the Light Bearer by the liturgy of Kadath, in the name of the Wyrm, in the solidarity of Nyarlathotep, and *do it now*. Make sure you get his two sidekicks while you're at it."

"What is the confirmation?" the dead mayor demanded.

"You mean the password?" Barlow laughed. "*I* don't have to give the likes of *you* the goddamn password. *You* don't even have the security clearance for it!"

"You are one of the Elevated Ones."

Barlow couldn't tell if that was a question or a statement. "Like I told you, this comes from a higher authority, which doesn't have to explain anything if it doesn't feel like it, and just now it doesn't feel like it one bit. I gave you an order. *Get on with it!*"

"By the hidden faces of the Nephendi, it shall be as you command. *Iä Shub-Niggurath!*"

"That's right. Shub—Shub—whatever you just said. Now get off this phone and do what you're told!"

Barlow slammed the receiver down and sat on the edge of the bed, shaking, drenched with sweat. His gut was worse than ever. He spent much of the rest of the night in the bathroom, but in the end he was clean, he was sure, of whatever poison his enemies had tried to slip him, and if the nano-thingies still remained in his brain, maybe he could find some use for them. Maybe he already had.

That morning, he caught up on desperately needed sleep. He awoke about three in the afternoon, showered, changed into his one and only set of spare underwear, threw the dirty ones in the trash, and went over to the motel office to check out.

He felt good. He had slept as long as he'd liked and nothing had happened to him. That he was still alive could only mean one thing.

He had played his wild card properly. He was winning the game.

When the motel clerk told him he'd slept so long past checkout that he'd have to pay for another day, Barlow showed the man his empty wallet and said, "My people will take care of it."

He walked out before the slack-jawed clerk could say anything.

Some while later, on the road, after he'd changed cars again, he heard something on the news about a backwater motel in Idaho which had been utterly destroyed by a fireball. From the sky, some people claimed. Investigators angrily denied it was anything more than a gas leak, but it was clear the UFO people were having a field day.

As well they might, Barlow understood.

He made his way southwest, checking into luxury hotels in major cities. Somehow bills were not a problem. He took a meandering route, stopping for tourist attractions and eating at the best restaurants. He encountered sly hints that *they* knew where he was. In a hotel room in Denver, he found an envelope on the bed, with a blank sheet of paper inside.

Don't report to me like this again. It is not secure. He wrote that in what he hoped looked like an angry hand, the broad strokes of someone with no patience for trifles. He sealed the envelope and marked it with his very own invented-for-the-occasion Arcane Symbol.

He stayed in that room that night, rather than switching immediately, as he might do if he were afraid. The essential poker strategy at this point was *not* to appear afraid. Later, when he returned from dinner and a concert, there was an American Express Platinum Card made out in his name on the bed where the envelope had been.

In the weeks that followed, he gambled in Las Vegas and won hugely. He partied with the stars in Hollywood. He even, on the spur of the moment, produced a movie, after a late-night, somewhat drunken conversation in Beverly Hills; the "somewhat" part being that the other guy was plastered while he, George Barlow, smart guy, remained cold sober. It was a gangster movie, which appealed to his sense of irony. But he didn't lose control even there. He made sure the flick was done under budget, with non-union workers, and that it made money.

He was beginning to enjoy himself; not merely to respond to threats, but to *do things*. Every once in a while he'd pick up a phone without dialing and whisper a message into the empty line, to have this person eliminated, or that one *changed* or replaced. He would get replies back the same way, or on seemingly innocent postcards, in graffiti, or, once, in skywriting, the words IT IS DONE spread out from horizon to horizon across the desert at dawn, their significance a mystery to all but himself.

He started a couple of wars and ended one. Just flexing his newfound muscles, he broke one of the oldest banks in the world and left some twenty-eight-year-old sap in Singapore as the fall guy.

He improved the quality of pizza in East Armpit, Idaho, sufficiently that the town became the number-one junkfood mecca west of the Mississippi.

For the longest time, no one seemed to check up on him at all. He laughed all the way to the bank, as the saying had it. Then he fired the management, emptied out the contents of the bank into another bank, which he already controlled, and moved on. Feeling the need for a vacation at the end of such labors, he took a world cruise, was gone for six weeks, and, by the time he got back, he realized he was within an inch of *owning* the world. Everywhere, limousines waited for him. His name or a wave of his hand sufficed in any situation. He didn't even have to show the Platinum Card anymore.

The credit statements never showed up either.

He, being a smart guy, wondered about that. Deep down inside, he was still uneasy. He knew that he was playing like a master, that he was ahead of the game, but this wasn't the sort of game where you could just scoop your winnings off the table and leave when you wanted to.

He'd have to play it through to the end. And win. Everything.

It was when he returned to his luxurious San Francisco penthouse from the world cruise and flopped down on the neatly made king-sized bed and gazed out the studio windows at the Golden Gate Bridge and the reddish-brown hills of Marin County beyond, that he was dealt the final hand.

The phone rang, once.

He picked it up wearily. "Won't you ever get this right? I don't have to pay attention to your kind. If you can't recite the complete Protocols of the Elders of Pnath, forget it, okay?"

"But Mr. Barlow," said the voice on the other end. "I *can* recite them in their entirety. I am sure you are a busy man, and don't wish me to waste that much time on the complete effort. The following should suffice." The caller broke into gibberish, but Barlow had no doubt it was *authentic* gibberish. *He*, Barlow, made up this stuff as he went along. He was quite certain that the other fellow did not.

He knew that voice. It sounded exactly like Vincent Price at his most suavely and silkenly evil. Good God, he thought. Vincent Price was supposed to be dead. Could it be…?

"Put the phone down and turn on your television, Mr. Barlow."

As he moved to do so, the light flickered, and it barely registered that, in this airy apartment on such a bright afternoon, no light was on. It was the sky. The sun flickered, darkened, and a false night settled over the Bay Area. Streetlights came on. Car headlights streamed across the Golden Gate Bridge as if no one had noticed anything odd.

He glanced at his watch and saw that it had stopped. That figured.

The face on the TV set wasn't Vincent Price's. Then again, the TV wasn't really *on*. The screen lit up, but inside, as if in a bubbling aquarium, a human head floated, attached to wires and pipes. Some of the fluid leaked out around the edges of the screen, puddling on the rug.

"Hiya, George."

"*Mongo?*" He sat down and covered his eyes.

"Look at me, George."

"Jesus God, Mongo. I'm sorry. What have they done to you?"

"Just what you told 'em to, George."

"No! I didn't mean it. I wouldn't—"

"You said the words, George. That was enough. But that don't matter no more, George." Eddie "Mongo" Riemer went on to explain, struggling quite hard to get past some of the bigger words and more arcane concepts, how the Owners had harnessed a vast network of human brains, even those of the likes of Mongo and Luigi Razors and Seymour the Flattener. Some were planted inside TV sets, as his was, or in telephone boxes on the tops of utility poles, or inside those railroad utility boxes marked DANGER! 50,000 VOLTS! that kids always dare one another to touch and nobody ever does. Agents of the Darkness were inside the world's mainframe computers, in Money Access machines in malls, anywhere information flowed. Information was power. It was harvested, for the benefit of the Masters, by those millions of slave brains linked by every conceivable means from tin cans and string to fiber optics, brains like cells in an Overmind, the consciousness of which was controlled from somewhere else.

A poker player, even when he knows he's lost, can only try one last, desperate bluff.

"Oh yeah?" George said. "Then how come more people don't *notice* there's heads in the TV set? I mean, you don't look like you belong on Showtime, or even the Fox Network."

"Most people can't see us, George. They're not attuned to the frequency."

"But I am, huh?"

"Yes, George. It was the pizza. Nano-something-or-other in the pepperoni. Our masters are very pleased with the way you've improved the quality of the pizza, by the way. It served their purposes admirably."

"Bullshit, Mongo."

"Everything you did, absolutely *everything*, served their purposes when it only seemed to serve yours."

"But—"

"I'm disappointed in you, George."

Barlow had begun to notice that this sounded less and less like Mongo Riemer talking, more and more like a superior intelligence speaking through the detached head inside the TV set.

He picked up the phone again. The same voice came from there too. Mongo seemed to be just mouthing the words.

"You didn't think you could get away with it, did you? You being a smart guy and all. All this time you have carried out the glorious missions of our masters without even knowing it. Even that movie you made carried our message subliminally."

"Okay, so why are you telling me this now?"

"Because at long last, George, you have outlived your usefulness."

"How's that?"

"You finally exhausted your American Express Platinum Card. There are no more nano-bugs left in the magnetic strip."

"I don't believe a word of this! *You* don't have the authority to lay this kind of crap on me! I don't care if this is a test, or what. *You* don't get to grade George Barlow, smart guy! I am going over your head. Get off the line and let me talk to Numero Uno, the Boss, the Big Cheese himself."

"Are you sure you want that, George?"

He screamed all the arcane phrases he knew or could make up, the Dhole Chants, advertising jingles from Yuggoth, something off a decoder ring.

When he finally had to catch his breath, the caller said, "Are you quite finished?"

"Yeah! Now get off the line!"

He switched off the TV and threw the phone down onto the rug. He paced back and forth in what now seemed a tiny apartment, a cage. He couldn't run away. This was it. He would have to play what was left of his hand to the end.

He paced, waiting for the phone to ring.

But the phone never rang. Instead, the floor shook. Books and bric-a-brac fell from the shelves. The enormous studio windows shattered inward, showering him with glass.

For just an instant he thought it was an earthquake, but then he saw that San Francisco Bay was *boiling*. The Golden Gate Bridge drooped and stretched like string cheese, but still traffic flowed over it, as if everything were relative and the drivers didn't notice a thing. Black smoke rose out of the bay, obscuring the view of Marin County.

He peered into the deepening darkness, fascinated as the city seemed to fall away like burning paper, crumbling like ash, the earth opening up to reveal what at first looked like infinite space, with a few dull-red stars guttering in the otherwise impenetrable blackness. The nano-things must have changed his senses, enabling him to see what others could not.

He saw shapes in the darkness, lakes of fire filled with the writhing damned, fortifications, cities of pain, circle upon circle as his gaze plunged ever downward. Another ring of dark towers resolved themselves into living giants, into titans who seemed to lower him gently in their hands down into Malebolge, the central pit where lies Cocytus, the Final Circle of the Abyss.

There, trapped waist-deep in a frozen lake, his ragged, useless wings fluttering in some indescribably foul breeze which Barlow was beginning to feel, was the Master. He had many other names.

The face of the monstrosity was as George expected it to be: hideous, filled with rage and madness, with infinite, malevolent awareness. Here was the Adversary, who reached out to corrupt all the universe. Between his teeth writhed certain traitors, who had doubtless once thought themselves smart guys.

In the end, George had to admit, there was a certain inevitability. He was ready for it.

What he wasn't ready for was the bundle of glowing fiber-optic cables patched into the creature's head, binding it like Prometheus to an enormous rock; or the gigantic telephone resting on a stone shelf at the lake's edge.

The phone rang, once. The Horned One answered. George knew they were talking about him, but for once he couldn't make out a word.

He screamed, but no one heard him.

Someone opened the door to his apartment and stepped inside.

He heard knives scraping across one another.

"Maybe you should have turned off the movie before the final reel," someone said.

He realized he wasn't such a smart guy after all.

The Great Escape

by Ian Watson

Perhaps the most paradoxical aspect of Hell is the participation of certain angels in its procedures.

I do not refer to those millions of fallen angels who became demons. I refer to our own select cadre of righteous, kosher angels who remain angelic, who are still endowed with the grace of the Quint, yet who are seconded by Him to serve in Hell for dozens of years at a stretch.

This is as though (to borrow a recent example) Nuremburg prosecutors or agents of Mossad must participate in the uninterrupted management of a Nazi concentration camp! As if vegetarians must collaborate with vivisectionists!

I am the Impresario Angel. My task is to fly low over Hell, bearing in my hands one of the special lenses—resembling a giant frisbee or frying-pan lid made of diamond—through which blessèd souls in Paradise are able to view the torments of the damned. (Some of these torments are indeed conducted inside of gigantic frying pans.)

When I reach a particularly atrocious scene, I hover there with the lens. I inhale the reek of cooking flesh or of voiding bowels. Shrieks of anguish assail my ears. The blessèd in Paradise are not assailed thus. The lens relays sights but neither smells nor sounds.

The demons who conduct the torments pay scant heed to me. Mostly they perform like automata. Out of the frying pan, into the fire. Out of the cauldron, onto the griddle. Essentially their work is monotonous and unimaginative. To devise ingenious new varieties of pain is no concern of theirs. Can it be that they refrain from doing so in order to frustrate the Deity, in a last, dogged show of rebellion?

Perhaps their lackluster performance is actually in response to my arrival on the scene with the surveillance lens.

Sometimes, as I approach, they seem to be gossiping. Quickly they become mute. Even if they did carry on chatting, only the screeching and wailing of victims would be easily audible.

I should not communicate with any of the demons, lest I be corrupted. Formerly—before my present secondment—I was a border guard between Hell and the higher domain.

As were my colleagues likewise.

I am the Impresario Angel. I present the hellish performance for the attention of souls in Paradise, although I have no idea of the reaction of the audience.

There is also the Trumpet Angel. He flies to and fro, sounding fanfares of exquisite purity on a long, golden trumpet. Each sufferer in torment may imagine that he or she is hearing the Last Trump, and that Hell might soon cease to function. He or she is wrong.

Then there is the Clock Angel. He tends the eternity clock. That clock, of diamond, rises from atop a crystal crag, taller than any skyscraper. The crag is much too smooth and sleek and sheer to climb. The clock is visible from many parts of Hell. Its four high faces lack any mechanical hands. However, the play of light within the precious substance of those faces constantly evokes the *appearance* of different hands—minute-hands, hour-hands, year-hands, century-hands, millennium-hands. Flying up and down one face and then the adjoining face, the Clock Angel cleans the clock by the beating of his wings. Otherwise, rising smoke and soot would dull the clock. Its diamond light is a source of illumination for much of Hell—supplementing the fires of torment and the faint phosphorescence of areas of ice.

Three other angels also serve with me in Hell, namely the Harp Angel and the Scribe Angel and the Ark Angel. Additionally, we each have a counterpart. These colleagues take over our roles as Impresario and Clock Angel and such during our session of praise. Since we do not sleep (nor, in Hell, does anyone), our half-day period of sabbatical is spent singing psalms to the Quint in a white marble tabernacle upon an alabaster island surrounded by a wide moat of quicksilver.

And while I am on duty with my lens, those counterpart angels are singing His praises. Hosanna, Hosanna. Thus does rapture regularly bless us all during our duties in Hell.

If demons try to cross that gleaming moat, their wings fail. Nor can they wade through it. On some previous occasion demons must have tried to fly or swim across: Submerged in the moat are several skeletons.

Sometimes these rise to the surface, where they drift like ramshackle rafts.

Although our departure from the island is always perfectly harmonized, return to the tabernacle is rarely simultaneous. Usually several minutes elapse between the arrival of the first of us and the last. Meanwhile our counterparts continue their enchanting, ecstatic praise.

After a sojourn amidst the misery, the singing has a powerful effect upon us. We yearn to join in. Indeed we must soon do so before our replacements can fly away, so that praise of the Quint will never cease for an instant. Yet there's often an interlude while we await a tardy colleague and prepare to hand over lens or trumpet. During this interval we are at liberty to engage in sublime discussion. *Colloquy* is a suitably dignified word for these occasional brief conversations of ours.

During a short interval twice every infernal day, no angel cleans the clock of eternity, or blows a golden fanfare, or plucks the silver harp; nor may the blessèd watch the torments of the damned. Recently I queried the Scribe Angel about the security aspect of these transitions between one shift and the next....

A word about time. In Hell there is neither day nor night. Nor does the clock of eternity possess hands. Nor do the salutes of the Trumpet Angel mark off minutes. Yet all of us angels possess perfect pitch. How else might we psalm the praises of the Quint? In matters of time instinctively we heed the chime of the Cosmos—that distant, quasar-like pulse of the Quint, cascading down through the realms. Successive veils of existence blur this pulse. That is why we do not return to the island in perfect synchrony. Our singing inside of our marble tabernacle readjusts this minor imperfection. The imperfection will recur. Is not Hell a place of blemishes?

I queried the Scribe Angel about security because, next to myself, she comes into closest proximity with the damned and with demons.

By contrast, the Trumpet Angel rarely dips near to the soil of Hell. I sometimes suspect that she blows her trumpet as often as she does in order to banish the cries of anguish from her ears! If demons conspired, *she* would never overhear their conversations.

The *soil* of Hell, did I say? It is hardly loam. Solid lava mingles with hot sand and with quicksands and with pebbles. Compacted excrement adjoins mud and glaciers. Black cones ooze molten rock. Fumaroles vent stinking steam, which coats the ground with flowers of sulphur.

By the nature of their tasks neither the Clock Angel nor the Harp Angel comes into close contact with the denizens. As for the Ark Angel, he presides over the boat-shaped fortress of timbers grounded upon Hell's only notable peak, to the east.

The Ark Angel stands upon a poop jutting high above the uppermost deck at the rear. He constantly surveys Hell, though from such an elevation and distance most details are indistinguishable.

The Ark is much vaster within than without. Decks descend beneath decks, plunging down, an abyss of a myriad levels. A myriad benches occupy each deck. Chained to each bench are inmates. Demons patrol with whips.

The Ark is at once prison-hulk and slave-ship, traveling nowhere except through the timelessness of Hell. Held therein are the ancestors of humanity. Pre-Men; hominids. Down in the bilges, in darkness and in fetters, hunch the two wizened, apish creatures known as Adam and Lucy. Punishment is only by whip in the Ark.

"Scribe Angel," I addressed her, "do you suppose that anything happens differently in Hell during the gaps each day when none of us are on duty? Do you suppose that the demons rest and that punishments pause?"

She consulted her great scroll upon which she forever records with the blood-quill the names of the damned and their tortures. Soon she would hand this scroll and the quill over to the other Scribe Angel. *He* always documented the torments of males. She, of females. She scanned her records, as if seeking some anomaly.

The psalming of our colleagues was approaching a transcendent climax, if indeed the sublime could top the sublime. Maybe it was exaltation which prompted her reply.

"A pause in the punishment?" she said to me. "Such would be the mercy of the Quint, descending even unto here!"

I spied our final colleague winging toward the moat of mercury. On this occasion the late arrival happened to be the Ark Angel. Just before he alighted, I ventured to ask, "What if the demons do something other than merely rest?"

"Surely the Quint would witness it!" was her reply.

"If so," said I, "why are *we* here as witnesses?"

"The Quint is ineffable," she told me with utter certainty. "He is inexpressible. He cannot be expressed. Therefore we are here as intermediaries. As ambassadors. This is the Embassy of Heaven."

The Ark Angel was landing on the alabaster isle. We must begin to sing in beatific chorus. We must proceed into the marble tabernacle.

We must hand over lens and scroll and blood-quill and trumpet.

What the Scroll Angel said was so true. The Quint—the Quintessence—is necessarily remote. Beyond the many angelic hierarchies—each more ethereal than the rank below—is the center-point, the Divine Core, the radiant quasar of all existence. That core, who is the Quint, is unknowable except to the Seraphic Sphere surrounding Him. Likewise, the Seraphic Sphere is unknowable except to the Cherubic Sphere.

Our duties, and our very existence, descend from on high. Yet could it be that the intentions of the Quint might be misinterpreted, as in the game of Chinese Whispers?

How could this be so, when intention is hardly ascribable to the Quint? He is Pure Being.

I decided to alight and address a demon directly. This went against my inner sense of my duty, but I was becoming suspicious of their zombie-like conduct.

By setting foot upon the infernal unsoil, would I be breaching a covenant? Would lightning rive the somber, smutty sky? Would demons be free to seize me and attempt to torture me?

What about the lens I carried? The lens would not sustain itself unsupported in mid-air. I must continue to hold it. I must not lay it down and risk it being stolen. Maybe I should angle the lens upward so that only the sky was visible? This might constitute a breach of faith with viewers in Paradise.

Therefore the blessèd must stomach an *interview with a demon*, particularly if they could lip-read.

A partial interview! Viewers would not see me, as holder of the lens. They would not read the questions upon my lips. They would only be able to lip-read the replies (if any) of my infernal interlocutor.

Gingerly—and gloriously—I alighted near to a gridiron. A sinner was suspended over this upon a rack consisting of iron winch and pulley and of rope black as tar. The naked man was stretched out excruciatingly. Beneath the hot gridiron a bed of coals glowed brightly whenever one of the two attending demons operated the bellows. If the rack was slackened, the man's buttocks would descend upon the hot iron. Hoist him again to relieve this pain, and his sinews would distend agonizingly once more.

Through cracked, dry lips the wretch would croak, "For mercy's sake, raise me." Soon he would gasp, "For mercy's sake, lower me."

In this manner he directed his own torment. The demon who turned the handle of the winch one way or the other merely complied mechanically.

When I judged that the victim was half-slack, I commanded, "Stop!"

The demon paused.

"Demon, by the grace of the Quint, I conjure you to answer me!"

The demon's expression was inscrutable. With his left hoof he scuffed at a ripple in the lava. With a long talon, he picked his yellow teeth. I was almost minded to unfurl my wings and leap aloft again. Yet I persevered.

"Demon," I demanded, "what do demons do when no angels are present?"

His reply, when it came, was in some language of grunts and barks and whistles and chattering which I had never heard before. Gifted with tongues though I am, this babble wasn't in my repertoire.

It sounded like some primitive mother-tongue which had preceded true speech. Not proto-Indo-European. But proto-proto. An ur-language preceding true language, and inaccessible to me—as ineffable as the Quint.

Thus did he mock me. He had answered me obediently. Yet I had no way of understanding the answer.

I was about to ascend in disgust. However, a second thought came to me.

Gloriously, and gingerly, I inclined myself and thus my lens over the face of the half-racked man. The Scroll Angel would have known the name of this person; but not I.

"Mortal," I addressed him, although, arguably, he was immortal now, his body repairing itself in order to be abused repeatedly. "Hear me, mortal: What do demons do when the Trump falls silent, and when the Harp ceases to twang?"

The sweating man stared up at me. From his expression I feared that he might be insane. Still, his mind must surely repair itself frequently.

"Water," he croaked. "Water—"

Give him a drink, and he would tell me... *something*. Where was there water in Hell, except boiling in cauldrons or mixed in mud?

An angel's cool, sweet saliva might serve—that same saliva which lubricated our psalms. I dribbled upon the victim's parched lips and swollen purple tongue which resembled a parrot's.

Promptly the bellows-demon resumed pumping. Coals flared. Choking smoke billowed. The winch-demon spun the handle, dumping my potential informant wholesale upon the gridiron. Feet and legs and buttocks and spine and head and outstretched arms all made contact. The moisture which I had donated shrieked out of the mortal.

The tethers of his wrists and ankles lolled loosely for the first time in what might have been centuries. As he lay writhing, those tethers began to smolder. They burst into flames. The rope was indeed impregnated with tar.

Blazing ropes parted. The man's squirming weight tipped the gridiron. Off he rolled, falling upon the hard lava.

The demons scratched their horned heads, as if such an event were outside of their comprehension. Surely their mime of stupidity was deliberate.

Despite his burns and despite his tumble, the naked man began to scrabble away, crab-like. To begin with, he proceeded slowly upon all fours, and then a little faster. He staggered to his feet. He lurched and limped. He tried to straighten. He was like some illustration of the evolution of humanity, commencing stooped over with knuckles upon the ground, then rising to become a biped. That biped was hobbling and hopping away. Both demons scratched their narrow, jutting chins. With that red gaze of theirs, they eyed one another. They shook their heads as though bemused.

Was it up to me—an angel encumbered with a lens—to recapture the absconder? In Paradise, were the blessèd praying that *I* would do so swiftly? Were more and more of the blessèd flocking to witness this unprecedented spectacle?

One of the demons grunted. His colleague squawked a response. At long last, hooves clicking upon lava, they did set out in pursuit. Ever so slowly and leisurely.

Leaping, and deploying my wings, I took to the air.

I followed the dawdling demons. Now and then I angled the lens so that it would show the faltering yet frantic progress of the fugitive. I was evoking a dramatic tension quite different from the physical tension of torture—yet akin, I suppose, akin. The maimed mouse being stalked by two lazy cats.

The man sprawled. He hauled himself to his fast-healing feet again. Nervously—putting on a pathetic spurt of speed—he passed quite close between two cauldrons. At this point he had little choice of route. A lagoon of molten lava bubbled to one side. A pond of pus, to the other. Trussed in nets which dangled from tripods, some children were being parboiled in those cauldrons. The demons who had been hauling the children up and down relaxed, to contemplate the runaway. They made no move to apprehend him. An inmate on the loose was too singular a sight to abbreviate.

I was paradoxically pleased with my lens-work. The angles I chose… The choice of "cuts" from demon to escapee—and back again. Whenever I focused upon the two stalking demons, anxiety must mount that maybe somewhere ahead and out of sight the man might have fallen or been forcibly halted. While I was focusing upon *him*, though, the unease was that the two demons might have broken into a sprint. Even now they might be rushing up from behind.

When the man had glanced from one boiling cauldron to the other, he had witnessed those netted children being raised and lowered, dripping and bright pink. His attention had mainly been upon the cooks—warily so—rather than upon the cooked.

As he wended his way farther, he seemed to become more attentive to the condition of the victims.

Presently he came to a place where a young man's intestines were being drawn out through his navel. The operation was occurring at a snail's pace by means of an automated windlass, powered by steam from a nearby fumarole. Not even a demon might have had the patience—or the obstinacy—to wind this capstan personally. So slowly, so monotonously, and with such regularity, did the evisceration proceed! The rate of extraction must correspond exactly to the rate of replenishment of new intestine within the victim.

The drum of the capstan was thick with coil upon coil of glistening, sausage-like bowel. Ooze dripped constantly from beneath the machine. This liquid soaked the compacted excrement of the soil, slicking the ground as if with diarrhea. Pressure from the outer coils must be squeezing the inner coils as flat as sloughed snakeskins.

The young man was crudely crucified against a timber framework in the shape of a letter M. This held him in position throughout his everlasting ordeal. Barbed wire secured his wrists and his outstretched ankles.

In a bizarre sense it looked as though he were escaping from that crucifixion via his own navel. The glossy rope of intestine resembled an ectoplasmic cord which might link a departed spirit to the body it had quit.

Our absconder paused near this young man. Were tears coursing down our refugee's cheeks, or only a swill of sweat? Outdistancing the demons, I flew ahead. I hovered above the fugitive like a gigantic white dove, annunciatory or pentecostal.

I did remember to pivot in mid-air and track the dilatory progress of the pursuers. If anything, that pair had slowed their pace. I returned my attention, and the focus of my lens, to the escapee.

He gaped up at me in my white splendor.

"Mortal," I called down to him, serenely and melodiously, "I do not intervene." Did he imagine that I might pluck him up—when I was already laden with a diamond lens—and carry him away to our alabaster sanctuary? (Oh, he knew nothing of that place!) I wished him to disregard me.

I suppose I *was* intervening to an extent simply by addressing him. Earlier, I had posed him a question. Now I strove not to thrust my presence upon him. I yearned to see what he would do.

He must have taken me at my word. His bleary gaze sank. He scrutinized the victim of automated evisceration. He stepped closer to the taut cable of intestine. His hands made nervous, aimless gestures. Was he contemplating unfastening the barbed wire and releasing the young man from that framework in an act of futile mercy?

"What did you *do*?" croaked the refugee to the victim.

Ah… perhaps our refugee wouldn't be willing to release the young man if, when alive, he had performed a truly vile crime, evil and perverted, such as the sexual murder of children, or, or… *abortion*! Abortion might actually have been the crucified man's crime, reflected by the endless dragging out of him of his own living tissue through an orifice close to where a womb would have been, were he a woman!

The victim seemed to be in a trance of torment, determined not to move—not even his eyes, much less his lips—in case the least motion multiplied his slow agony. He remained silent.

Our refugee stared about him at the landscape of Hell—and at those two laggardly stalking demons. He must have realized that ultimately he had no hope of escape.

"Let me take your place," he begged the young man.

This sounded like a saintly offer, except for the wheedling tone of voice.

Our refugee imagined that he could endure slow, automated evisceration more easily than the constant bump-and-hoist of alternate racking and broiling—because this other punishment would be uniform and unvarying! The younger man seemed to have achieved a meditative stupor of misery, which must surely be lesser than rack 'n' roast. The young man was privileged in that he was devoid of the constant attention of demons.

No doubt demons must unload the drum of the windlass now and then, disburdening it of the accumulating weight of compacted bowel. Otherwise the torment might have slowed eventually, and even stopped. Aside from such intervention, the young man suffered in peace.

"Let me take your place!"

Feverishly our refugee knelt. He began to prize apart the rusted barbed wire looped so tightly around one ankle. His fingers bled. He licked the moisture.

Did he imagine that he might succeed in unfastening the young man completely before his own personal demons arrived? Did he fantasize that, like a midwife, he might sever the long umbilicus with his teeth? That with the sharp barbs of wire he might make an incision through his own belly-button, hook out some of his own upper bowel, and knot that to the disconnected trailing end? That the young man would agree to crucify the refugee instead?

All this—without the two demons arriving prematurely, or objecting to the substitution?

A suspicion began to dawn that I was being led astray by a charade. Astray from my original question! The end of my shift might arrive before I witnessed any finale. In waiting for a climax, my question would remain unanswered.

"Mortal," I boomed, "what do demons do when no angels watch over them?"

The refugee cowered from my voice. His bloodstained fingers plucked frantically at the wire.

Might I make an offer of amnesty in exchange for a reply? Might I promise to carry him away across the mercury moat to our island, where the harmonies issuing from our tabernacle would fill him with everlasting ecstasy as if he were truly in Heaven?

If I held him in my arms, he would need to hold the lens on my behalf. His fingers would be slippery with blood. His blood would stain the view enjoyed by the blessèd in Paradise. The lens might slip from his grasp and fall into the mercury moat. How could I ever retrieve it? Would a raft of demon's skeleton bear my weight? What could I use to grapple for the lens? A web of hooks made of barbed wire? I might fish for half of eternity, like some pagan condemned to fill a pitcher with a hole in its bottom and carry it up a slippery slope! Would my wing-feathers or my psalmist's lungs tolerate immersion in mercury?

How could I possibly bring a naked wretch to our beautiful island? The constant sight of him would untune our hymns.

I could not make such an offer.

"By the Quint," I bellowed, "I command you to answer me!"

Fingers scrabbled at the barbs, shredding skin faster than it could possibly heal. The man was dementedly obsessed by this one activity.

At last the crucified man summoned breath. Softly he implored, "No, no—" How it pained him to speak.

The demons had arrived. They were chuckling. I'd forgotten to jump-cut to them.

Nearby the trump sounded, long and grandly. I ascended, to stare faraway at the shining, timeless face of the clock of eternity. Within me welled the urge to commence my return to the isle.

Later, none other than the Ark Angel confided anxieties to me.

This time it was the Harp Angel whom we were awaiting. Unlike the Trumpet Angel, she never transported her instrument along with her. The Harp was much too huge. Twenty times larger than herself, it was a veritable precipice of strings. She would fly to and fro across these—like a white moth across a great grille—plucking with her outstretched hands to sound the chords and arpeggios, brushing with her wings to rouse the swishing, swirling *glissandi*.

"Impresario," the Ark Angel said softly, "I fear that something furtive is afoot in the Ark."

Thinking of that fugitive from rack 'n' roast, I suggested, "A hominid may have broken free. An ape-man could scuttle about for ages on his knuckles beneath all those benches on all those decks. The demons might be too lazy or clumsy to catch him—"

"It is not that. There are too many creaky noises below decks."

"Rattling of fetters? Shifting of hairy bums on benches?"

"I'm familiar with such noises, Impresario. There are new noises."

"Increased use of the whips?"

"That would cause more shrieking."

The Ark Angel's rightful place was upon the poop, as a kind of honorary pilot and look-out. He was much too large to go belowdecks in person. The most he could accomplish by way of scrutiny would be to stick his glorious head down one of the uppermost hatchways. In the Ark, decks descended, and descended again. Such is the design of Hell. Its topography can be crudely described as *fractal*; hence its capacity for prisoners. This fractal quality is inevitable, since Hell is an unwholesome dimension. It cannot possess anything remotely equivalent to the singularity of the Quint, or to the integrity of the angelic realms.

There was urgency in the Ark Angel's request to me:

"Impresario, during our next tour of duty, will you kindly join me upon the deck of the Ark with your lens? I would value your insights."

My insights...

Did the Ark Angel suppose that by means of my lens we would be able to spy belowdecks? That was not at all how the lens functioned. I must take it on trust—as an act of faith—that the lens does serve the purpose which I ascribed to it. Yet since I must believe that it does, the most I might achieve by thrusting the lens down a hatchway would be to reveal to the blessèd in Paradise a limited, dingy view of the limited, dingy sufferings of some of the primitive ancestors of Man, and of Woman.

I did not wish to disillusion the Ark Angel, however, since his suspicions reinforced my own about the conduct of demons.

"Of course I shall come! Do you suppose your counterpart has noticed anything peculiar?"

"I scarcely have time to ask her—"

It was out of the question that there could be any complicity between the female Ark Angel and the demons of the Ark. No, it was during the *intervals* that whatever was happening took place.

The Harp Angel was coming in to land. Our colloquy must cease. Soon we must start to sing.

I alighted upon the poop deck with my lens. At his post, the Ark Angel awaited me.

He gestured at the main deck. Surrounded by demons, a large *device* was bolted massively to the timbers. The contraption was built of parts of racks and of gridirons, and of clamps and screws used in torments. Mirrors used for burning also played a role. The apparatus cradled a hefty tube, angled vertically. Under this, a demon lay upon his back. He peered up through the tube, busily adjusting screws.

"That," Ark Angel said, "is new."

Here for the first time might be evidence of aberration!

Yet I suggested, "Maybe that is a new instrument of punishment for hominids?" Maybe a hominid would be placed inside that tube, and screws and clamps would be tightened.

"Pre-humans are only ever punished with the whip," the Ark Angel reminded me. "Such is the clemency of the Quint."

We descended a grand stairway to the main deck. We approached the infernal machine. Demons clustered protectively. They exhibited a kind of stubborn insolence.

The main deck vibrated subtly under our feet. It was as if some engine throbbed deep in the bowels of the Ark, or as if some coordinated activity or rhythmic exertion were under way. How could this be?

A red demon appeared to be some kind of foreman. "In the name of the Quint," the Ark Angel called out to him, "what is this contrivance?"

I quite expected to hear some gibberish. But no. The red demon seemed flushed with confidence and effrontery.

"Wise One," he sneered, "we call this a *theodolite*. From the ancient words *theos*, signifying God, and *dolor*, signifying misery."

"What does it do?"

"Ah," came the reply, "it measures the distance and direction of the Quint!"

I stared up at the sooty sky—as if that tube might somehow be burning a channel through the welkin of Hell to reveal a glimpse of the realms. The sky remained as stygian as ever. This theodolite must operate in some different mode.

"What might that distance be?" I asked derisively, my lens held upright to capture the foreman demon's image.

The demon leered at me, and announced:

"It is one hundred and eighty parasangs. If you know what a parasang is."

Of course I knew. One parasang is equal to one hundred and eighty billion times the polar diameter of the Earth, as revealed in the Jewish

Shiur Qomah, otherwise known as *The Measurement of the Height*. So therefore the distance to the Quint, as calculated by demons, was one hundred and eighty times that figure....

"A bit less by now," said the demon.

What did he mean?

Such a smirk. The deck vibrated underfoot. All of Hell seemed to quiver, as if a mild infernoquake were occurring.

"This Ark," bragged the demon, "is now underway toward the Quint."

During the interludes demons had secretly been carpentering oars from the ever-available stocks of wood intended for racks and gibbets and bonfires. Demons had brought these oars on board the Ark unobserved. They had equipped all the hominids' benches with rowlocks fashioned from fetters. They had trained the hominids to be galley-slaves. This operation must have taken a century, or, in view of the fractal nature of the Ark, maybe a millennium. Within this vessel, those slaves were now rowing in unison, pulling the great oars to and fro!

The brutish ur-speech which that other demon had used had been the primitive proto-language of hominids. Those hominids, stretching way back to Adam and Lucy, could not possibly have initiated this project. The concept would have eluded them—though, since punishments of pre-humans were mild, their bodies retained stamina. No, the demons were using those precursors of Man and of Woman as inadvertent insurgents. How devilishly sly this use of the ancestors! It evaded the whole etiquette of Hell.

Our demon informant taunted me: "By now, the distance to the Quint is only one hundred and seventy-nine point nine parasangs!"

The demon who lay under the theodolite corrected him. "Point nine nine."

"Progress is being made!" snarled our demon.

I hastened to the rail of the Ark. Averting my lens, I stared down the side of the vast vessel. The Ark was exactly where it had always been since prehistoric times. No banks of oar-blades jutted from newly revealed slots in the bulwarks.

Nevertheless, we were under way.

Although the oars were enclosed inside of the Ark, the rowing of the hominids was propelling us! The Ark was shifting in the direction revealed by the theodolite, which doubled as compass and rudder!

Rooted in Hell, this Ark would never cross the line between the infernal region and the lowest of the heavenly realms. No border guards with shining swords would rush to board her, because no demon was attempting to leave the territory of Hell.

The whole territory of Hell itself was on the move!

Impelled by the Ark, by the muscle-power of subhuman hominids, Hell itself had begun to travel upward so as to pass through the domains, carrying with it all the evolved descendants of those hominids who writhed in torment ordained by the Quint through His intermediaries.

Did I hear, for the first time, a chime sound from the clock of eternity? Or was the Trumpet Angel sounding a note which had altered in pitch?

Ours would be a long journey—of two hundred and fifty-five point nine six quintillion miles, I calculated. That many miles to reach the quasar of the Quint! En route we would travel through the choirs of Angels, Archangels and Principalities. Then through the choirs of Powers, Virtues and Dominations. Finally we would cleave through the choirs of Thrones, and Cherubim, and Seraphim....

Oh, but already the distance was slightly less than that amount. And no doubt, as realms became more rarified, we would accelerate rapidly.

Agonies will continue. Torment is an aether into which the hominids dip their oars, and through which they haul. The demons seem contemptuous of us angels. Yet we still have our roles. Now that Hell has shifted its location, no other angels will know how to enter and replace us.

I am both appalled and elated.

Appalled, because during this journey the demons intend to convert a percentage of gridirons and racks into great harpoon guns. These they will mount on the main deck of the Ark, to be fired at the Quint.

Yet I am also elated — because contrary to all expectation for anyone below the rank of Seraph, I and my humble angelic colleagues and counterparts will come directly into the presence of the Quint, when Hell harpoons that pure Being and then collides with Him.

Such hymns we will sing as we near His radiance—Hosanna!

Hosanna in the Highest! And all will be revealed.

If only I could understand the language of the hominids, originating before the time when the Quint became manifest.

Unfortunately, I am too bulky to descend any of the myriad ladders of the Ark with my deaf lens so as to interrogate Adam and Lucy. Besides, their speech might brutalize my psalms.

Hell is for Children

by Nancy Holder

He was six years old. He was six years old. He was six years old and I ran over him.

Jason Dalton screamed with grief. He had been screaming for ten thousand years. His voice was wracked with remorse as he wept, "I'm sorry. I'm so sorry. Can I ever be sorry enough?"

It was six weeks old. It was six weeks old. It was six weeks old and I aborted it.

Through the flames, Mérida Guzman writhed and whispered, "I didn't know. I didn't think. *Santa Maria*, please, please forgive me."

Around them—and around thousands of others—a chorus of the damned shrieked and wailed:

I did it.

I stole it.
I killed him.
I put the kitten in the—
Don't let me think of it.
Don't make me think of it.
End this torment.
End this.
End this!

And then: silence.

A calming peace stole over Jason Dalton. His tears stopped with a gasp, so shocked was he at the reprieve. He clasped his hands together in gratitude and sank to his knees.

"Oh, praise to you, Mother of God," Mérida Guzman whispered joyfully. Her guilt lifted from her like a weight of feathers. A *bad dream*, she thought. *I didn't really do it. It never really happened.*

Kenji Sunamoto.

France-Marie Mueller.

Tutu Mbongo.

Thousands blinked and wept and said, *It didn't happen. I dreamed the whole thing.*

Others cried:

I am washed clean.

I am saved.

I am forgiven.

But what they didn't realize was that there was nothing to forgive. They had done nothing, except to surf the net between 12:00 and 3:00 A.M. the prior Friday the thirteenth. This had run a program entitled alt.kingdom that in a terrible way ran *them*. Now, at unpredictable moments and in random locations, and with the utter cruelty that accompanies chaos, they descended into hell for an eternity that could be an hour, a minute, or a day.

Washed in the green glow of her screen, Regina Fullerton, knowing this, savored a good evening's work at the keyboard and laughed until she cried.

Regina—peaches, cream, and strawberry blond—was sixteen and change; she knew she had conned everyone except a few kids she hung with now and then. Her parents were delighted with their quiet, good daughter, who was the antithesis of her twin, Juliette. Purple-haired Julie pierced her nose and her navel and the space between her thumb and forefinger, and sneaked out at night and went to clubs and came home reeking of sex, drugs and rock 'n' roll. Not Reggie. "Our little computer nerd," Regina had heard her mother say of her. "We're so glad she's a, well, a geek." Her mother had laughed.

In retaliation, mostly for her being so stupid, Reggie was working on incorporating alt.kingdom, her Hell Virus, into her mother's interactive Celtic library, a shareware product she was developing with some old boyfriend in Glasgow. The library was a source of contention between her parents, this collaboration with a former lover, and Regina loved the tension that *crack-cracked!* like the ratcheting of a shotgun every time the subject came up.

So while she typed merrily away, causing at the least bad dreams and at the worst—or rather, best—prolonged stays in psychiatric clinics, her parents worried themselves sick over Julie the evil twin. About the violence that could be done to their demon child because she always lied to them about where she was going and what she was doing. Nightly the TV dripped with horrorshow poison: carjackings, assaults, rapes, kidnappings.

Regina could see them shaking with terror. It was their own hell, and she knew Julie hated them for descending into it on her behalf. Julie didn't want anyone to feel anything because of her. To prove it, she would do things like stick cigarettes against her forearms or shave her head. The folks were sending her to a therapist, who said their daughter was "very, very conflicted."

Because her parents felt so guilty about this family disharmony and sibling dysfunction, they bought Reggie all kinds of computer stuff: hardware, software, vaporware. She was fully loaded. She was self-sufficient. No confliction here, babe.

And they had no clue that their good daughter the geek *in*flicted more violence with their indulgences than all the TV horrorshows edited together into one interminable epic. Doleful city, hell; she had created a doleful cyberverse. Nightly, she enhanced it, making it stronger and more real to her victims. Used, meet user. Beyond virtual reality, beyond any of the drugs that Julie needed to keep herself going. That stuff only messed with your mind. Regina messed with your whole system. *Leave all hope, ye that enter.* As Frank Herbert had said in *Dune*, fear was the mindkiller.

Right on, as her parents used to say when they were young. If they had ever really been young. Or maybe that was just a program they ran, blah-blah-blah, when they wanted to pretend they were actually human beings.

Her phone rang. She jumped. Sitting in the dark with the screen glowing like a jack-o'-lantern, she waited for the answering machine to get it; anyone she cared about—term applied loosely—used e-mail.

"Reg? Pick up."

Her spine tickled at the base. It was Leon, the new guy at school who had started to hang with the kids she hung with, when she hung.

She hadn't given him her number. Someone else must have. She didn't know how she felt about that.

What a crock. She knew *exactly* how she felt about that.

Eagerly, she punched on the speaker-phone and crossed her ankles on top of her desk. Julie's post-post-post music suddenly throbbed against the wall. Oh, joy. The family's clinically possessed poster child was home. "Yeah?"

"How ya doin'?" Leon was from New York. He had an appealingly ethnic aura about him—blue-black hair, dark eyes and a square chin, said chin stubbled every day no later than the three o'clock bell. He knew more about computers than she did. He had broad shoulders and little buns.

"Fine."

"Cool. Listen, somethin' weird happened to my box. It's, like, flashing messages at me or something."

She dropped her feet to the floor and sat up straight. "Like what?"

"Well, it's mostly garbage but there's these embeds, like. 'Melancholy, misery, sin.' It's somethin' very strange."

"Don't look at it!" she shouted, then realized with a sick, heavy thud in her stomach that she was giving herself away. And also, that he should not be able to read any of it. It was designed to lure you in fast, psych you into a state of deep hypnosis, but keep you ignorant of what had happened.

And it was only supposed to work on Friday-the-thirteenths. The most recent one had been three months ago. She had calculated them out for this year and the next three years.

Today was Wednesday, the fifth of April.

"Shut down," she said, more calmly. "I've heard about this. It's a bad virus. Tomorrow it'll probably be gone."

"But it's already in my works."

She licked her lips. "I think you should shut down."

"Damn. I was in the middle of something." She heard clicking, an electronic "goodbye" from his computer as it turned off. He had a totally power-user portable. If she told her parents she wanted one, they would probably get it for her. Julie hated her for things like that.

Julie's music throbbed. God knew what went on in that room. Reggie hated Julie back, both on general principle and because Julie was so nuts.

"Maybe you could take a look?" he asked. "You doin' anything? I could bring it over."

Her stomach did a flip as she looked at her clock. It was eight-thirty. She thought of what her parents might think about Leon. The jig would be up. He had tattoos. He had earrings. He was the kind of guy they would expect Julie to flaunt at them. Reggie was amazed her sister hadn't already snagged him.

She thought of telling him to start back up so she could try to check things out remotely, via modem. But that wouldn't work; she didn't know where the virus was and why it was acting up. If it even was her virus. Maybe someone else had broken in and changed it.

"Reggie," he said softly, and her body tingled. He was so adorable. She had never had a boyfriend. It was a point of pride with her. But all rules everywhere were made to be broken.

"I can come over there," she said, even though it was too late. She had some dim memory that he lived on the east side. Though she was old enough, she hadn't gotten around to her driver's license, and it would take forever for her to get there on the bus. Her parents trusted her; they would forgive one late night. They would be in major shock, but they would let it go.

Fear is the mindkiller.

She would have to be careful.

"I'll be there soon," she added, smoothing her hair as she gazed at her screen, as if it were a mirror that could tell her how she looked.

It was bad where he lived. Taggers had sprayed the jade stucco walls of his building, and all the windows were barred. For a second—make it a nanosecond—she thought about making a dash back to the bus before it got too far away, but once she got that under control, she hauled herself to the front door and buzzed his apartment.

A woman's voice crackled, "Yeah?" in the intercom. It had to be Leon's mother. He had no father.

"Is Leon there? I'm Regina Fullerton."

"Oh, yeah. C'mon up."

Wonk of the security buzzer, and she was in.

Leon came halfway down some cement stairs and gave her a wave. He wore jeans and a black sweatshirt, no shoes. Behind him wafted the odor of baking.

"Hi. My mom's making cookies." He gave her a lopsided grin as if to say, *Can you believe it?*

"I like cookies," she retorted, and came up the stairs. He didn't move right away; she held her breath as she stood one step beneath him, looking up at him. He smelled like soap, like he had just taken a shower, maybe while she had been on the bus.

"Where's your box?" she asked, as Leon pushed open first the screen door and then the wooden door that led to the apartment. Whoah, lots of religious pictures, saints and Jesus and a gilt crucifix. Regina had no time for organized religion, nor for Christianity in any form. How could she, and do what she did?

She surveyed the living room: coffee table, couches, a dinette near curtained windows. A Formica breakfast bar, and behind that, the kitchen: the Mom. Very Italian, dark hair, dark eyes. The Madonna. She smiled a big smile at Regina.

"Hi. I'm Mrs. D'Angelo. You kids go on with your project."

Leon said, "This way," and led Regina down a short hallway to the left.

His bedroom was the third of three closed doors. The walls were bare except for one poster of Jean-Paul Sartre—that was cool—and the floor was littered with packing boxes. She tried not to look at the rumpled sheets on the bed. Instead she focused on the neat configuration on a work desk, screen dark as she had instructed. Now what?

A cuckoo clock started singing. Reggie jumped and glanced in the direction it seemed to be coming from, seeing no clock but a statue of the Virgin Mary on Leon's dresser, and a crucifix on the wall above it. Or Her. Whatever. An image of Jesus Christ going "coo-coo, coo-coo" flashed through her head and she had to stifle herself with a cough. "Nice clock," she rasped into her fist.

Leon grunted. "It's an antique. I'll show it to you when we're done."

When we're done. She rubbed her hands together and cracked her knuckles. With a flourish she pulled out the chair and sat down.

Leon booted up the machine and leaned over her shoulder. She swallowed hard and closed her eyes. If he didn't see Hell, she would open them.

"Reggie?" he asked after a moment.

She looked not at the screen but at him. He seemed fine. She hazarded a glance, another. He leaned in closer, his breath warm on her neck.

"Where was it?" she asked.

"I opened up a file, um..." He hesitated. "Well, I snagged some shots of naked cartoon characters off the net."

"Leon, you pervert," she cackled, not shocked, just amused.

"Shut up." He sounded mortified.

"Take me there." She took her hands off the keyboard and scooted out of his way. Closed her eyes. His hands went *tap, tap, click click click*.

"Okay."

She counted five and opened her eyes again. Snow White appeared topless before her, surrounded by bunnies and duckies and birdies. She snorted. "No wonder you're flunking biology. This isn't what girls look like."

He gestured to the screen. "It was right there. The garbage. I did a virus check before you got here," he added as an afterthought.

"Before you phoned me." She couldn't help but needle him.

"Yes. Of course."

"Because you didn't want me to come over here for nothing."

"Yeah."

"Tell you what. Type this in, all upper case: Alpha and Omega."

"*The Book of Revelations*?" he asked, complying. "But why?"

"I heard something about a new virus. On the net somewhere," she said vaguely. "Maybe it's what you've got."

Nothing happened, but nothing was supposed to happen. That was the code that protected the user.

Leon glanced at her. She shrugged, held her breath. "Try alt.kingdom."

"Nothing."

That was odd. "*Rev.* 9:5." That would run the debugger.

"'And to them it was given that they should not kill them, but that they should be tormented,'" Leon said as he typed.

"What? Those words are there?" she asked, still avoiding the screen.

"Naw. I know a lot about the Bible." He grinned at her. "We're Italians. Big-deal Catholics. My uncle was a priest. I was an altar boy."

"Oh." She didn't know what to think about that. It was her opinion that of all the varieties of Christianity, Catholicism was the most outdated. She had used Bible verses for a joke. Irony. Sarcasm.

There was still nothing on the screen. Leon pushed back in his chair. "Maybe it was a one-shot thing."

"Yeah." Nervously she licked her lips. "It's probably okay now."

"So you did come out here for nothing. I'm sorry." And he took her hand, just like that, his warm fingers gripping hers. Reggie's knees almost buckled.

He rose and put a hand on her shoulder, drawing closer. He said, "Maybe not for nothing after all." Reggie swayed. He came closer.

There was a knock on the door.

"Kids? The cookies are ready."

"Yeah," Leon said, gave her a lopsided grin, and pulled away.

They filed back into the living room. The statues and crosses seemed to follow Reggie with their eyes. She noticed for the first time that Leon was wearing a cross. So was his mother.

A big old painting of Jesus eyed her.

Mrs. D'Angelo said, "My brother painted that. He was a priest." She sighed. "He died last week."

"Oh, I'm sorry," Reggie said, and maybe she was a little, because the man had been Leon's uncle. Uneasy, she murmured, "Gotta get the last bus."

A few minutes later, Reggie was out the door.

For the first time, she felt something that was as close to a pang of conscience as she thought she could get: What if the virus came back and zapped Leon?

"Altar boy," she murmured, and watched the dark streets and shadows blur by.

Her parents didn't even notice that she'd been out. They were too busy screaming at Julie, probably because she had done something like torture a cat. Reggie ducked into her room and automatically sat before her computer, reaching out to flip it on before it occurred to her to stop and think this out.

The phone rang.

"Reg, pick up." It was Leon. She picked up. "It's back."

"What? What's it saying?"

"'I am the Lord thy God. Thou shalt have no other gods before me.' It's the Ten Commandments."

"Damn," she said, alarmed. It had to be another hacker. Someone who *knew* what she'd been up to. Or rather, knew what *someone* had been up to; maybe it couldn't be traced to her.

Who was she kidding?

But surely they had no idea what kind of power lay behind the program.

"Reggie?"

Her heart was pounding. "Can you capture it? Print it out?"

"I don't know. I can try." There was a gasp.

Reggie cried, "What?"

"Reg... Regina, I see... I see *angels*."

"On your screen?"

"Angels. They're beautiful. Oh, my God. My God." There was a clatter.

"Leon?"

She heard him as if from far away. "Blessed am I, blessed, oh, Hail Mary.... Turn on your computer."

"*Leon!*"

"Turn on your computer," he said again. "Oh, Reg, just do it."

"Is this a joke?" she shouted.

Silence. The line went dead. "Leon!" There was no answer.

"Great." She spoke the word as if it were profanity, and angrily kicked on her machine. "Leon, you jerk," she said. "All that way on the bus. April Fool's is over, dude." But in her mind she envisioned someone else messing with her creation.

The screen lit up. On it was written: I AM THE LORD THY GOD.

"Yeah, right," she muttered, getting into her word processing software. *I* AM THE LORD *THY* GOD, she typed. Then she realized she should get out and turn her computer back on. It could be the FBI entrapping her. Or some other agency so secret she didn't even know about it.

She closed the file and punched the power button.

The computer stayed on.

I AM THE LORD THY GOD.

She punched the button again. Again. Again.

"Damn it!" she shouted. Clearly it was stuck.

BOW DOWN BEFORE ME—

"Okay, I'll play," she said between her teeth as she typed, BETTER TO REIGN IN HELL THAN TO SERVE IN HEAVEN.

The screen blanked and read: HE THAT LEADETH INTO CAPTIVITY SHALL GO INTO CAPTIVITY. And suddenly her mind filled:

I did it.

I stole it.

I killed him.

I put the kitten in the—

Don't let me think of it.

Don't make me think of it.

End this torment.

End this.

End this!

Screaming, she grabbed her head and said, "You're not God!" as she felt her skin flush, grow hot, hotter, as she saw an aura of flames around her hands and arms. As her legs burst into flames.

INASMUCH AS YOU DO THIS TO THE LEAST OF THESE, YOU DO IT UNTO ME.

UNCLE WENT ON THE NET LAST FRIDAY THE THIRTEENTH, REG. SUICIDE.

The door to her room opened. Her mother froze on the threshold and began to scream.

Regina held out her burning arms, smoking, sizzling, and shouted, "Mom, it's not real. It's not! Leon's doing it!"

Don't let me think of it.

Don't make me think of it.

Her mother started shrieking for her father.

Then everything erupted into the fires
of Hell.

The phone rang.

"Reg? Pick up."

Her spine tingled. It was Leon, the new guy at school.

Julie grabbed up the phone and said, "Leon, gee, Reggie died last night."

Leon blurted, "Oh, my God, no. H-how?"

She shrugged innocently, though it was all she could do to keep from laughing. "No one knows. She got burned up."

He gasped. "I asked her to come over last night, but she never showed. Maybe if she had come, she wouldn't have…" He trailed off.

Maybe she wouldn't have kept staring at that damn screen, Julie silently added. At that *damned* screen, ha ha, until Julie's own special enhancements had kicked in and Reggie had *believed* herself into oblivion. It had been so easy to mutate the Hell Virus. All this time, everyone in the family had thought she was at clubs and with guys, wasting her time. If only they'd thought to check the night school computer classes…

She snapped her fingers. "Spontaneous combustion. Like magic." And with that, the coast was clear for all Regina's computer equipment, as well as this incredibly handsome guy. It was Reggie's own fault, of course; if her stupid sister had been nice to her once, just *once*, Julie would have spared her.

"I just can't believe it," Leon went on.

"Unfortunately, it's true." She smiled to herself and applied another cigarette to her forearm. It didn't hurt. It would never hurt.

You can't hurt the Devil.

Especially if she's computer literate.

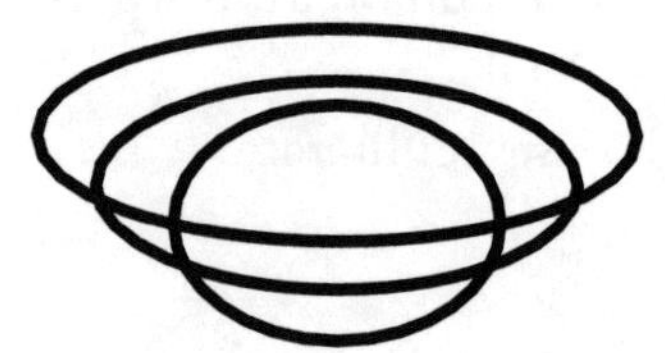

DANTE'S

DROPOFF

by Brian Herbert and Marie Landis

Tom Mullen's memory of his childhood summers was a farrago of frightful nights, sunny days, a large lake and his Mummy's screams.

He was thirty-three years old now, but her screams still reverberated in his head, distant, indistinct echoes. Sometimes he thought they might be no more than a mild tinnitus, a buzzing in his ears. But once in a while her words would come back to him in dreams, loud and grating as a fire-truck siren, and he'd awaken damp with sweat.

"The dropoff will get ya, Tom. Ya hear me?"

Her voice rasped his memories like metal scraping a blackboard, and with it came the image of her face, wide with small eyes set close together above a stubby nose and cheeks tinted with round circles of pink rouge. The same color that covered her ever-moving mouth. A *cookie face*, he thought, *decorated with two raisins and colored frosting*.

Her resonant voice belied the rest of Mummy's physiology. She'd possessed a tall, angular body with shoulders wider than his father's. Mummy could have lifted his short, flabby father off the floor any time she'd wished to do so. He wondered if his father had recognized how vulnerable he was.

Tom was glad he'd inherited Mummy's body structure, one of the few things he appreciated having received from her.

When Tom was young, his family spent summers at the lake. At least he and his mother did. His father was only there for evenings and weekends, while the rest of the time he worked as a bartender in town.

They stayed in a log cabin that had once belonged to Grandpa. The structure tilted to one side, as though foundering in the sea of weeds that surrounded it. The interior smelled of mouse droppings and rotting wood. The stench never seemed to bother his parents, who, for the better part of the summer, stayed drunk and unaware of their environment.

It was difficult to conjure a pleasant picture of the cabin. It sat in naked ugliness upon a piece of land cleared of everything but stumps and weeds. Beyond the structure lay a serene body of water, a large lake surrounded by a forest of fir and cedar and coarse ferns. A low dock jutted into the lake from the shoreline, a place where you could tie a boat if you owned one, or read a book, or sunbathe, or watch sunsets.

His family never did any of those things. Mummy and Father stayed inside the cabin and played cards and drank beer. There was never any breakfast or lunch, but for dinner they ate pork and beans and Mexican corn from cans. His parents drank beer and puffed on their "ciggies" and, if Tom was lucky, they might give him a puff of a cigarette or come up with an Orange Crush for him or, on a good day, a Hostess cupcake. The rest of the time they kept him locked out of the cabin.

Good day? When had he ever had a really good day? There had only been one in Tom's recollection. He always called it his "special day." His awakening.

"Isn't this fun?" Mummy had said as they sat inside the stuffy cabin scraping cold beans from the bottoms of cans. "Life doesn't get much better than this." She swilled a can of beer and threw it on the floor, where it clattered off into a corner. Her long, square fingers riffled a stained deck of cards. The big diamond ring on her right hand glittered.

Five-year-old Tom liked to watch the light dance along its facets, watching the blue and pink colors that flashed at him. On impulse he reached out and touched the ring.

She screamed and swiped the back of her hand across his cheek, sending him reeling. "Be careful!" she said. "This is an heirloom! It belonged to your grandma."

Tom's cheek stung. He reached up and touched it, and when he looked at his fingers they were covered with blood. He wiped the blood on his shirtsleeve.

Mummy flew into a rage. "Dammit, now look what you've done. How the hell am I supposed to wash anything out here in the wilderness? Can't even take a damn bath." She spewed bad words at him, like venom from a snake.

Tom wished he were someplace where there were carousels and clowns and swings and ponies to ride and other kids with whom to play. Instead of inside this stupid cabin that reeked of stale booze and cigarette smoke.

"Tom!" Mummy howled. "Can't you smile or speak or react in some way when I talk to you?"

He couldn't think of a proper reply.

She leaned over and said, "Now listen, you little shit, we came all the way out here on your account, so you can see what it's like with all this nature around you, and you don't say a thing. Not a thank-you or even a good-morning. You know what? I don't give a doodle damn if the dropoff gets you or not."

That night his parents slept inside the cabin. There was only one bed and, no, they'd told Tom, they weren't going to share it with him. He was a big boy, and he could sleep outside by himself. So he'd slept on an old mattress on the porch, under a single blanket that didn't provide much protection against the wind and rain and dew.

He hated being alone in the dark. The night sounds frightened him, those unidentifiable squeals and grunts and whistles that crawled through the shadows toward him. On this night the sounds seemed closer, and they kept him awake with chuckles and words, the bad kind Mummy had told him not to use. It didn't seem fair that she could use those words but he couldn't, that she could drink and smoke and have all that freedom while he could only do what she said was okay. Tom liked to say the bad words sometimes, but only when she wasn't listening. He could write one of them, too, in the sand with a stick. But always he smeared the sand to cover up when she approached.

Tonight the bad words frightened him. Who was speaking them? The wind? He couldn't run inside and tell Mummy because she'd only scream and send him back outside again. So he pulled the blanket over his head and didn't come out until morning.

The following day, the special day he would remember for the rest of his life, he'd awakened in the morning and run to the lake's sandy shoreline. Life was much better in the daytime. He was allowed to wade in the water, but not permitted to advance more than a few feet from shore. The lake's clay bottom was slippery and silky, like wet skin, and he pretended he was walking across a giant's body, an invisible friend who lived just beneath the surface of the lake.

Someone who could protect him against Mummy.

And just about the time he was beginning to forget his night terrors, he heard Mummy scream from the door of the cabin, "Watch out or the dropoff will swallow ya up, Tom, and we'll never see ya again!"

He wasn't certain what "dropoff" meant and had been afraid to ask her. Whatever it was lay in waiting just beyond the end of the dock, she said. Was it a giant fish, like the one he'd heard about at Sunday school, the one that had swallowed Jonah?

Or something worse?

The dock was another place he was not supposed to go, but he very much wanted to walk out there one day and see the dropoff. When Mummy wasn't looking.

Wearing a green-and-white calico dress, Mummy staggered toward a beach chair not far from the shoreline. A big floppy hat was tipped over her face to shield her from the sun. She held a beer can in one hand and a cigarette in the other. "Don't give me any problems today," she shrieked. "I have a headache."

He waited at water's edge, where the waves lapped gently against the sand. After a while, Mummy's mouth dropped open and her cigarette slipped from her fingers, but she still clutched the can of beer as she slept, making loud, wheezing sounds.

As for his father, Tom figured he was in a similar state inside the cabin, smelling like beer and cigarette smoke.

The boy climbed up on the dock.

Timidly, he walked out on the structure, which had a few missing planks. At the end, way out over the water, he peered down into the lake. It was blue and clear. A school of miniature fish clustered near the dock pilings. He looked a little farther out and saw that the water was a deep blue there, almost black, and he wondered if that was where the dropoff lived. What sort of creature was it?

Something padded up behind him. Frightened, he turned. There was Mummy clutching for him and screaming, "I warned ya! I warned ya!"

Quickly, Tom danced sideways and ran back toward the shore. But she caught up with him, passed him and blocked his path, her legs stretched wide, a barrier across the dock.

"Where do you think you're going?"

He turned and ran back again, toward the end of the dock, the only direction to which he could retreat.

She screamed and rushed him, and he danced sideways once more.

She slipped, and for a moment that Tom would forever remember she balanced on the edge, teetering and tottering. Then Mummy fell into the lake. Her eyes were filled with drunken terror, and twice she screamed out, splashing and flailing as the lake water spun wildly around her.

The dark coolness embraced her and pulled her into its world. She cried out for help, then gurgled and slipped beneath the surface.

Everything was quiet again.

A piece of green-and-white calico bobbed to the surface: the belt of her dress. Then a raging whirlpool took it down where Mummy had gone.

For a long time the small boy sat on the dock and watched swirls of dark water. Bored, he turned his attention once more to the little fish that swam around the dock. After an hour or so he wandered back to the cabin and awakened his father.

"The dropoff swallowed Mummy," Tom said.

His father lay on the rumpled bed. He reeked from lack of bathing, and his jeans and torn T-shirt were spotted with stains. A stubble of beard covered his face. Slowly, he came to awareness and sat up.

"What?" he asked.

"Mummy fell in the lake and didn't come back up."

"Jesus!" His father ran outside and down to the end of the dock.

The boy followed.

"I don't see her!" Father said, anxiously. "Where did she go in?"

Tom had put his thumb in his mouth. He removed it long enough to point and say, "Right there. You better jump in and get her."

The dropoff got Father, too.

Tom thought of his parents often, as he was doing now. He parked his aging Plymouth as close as he could to the old cabin and walked across a weed-infested yard to the structure. The tattered mattress that he had slept upon as a boy was even more torn and stained than he remembered, and was draped over a table on the porch. The front door hung by one hinge, and there were gaping holes in the roof.

He went inside.

The floor creaked and there were spider webs and evidence of infestation by rats and other creatures. Something small and unseen scurried for cover. Beer cans and pork-and-beans cans still lay on the floor and on the kitchen table, much as he had last seen the place, except everything looked dirtier and more decrepit and forlorn. An old sideboard was missing. A couch was missing, too, and so were the chairs they'd sat upon.

He opened cupboards and found only a few broken dishes, some old paint cans and a rusty, broken screwdriver. The place had been ransacked, but obviously the thief or thieves had found little of value.

Although Tom had never sold the property, he no longer owned it, having lost it to the guillotine of unpaid taxes. The county owned it now, as shown by a sign that had been posted out on the road. Apparently the place was of little interest to its current owner or anyone else, undoubtedly due to its remote location and the poor economies in nearby towns.

This was the first time Tom had visited the place in twenty-eight years. He'd come because the eternal resting place of his parents was beneath the surface of the lake just offshore.

"I'm here to pay you a little homage," he said aloud. "Ya hear me, Mummy?"

But most of all he'd been thinking of something else, something that could help him overcome the monetary difficulties that had driven him close to bankruptcy.

He was at the window now, gazing out at the dock, which had been in disrepair in his youth. He could see signs of some repair work, but in general the structure didn't look much better than it had so long ago. It still had immense holes and missing planks, and sagged and drooped toward the water.

Mummy and Father were out there just past the end of it, in the dark water.

So was Mummy's huge diamond ring. It belonged to him now, and he had to go find it. He didn't know what his chances were of locating it, but he had brought diving gear and metal-detecting equipment, as well as a powerful underwater flashlight. He wondered if his parents' bones were still down there, or if fish and water currents had spread them around like pick-up-sticks.

The dropoff. How foolish he'd been as a child to imagine that it was a living creature, perhaps a large and ferocious lake fish. He knew better now, and that his parents had undoubtedly been unable to save themselves because of their drunken stupidity.

He thought about the cold pork and beans and canned Mexican corn of the old days, food he would never touch again, no matter his financial difficulties. In his car he had two bottles of good white wine, purchased when he'd had more money, and he'd brought along some Camembert cheese and French bread.

"I have better taste than my parents," he said to himself.

At one time, he'd owned a BMW and a nice townhouse condominium and had eaten in the better restaurants without worrying about the cost. He'd used to travel freely.

Then things had turned sour.

Now he had a hot tip on the stock market, inside information about a company whose stock was about to go through the roof. Mummy's diamond ring must be worth twenty thousand dollars or more. He could use that sort of cash right now.

He didn't miss his parents, not one bit. Mummy had been the worst. Tom had forgotten a lot of things about her, but memories were returning to him now: the mean things she used to say to him, and the time she hit him across the face, cutting his cheek with her ring. He still had the scar to remind him each time he looked in the mirror of how much he hated the woman who'd given him life.

He remembered a social worker who had spoken of how irresponsible his parents were, and how they had abandoned their son in a cabin and run off, bound for who knew where.

Tom hadn't told them anything different.

Most of all he'd hated the way Mummy had enjoyed scaring him with the dropoff story, the way she hadn't explained anything to him and instead let his child-mind imagine the worst.

A dropoff, he knew now, was nothing more than a change in the topography of the lake's bottom, an incline, a deviation. It wasn't an undertow. It wasn't a monster.

It was time to find his parents' bones and the ring.

He went back to the Plymouth, pulled off his expensive clothes and put on his swim trunks and an equipment belt. He located the flashlight, secured it to the belt, and then as an afterthought buckled on a hunting knife too, for reasons that eluded him. Did a small part of his mind still think of the dropoff as a threatening monster? Of course not! Still, the knife provided him with a level of comfort. He would go in the water first without diving gear, just to look around. If luck was with him he would see the diamond ring, glinting at him, inviting him to pluck it up and take it away.

Maybe Mummy was still wearing it. He envisioned the ring on a bony finger.

He walked across weeds toward the shore.

It was quiet here. No sound of passing traffic, no people, no screams. His therapist had told him many times to face his past. Well, here he was, doing exactly that and hoping to turn a profit in the bargain. He'd learned to swim in the Pacific Ocean through riptides and immense waves, and he could hold his breath underwater for more than four minutes. A swim in this lake would be easy.

He popped soft plastic earplugs into his ears, then waded out into the lake. He swam a few feet out from the end of the old dock, where he trod water for a short time. Then he inhaled a giant gulp of air, jackknifed his body and plunged down, using strong breaststrokes to propel himself toward the bottom.

At first the water was translucent, a crystal ceiling overhead reflecting sunlight, but as he pushed deeper the water grew darker, more opaque.

He continued to swim, seeking the bottom. As he went down, smooth walls of rock became apparent around him in a wide, continuous circle. An underwater formation—it was like a giant wormhole, wide at the top and narrowing at the bottom. Like a funnel. He felt his heart pounding. Had his parents come this way? Should he go back for the diving gear? He would explore for just a few moments more.

I'm in some odd sort of crevice, he thought. *Got to conserve my air.* He burped up a little from his stomach, a trick he'd learned from a lifeguard. After thirty seconds or so, he'd burp up some more.

Below he saw a faint illumination, and it grew brighter as he went deeper. There was little room in which to navigate, but he tucked his arms against his sides and paddled his feet. Down, down and down. God, where did this funnel end?

Sudden confusion came over him, and the fear he'd been down too long. His lungs ached and he lost all sense of direction. Though he'd thought he was descending, he appeared to be surfacing, for the light was getting bright now, like sunlight. Was he about to emerge?

A quick glance at his waterproof watch told him he had been under for a little over two minutes, half of his air capacity. Better figure this out quickly.

He popped his head out of the water, sucked in air with relief and climbed up a wooden ladder that hung off the side of the dock. He sat down for a few moments with his feet dangling over the edge.

How could he have lost track of up and down?

He heard the shriek of a female voice behind him and, turning, saw a woman on the porch of the cabin. The old abode, while weathered and leaning, was in better condition that it had been only a few minutes before. There were no holes in the roof. Likewise, the dock on which he sat wasn't sagging as badly as it had been.

The woman wore a green-and-white calico dress. She was familiar. Tom's heart raced, telling him what his mind withheld.

"Tom!" she screamed. "I told you to stay away from that place! Do you want the dropoff to get ya?"

Mummy? And now she was running toward him, bounding across the yard with her long legs. She held a heavy stick.

Instinctively, Tom took a deep breath and dove back into the water.

This time the lake was different, and all around he saw jellyfish-like creatures, similar to those he'd seen when diving in ocean water, but unlike anything he'd ever seen in a lake. The jellyfish swam toward him rapidly, a great cloud of them. As they neared he saw that they had human eyes and sharp canine teeth and didn't look anything like regular jellyfish. Their dangling tentacles were arms and legs and obscene appendages, waggling and wiggling as they approached.

Frantically, he kicked his legs and stroked with his arms, propelling himself deeper.

A faint light became apparent ahead. Something stung his back and then a leg, and he swam faster. His lungs screamed for air. The light grew brighter, and presently he emerged, gasping for breath.

He was back at the dock.

It relieved him to see that the dock sagged and drooped into the water, and that the cabin was in a similar state, with great gaping holes in the roof and a run-down porch. His old Plymouth could be seen parked beyond the cabin. Everything was as it should be.

Forget the damn ring, he told himself. *Get in the car and get the hell out of here!*

He reached the shore and stepped out of the water onto the beach, where long ago he'd used a stick to scrawl bad words in the sand.

Stick.

His mother had chased him with one, in the other place, the world on the other side of the water.

"Tom!"

It was only a whisper from behind, but spoken urgently. A chill coursed his spine, and he whirled to look out into the lake where his parents had drowned so long ago. Sunlight on the water made him squint.

"Cold!" the whisper said, this time coming from another direction, from the cabin. Perplexed, Tom looked that way. His mind seemed to be playing tricks on him today.

"Warmer!" the voice said.

Cautiously, Tom headed toward his car. To get there he had to pass the cabin. He felt like breaking into a run, but thought better of it. Best not to show fear. Walk, and appear calm. Someone was playing games with him. Whoever it was, he didn't want that person to sense his fear. Animals and people attacked when they smelled fear.

"You're getting warmer!" the voice said, in a loud, throaty whisper.

The cabin was only a few feet away. A cloud passed over the sun and a cold wind whipped his hair.

Suddenly a stocky old man emerged from around the side of the cabin, between Tom and his car. The man, in blue jeans and a stained T-shirt, held a hatchet. A stubble of beard covered the man's face. The eyes were crazed and wild. Tom's mind struggled to comprehend.

"Father?" Tom said, hardly able to speak the word. If it was, the man had aged severely. Had he been alive all these years, living on this place?

"Mummy's here, too!" a voice screeched from the porch to Tom's right.

Looking in that direction, Tom saw an old woman in a tattered green-and-white calico dress—a much older version of the woman who had chased him with a stick only moments before, in the other place.

The old man moved toward Tom with surprising agility and speed, wielding the ax. The old woman moved toward him too, carrying what looked like a piece of iron bar.

Terrified, Tom turned and ran toward the lake. He waded out in the water to the end of the dock, took a deep breath and dove in. Down he swam, deeper and deeper. His mind raced, searching for answers, and he knew he had only a little over two minutes until he reached the other surface, where the other Mummy was, and the other Father.

The jellyfish surrounded him, and he could see them more clearly. They wore nasty, knowing little grins, and their bodies were bright red, and their long tails flipped back and forth as they accompanied him.

To where?

They whispered and chuckled the answer.

Mummy and Father were waiting for him. They would drive Tom back into the lake, and he would seek the surface again and again. But they'd always be there, wherever he appeared. He was caught in a hellish funnel that ran in both directions.

The only escape he had was in the coolness of the lake, in the swimming interval between worlds, a few minutes at a time.

That's all he would ever have for eternity.

CANTO (EVOCARE!)

by James S. Dorr

"I am the serpent Sata, the dweller in the uttermost parts of the earth. I lie down in death. I am born. I become new, I renew my youth every day."
—The Egyptian Book of the Dead

I am Eternity, the Serpent-Earth
    Encircling all; I, cast forth to the dark,
    Am the Forever. Hear now of my birth:

From night I came, to night I still embark,
    I, born of ocean, spawn of *His* cast seed
    In foam and blood became, in blood, the spark;

The fire, the *Lucifer*, Sathanas, Set,
    The Adversary; slayer of the sun,
    Osiris' bane; the encompassing greed;

The fire of Moloch. I, scaled Python one
    Of many names, brought wisdom, knowledge, lore
    Of good and ill. I am the evil son.

I am the Cain who, knowing Man too well for
    Adoration, spited God's command
    To worship this, *His* creature. Better, war!

Yes, better death than blind obeisance
    In this, *His* first request, far better to
    Be cast in flame—
                                        Evocare! Be called forth, hence

To hear my word. Forget *His* measured rhyme,
    His cadenced hymns to glory, hear instead
    This my canto: I, born anew, to conquer time,

To recreate the world; thus was I wed
    To Aphrodite, Charis, dark Nephthys—
    To Night and Beauty; I, safeguard of the dead

Who pay me heed; to those who live, the key
    To riches, pleasure, all things one may wish
    Of this wide universe *sans* let or fee;

The Lord of Man, of beast, of fowl or fish
    That dwells in my earth-ocean, air or fire,
    That lusts, that loves, that procreates; that rash

And filled with equal arrogance and ire
    Seeks blood to flow, seeks flame and sword and rock
    To crush his enemy; that, gluttonous, would mire

Himself in excess, thus to taunt and mock
    Or be himself mocked, eyeing all through green-
    Tinged glass another's gain; that brings forth pox

On self and chattel as, content to dream,
    So fails to act; that, chief of all, to pay
    The bitch-wolf avarice that which *she* deem

Her part, will clutch and grasp, frenzied, betray
    Even life, death, pride, that which one most loved,
    And thus subsume the whole:
                                        Evocare!

Be called forth at command! Forget this rhyme,
    God's measured tread, each one of you who read
    These lines. Forget the measured rule of time—

God's time—and hear instead of history
Spawned, as myself, in hate and bile, in blood,
In fire and blackness, chaos, word and deed:

I bear the mark of Cain, I who once stood
At *His* right side? I who, myself, betrayed
By my own brother Michael at *His* Word

Was cast in Hell? I who did only say,
"That work does lack perfection." Hear me now,
You child of Adam, creature made of clay,

Not even sperm as Michael, I, the rest
Who came before, not even ocean's foam-
Absorbing Oneness, think you now—

Forget this rhyme! —think you now that you came
In God's *perfection?* See now as I show
The lot of Man: See river flood and death

That there might sprout yet life anew, as I,
Who lie down dead that I may be reborn
With each new day, in serpent form devour

The sun. See how I am myself attacked
By vengeful Horus, Isis' child and love,
My body torn, consigned beneath the ground.

Then see, to Egypt's east, how I, renewed
Again in youthful beauty, take the name
Of Iblis-Shaytan, Apollyon, of Baal;

How, brazen-cast, my image rises high
By hand of Man; my belly, made a pit,
Now houses fire; my appetite for death

Is sated only by the sacrifice
Of Man's own children, flesh of Man's own seed,
By Man and Man's priests—not by *my* command.

And yet will that suffice to fill Man's need
For blood and torture, all in name of gods—
Or *God*—in piety and zeal to feed

The yawning pit of earth? See now the wrath
Of nomad tribesmen. See proud Jericho
Laid waste, while east yet of this place

New armies gather, taking Persia's wealth
And leaving chaos. Now still others rise,
Strong Rome, to conquer all the world in blood,

To bring the faith of *Him*, which they pervert
To cover acts of rape, to rob and burn,
While north yet others mass. See now the sack

Of cities; see how Nature, too, reaps wild
The crop of death; how Pompeii, blasted, falls;
How rivers flood again, how famine reigns.

Yet priests are priests. Now superstition turns
To knowledge blessed while wisdom is condemned,
And those who teach the ancient truths are burned.

The world turns upside down: More fires are lit
As faith fights faith, as tortured people scream
As flesh is torn, blood boiled, bone crushed

And bodies heaped in abattoirs of shame—
The Inquisition! —Holy, foul, yet then,
As if what *He* wrought lacked sufficient blame,

The voyages to New Worlds now begin.
    Oh, see the filth, diseases spread the earth
    As brand-new races come to lust and sin,

As slaves are stolen, new slaves bred from birth
    To death; greed fed anew; pride raised again
    And envy, sloth, the glutton gain new worth;

And always war. The wrath of nations when
    The wealth *I* offer yet fails to suffice,
    The powder, bombs, the guns, the wholesale sin

Of slaughter: As a lion makes war on mice,
    So Adam's spawn now seeks to decimate
    His own cursed race, for neither gain nor vice

Nor even love made wrong—one does not hate
    Whom one knows not! Yet still the cabaret,
    The carnival of blood will fail to sate

What *He* who dares condemn me, Satan, laid
    Upon this fair earth. Man! The worm! The foul!
    And you who read these lines—*Evocare*.

I harrow Hell.
                Ab Infernis evoco te:
    Beelzebub, Prince of the Seraphim,
    Evocare; Leviathan, of heretics

The chief, be called to me, *Evocare;*
    Bright Asmodeus, of the wantons lord,
    Evocare; and Prince of Cherubim,

Fell Balberith I call, *Evocare;*
    Evocare, be called to me as well
    Astaroth, Prince of Thrones; and Second Prince,

Verrine of Thrones; and Third, Gressil; and Fourth
    Sonneillon, Prince of Thrones call I, *Evocare*;
    Evocare, of Powers the Prince, Tarreau;

And Carnivean, also Prince of Powers,
    Be called forth to my side, *Evocare*;
    And Oeillet and Rosier, the First

And Second Princes of Dominions both
    Fetch I, *Evocamini;* and Verrier,
    Of Principalities, lastly, the Prince;

I call them each! Drink now of Satan's power
    On Earth and Hell: The others call I too,
    First Hitler, Stalin, minions of my bower,

And Torquemada, giving Faith its due
    To be perverted; Nero, Constantine
    Who would bring hope by sword I bring in view;

And Thaïs, Cleopatra, lustful Queen
    Of my own Egypt call I to this dance,
    To Carnival. *Man's* City. Have you seen

Enough? Might Croesus please your eye by chance,
    He who could never gain his fill of wealth;
    Or Isabella, who in envied pride

Reconquered Spain, then fell too in her quest
    For other nations' gold? Or those whose health
    Is ruined by surfeit—Rip Van Winkle, yes,

Who slept through Revolution; Frederick
    And Arthur, napping through their countries' need;
    Or glutton Nicholas, once Myra's Saint,

Grown stout of late, who yearly plants the seed
    Of avarice in children? Covetousness?
    And always pride and wrath and lust. The Creed

Of Carnival is this: In all, success.
    In all you ask, I bid you prosper—may
    Your wishes, wants, desires, your hopes be blessed

To come upon you threefold, fourfold, nay,
    A thousandfold the pleasures I grant you,
    Who would but ask, who read these lines. I say—

I, Satan—Sata—Serpent—thus endue
    To thee the world:
                                        Evocareque tu!

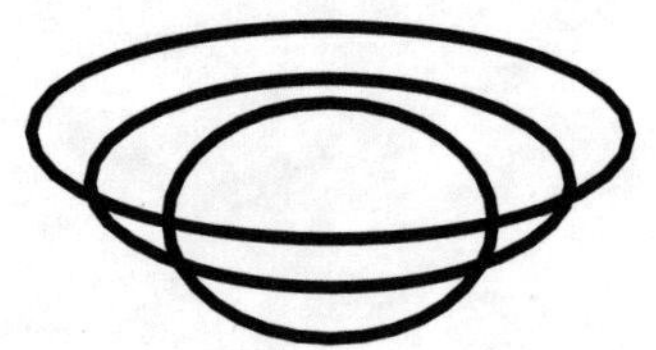

DANTE'S

TUNNELS

by Rick Hautala

The cop was pretty fast. Ace had to give him credit for that, at least; but a few too many jelly doughnuts and being at least twice Ace's age was slowing him down.

Ace scurried down the stairs into the subway station, cleared the turnstile with an easy vault that barely broke his stride, and was already weaseling his way through the mass of people waiting for the train on the platform before the cop was even halfway down the stairs. Ace thought he could hear the cop shouting out for him to stop, but that was the last thing he was going to do. He figured he could have been moving even faster if it wasn't for the backpack loaded with cans of spray paint that was weighing him down.

Too bad about Flyboy, though, Ace thought with a slight shiver.

It had been too dark for him to actually see Flyboy hit the pavement, but he'd watched him go over the iron railing backward, his hands clawing at the air as if he could catch it. Ace figured it was at least twenty feet down to the street.

Too bad Flyboy couldn't really fly.

If the fall hadn't killed him, he sure as hell was going to be one racked-up, sorry son-of-a-bitch.

But Ace told himself not to feel *too* bad about it.

Shit happens.

Everything has its risk. Flyboy had been out "bombing" plenty of times before, so he knew the chances he was taking. Either he was dumber than Ace, or else just a little less lucky.

That's all there was to it.

Panting, but still feeling strong and wired with adrenaline, Ace paused a moment and looked first left, then right.

Fifty-fifty, either way.

Chances were some do-gooder, white-collar asshole was going to tell the cop which way he went, anyway. It all depended on just how seriously this cop wanted to catch his ass. The only thing bugging Ace was that he hadn't had a chance to finish his piece. He and Flyboy had just started spraying the outlines of their logos when the cop saw them and gave chase.

That's when Flyboy slipped and fell.

Jesus, just don't think about it! Ace told himself.

He licked his thin lips as he looked around. He wasn't familiar with this particular Orange Line station, but—hell, they were all pretty much the same. After one more quick glance over his shoulder to make sure the cop hadn't spotted him yet, he headed off to the left.

Ace felt better as soon as he rounded the corner and was swallowed by the cool, vibrating darkness of the subway tunnel. A chill breeze from a nearby ventilation shaft raised goosebumps on his thin, pale arms. His body was still tingling from the rush of the chase.

Ace was never afraid to be alone in the tunnels. In fact, he liked the way the darkness closed down over him like a lid that shut out the glaring lights, the noise and bustle of the city. He liked the way the *scuff-scuff* sound of the brand-new Reeboks he'd ripped off just last week echoed from the piss-yellow tile walls in the throat of the tunnel. And he liked how he always seemed to be able to hear the faintly echoing *click-clicking* sound of dripping water somewhere deep in the darkness. Sometimes he thought it sounded like a huge, dark animal, lapping up water.

Within seconds, though, the echoing silence was shattered.

Everything was suddenly drowned out by the bone-deep shudder and rumble of an approaching train.

Feeling more than seeing his way along the edge of the cat-walk that ran five or six feet above the tracks, Ace looked up ahead for a service niche in the wall where he could hide. There had to be one close by, but he didn't see it before the train roared around the corner.

A bright light speared the darkness and swept like a searchlight over Ace. He felt like an insect specimen pinned to the wall as the train came straight at him. The sound of grinding metal against metal was deafening. Ace watched, fascinated, as the train rushed at him. White sparks snapped and flew like exploding squibs from underneath the wheels.

Spreading his arms out wide, Ace flattened himself against the cold tile wall, but the backpack pushed his stomach out a little too damned close to the train for comfort. For a single, shimmering instant, he was afraid that the front of the train was going to scrape him up like so much dog shit; but then, with a roaring suction of hot wind, the engineer's car took the turn and zipped past him. Ace couldn't help but laugh as he wondered what the engineer thought, seeing him appear so suddenly from out of the darkness.

The passenger cars clattered past, and Ace stared at the dull lemon light inside the train that flickered like an old-time movie through frame after frame of grime-smeared windows. He caught quick, blurred glimpses of the people, either sitting down or standing, hanging like apes from the hand grips.

The screeching sound was all-encompassing. The chatter of rails and grinding of steel wheels shook Ace's body. Just for the pure rush of it, he threw his head back and started screaming as loud as he could, even though he couldn't hear himself. Sweat was running in icy streams from his armpits down the inside of his T-shirt, tickling him. The dark air was filled with the choking stench of exhaust, the sting of ozone, and other, unnameable things that swirled in a blinding cloud and tugged at Ace like strong, urgent hands that wanted to drag him under the train's wheels.

But Ace hung on and kept right on screaming until the train was past him.

Then, his ears still ringing and his body trembling with excitement, he watched as the train's taillights were swallowed by the darkness. Then the dull echo of the passing train faded to a low, steady, clacking pulse that Ace felt in his blood more than heard.

"Fuckin'-A!" he shouted.

He raked his hair back out of his eyes with his fingers, then took a deep breath of the foul-smelling air, smiling with self-satisfaction. He was confident that no cop was desperate enough—or *stupid* enough—to follow him down here. The only problem he could see was if Flyboy had survived the fall. The stupid asshole would probably be so scared about saving his own ass that he'd give Ace up.

But if the cop was desperate enough to come after him—well then, maybe Ace's luck would hold, and the train that had just passed by would clean him out.

That'd serve the asshole right!

But Ace knew he couldn't take a chance that the pea-brained son-of-a-bitch *wasn't* coming for him.

Hell, if Flyboy died from the fall, they might try to pin a murder rap on him. More than likely, though, the cop was just going to wait back at the platform. Maybe he had already called ahead to the next stop to alert the police to keep an eye out for him.

But then again—maybe the asshole would just keep coming down the tunnel after him.

The only thing Ace could do was keep walking—no matter how far it was—to the next stop.

Maybe on the way he'd take a break and smoke some jib.

Maybe he'd throw up a logo, too, just so anyone who came through would know that he'd been here. Once he was sure it was safe, he could catch the train back to Park Street Station and then get the train back to the 'hood.

As he walked along the service walkway, moving with a spider's supple grace, Ace never stopped to wonder if this was ever worth the effort.

Of *course* it was... even if Flyboy got his ticket canceled, it was worth it!

Ace was one of the best graffiti writers in Boston. Hell, he'd bombed half of Beantown by the time he was sixteen. He'd marked his logo on billboards, city buses, trains, subways, storefronts, restroom stalls, construction sites, sidewalks... just about anything in Boston that would hold enamel paint.

And he knew he was good—*fast* and good.

He took pride in his work, and he had the scars to prove it. His arms, legs, face and shoulders were ribboned with thin white lines where razor wire, chain-link fences, broken glass, and pavement had cut him. The six-inch scar on the left side of his head that made his left eye droop down was where a cop had whacked him with his nightstick last summer. Ace called it getting a "wood shampoo."

But he kept bombing because he knew it was worth it.

There weren't many—hell, no! There weren't *any* better graffiti writers in all of Boston!

As Ace walked along, he kept his eye out for a good place to tag. It had to be someplace where the engineer, at least, would see it as he made his turn. Up ahead, where the wall curved gently to the right, looked like a good spot; but before Ace got to it, the tunnel echoed again with the distant squeal of another train. This one was approaching from behind.

The sound of grinding wheels set Ace's teeth on edge. He saw the signal light on the tracks change from red to green. In the dim light, he also saw a wide, dark opening—a service bay—not more than fifty feet ahead. He started running, hoping to make it to cover before the train. He wasn't afraid of falling under the train, but he wasn't too keen on the engineer seeing him, either. If the cop who'd been chasing him had notified the engineers to keep an eye out for him, it'd be just as well if he stayed out of sight.

A dull spot of yellow light swung around the corner behind Ace just as he reached the niche and ducked inside. He couldn't see for shit in the sudden darkness, and he tripped over something and almost fell. He caught his balance and muttered a low curse as he brushed his hands on his pants legs.

"Yeah, well, fuck you too!"

The suddenness of another voice, coming from out of the impenetrable darkness, startled Ace.

For a flickering instant he thought he might have imagined the voice. His whole body tensed as the sound of the train grew steadily louder, echoing with a strange reverberation in the bend of the tunnel. Clenching both hands into fists, he got ready to fight if this tunnel rat, whoever the hell he was, gave him any shit. Ace wasn't very big for his age, but he was street-tough and wiry. Not many people fucked with him and didn't regret it.

The tunnel rang with grinding metal as the train roared by; then a deep silence clamped down in the darkness again. Still tense and ready to fight if he had to, Ace started backing toward the opening.

"Sorry, man. I din't know you was down here," he said with only the slightest hint of nervousness in his voice.

"What, you mean you can't see where you're going or something?" the man asked.

This was followed by a low, gravelly laugh that ended in a raw fit of coughing.

The voice sounded old and cracked, kind of creepy coming out of the pitch darkness.

Ace leaned forward, trying to get a better look, but there was nothing there—just thick blackness. He was pretty sure this had to be just some homeless wino, but he didn't like not being able to see him. A vague sense of unreality swept over Ace as he shook his head and tried to convince himself that there really was someone there; but no matter how hard he stared into the well of darkness inside the niche, he couldn't catch even the faintest hint of a shape that might be a person.

"So what the fuck're you doing down here, anyway?" the voice asked.

The last word reverberated with a dull, steady pulse that hurt Ace's ears more than the sound of a passing train.

"Jus' hangin.' Tha's all," Ace replied, his voice low and tight.

"Doing a bit of writing, too, I suspect. Huh? And maybe running away from the *po*-lice."

The man pronounced the last word the way the brothers say it, heavily accenting the first syllable.

"I ain't running from no one!"

"Is that a fact? Well, maybe you think you're some hot shit because you got away tonight, unlike your friend, huh?"

Ace had no idea how this guy could have any idea what he'd been doing, but he wasn't about to say a word. For all he knew, this might be another cop, setting him up to nail his ass.

Suddenly a scratching sound followed by a snapping *crack* filled the darkness as a small flower of orange light cupped inside the man's hands burst through the darkness. It underlit the features of the man's face as he raised the match to the tip of the cigarette in the corner of his mouth and puffed. Ace stared as the light glowed for a few seconds, and the man took a deep drag. With a quick flick of his hand, the light went out, plunging the niche back into darkness. A vibrating green-and-black afterimage of the man's features drifted in front of Ace's vision, no matter where he looked.

"You think you're some hot shit writer, huh? Or should I say *graffiti* artist." The man chuckled softly. "Is that what you think you are? An *artist?*"

He exhaled noisily, and a funnel-shaped plume of blue smoke appeared like magic from the darkness and blew into Ace's face, stinging his eyes. Ace waved the smoke away with both hands but said nothing. He sure as fuck didn't have to brag to anyone… especially not some burnt-out tunnel rat.

"Say, why don't you do me a favor," the man said.

His voice sounded mellow enough, like he was going to make a simple request; but there was also a harsh level of command just below the surface that Ace didn't like.

"Look, man, I don't owe you shit, you unnerstand? Who the fuck you think you are, anyway?"

Although he couldn't see the man and had no idea if he was getting set to jump him or not, Ace bounced up and down on his toes, his fists clenched at his sides and ready.

"Hey, all I'm asking is one tiny favor," the man said, not sounding at all like he was rising to Ace's challenge. "Just do me a quick throw-up. Show me your stuff."

"You're fuckin' crazy, man," Ace said as he backed closer to the edge of the walkway. He wanted to turn and leave, but something warned him not to turn his back on this guy. The flesh at the back of Ace's neck began to tingle as though tiny worms were crawling just beneath the surface of his skin.

"If you think you're so damned good, show me what you got," the man said.

"I don't *think*. I fuckin' *know!* I'm tops in this fuckin' city. D'you know of one block in Boston that I ain't tagged in the last ten years?"

"I'm something of a writer, too, you know," the man said.

He paused and inhaled on the cigarette. The glowing tip illuminated his face with harsh black lines. When he exhaled, he made a soft, satisfied sound in the back of his throat that might have been laughter.

"Tell you what," the man said. "Give me a can or two, and we'll both do one. Just a quick mark so they'll know we've been here."

"I don't need this shit," Ace said, shaking his head and backing away.

He dropped his right hand to his pants pocket and felt for the bulge of the switchblade he always carried. He was more than willing to cut up this motherfucker if he didn't shut his face.

"Let's call it a little contest," the man said, sounding friendly, almost cheery. He took another drag of the cigarette, then flicked it away with a quick snap of his finger. The glowing tip hissed and spun end over end like a whirling comet inches past Ace's ear before it landed with a dull sputter between the tracks.

"Yeah, 'n what's the prize?" Ace said.

"Show me your best work, and… oh, I dunno. Maybe—if it's as good as mine—I'll let you leave here… alive."

Ace sniffed with laughter even as cold tension coiled deep in his stomach.

"You don't scare me, motherfucker," he said, squaring his shoulders and taking a threatening step forward.

"And you don't scare me, either," the man said. "I'm just not sure I like the way you left your buddy back there."

"What—Flyboy?" Ace said. "He's a cold turd. If he can't climb, then he ain't worth the effort it's gonna take to shovel his guts off the street."

"You mean you didn't push him?"

Ace was about to say something, but then stopped himself cold.

How the fuck could this asshole know anything about what had happened up there on the bridge?

Okay, once he saw the cop, he might have nudged Flyboy a little so he could clear the bridge railing first, but he sure as fuck didn't *push* him.

For several seconds, the tunnel was tomb-quiet. Ace couldn't even hear the man breathing. Then he swung the backpack from his shoulder, unzipped the top flap, and grabbed a few cans of paint. Not caring what color they were, he threw them into the darkness, only guessing where the man was. He heard two loud *smack* sounds as the man caught the cans, then a loud rattling as he started to shake them. The ball bearings inside the paint cans jangled like alarm bells.

"So where do we write?" Ace asked. "I can't see for shit back here."

The tension in his gut was steadily tightening, but Ace chose to ignore it.

He knew he was the best.

He'd have a whole fucking mural done before this burnout figured out how to pry the lid off the can.

"Why not right outside here on the wall?" the man said.

Ace heard a low, shuffling sound as the man stood up. Then, like a photograph gradually developing, a face resolved out of the darkness mere inches from Ace.

"What the fuck—?" Ace said, taking a quick step back and raising his hands defensively.

He was surprised that the man didn't look anywhere near as old as he had in the glow of the match. Ace guessed the man was in his mid-thirties. His face wasn't lined or wrinkled at all. In fact, his skin glowed with a white smoothness that made Ace think of polished marble. The man had a solid build, too—lean and muscular, without an ounce of fat. Ace was damned glad he hadn't tried to fight him. He looked like he could have picked Ace up and broken his back with one hand.

Ace's hand was trembling as he took a can of spray paint, snapped off the cap, and shook it. Side by side, he and the man walked out of the niche and stood on the catwalk by the wide, curving cement wall.

"Wha'do yah want?" Ace asked, trying to control the tremor in his voice.

"Anything at all," the man said, sounding like he was trying hard not to laugh. "Just give me your best shot."

Ace cocked his hip to one side and stared at the grime-stained wall for a moment. He always liked to study the space to see what shape suggested itself. After a moment, he inhaled sharply, stepped close to the wall, and began to spray.

His arm moved in wide, controlled sweeps. The hissing of the spray can was all he heard or *wanted* to hear as he lost himself in his work. The smell of paint fumes tingled his nostrils, making him feel higher than any other drug he'd ever tried.

Within seconds, Ace had outlined his name in tall, fat-bellied black letters. He placed the can of black paint down by his feet, grabbed a can of white from his pack, and started filling in and high-lighting the outlines. Ace soon became so involved in his work that he paid not the slightest bit of attention to the man working beside him. He was only vaguely aware of the hissing of the man's spray can.

This is too fucking easy, Ace thought.

But all the time, he couldn't stop wondering if the man had been joking, or if he had really meant what he'd said about not letting him leave here alive if he didn't like his work.

Ace barely noticed when another train rattled by. After several minutes, he capped the white, picked a can of red paint, and began adding five-pointed sparkles on the tops and sides of each bulging letter. He jumped and actually squealed out loud when the man's voice suddenly broke through the hissing sound of spraying paint.

"Well, I'm about done," he said.

"What the fuck—?"

Ace finished the stroke he was making, then stepped back so he could see what the man had been working. He gasped with utter amazement.

"No way… No fuckin' way, man!" Ace said, shaking his head in wonder as he stared at the man's artwork.

"You had that started before I got here. I jus' din't see it before, is all. No fuckin' way you could've done that so quick."

The man regarded Ace steadily, his eyes gleaming wickedly in the soft glow of light.

"Like I told you," he said in a low and teasing voice. "I used to be something of a writer myself."

"No shit! With work like this… and you know… I think I seen it before."

Ace couldn't disguise the awe he felt as he regarded the man's artwork. He had always prided himself on how easily he could make his letters look three-dimensional, but what this guy had done made everything Ace had ever written look flat and amateurish—nothing more than childish scrawls.

The logo was six feet tall, and more than ten feet wide. Wide, angular black letters were highlighted by pointed streaks of yellow and blue. In the dim lighting of the tunnel, they looked alive with jagged forks of lightning that throbbed with a rich, vibrant life of their own. Ace couldn't quite make out the name the man had written, but he sounded out each letter.

"*L-E-G-I-O-N*. Leg… Leg-ion? 'S that what it says?"

The man shrugged as if it really didn't matter.

What Ace saw—and couldn't help but appreciate—was the absolute genius of the work. The word seemed to jump right off the wall. Ace thought, if he reached out and touched it, it, would feel as hard and dimensional as freshly painted blocks of stone.

"No way, man… I don't like this shit." Ace turned to the man. "You're dickin' around with me…."

The man smiled at Ace, his flat, white teeth glistening wetly in the semi-darkness.

"So what… what's it mean?" Ace asked tightly.

The man didn't reply. He walked up to his artwork, reached out, and gingerly touched the center of the letter G. For a moment, the contact of his fingers with the wet paint made a slight *tick-ticking* sound.

Then something strange happened.

Ace knew it had to be a trick of the eye.

Maybe there was a crack in the wall he hadn't noticed, but—somehow—the man's fingertips disappeared into the design as if he had thrust his hand into a darkened doorway.

A sensation of stark fear slithered up Ace's back as he watched the man lean forward, reaching farther into the darkness until his hand disappeared up to the wrist in the solid blackness.

Looking at Ace over his shoulder, the man grinned again: a smile so wide the corners of his mouth almost touched his ears.

"What the fuck're you doin', man?" Ace said. "I don't like people fuckin' with my mind."

Powerful shivers danced up Ace's back and gripped the back of his neck.

"Go ahead," the man said, stepping back and waving toward the artwork. His teeth were gleaming like ancient bone in the moonlight.

"You can touch it."

All Ace wanted to do was get the hell out of here, but he felt strangely compelled to touch the artwork, if only to prove to himself that's all it was—just paint on a grimy cement wall. It was an illusion, and nothing more!

But no matter how long he stared at them, the black letters seemed to extend backward into thick, impenetrable darkness.

Ace tried to control his trembling hand as he reached out to the wall. A numbing chill zipped up his arm to his neck when he touched the wall, and then his fingers disappeared into the blackness.

"What the fuck—?" he muttered, vaguely aware that the man beside him was snickering softly.

Ace leaned forward, reaching further into the darkness and waiting for his hand to hit solid wall; but his wrist, then his forearm, disappeared so completely it looked like his arm had been cut off.

In Ace's peripheral vision, the jagged yellow and blue streaks surrounding each letter slithered on the wall, crackling like pale, electric fire. Ace told himself this was just an optical illusion, but his body suddenly felt charged. Every nerve and muscle twitched and vibrated with a deep, humming energy.

"This is… this is totally *weird*, man," Ace sputtered. He tried to laugh when he leaned back to pull his hand away, but a numbing coldness gripped him and held him there. In the first, sudden flash of panic, he thought he could feel a cold, scaly hand from inside the wall, gripping him firmly by the wrist.

"What the fuck, man." Ace's voice had a high, baby-sounding pitch.

"Well—you know what they say: Sometimes the artist has to *become* the art." The man's voice sounded muffled and hollow, like far-off thunder.

Frantic with fear, Ace struggled to pull away from the wall, but an irresistible force was pulling him closer and closer to it. His new Reeboks squeaked loudly on the cement floor as he braced himself and yanked backward as hard as he could, but the thick, churning blackness was getting inexorably closer. Its coldness spread up Ace's arm and through his body like a blast of ice water.

"Come on, man!" Ace said, his voice breaking on every syllable. "Whatever the fuck you're doin'? Make it stop! Please! Make it stop!"

"I'm afraid it's too late," the man said. "Maybe it wasn't such a good idea for you to reach into it."

Ace's legs pumped furiously as he tried to get a solid enough footing to thrust himself away from the wall, but he could feel himself being absorbed by the darkness. His arm had disappeared all the way up to the shoulder. He tried to look away, but his face was being pulled closer… closer to the vibrating blackness.

When it was less than an inch away, Ace sagged forward, suddenly drained of all strength. The bones in his hands felt like they were being crushed into a pulpy mush. Wave after freezing wave of pain shot through him.

"Shit, man!… Please!… Help me!… You gotta… *help me!*"

Hot tears gushed from Ace's eyes and flowed down his face, but the man did nothing.

"Help you? You mean, the way *you* helped *Flyboy?*" he asked.

"It was an accident!" Ace wailed. "Jesus Christ, man!"

The man sniffed with laughter.

"No. I'm sorry," he said. "I think you're talking to the wrong person."

The darkness opened like jaws inches from Ace's face. Churning with a cold, raw energy, it sapped what little strength he had. The stench of raw, rotten flesh filled Ace's nostrils the instant he was pulled into the surrounding darkness. He wanted to scream, but his voice choked off. He was himself dissolving… spreading out… lost in the utter, impenetrable darkness that engulfed him.

He had no idea which way to turn.

It wasn't long before the only sound he could hear—other than his own labored breathing—was the faint *click-clicking* sound of dripping water. It sounded like an animal… huge and unseen… somewhere in the darkness… lapping up something….

Hell is a Personal Place

by Brian Lumley

The uniformed man in the bunker gave a last stiff-armed salute—or it should have been, but most of the stiffness had disappeared now; and the uniform with its black leather cross-strap was less than crisp, indeed it was dusty with a fine layer of concrete powder, which kept drifting down from the low ceiling as the thudding concussions crept closer and closer—and put the muzzle of his pistol to his head. With feeble cries of *Heil Hitler* ringing in his ears from those whose pale, sickly faces surrounded him—cries *so* feeble and faces *so* sickly he felt he really should shoot these knock-kneed imbeciles first, or even instead; except that would mean being alone, and maybe not enough ammunition left to finish the job—he pulled the trigger.

It was so simple it was great, he thought. Even glorious!

At the last moment he had closed his eyes. Small in stature but hardly insignificant, *not now, anyway*, with his hair parted in its distinctive style, *which so bloody many enemies of the Reich found so bloody funny!*, he reeled from the expected devastation of his brain, the hammer bullet falling on his grape head…

…And reeled again as the realization dawned that he'd felt nothing!

"What?" he cried in astonishment, and then rage: "*What!* What, what, WHAT? A gun that doesn't work? But should I be surprised? Of course not! Why should I be surprised? My army didn't work, my navy didn't work, my air force *certainly* didn't work, so why should one small pistol? Am I the only one in the entire bloody *Vaterland* who *has* bloody worked?"

He turned to hurl the offending weapon in the nearest sickly face, only to discover that his hand was empty and that the nearest face had no flesh, sickly or otherwise.

A tall, thin figure in black sat on a flat-topped rock and gazed at him through empty orbs from beneath the peaked cowl of his robe. At his feet there lay a rusting, neglected scythe and a bone-dry whetstone.

"What?" said Hitler. "What?"

"I didn't say anything," said the man in black. He shuffled his sandaled feet a little, and the knuckles of his toes gleamed bone-white through a lattice of ancient leather.

"Explain!" Hitler cried, advancing a short, sharp pace. But then he paused, looked beyond the somber figure seated on the rock, gazed upon three distinct arcs of a distant horizon. One arc lay in a dark blue, near-impenetrable shadow.

"Limbo," said the skeletal man in black. "For those who are blameless but desire only rest—an eternity of rest."

Hitler's eyes went to the next arc of the horizon, where golden rays lanced skywards into azure heavens from the gleaming minarets and domes of a city unthinkably beautiful. And the cowled figure explained: "Reward—for those who have loved and aspired to even greater love, and who now in their turn are loved."

Finally, there remained only the third arc. Red and yellow fires leaped there, and a faint wind brought a sulphur reek, mixed with which Hitler believed he could hear, very distantly, tumultuous cries of torture and terror. It seemed a familiar sort of place, and the man in black offered no explanation but merely gloomed on Hitler from the deep, dark sockets of his eyes. He stood up, and Hitler saw how tall and thin he was. But of course, he would be.

"So you are Death," the little man mused. "Strange, I never really believed in you—not for myself.

"But for many, *many* others," Death answered. "So many, indeed, that I was beginning to think you'd be the last of all. Why, you're a legend!"

Hitler preened a little. "I am?" Then he frowned. "But of course I am! I know that!"

"You very nearly did me out of my job," Death went on. "They came so thick and fast I couldn't keep up! See my scythe there, all rusted where once it gleamed silver? Ah, well, and now I'll have to get it bright again. But yes, you are a legend. So was Atilla, and the Asian wizard who first created the Black Death and sent it scurrying westward, and Cain, who was the greatest murderer of them all."

"Cain?" Hitler wrinkled his brow. Who was this upstart Cain?

"With a single stroke, he killed one fourth the world's population," Death explained, as if he'd read the little dictator's thoughts. "Even you haven't managed that!"

Hitler struck a pose, peered at the three different arcs of horizon. "That was never my intention," he said (Death's wit escaping him entirely). "I intended only the elimination of certain—or several—ethnic groups. *Large* ethnic groups, true, but—" And he paused, then scowled, then looked amazed as he took a first involuntary step toward the arc of smoldering fire and sulphur stench. Involuntary, yes—invoked by the will of some Other.

"Your time's up," Death explained.

Hitler looked again at the three distinct horizons, keeping till last that direction in which he felt compelled. The way to Limbo was a broad swath of deep green grass, blown languidly in a cool, pleasantly-scented breeze. The way to Just Reward was paved with blue crystal tiles of infinite delicacy, where fountains played every now and then, and strange, delicious-seeming fruit grew on low golden bushes by the roadside. Alas, the path to Hell was parched, where the earth was cracked open and scarred like scrubland in a drought.

The ex-dictator fought against the next step, leaned back against its pull, to no avail. His jackboot came up, moved forward and plumped down, pointed him unmistakably along the desiccated track. He stumbled, half-turned, said: "Wait! I have not interrogated—I mean questioned—I mean you have not *told* me the things I need to..."

"There is nothing else," Death was brief. "The rest lies in the hands of *der Führer*."

"*Der Fü—?*" Hitler was astonished, outraged—his blood boiled! He would have stamped his foot, but when he lifted it, it took another involuntary pace toward Hell. "Is that what he calls himself, this... this *devil?*"

Death came pacing after, loping like a long shadow to overtake Hitler's ever-quickening march. "Hell is a personal place," he said, "and Satan has many forms. One for every damned soul. For yours he is *der Führer*."

Hitler paled a very little. "What's he like, this Satan?"

"Very handsome," Death shrugged, walking alongside the new arrival. "And not a little conceited. Alas, that was always his trouble. Oh!—and of course he's *not* an Aryan..."

"Not an Aryan?" Hitler repeated him, dazedly. Then his eyes suddenly brightened into feverish intensity. "Not an Aryan!" His nostrils flared. "Hah!" he gave a stiff-armed salute. "Then it's time there were some *changes* around here! Big changes!"

Death chuckled, however humorlessly. "But aren't you a rather small man, Adolf," he said, "to be dreaming of such sweeping changes? After all, *he* is very big."

"I was small once before," Hitler snapped. "But a man's destiny is fashioned by his dreams, not by his stature."

"That might well be true," Death answered, "but where you're going Satan fashions the dreams. All of them. And each and every one, a nightmare! And before I forget—" he produced a black patch in the shape of a six-pointed star and quickly slapped it on Hitler's left breast just under the cross-strap. The star at once seared through jacket and shirt, burning itself into flesh.

Hitler yelped, tore open his smoking jacket and shirt, then tucked in his quivering chin and stared down in horror at the star which was now part of him, like a great black birthmark or some hideous melanoma, made that much more hideous by what it conveyed.

"Preposterous!" he sputtered then through tears of pain and rage. "I am not a Jew!"

"And I repeat," said Death, enigmatically, "that Satan is not an Aryan. But in Hell, each has his role to play."

Hitler's shoulders slumped, but his jackboots kept marching. The fiery horizon was that much closer now; heat came gusting in scorching waves, carrying the worst possible stenches; the cries of tortured millions were loud and growing louder.

"*Verdammt!*" Hitler's frustration overflowed. "Where is my Third Reich now?" Tears, apparently of anguish, flowed down his face.

"Gone," Death answered his question, "but the Fourth lies directly ahead. Except it is not yours. *Vorwärts!*"

Then the Grim Reaper came to a halt, and watched as Hitler went striding off toward his ultimate solution. The ex-dictator glanced back once, fearfully, at Death, but already the gaunt figure of that timeless being had been left far behind. Hitler sighed his resignation and faced front.

In the near distance, curling over the balefires, a huge black swastika was blazoned on the sprawl of a vast scarlet flag....

The Kingsbury Technique

by Sean Doolittle and Wayne Allen Sallee

Unfortunately, when the Torso Murderer stepped back into the oblivion from which he came, he took his secrets with him.

—Steven Nickel, on the Mad Butcher of Kingsbury Run

But a few words about Oblivion.

At least this one.

It was inhabited by a minor demiurge, whose name translated most efficiently into the single word "Unruh." The oblivion had rooms and chambers and secret passageways; for a time, it had materialized as the Torture Castle of H. H. Munro, located at the corners of Sixty-Third and Wallace in Chicago. The demiurge had assisted Munro in his dismemberments. In that case, during the last decade of the nineteenth century, it hadn't even been necessary for Unruh to use his powers to infect the killer's mind.

Even so, there was always a price.

And there was always a plan.

For Unruh's trouble, Munro was required to introduce him to society officials, petty and despicable big-city politicians among whom he might one day cull deals. Usually, Unruh's deals were double-edged swords.

The phrase "damned if you do, damned if you don't" was put down on paper for good reason.

Munro had his own uses for his victims. But Unruh harnessed their fear. With enough years and enough accumulated terror, he might attain the strength required to break the plaster of his own caste. For even in oblivion, there existed a hierarchy, and Unruh intended to climb. The name of the demon who occupied the next level was irrelevant; he was as good as overthrown.

It was never up to Unruh how the victims were selected and how their lives were disposed of. He was simply called up from his Hell of

Many Mansions to infiltrate the mind of a borderline psychotic, sometimes even an obsessive-compulsive member of the world's everyday, normal workforce. Munro was the only time he had deviated from standard strategy, choosing this time to materialize as a steerer—an old Chicago tavern term for someone who pulled people in. Munro, a.k.a. Herman Mudgett, was the Jekyll-and-Hyde killer of the 1893 World's Fair. Each of his decapitated victims was eventually dissolved in lime pits.

Unruh the demiurge could only exist in corporeal form while his host predator, for want of a better phrase, was still alive. This was the nature of hierarchy: Each level had its conditions. Still, before Munro's hanging, Unruh, in the guise of a Levee District brothel owner, managed to befriend several important mortals. "Big Jim" Colosimo. "Polack Ben" Colgcsaz. Alphonse "Scarface" Capone.

If he'd been prone to ridiculous behavior, Unruh might have squealed with glee. What better playground than this? The grimy ash of corruption inherent in the Jazz Age was sweet food; from it Unruh would ascend to the highest ranks of all the demons. And Chicago would be his gateway to hell.

Things had panned out after all: Reinhardt found Detective Blackmur sitting by himself at the end of the bar.

It was her first time inside the place, a dark and sparsely populated pub with its name in buzzing cobalt neon—*Ninth Street Blues*. Her colleagues, when they invited, tended to favor Lazlo's, in the somewhat more academically acceptable historic district known as the Haymarket, because the place brewed its own beer. Sheila Reinhardt favored neither beer nor her colleagues. And none of this was the least bit relevant to her reasons for coming here.

Even through the smoky haze, Blackmur looked like a man who had been stomped by some cosmic shoe: He slouched in on himself atop the narrow stool, staring blankly into the polished surface of the bar. One hand curled around an empty shot glass. The other rested limply at the base of a mug that contained more foamy dregs than beer. He was a big man; even slumped, his shoulders were thick and broad. He was wearing a T-shirt and jeans that looked like they'd been unwadded from a pile.

Reinhardt unshouldered her attaché bag as she moved, cutting a swath through the general chaos. There was a football game on the big screen at the back, the staccato clack of pool balls to one side. The patrons ranged from animated to comatose, shouting at the screen or lurking in shadowed nooks. The gender ratio here was overwhelmingly male; she pretended not to have heard the chivalric drink offers made by what looked like eight happily shitfaced construction workers jammed into a single booth.

One stool down from Blackmur, within easy distance but not obviously close.

Not that strategy seemed to matter. His eyes were flat and oblivious; she might as well have straddled his lap for all the acknowledgment her presence received. From here she had a better view of him: craggy experience in the face, and short, dirty-blond hair that at the moment was standing out from the back of his head in coarse, errant tufts.

"How 'bout it, miss?" The bartender had a cocktail napkin in front of her within seconds. He was tall and moderately handsome, anywhere from twenty-five to thirty-two. He had a friendly face, open and clear, looking pleased just to have something to do.

"Gin and tonic," she said. "No ice, no tonic."

The bartender grinned. "Atta girl." He glanced to his left once before moving off.

"Lem?"

Blackmur didn't look up. Just one tired, barely perceptible nod.

Sheila fiddled with the napkin while she waited, tearing little tabs from the corners and letting them flutter to the ground. Julian—identified by his nametag—ambled back in a few minutes with three drinks clutched deftly in his hands. When he'd divided them up—tumbler for her, another boilermaker for the detective — she pulled a twenty from her purse and slid it forward.

"I've got these," she said. Julian gave a polite nod and took the bill, moving down the bar toward the register again.

Blackmur glanced up, briefly, once. He said nothing. And that was all.

You expected it to be easy?

No.

So take a breath. Forge ahead.

"Lemuel Blackmur?" Sheila turned on the stool, half-facing, half-casual. She took a sip from the tumbler, licked the burn from her lips and set it down beside her.

He might have sighed. He might not have. "What."

Engagement. Sheila paused, testing potential responses in her mind. None of them sounded any better than another, so she decided on one that she hoped seemed least imposing. "You look beat."

There was a long moment of silence for her to wonder whether or not she should have gone with another line. Julian hung back on the periphery, pretending to be seriously involved with the glass he was wiping. A good minute passed, enough time for Sheila to consider trying again. Then Blackmur looked up at her, the way a very tired person might look at a ringing phone.

"Since there's only one paper in this town," he said, "I guess I don't need to ask which one you're from."

Sheila shook her head. "I'm not a reporter. Exactly."

Blackmur smirked, bobbed his head. *How entirely lucky for me.* He knocked back the whiskey and put the glass down firmly, not bothering with the chase.

"Look," she said. "I don't mean to bother you."

"Yes you do."

Sheila grinned. Took another drink, eyeing him over the rim of the glass. "Okay, that was stupid. Sorry."

Blackmur rolled his eyes.

"I'm a professor at the university," she said. Indirect was going to get her nowhere, that much seemed like a bet. She decided that she might as well cut to the point. "Criminology."

"How nice for you."

"My name is Sheila Reinhardt." Keep moving. Stay on your feet. "And I know you'd just as soon be left alone, and believe me, I can understand that."

Blackmur took a long pull from the mug. Wiped his mouth. Stared at her hard. "Then I suppose that leaves me with one question."

"Why am I sitting here."

Blackmur smirked again.

"I'd like to talk with you, Detective." She scooted her stool a few inches closer when Blackmur dropped his eyes. "I don't expect that you'd much like to talk with me, so I'm apologizing up front. But I've got to tell you, this isn't really about what I'd like. *Need* is closer to the truth."

Sheila stopped here, hung back. Watched him expectantly, held in a breath. She had officially entered tricky waters, and she projected possible scenarios in her mind. He would either respond, or he wouldn't. Supposing he didn't: *How to get him back?* Supposing he did: *What was she going to do to keep him on the line?* This thing could go any number of ways, and each move she made was crucial, each word the possibility of losing him for good.

“Hey, Lem.” Julian had appeared, his smile easy and broad. “Why not cut the lady a break?” He reached forward with the bottle of Cutty Sark he held, filled Blackmur’s shooter again. “You aren’t exactly keeping me company, here.”

Blackmur snapped his head up; his eyes were glinting. “Who the fuck asked you, Jule?”

Julian took a long step back, hands palm out in front of him. *Hey. Pardon the shit out of me*.

Then Blackmur turned his gaze on her.

“Lady, I’m sorry. Whatever you’re after, I don’t think I’m up to it. Okay?”

Sheila met his eyes. One hand on her drink, the other on a knee. “Please.”

Blackmur looked at her for a long, icy moment. Then his entire body seemed to deflate.

“You aren’t going to leave me alone,” he murmured. “Are you?”

“No.”

“I could shoot you.”

She laughed.

“Jesus,” Blackmur said. Downed his shot. “What.”

Yahtzee.

“First thing,” she said. “I’m not out to grill you, or judge you, or anything like that. Honestly. This is about my work.”

“Mm-hmm.”

“Most of my research,” she went on, “and virtually everything I’ve published, deals with cases similar to the one we’ve got going on here.” She downed her drink, nodded to Julian when he arched a brow. “Serial murders.”

Blackmur dropped his head to his forearms.

“But not the murders themselves,” she said. Took a chance, put a hand on his arm. “Or even the murderers. It’s all redundant, all bullshit. All being done by a thousand other people. My work,” she paused long enough to pay out from the pile of change Julian had left by her hand, “my work deals with the *investigators* of these cases. The relationship. Especially in cases that have gone…”

Great. Oh, just beautiful. She stopped abruptly, too late; her mouth was already stuffed with her own unspoken words.

Blackmur finished the sentence for her. “Unsolved?” He’d lifted his head slightly from his arms, cocked it inquiringly her way.

It wasn't a bad touch.

"I'm sorry," she said. Radiant frustration-heat in her cheeks and forehead. "I really didn't mean to imply what I just implied. That was rude."

"It doesn't matter."

"No, it *does*." Her voice had slipped up a half-step, and at the sudden inflection Blackmur looked up at her again. "It does matter."

Sheila leaned forward, one elbow on the bar. Put her palms together in front of her as a gesturing tool.

"I think I know how this is going to sound to you. But I wouldn't have come here if I didn't know it was important."

Blackmur looked at the ceiling for a second, then took another pull from the mug. He sat up, then, and turned her way. His expression was flat. But it wasn't a refusal.

Sheila went on while she had the chance. "I've made a career out of studying the implications of crimes like these for the people who, by profession, have been held responsible for stopping them. Everybody from academics to the tabloids focuses on the killers: What kind of monsters are they? What are the psychological triggers, what kind of childhood did they have, every other goddamn thing."

She looked at him. He looked back.

"Nobody," she went on, "considers the other end. What it means for the investigator who must meet an aberrant psychology on its own ground. And who becomes, in the public eye, with each new murder, almost more of a scapegoat for the crimes than the criminal."

"That's sweet," Blackmur said.

"Detective, this is an opportunity to do some of the most illuminating work this field has ever seen."

And Blackmur laughed. It was a deep, unpleasant sound.

"Let me run this back to you," he said, finishing off his beer. "See if I've got it clear in my mind. You'd like to interview me."

"Yes."

"Kind of like history-in-progress, right? A case study in our very own humble town."

"Yes."

Blackmur grinned wanly. "I guess it's lucky for you this motherfucker is still running around, then, isn't it? I mean, career-wise."

Sheila leaned back again. "I told you. I know how it sounds."

"Hell, it's even lucky for *me*. Here I am with the chance to be a part of the most illuminating work the field has ever seen."

Her turn to smirk, this time. She took out her wallet, pulled out three more twenties. "I had that coming," she said. "And the drinks will be on me."

Blackmur put up his hands. "Well, shit, then." Sarcasm in dripping layers. "Hit us again, Jule. Matter of fact, why don't you just bring up the whole goddamn bottle."

Julian nodded, glanced at Sheila once. Rolled his eyes. He took Blackmur's mug to the tap and filled it, tilting the glass to reduce the foam. Then he returned with it and two bottles, one for each of them. Beefeater in front of Sheila, the Cutty in front of the detective.

"Okay, Sheila Reinhardt," the detective said, pouring a shot for himself, then reaching forward to fill her glass again. "I'll make you a deal."

Sheila nodded, answered with a raise of her glass.

"It'll be like a contest. Fair?" He held up his own glass. "You see if you can ask all your questions before I get tanked enough not to answer them."

Reinhardt grinned. "Fair." She pulled up her bag, settled it on her lap. Retrieved a pen and a legal pad. And a tape recorder, which she placed between them on the bar. "Thank you, detective."

Blackmur had killed his shot and was filling the glass again. "Lady, you're already behind."

According to the 1990 census, Lincoln, Nebraska, recorded approximately three murders per hundred thousand citizens per annum. Percentage-wise, at nearly 200,000 citizens and 365 days in a year, it was barely worth the trouble to do the math. That was in 1990. Since '93, the statistics had changed.

Over two years now since the first of the murders, which had slapped the people of Lincoln like a gloveless hand. The following twenty-six months had produced sixteen victims total, counting last week, and a dark paranoia had descended on the city like a towel. This was the stuff from which urban legend was born; people had stopped doing things like running down to the corner for smokes in the late hours of the evening, and parents forbade their children to walk to school. The city council, at their wits' end, had finally issued a mandatory 9:30 P.M. curfew for all minors, and retail sales of pepper gas and handguns had increased 425%.

The newspapers had been quick to dub the plague the "Capitol Crimes." This was a pun, not a misspelling; one of the principal things that each of the victims held in common, besides being women, was that all had ended up nude and in a sitting position at the base of the capitol building's granite steps. This, however, was only one facet of the inevitable display: In every case, the women's breasts had been removed with a cleanliness and precision that bordered on surgical. There was no end to the Freudian speculations regarding this, hopelessly compounded by the fact that the four-hundred-foot shaft of the capitol's tower resembled nothing so much as an enormous penis. What resisted logical analysis, however, was the fact that—also in every case—the breasts had been replaced with other objects. Hubcaps. Styrofoam cups. Last week's, perhaps, the most bizarre of all: The killer had planted a marigold in the red, meaty center of each ragged stump.

Sheila Reinhardt had built a career as a historical analyst of cases just like this. And the way Blackmur had sized her up, shrewd and superficial and premature… that had been uncomfortably close to the bone. There were, by necessity, a few philosophical floor routines involved in keeping a perspective on her work. Ethical and emotional gymnastics toward remembering—and re-convincing herself—that she was a scholar and not a ghoul.

There were those who considered both to be equally parasitic. Perspective could be funny that way.

Detective Lemuel Blackmur was beyond relevant to Reinhardt's research. She'd made some random notes over the past few months, sketchy comparison profiles between the Capitol Crimes and similar sprees of the past. The Grant Park Axe Mutilations in Chicago, 1973. Others. This was more by way of warming up than anything else. The killings were a collateral issue, and there were too many comparisons to be made.

The real comparison was Blackmur. Reinhardt's interest in the investigators of serial murderers had developed early, in graduate school. She'd written her doctoral thesis on the miraculously unsolvable murders committed in Cleveland, Ohio, during the better part of the 1930s. There was a mysterious, Jack-the-Ripper quality to this case that had appealed to her—but in the course of her research regarding the phantom known as the Kingsbury Run Torso Murderer, Reinhardt had discovered an infinitely more intriguing story than the killer.

His pursuer. Eliot Ness.

Ness arrived as the Cleveland Safety Commissioner in 1934 riding the crest of his own legend. He was the Golden Boy. A public hero. The

Man Who Got Capone.

The thesis had mutated, and in the following years Reinhardt had expanded it into a book. God was in the details, specifics were between here and there, and there had been enough of both to fill four additional years. Nutshell: Not all the victims of the torso murders had been physically mutilated. The same crimes had also been the downfall of Eliot Ness's career.

Her only regret was that the book had already been published, out of Rutgers UP in 1982.

Sheila didn't believe in a supernatural universe. She didn't believe in fate or intervention, divine or otherwise. But sometimes it was hard not to reconsider. That she had ended up in Lincoln, Nebraska—with the intellectual opportunity named Lemuel Blackmur—seemed almost too coincidental to believe.

The parallels were stunning. From a criminologist's standpoint, Lincoln was at present a card-carrying volcano. The Capitol Crimes *themselves*, in fact, seemed almost to be an incentive for the additional fact that, in two weeks, the state would be charging the electric chair for the second time in forty years. The last had been only a handful of months ago, when Walkin' Willie Otey had died amidst a carnival of controversy and media hype. Next up: the son of a wealthy Midwestern cattle family named Richard "Corbie" Edwards. Edwards had been pre-med at the University of Nebraska at Lincoln when he was convicted of the murders of six heterosexual couples between the months of April and September of 1976.

It had once been fashionable to get laid in the early-morning dewy grass of Antelope Park. Corbie Edwards had beheaded all six naked lovers with a twenty-inch machete—an implement better known to those in outlying farm communities as a corn knife. After the first murder, coupling in the park became the kind of thing drunken college dares were made of. The press had been less clever with nicknames, it seemed, in those days. "The Anteloper" had been convicted in 1978. Apprehended by Detective Blackmur. And sentenced to death largely on the basis of his testimony and criminal profiling.

From this case, Blackmur had compiled a report that had eventually found its way to Jessica Winger at the Omaha branch of the FBI's Behavioral Sciences School. Reinhardt had discovered that she wasn't the only expert on Cleveland criminal history trivia. Blackmur's report had been titled "The Kingsbury Technique," and was incorporated into the curriculum as a required text for any field agent trained in the investigation of mutilation crimes.

And now, seventeen years later, he was looking at what the city referred to in whispers and furtive moans simply as Number Sixteen.

Reinhardt wondered what Blackmur and Ness might have had to say to each other, now. She wondered how quickly they might have become friends. So much in common, between them.

Or would they even have talked shop at all, knowing there was nothing to be learned?

It was just the way it happened, when you became an expert at something. People always expected you to save them.

Unruh watched Reinhardt and the detective from the shadows of a corner booth. He smiled when the woman had to reach out quickly to keep Blackmur from toppling off his stool.

He'd dressed in jeans and a casual sports jacket over a white shirt, had no problem blending as he'd followed her from her apartment. It had surprised him somewhat to see her leave the little white Nissan parked in back, opting instead to walk the twelve blocks—at night—alone. And then it hurt his feelings. Finally, it simply pissed him off. In a paranoid, trembling city, her singular lack of fear was frankly insulting.

Unruh took consolation in the fact that this bright woman, attractive in a peach blouse and flats, wasn't quite as intelligent as she considered herself to be. She had no idea about so many things.

It entertained him to see her sitting with Blackmur. It entertained him to see Blackmur with her.

Did Reinhardt know the circumstances regarding how Corbie Edwards' victims had been discovered? Maybe. Maybe not. It didn't matter; Unruh hadn't the least bit to do with the charming, if uncreative, spree of the lad who in prison had grown long hair and a beard. Unlike Oswald, Corbie had been the lone gunman—rather, samurai—during that long summer of 1976.

Not so with the killings of late. For it was Corbie himself who had called Unruh back to this plane. Out of oblivion, as it were.

Just as he'd been called by Alphonse Capone almost fifty years ago today.

It entertained him to muse over all the things Sheila Reinhardt didn't know.

Unruh watched them from the booth, nursing his beer. It was warm and foamy and pleasing: He'd changed it to urine the instant it had been served. Not exactly water to wine, but similar in principle. And over the centuries, he'd found the acidic tang of piss to be much closer than blood to the taste of fear.

After a while, he grew bored with the entire thing. Unruh finished the mug and strolled out of the pub. Into the streets. He whistled as he wandered the alleyways, finding himself eventually at the base of the now-legendary tower. The bronze sculpture atop its tarnished metallic dome was known as the Sower, named for the bag of seeds. Unruh found a place where he could sit, in the spring mists that rose from the sweaty streets. And gazed up at the pulsing red light between the Sower's legs. Past. Into the purple night sky and its beatific puncture wounds.

In the garish white light of the toilet stall, inside the closet-sized men's room of Ninth Street Blues, Lemuel Blackmur slouched against the coolness of porcelain and waited to puke again.

What kind of fingernails were those? His arm was pinned uncomfortably beneath him; Blackmur stared idly at his own left hand, which had somehow wound up six inches from his nose. Hygiene, for fuck's sake, hygiene.

And the room reversed its slow spin.

As the toilet bowl hissed, filling, Blackmur arranged himself and thrust his hands into the rising tide of fresh water. It was gloriously cool. He scrubbed his nails, attacking the thick half-moons of gunk beneath them.

The dirt broke free in clumps and dissolved, spreading tendrils. Thin red threads in the clear water. Through the booze-cloud, Blackmur was dully intrigued by how much they looked like blood.

Eight blocks away, beneath the stern, judicial gaze of the Abraham Lincoln statue at the bottom of the capitol steps, a good-looking young man in a sports coat whooped gaily in the air. The group of college kids making their way to bars downtown had no idea what the guy was doing when he pulled an invisible lever and said, *ka-ching ka-ching*.

The steps were as grand and vacant and echoing as the legislative corridors inside. In the yellow light cast by nearby sodium-vapor lamps, shadows turned Abe into a leering skull, danced in the pockmarks of surrounding stone. From where he sat with a tranquil grin, Unruh could almost hear the screams.

But no.

The sounds were only the drunken revelry of still more students, careening past in Escorts and Geos and Jeeps, heading for the bars lining O Street and beyond. Windows down, radios blaring. Never noticing the weird cat lounging on the same steps where bodies kept turning up.

Amend that: There was one. A hairsprayed blonde in a fraternity sweatshirt, gazing from the passenger window of the car that had stopped at the traffic lights of Fourteenth and G. Unruh locked eyes with the girl, gave his most charming grin. She yanked on the arm of the driver, who leaned forward and turned his crewcut in the direction she was pointing. Perhaps they might have reported the Suspicious Person, had they not been in such a hurry to get home and fuck.

Unruh watched them pull away, extracting what he could from the girl's brief flash of paranoia. The spark was frustrating, little more than a tease. Washed away by the exhaust fumes of a slowly trolling pickup truck, bed crammed to capacity with bulging boys in Wrangler jeans. Unruh caught the music wailing from the cab, a song by someone the deejay announced as Brooks & Dunn. About a guy who had never missed work at the plant in fourteen years and was a volunteer with the fire department and all those lovely things, who on the weekends got snookered on grain alcohol or whatever in hell hillbillies drank.

Unruh thought of Blackmur as he listened to the lyrics. And he couldn't help but grin again.

The chorus explained that this was how Barney Jekyll turned into Bubba Hyde.

All things considered, Blackmur was holding up surprisingly well. How much longer? How long before the man split from the frustration and pressure—before he cracked beneath the weight of his dreams? On the top shelf of the man's closet, wrapped in a pair of panties that had been drenched with the discharge of fear, Blackmur kept his gun. A throw-away piece, they called it on the force—the back-up that cops never accounted for to their superiors. Would Blackmur begin making connections? How long before he decided to eat his gun—and how much could Unruh bleed from the man before he did? Would there be a hostage situation, a stand-off with nearby innocents killed? One could hope.

It was fun to speculate about these kinds of things. And fun to remember the past.

Ness—for all the trouble the sniveling petunia had caused, Unruh had to admit that Ness had been great fun. But this one, Blackmur? A singular masterpiece. Unruh found it hard to believe that he hadn't come up with this twist before.

Maybe things had worked out for the better after all. What Unruh had always considered to be an infuriating setback now seemed like a much more comprehensive plan.

In those early green and salad days, Herman Mudgett had contacted Unruh with more than enough raw material to begin cultivating Chicago for real. The advent of Eliot Ness and the Untouchables (oh, that was *still* rich) had been annoying, but interesting in the end. When Ness finally put Capone away on charges of tax evasion, Scarface was already equipped with all the subconscious knowledge he'd need for the eventual conjuring. Unruh had planted the seeds long ago, in anticipation of just such a case. The two of them had shared ample opportunity for such exchanges at the Four Deuces, which had been Capone's headquarters at 2222 South Wabash.

The fat gangster had been convicted in October of 1931. It wasn't quite two years after that when Unruh had finally been called. He met Capone in his minimum-security cell just outside of Marietta, Georgia. To talk of terms and tallies at last.

A bit of an anti-climax. Capone had read in the *Atlanta Constitution* that his nemesis had taken a job as Safety Director of Cleveland. Unruh remembered visualizing an industrial dirt-basement in shades of brown, unlike Chicago's own bright sheet-metal-gray facade. Damn that pudgy doughnut Capone for wanting to make a killing ground out of *Cleveland*.

But damned he already was. For a man already on the road to Hell, what was one more deal with the devil?

All in all, the aggravation was relatively minor. The whole thing interrupted Unruh's work in Chicago, but that hadn't worried him so much, back then. Put the tallies on hold—he'd only be gone for a decade or so. Capone wanted Ness to be ridiculed from without. Tormented from within. He wanted Unruh to fashion the kind of monster that ultimately inspired American tabloids and assorted media to begin giving their monsters catchy names.

And so he did.

On the same mid-August day in 1934 that Mr. Ness took his new job, Unruh infected the brain of a second-generation Hungarian alcoholic named Dolezal.

The Mad Butcher of Kingsbury Row.

The Headhunter. The Torso Murderer. There were other names.

All drafted in sweet fear to refer to the berserker created from the fodder that was Capone's hatred for Eliot Ness.

Ness hadn't even unpacked his boxes when Dolezal slipped into his first fugue. Result: one dead whore at Tenth and Scovill. Dolezal spilled the limbs and other assorted cuts into the Cuyahoga River, where they drifted for two weeks before washing up on Euclid Beach.

5 September 1934. "The Lady of the Lake" made headlines.

And always, there was a price.

Capone got his wish. He also got the brain shakes. In the same instant Unruh gave Dolezal his dementia, he gave Alphonse Capone a staph disease called syphilis. The idea was simple and artistic: As the brain cancer progressed, so would Dolezal's condition—and so would the frequency and brutality of the murders. The only drawback: Time for everyone was short. Blasted conditions again, and a moment of careless vanity. Unruh the demiurge could only be corporeal as long as his summoners were alive. The syphilis would kill Capone before the bloated ex-mobster was fifty years old.

Unruh was not unduly flustered; to turn a phrase, there was plenty of time to kill. And there was really no telling what the coming years might bring—always the chance he might line up another summoner by the time Capone expired.

So he set about things with some diligence, collecting all the energies he could. The first seed planted on Euclid Beach, Unruh decided to let saplings grow. And he took his Hungarian to Youngstown on the Lake Erie Rail. From there, thumbed through Gallipolis into West Virginia and the armpit of Kentucky. Tallies ran high along this trail; quick fear, random and impromptu, was sometimes the finest kind. Throats slit and firm flesh carved, grain haulers and truck-stop whores. Three in Barboursville and Savage Branch; fifteen in the Kentucky coal valleys of Catlettburg, Ashland and Riverton.

Unruh was in no particular hurry to steer his drifter back to Cleveland and Kingsbury Run; Capone was still as healthy as he'd ever managed, and was negotiating prison life admirably. Unruh knew the man had no intentions of Doing the Dutch, as his kind were wont to speak of suicide. And Greasy Thumb Guzik watched from outside, Capone's personal insurance policy against the kinds of... accidents one sometimes encountered in prison.

The location was safe enough, no random selection in that—there were senior officers in the Kentucky State Police who were running, as it so happened, a snatch-and-snuff ring as far west as Covington. Blanket cover-up guaranteed, to cover any asses that might have been exposed. So Unruh felt free enough to run this line until the quick hits lost their novelty. After almost eleven months, he took Dolezal back to Cleveland on the Ironton Railroad.

They started relatively slowly, working into things. Of the first three victims, two were left intact enough to be identified. Polillo and Andrassy. Ness banged between walls for five months, seething at the lack of progress on the case. When the third unknown floated beneath the Third Street Bridge in June of '36, Ness went on a two-day binge.

From there, a fairly uneventful list. Between the months of July 1936 and June of '39, twelve more victims who were logged by one appropriate and familiar identity term: *Unknown*. The gender mix had ended up slightly in favor of the males.

Climax, denouement:

1938. Cleveland coppers pick up Dolezal on a fluke. They conclude by beating him senseless in his cell. The cops don't mean to kill him, it just sort of happens that way. Unruh milks the immigrant for every last spoonful of fear and desperation he gives.

By this time, Ness has already begun his serious drinking. Oh, and womanizing, too.

1939. Capone's syphilis is acutely advanced, just this side of full-blown. The man called Scarface is bounced around to facilities across the country. From Terminal Island, California, he gets on a plane to Florida.

Ness has forged ahead. Taken a man into custody. He meets with "the killer" face-to-face, as planned; a deal is cut with City Hall. As a result, Gaylord Sundheim gets committed to an unnamed asylum. Ness has conniptions; in Florida, Capone drools with delight when the morning nurse reads the newspaper story to him.

All of it pleases Unruh immensely. Certainly, Chicago is still the front gate. But for the first time he begins to think of Cleveland as a potential back door. After Dolezal, even though they'd had nothing on the man, the police were quick to suspect a copycat. They weren't so dimwitted after all; Unruh had given in to an ironic urge and recruited one of Andrassy's manic-depressive friends.

Knowing that the discovery of every single solitary last torso would place the onus—ahem—on the head of Eliot Ness. Three more murders in Youngstown. Six corpses in a swamp in New Castle, Pennsylvania.

1940-1. Unruh stays in McKee's Rocks and Pittsburgh. After vicious public ridicule, Ness leaves office in Cleveland. Capone gives Unruh a wink with one swollen eyelid, even then not suspecting a thing. The hot-shot Mob doctors and skull carpenters still have the fat fuck believing he is going to get The Cure.

And Unruh travels. Leaves Andrassy back in Cleveland, a crumpled heap. Picking at random now from the emotionally weak. He causes motorists to be shot dead in Baltimore. Mass suicides at Bethesda Naval Hospital. Satanic rituals in Baton Rouge, Bayou Goula and New Orleans.

Why *not* Lincoln, Nebraska? Why not build the door, and leave escape hatches from sea to polluted sea?

He grows stronger by the mile.

On his own, Unruh leaves a brain tumor in an infant by the name of Charles Whitman, adds magnesium and aluminum to the cerebral cortex of a toddler named Richard Speck. Both end up insane in the summer of 1966, leaving bodies in Austin and homeland Chicago.

He scalped Indians in Rapid City.

Ate children in Seattle, Olympia and Portland.

By 1947, Capone was gurgling prayers. And Unruh, sensing that time was slipping, decided to go out swinging for the bleachers.

On 13 January, Elizabeth Short met a hormonally imbalanced man named Harold Blane and took him for a quick roll in the hay.

Her torture, on the other hand, was anything but quick.

For two days, the woman the media would call Black Dahlia was beaten and burned, finally eviscerated. Her bisected torso, in the tradition of Kingsbury Run, was dumped in a deserted Los Angeles parking lot at Thirty-Ninth and Norton.

The memory made Unruh nostalgic. The very thought came in the voice of Frank Sinatra, whom Al Capone had dearly loved.

Forget this shit about where you were when Jack Kennedy was killed, okay? The Dahlia was it, baby. She was the goods.

There would be copycat killings in greater L.A. that year, and Ness was mercilessly aware of each.

But by that time, it was over. Unruh had receded back into Oblivion. Alphonse "Scarface" Capone died on January 25th.

Ness, pathetic and broken, would follow him as far south as Purgatory. On the 16th of May in the Year of Our Lord 1957.

Reinhardt nodded toward the television, an ancient console RCA.

"I suppose they're warming up," she said. She'd become surprisingly comfortable on this couch, stocking feet curled beneath her and drink resting between her hands.

Blackmur stared darkly toward the floor, distracted and slipping into a mood. "I suppose."

Sheila leaned forward, stretched her hand across the channel of dingy olive carpet separating the couch and the La-Z-Boy. She patted him twice on the arm, leaned back once again.

They were finished for the evening, unwinding. Sipping drinks in the musty solitude of Blackmur's apartment, gin and whiskey respectively. It had surprised her, a little, how readily the detective had opened himself in the end. After all the gruffness, the hardnosed-cop routine. Somewhere in there was a tormented man, desperate to share the weight of his psychic baggage.

In a double handful of late-night sessions, conducted over the past two weeks, Sheila had filled two spiral notebooks and three ninety-minute Maxell high-fidelity cassettes. The work was staggering, richly pure; Blackmur went through rage first, the infuriating aspects of the case, police procedure, the media. Eventually, he moved on to guilt—the feelings of responsibility, failure.

There was a small alcove serving as a den in the apartment. Blackmur showed her the wall above the desk, where he'd taped body counts. For each victim, one newspaper clipping and one crime scene glossy from the lab. They were stark and lurid and horrifying; the cumulative effect—so *many*—was akin to emotional overload.

All placed at eye-level on the wall, for Blackmur to return to each day. The whole thing was eerily like a shrine; Blackmur talked about the neural strain of stalking a killer. Hunter: Know thy prey.

And Reinhardt scribbled at the top of one page: *Theory of Transitivity: If A=B=C, do A and C know each other, too?*

Long hours. Rocky ground. Reinhardt began to worry herself, a bit, about the stress involved. The friction between their sessions and his daily work. Eventually, Blackmur had insisted. He'd begun to talk about his blackouts. And his dreams.

Corbie Edwards was scheduled to die at midnight tonight. Sheila and Blackmur knocked off early. Not a conscious decision, just something in the polarity of the air.

This morning, two more bodies had been found on the steps of the capitol. They had been positioned in an awkward embrace, chest wounds together. This time, their flesh had been intricately carved. Fiber-thin red lines, in geometric designs. Once again, the corpses were pristine. Devoid of trace evidence, not so much as a strand of hair or errant flake of skin. Both women alone in the city, no family and relatively few friends.

It was almost as if the killer were aware of the sudden shift of attention, and refused to be upstaged.

LPD, at last, had gone to the bullpen. After twenty-six dismal innings, Blackmur had been taken off the case.

Sheila got up from the couch, padded across the room. She knelt down and snapped on the tube, waited for the picture to bleed in. Channel Ten had already begun its pre-game. The crew was in the parking lot of the penitentiary, amidst a pond of protesters and supporters, frat boys hoisting their girlfriends to their shoulders and aping for the cameras.

"Come on," she said. Tried a consoling grin. "I'll make some popcorn or something."

Blackmur was quiet for a long time. Still gazing into the floor.

At last, he looked up at her. Gave a wan smile. Said, "I think I should be alone."

Sheila nodded. She gave his hand a squeeze on her way past; he squeezed back. Then she gathered up her things, pens and pads and the recorder. Stuffed them into her bag. Grabbed her coat. And went to the door.

Before making her exit, she paused one last time. "Lem? Sure you'll be all right?"

Blackmur nodded in the darkness. He had turned to the screen. "Yeah, kid," he said. "I'm sure."

Ellipsis: the near future.

The gun was, in fact, in Blackmur's closet. Wrapped in panties he didn't recognize. On the top shelf. It was a Sig Sauer .45 caliber auto with black matte finish and pebbled grip. Model 220. Seven rounds in the clip.

Corbie Edwards received neither pardon nor stay.

At precisely 12:01 on the twentieth of March, 1995, three things happened. At the exact moment a great cheer rose into the night from the parking lot of the State Penn, a man wearing slacks and a suede jacket, who was standing next to the barricades, shouted "Fuck!" and disappeared. And forty blocks away, Detective Lemuel Blackmur snuggled the barrel of the Sig against the roof of his mouth. Hooked his thumb around the trigger. And squeezed.

Later, his personal effects—including the footlocker from beneath his bed—would be shipped to his mother in Shreveport, Louisiana. There was no key for the footlocker, and Helena Blackmur refused to defile the memory of her son by having the thing pried. It went into storage in the basement, where its contents continued to wither with the passage of time. Eventually, even the most recent additions resembled nothing more than small leather coin purses. Or irregularly-shaped coasters. Or any number of other things.

It took nine uneventful months before the people of Lincoln began to hope—for the first time, with reason—that the horror had come to an end.

Time enough to have a baby. Sheila Reinhardt finished her book the following December, titled *Kingsbury Oblique*. The volume was promptly published by Rutgers as a follow-up. Reinhardt was given awards in the fields of sociology, psychology, criminology and by the Academic Women's Guild.

And Unruh stepped forth from Oblivion long before any of this, at the summons of an inmate who had studied the occult. The illegitimate son of an Oak Park photographic artist, Elmo Coombs had sacrificed twenty cocktail waitresses to the Horned One, whom Unruh did not personally know.

Still, young Elmo wept with joy when the demiurge came to his Statesville cell.

Spring, 1995. Chicago.

It was certainly fine to be home.

—*For Robert Bloch*

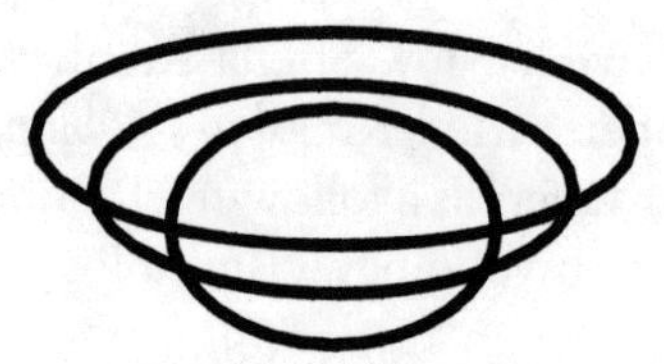

DANTE'S

The Bridge on the River Styx

by Jody Lynn Nye

Colonel John Perkins straightened his back to a parade-ground attitude of attention and winced. For a blissful single moment, while he heard his wife crying and calling his name, nothing had hurt. Now everything did: his rheumatism, his chest, even his bloody war wound, and that was over fifty years old. Well, that wasn't going to stop him tearing a strip out of whoever had taken him away in the middle of his own dinner party and deposited him here. Rotten joke.

"Hello!" he bellowed at the empty, flat, gray landscape. "Hello! I demand to see whoever is in charge here!"

Only a faint moan like a soughing wind answered him. He peered out through the cold mist that seemed to rise from the broad river at his back. The boatman chappie that he thought he'd seen for a moment was gone. Probably pissed off the second Perkins had turned away. Was he alone in this miserable place?

No, he could see human shapes in the fog. He strode toward them.

The moaning grew louder as he approached, and as the fog parted the figures took on more detail. Perkins knew that he was looking at the damned.

Clad in clothing of every description, rags or nothing at all, men and women from youth onward wandered aimlessly to and fro. When two of them met, they raised their heads for a moment, then disinterestedly changed direction. Many of them were missing limbs, or were grotesquely deformed. It looked like a macabre country dance in slow motion. Perkins shuddered.

"What in hell am I doing here?" he asked out loud.

A burst of hot yellow blazed at his feet, making him jump back in spite of the hobbling pain in his legs. It grew into the figure of a gigantic demon with blazing eyes.

"You are here to serve your term of punishment," Satan intoned.

"There's some mistake," Perkins said, mentally ramming an iron rod down his spine to prevent it buckling with fear. "I… I demand to have my paperwork reviewed. I'm a good man. I don't belong here. If I am dead, you must send me on to the other place." He gestured back toward the river, and knew without looking that his hand was shaking. Damn it. "There."

Satan's own hand swept down and swatted him as effortlessly as a tennis player returning an easy serve. Perkins flew backward and landed almost at the feet of one of the gray men. He cried out as his body caught fire from the spot on his cheek where Satan had touched him. His arms, his legs, even his face, were consumed by dancing flames that seemed to laugh as they fed. The agony overwhelmed any pain he had ever felt during his life.

"You are here at my pleasure," the rumbling voice said. "You are strictly bound by my rules." Perkins lifted a crumbling hand, asking wordlessly for mercy, unable to ask what the rules were. The hot yellow blaze leaped upward to giant size, then shrank to a pinpoint that went out. Perkins saw no more.

A moment or an eon later, he felt his body reconstructing itself from the scattered ashes. Soon, sight returned to his eyes, and he could watch what was going on around him while the rest of him pulled itself together. Should he have to put up with an eternity of this? Certainly not! There must be an appeal process. He couldn't see divine justice being so arbitrary as to trap him here forever. He had been a good man. He had served his country through the Second World War. Never in all the years of his sometimes onerous marriage had he ever strayed from his wife, not even when faced with the fleshpots of Paris and Rome. He fancied he'd been a good father and grandfather, so why Hell?

The devil had quoted rules at him, so there was more than just arbitrary choice at work. Hell was a bureaucracy, but if his request for review was turned down so painfully once, he was likely to get the same any time he asked. By now his neck muscles had regenerated somewhat, and he could turn to look across the river. He saw the faint gleam of whiteness. There lay Heaven. He rested his cheek on the gray sand, drinking in the dim light. This was punishment indeed, to be in sight of eternal reward and unable to reach it.

But who said he couldn't reach it?

Blessing the remnants of a classical education, he seemed to recall that there were concentric circles of Hell. If that was true, he was in the outermost one, meaning that he was only just damned. Perkins was as certain that he fell on the good side of the measure as he was that he still had a soul. It also meant that Satan, who was only a fallen angel, after all, had many demands on his time, and couldn't go haring away after those guilty of peccadilloes when he had mass murderers and tyrants to punish. Escape must be possible. But he couldn't do it alone. He raised himself painfully to his feet. They held him. The rags of flesh continued to knit, although his dinner suit would never be the same again.

Thousands of the gray people meandered around him. Some nearly touched him, but continued on their aimless way. Perkins turned this way and that, trying to catch their eyes. None would raise their heads far enough to meet him. His heart sank.

I have never felt so alone, he thought gloomily, then frustration hardened his resolve. *Right*. His commanding officer in Covert Operations during the war, General Hartley, had always said Perkins was at his best when things looked hopeless. He reached back into himself, trying to strip away fifty years of soft living, to the time when Jerry had threatened everything he held dear. He could help these people, and they could help him, but they wanted organizing. He took a deep breath, yanked his shoulders back, and tucked his hands neatly behind his back.

"All right, you lot!" he shouted. "Tenn-hutt!"

His voice echoed over the heads of the damned. No one paid attention. They were too immersed in their own misery. He drew a deeper breath into his lungs, and let out a bellow calculated to swing a division around.

"A-tennnn-*shun*!"

A few of the misty heads turned vaguely toward him. Perkins sensed that the last vestiges of their memories of old military service were being nudged awake. Better build on this before it vanished again.

"Come on, you slackers! Jerry's on the doorstep, and look at the lot of you! Present yourselves! Straighten up there," Perkins admonished one pale spirit, who stumbled toward him on a single foot and a stump. Gradually, a dozen spirits gravitated toward him out of the crowd, some with purpose, others only following a source of energy.

"*That's* better," he said encouragingly. In truth, he felt better himself. He wasn't just dissolving away, and if he could keep his brain alive, he wouldn't.

The raggle-taggle souls assembled before him reminded him of the

Home Guard who'd patrolled the village when he was a boy. They'd had nothing but hay forks and birding guns for weapons, but, by God, they were *willing*. That was what lacked here: will. Well, where self-direction lacked, orders would do until initiative grew up again. He'd set a good example.

"You!" He pointed to a misty form that hovered in front of him. The lad was barely solid. What was left of his clothes looked like a World War I American uniform. *Good men*, Perkins thought, as his heart gave a wrench. *Good boys*. This fellow couldn't have been more than sixteen when he died. Perkins pointed to a rock by his feet. "You, lad, pick up that stone."

The boy's vague eyes focused with difficulty. Perkins shook his hand impatiently until the boy saw the rock and hefted it, straightening up.

"Well, don't just stand there, lad," Perkins said, wishing he had a swagger stick, or something to flex between his hands. "Put it… over there." He pointed at random to a spot near his feet. "You lot, help him!" He singled out three more, and directed them which stones to pick up. A heap of rocks there wasn't useful for anything, but it began to build connections in the minds of his troops.

Hundreds of lost souls were drawn to the site of activity. Perkins shouted himself temporarily hoarse at them, but they wouldn't help, and, tryingly, they would not go away. The men who had shown some glimmer of light were starting to lose interest. Perkins felt overwhelmed.

"Sah!" The colonel spun about and looked down. Behind him was a scrawny rat of a man with a narrow face, dressed in a field uniform Perkins would have known anywhere. He put his arms behind him again, feeling the tiny warmth of joy in his belly.

"Corporal?"

"Sah, request permission to carry on, sah?" The little fellow gestured at the rock carriers.

"By all means, Corp," Perkins said. A *live one*, he thought with delight. A *mind that hasn't died*. "What's your name, lad?"

"Danby, sir," the little man said, after a moment's thought. No one had asked him a question in ages. "Bob Danby."

"Well, Corporal Danby, I am Colonel Perkins. Carry on, then!"

"Sah!" Danby threw himself into a crashing salute, then whirled and advanced upon the dozen or so who were hovering around the rockpile.

"All right, you lot, show some spark! You, get that one. Come on, your hands aren't falling off, are they?" He stuck his narrow little face into the broad, flat face of a dark-skinned man in modern American uniform. Perkins saw with dismay that the little man's back was hollow, as if it had been burned right away. He'd been a sapper, and his job had surely killed him. Perkins felt a pang for Danby. He'd been following orders, and yet he had ended up here. Well, if there was any hope of Heaven, he'd get Danby out, and anyone else he could. The devil should not keep Englishmen nor their allies in Hell. He turned away to recruit more soldiers from the now-curious damned. They were going to need plenty of help to escape.

"Sah!" Danby said, after rounding up the new men and women and making them stand to attention. "Will the colonel pass on review?"

With understandable pride, the little man gestured at the heap of stones. They had fashioned a parade-ground stand for him, about three feet high, with steps to one side. Somewhere, someone had found a long stick, stuck it in the ground, and tied a rag to it. On earth Perkins would have thought it looked pathetic, but here it was the handsomest regimental banner he could ever hope to see. He forced his words past the lump in his throat.

"A most creditable effort, men," he said, swallowing hard. "Well done." The original twelve conscripts straightened up just a little more. Perkins twisted his lips to keep from smiling outright. To do them honor, he marched toward the platform with perfect military precision, took a sharp left, sharp right, sharp right again, and stepped up onto it as if he'd been doing it every day for years. He assumed parade rest, and Danby screeched an order at his lines. They only relaxed a little.

"I will tell you why we are all here today," Perkins began, pitching his voice so even the spirits at the back of the milling crowd could hear him. "We are in a state of war with the enemy, and it is up to us to get back to friendly territory. Are you with me? Eh? Are you with me?"

"Yessir!" Danby shouted. A few more of the damned stirred.

"Are you with me?"

"Yeah!" A few rusty cries of approbation came from the ranks. Then more voices joined in, until Perkins's exhortation was met by a satisfactory roar.

"Then here are my orders."

"Approach," said the awful presence of Satan. The junior demon hurled himself flat on the burning stones at his master's feet.

"An escape attempt, in the outermost circle, Your Eternity," the demon babbled.

"What?" the great voice thundered, and the little demon flinched. Satan concentrated his attention on the rim of his domain. The tiny soul who had dared demand an audience of him was mustering a force of the damned and—bless him for a minion of God if they weren't trying to build a bridge! "The pest of him, he's actually making progress. Go and stop him. Use whatever means necessary, but don't pull anyone away from the important efforts. We have truly evil souls to punish. This one is marginal at worst."

"Yes, Your Eternity," the demon said, scrabbling up to his knees. He rushed out of the presence before his master could inflict pain on him for not thinking of it himself.

Masses of the damned clustered around the men and women who were working under orders. Perkins ordered them all away again and again, but they always came back.

"Where would they go, sir?" Danby asked. "Let's fence 'em orf, then they'll have to stay out of our way."

"Good man," Perkins said, resisting an urge to pat the corporal on his scalloped back. "See to it."

The struts of the bridge were rising nicely. Even though the souls were not able to enter the water, it was possible to drop supports from the existing span and build to them. Once that was secure, they would extend the span and drop the next support. The twisted, dried-out trunks of trees all over the ninth circle were ideal material, since they seemed as hard as iron and heavy as lead. It had taken a long time to cut the first four, using broken bones and shattered rocks as tools. A crippled Swiss lumberjack who had died when a tree fell on him in the late 1800s joined the growing force, and showed the rest of Perkins's army the correct way to fell a tree. The souls who were the most recent and hadn't lost hope yet were the best pupils, but there were unexpected gems like Danby who came from farther out of the past to help. With every stone that was piled on stone, their optimism grew. They began to talk more, and their wavy gray outlines fleshed out, even taking on some color. The bridge grew to three spans.

Perkins had no real idea how long they had been working. Day and night were alike, no more than gray gloom unrelieved by so much as a change in light levels. He realized how very much he missed the little sounds: birdsong, the clatter of the milkman's wire basket, the voices of the neighbors. Apart from the neverending moan of misery, Hell was quiet. Perkins tilted his head back. He'd have given half his heart for the sight of a cloud in a blue sky.

Then, suddenly, there was a rending noise like a crack of thunder. The workers scrambled to get off the bridge as it split in half and collapsed into the waters of the Styx. Three small, blazing figures on the spans danced up and down, spreading fire where they went, and laughing in shrill, maniacal voices. Some of the human souls sprang forward to attack them, but had to withdraw against the heat of hellfire. A few of them got the bright idea of throwing water on the burning spans. The fire was so hot the water burst into steam in mid-air. Perkins raged at the demons in fury for a while, then let himself calm down. There was nothing he could do. When the demons had done all the damage they could, they jumped off the ruin and skated over a layer of steam on the surface of the river, disappearing rapidly out of sight. As one, the despairing souls turned to Perkins.

"We just have to start over, men," he said, resignedly.

Strangely enough, the destruction of the first part of the bridge actually steeled some of the dead to their work. Now that they knew there was an enemy to fight against and not just their own unending misery, they rallied heroically. Some of the men and a few of the women who had had military experience started their own troops under Perkins. Against his own initial reluctance, Perkins discovered a deep respect for one Captain Robin Dale, of the United States Air Force, who had been in Hell since 1976. She had been killed by a munitions accident in California. It took a tough man, let alone woman, to volunteer for ordnance training. She became a good ally, and Danby, too, liked her in a shy, offside way. Perkins guessed that his corporal had never had a sweetheart on Earth, and felt sorry for him.

Perkins sat on the stones to one side with Danby while the work gangs under Dale's command struggled to pull down the damaged piers and clear the work area.

"Damn them, we were making such good progress," Perkins said, surveying the ruin.

Danby sucked his front teeth. "Well, they can't let us succeed, not on purpose, right, sir? That's why we're stuck here, instead of with the harp music and white nighties."

Perkins shook his head curtly. "It's frustrating. If I were alive, this would play merry hell with my ticker." He looked up at the sky. It was the usual featureless gray, although he spotted rising smoke from some distant fire. "I wonder if it's teatime. Do you know, I miss having something to eat. You don't really need to eat or sleep here, but eating would help to break up the day, wouldn't it?"

"Too right. I'd give anything for a smoke, sir."

"Bad for you, son. It shortened my life, a little." Then Perkins realized the absurdity of his lecture, and stopped. "Certainly *my* heart would have held out a few more years if I hadn't been a tobacco man." It was odd to talk about his life as if it were past. His mind was as clear as it had been before that moment when he had had that fatal heart attack, if not clearer.

He felt as if he were back in his combat days. There wasn't a lot of difference between then and now. They'd faced hard situations, men and women having to rally together against the enemy. The chief difference was that they didn't know what was on that other side of the broad river. The only thing they knew was, they had to get there. That goal alone was keeping him sane.

"May I ask why you're here, Corp?" Perkins asked, suddenly. Danby hesitated, and Perkins realized what a personal question it was, to inquire into the reason one had been damned. "I'm sorry. You needn't answer. Unforgivable of me to ask, really." But Danby had only paused to think.

"Dunno, sir," he said, scratching his head. The colonel noticed that he was also missing part of his right hand. "Thought I deserved my eternal reward, but it didn't come. I mean, I was crawling under that 'ere wall in '42 with the charges in tow, then the whole world goes to hell." He grinned. "Or just me. I dunno. I went to church my whole life, tried to listen to vicar, and do good, but here I am. Maybe I took too many people with me when I went, and murder's a sin even if it was in wartime. That's all I can figure. How about you, sir?"

Perkins searched his soul as honestly as he could. "I still don't have a clue, Corp. I think there was a filing error when my rotten ticker stopped. I'm determined to put my case before the Throne, if I can. And yours, too," Perkins added. "I'm sure there are thousands of similar errors wandering around in this outermost circle. If that appeal doesn't clear me, well, I'll take my punishment like a gentleman. But I'm dam—dashed if I'll stay here endlessly if I've been filed in the wrong place like a blasted document. I thought one could expiate one's sins and go on, but the chap who was here didn't say a thing about that." He rubbed his jaw where Satan's hand had struck. It still hurt.

"You already done *me* a good turn, sir," Danby said, his normally narrow eyes wide with sincerity. "I been here a long time. Thought I'd never hear a friendly voice again. These people are self-involved, like. They grumble to themselves for a while, then they stop talking sense. I thought the devils would be at you and at you all the time, but they can't get into your secret thoughts. I been burned by the little demons, and all the time I tried thinking, "I love you, you know. I just love being hurt. You can go on doing that all day," but they just went on. They couldn't tell, a'cos they'd have stopped if they thought I liked it. Your *self* is all right, no matter what happens to your body. That's what I hold onto."

Perkins sat back. "So they can't hear what you're thinking, eh?" Danby shook his head. That gave him choice food for thought. "My G-g-g… you can't say The Name here, can you?"

"No, sir."

"Well, anyhow, I think we have just found the advantage we need. They're going to go on hampering us as they can, destroying what we've done. We just have to minimize what they know in advance. Do you read me?"

"Like a newspaper headline, sir."

"Good man," Perkins said. "Now, here's what I have in mind."

From his review platform, Perkins addressed his troops.

"Men, and ladies," with a little bow to Captain Dale, who frowned. He'd have to ask her later what form was current in the United States army. "The enemy has caused a setback in our plans, but we will not allow that to deter us from our eventual goal. We must dig the pilings in deeper, and make the spans wider. That way, when we have completed our mission, there will be a bridge between Heaven and Hell that anyone can walk in safety. I'm proud of your efforts, men… troops! Carry on! Corporal Danby and I will assign tasks to each work group. Report to one of us after this briefing. That is all."

Danby and a few structural engineers from various eras of history were examining the pilings yanked out of the wreckage of the bridge. Perkins picked up a loose twig and found it made a tolerable swagger stick. He tucked it under his arm.

"No good, sir. They're ruined," said a black engineer from Zimbabwe, showing him the charred ruins of the piers.

"Well, we've used up all the trees in this part of the circle," Perkins said, swinging his stick at the terrain. "Send out a detachment to find more. Captain Dale, will you lead a foraging expedition?"

Dale snapped to attention, gratitude replacing the hovering peevishness. She had undoubtedly been waiting to lecture him on the 'ladies' gaffe, and now forgot all about it in the light of special treatment.

"I will, sir. How many pilings do we need?"

Perkins leaned back on his heels to think, and stood up straight when the rheumatism in his knees gave him pain. "Let's start with fifty. Send them back in detachments, and we'll go on from there."

"Right, sir!" She snapped another handsome salute. Perkins touched his brow with the stick, and turned away.

The crowds continued to press around them, and the moaning began to get on Perkins's nerves. The head office must have taken note of his antipathy to continuous noise, because the cacophony increased. While he was trying to give some orders regarding the bridgehead, voices high above them broke into a cadenced series of shrieks Perkins recognized with dismay as opera. It built in volume until no one could hear even his most powerful bellows.

Confound it, Perkins thought. He'd always despised opera. His wife had made him go with her, but he always fell asleep before the first act was out, embarrassing her with his snores. Was this his punishment for not behaving himself when he knew the old girl was counting on him? If so, he was paying. If he considered it part of his punishment, he ought to be working toward heavenly respite, and that made it worthwhile. He looked up at the sky and smiled. The song halted abruptly.

"Got you, you bastards," he said.

Painful music was only the first of the trials that Satan's minions had prepared for them. Flying demons with ragged bat wings swooped out of the gray sky and snatched up souls, carrying them away screaming. Some of Perkins's remaining workforce flung itself to the ground, demoralized.

"That's just what they want to see! Don't give up, troops!" Perkins cried. Gradually, the men and women got onto their feet and back to work.

Danby appeared beside him and threw his energetic salute. "Under the crust it's about boiling, sir, but firm enough for all practical purposes."

"Right," Perkins said. "You do your job, and I'll do mine."

Some of the obstructions the troops met weren't sent by Satan at all. A scrawny madman in tattered robes hung around the worksite for shifts on end, haranguing them in a shrill voice.

"You'll never succeed! Doomed! Doomed to fail!"

Perkins, dealing with the huge mounds of gray earth left at the bridgehead by the excavations, managed to ignore him in the same way he'd always shut out grand opera, but some of the troops were slowing down to listen to him. Perkins saw the dismay on their faces and hurried over to pull the man away.

"Doomed to fail!" the man howled over his shoulder, as Perkins yanked him along to the barrier. "Doomed!"

"Old chap, I'd tell you to go to hell, but you're already here and you seem to like it," Perkins closed the gate between them, "so just push off, won't you?"

"You'll fail!"

One of Danby's engineers, grimacing, scooped up a clod of steaming mud from the heaped tailings, and flung it expertly at the doomsayer, striking him in the middle of the chest.

"*You've* failed, you limb of Satan," he intoned in a mighty voice. "Get ye gone."

"Right, you blighter, orf with you!" Danby joined in target practice with glee. His first clod of earth fell short, but the next one hit the apparition in the shoulder. Even through his madness the ancient realized he'd had the worst of the encounter, and hobbled away as fast as he could.

"Carver!" Perkins shouted, addressing the broad-chested engineer who'd thrown the first missile.

"Sire?"

"I am appointing you morale officer," Colonel Perkins said. "Keep up the good work."

The big man produced an even bigger smile that revealed several missing teeth.

"Pleased to, your worship." He looked around him at the rest of the workers, who waited expectantly. "All right, friends, let us join in a hymn. If you don't know it, listen the first time through. We'll give them evil ones somewhat to think on."

Perkins stayed around for a while, enjoying the rousing song of praise with all the Holy Names expurgated. The others must have felt as nicely naughty as he did, coming close to blaspheming where Hell was concerned. They all joined in the second chorus with gusto. *Another trial vanquished*, Perkins thought with pride.

Some of the troops simply vanished from time to time. Perkins lost his best engineer, and a couple of other nearly irreplaceable ones, including a man from the German Axis with whom he wouldn't have so much as shaken hands on Earth.

"Where's the chap gone?" Danby demanded. "I was watching him meself—so were you! Slap into thin air, gone."

"Haven't a clue," Perkins said, sadly. "There's not a single indication as to the direction. Satan must have snatched them up and dropped them somewhere else. We can only hope they make their way back to us, Corp. We've a hundred others to think of."

"Yessir," Danby said, bowing his head.

"All right, lads, another song!" Carver said into the heavy silence. "A mighty savior is That One, with relish never fail-ing...." The voices took up the melody, weakly at first, but more energetically after a while, resonant with hope.

Dale reappeared at the head of a troop triumphantly hauling thirty rough-hewn pilings. The sixty she had already sent had been installed, or destroyed by Satan's minions, but here were surely enough to finish the bridge.

"Well done, captain!" Perkins said, returning her salute with relish. "I applaud your efforts. I am most impressed."

"Thank you sir. There's a blighted forest at the edge of the next innermost circle with plenty…" Her voice died away as she swayed.

"Are you all right?" Perkins asked, peering at her. She seemed more translucent than usual.

Dale put a hand to her head. "I don't know, sir. I feel… good." Perkins hurried to grasp her upper arms to steady her, but the stuff of her body dissolved between his hands like smoke.

"Another foul trick!" the colonel exclaimed. "We'd da—dashed well better succeed, before Satan's swept away all our workforce."

Dale's second-in-command, a compact Japanese man in a civilian pilot's zip-up coverall, stepped forward and presented Perkins with a ripping salute.

"I'll take over, with your permission, sir," he said.

"Carry on," Perkins told him. He was grieved about Dale's disappearance, and wondered if there was any way to rescue her from the demons and complete their escape plans at the same time.

"We'll meet again, sir," Danby said, although his voice held out little hope. "That's like the song said. Got ter keep thinking it, sir."

"Right you are, Corp," Perkins said wearily. For once he was unable to ignore the pains of his rheumatism and angina. "The last push now. We'll either make it, or not, as of now."

The bridge had reached fifty spans now, and at the end some of the troops scrambling back reported with delight that they could see a bright city in the whiteness on the other shore. That raised morale among the rest of the workforce as nothing so far had been able to do. Everyone was singing or humming as they went about their work.

"It's been too quiet," Perkins said to Danby. They had avoided writing down any of the assignments not strictly required by the builders, and all the plans were on a need-to-know basis. Perkins kept everything in his head, except for what he confided in Danby. "The final blow will come when we've nearly finished, just to destroy hope."

"We'll be ready, sir," Danby assured him. "They won't beat us, not now."

A minute imp, the size of a fingernail, overheard their words, and hurried back to report to the junior demon in charge of demoralizing this gang of lost souls.

"Now," the demon said, rubbing his taloned hands together. Oh, his master would be pleased with him. "Now! Now!"

Winged fiends converged on the building site, carrying off timbers and men. Perkins and the others stooped to throw clods of earth and rocks at them. The saw-wings looped around and opened their obscene beaks to breathe fire on them.

Flame demons danced out onto the spans of wood, stone and clay. They seemed to experience glee when they encountered the huge buckets of water set out at intervals to prevent fire. Several of them ringed one tun after another, whirling around and around until their body heat caused the water to boil off in a huge, hissing cloud of steam.

"After them!" Perkins cried. The workers seized buckets full of water from the banks of the Styx and ran at the enemy. The demons laughed with delight, picking out trails of fire along the carefully hewn timbers as they flew. Tiring of the chase, they stopped at around span thirty-six and set both uprights ablaze, like the lintels of a fearsome doorway. The humans stopped. The chase reversed itself, with the demons now in pursuit. The junior demon in charge soared down on the back of a winged lizard, urging his imps and apparitions to greater terrors.

"Don't lead them in here!" Perkins shouted as the troops dashed back along the burning bridge. He stood in front of the slagheap, where all the tailings, sawdust, fragments of wood, charcoal and clay had accumulated over the ages of constructing the bridge. "It'll burn like Chinese New Year!"

That was exactly what the junior demon wanted to hear: fear. He directed all of his forces to converge upon the gigantic heap of burnables.

"We'll show them what Hades really means," he hissed gleefully. The humans flung themselves away from the fire demons, who hurtled toward Perkins. The colonel only just managed to throw himself out of the way before they struck.

The hillock exploded into glorious, roaring flames that burst out in every direction. The fire demons reveled in it, some diving in to scoop up fire with their bare claws. They threw it up in the air, rubbed it on themselves and rolled in it, shouting with glee. It spread outward in a series of blasts until it engaged the bridgehead, causing the painstakingly made pilings to catch roaring fire like pitch-soaked torches. It was so hot the stones of the spans began to melt into the Styx, raising blinding clouds of steam that warred with the roiling smoke from the slagheap fire. The flames raced from piling to piling until the first third of the bridge was burning. The curious dead souls crowded in close to see, and were burned to ashes in droves.

Perkins must be going mad at this moment, the junior demon thought, turning his steed to locate the upright figure of the commanding officer who had spent decades of his afterlife building this hopeless cause. He suddenly had an urge to see Perkins's misery and defeat.

He swept the protesting lizard low through the smoke, and discovered that the area was nearly empty of damned souls. He gulped when he saw where the rest of them were.

"Your Eternity," another imp reported, taking delight in the discomfiture of one of his rivals for Satan's approval, "they've escaped!"

"What?" Satan demanded. "But I have had my Eye on that bridge for years now."

"And more than forty others with him. The bridge was a tactical diversion, my lord," the imp said. "They left through a tunnel under the Styx. It looks like it's been there since they started, Your Eternity."

"But the ground underneath is molten!" Satan exclaimed. He checked his inventory of souls. "That English sapper is gone with him as well. He gave Colonel Perkins the expertise. Incredible. I thought his mind was gone. You can never tell with these non-comms. I should have had him building traps for me."

"We pulled a half-dozen out of the mouth of the tunnel. Should I send firesnakes after the rest of them?"

Satan shook his head. "Once they're halfway across, they're no longer mine," the Devil said, thoughtfully. "And I don't want that man here any longer, no matter how much of his punishment was left to expiate. He has the power to stir up even the souls of the damned. He might be telling me what to do next. One thing I've never been able to tolerate is that holier-than-thou attitude. I get enough of it from you-know-Who."

The imp clashed his claws together nervously. "Yes, Your Eternity."

"Hurry," Dale's voice said in the darkness. "This way! You're nearly there!"

"By God, she's right!" Perkins said, seeing a bright white light ahead of him in the tunnel as he scrabbled on hands and knees through the hot mud. His rheumatism pain was fading like the rest of the awful nightmare. "Listen to me, Corp! I said it! Carry on, men! By *God*, we made it! There are other bridges than spans over water."

"Right you are, sir," Danby said fervently, clambering after him. "Right you are."

ISLINGTON

by Ian McDonald

Hong Kong was full of Arabs, Prague stiff with Americans rediscovering the *Grand Siècle*, so Natasha and Iain went to hell for the weekend. It beat out the new private-security company premiums and the threat of the Channel Tunnel rail link as the topic of conversation around Natasha and Iain's stripped-pine table at Sunday lunch.

"You mean, hell?" asked Clytemnestra, the interior designer who sat underneath Natasha and Iain's de Koening print because it offended her sensibilities.

"As in, *hell?*" her husband Hugh added. He wore a waistcoat and was trying to grow a beard. He felt it expressed his status as an occasional cinema reviewer for the quality Sundays.

"A hell," Natasha said, passing the Marks and Spencer's sun-dried tomato *ciabatta*. Maya, on her left, declined. She had been told she was allergic to vine fruits.

"You mean, you can pick and choose?" Maya's partner Ryan asked. People paid him to be a barrister, but he thought of himself in his soul as a stand-up comedian. Many of his clients had reached the same conclusion. "Like there are resorts? Do the Germans grab all the best torments before breakfast?"

"There are all kinds of hells," Iain said.

"Like Dante," Jonathon the consulting engineer commented. He and his wife Jessica were enthusiastic patrons of the Rotary Club bondage nights. The idea of a weekend in hell appealed to them very much. "Seven circles."

"Dante's is just one of them," Iain said. "All the hells that have ever been imagined by the great hell-describers of history are there, and a lot more no one's ever thought of."

"How do you get there?" Ryan asked. He held up his glass for more Southeastern Australian un-oaked Chardonnay. He was firmly in stand-up comedy mode now. "Does a trap door open in the floor of the travel agent, and down you go? Where the hell—ha ha—do you go to book something like that anyway? It's hardly in the Kuoni Long Haul brochure."

"Actually, it's in the small ads in the Sunday Independent Color Supplement," Natasha said. She despised Ryan in comedian mode. She despised him equally in barrister mode. "Holidays in Hell, Limited. And you get there by elevator."

Ryan choked on his un-oaked Chardonnay.

"Now you are taking the piss. How would madam like to pay? Check, charge or soul? And I suppose there's a little guy in a red lycra suit with a neat goatee and horns to meet and greet you in reception?"

"You can be such a fucking bore, Ryan," Jessica the aromatherapist said. "Just shut up and let Natasha and Iain tell it their way. I, for one, am dying to know what hell's like."

"Pun intended," Ryan said. "All right, I'll shut up, if you pour me another glass of this quite acceptable little Aussie brew."

"So, where shall I start?" Natasha said, mentally drawing herself into performance. She was an actress. The theatre, she said too frequently, is like the True Church: invisible, present all around in all places and circumstances. Her last acting job had been in a fabric conditioner commercial. The company was still running it, though they had over-dubbed her voice with a real celebrity's. "In Harrow. It's all very discreet, very low key. They run the company out of an office above a shopping center in Harrow. And no, Ryan, there are no little men in red suits taking a mortgage on your soul, or hellish laughter and screaming on the Muzak speakers. And no brimstone potpourri."

"What is a brimstone anyway?" Hugh asked.

"We dealt with a Mr. Conway," Natasha continued. "Very charming man—about our age, mid-thirties. Holding onto his hair well. Better than some of his contemporaries." She looked at Ryan. He smiled sarcastically at her. "Gave us coffee and biscuits while we watched the promotional video and looked through the brochures. Said we could take any of the material home we liked, if we wanted to study it at leisure, but we thought not. Well, some of the material was rather… lurid?"

"The kids," Iain said. He was a telecommuting ad-boy and house-father, which meant that he employed a nanny, Nanny Bernie, from Ireland, who knew all the passwords to his computer system, but Iain was too lazy to change them.

"We were very lucky," Natasha went on, telling her story. "They had a late cancellation for that weekend—demand has been ferocious; they've been booked solid since they started to run the ad campaign. It's not that hell gets crowded, it's demand on the elevator. It's like charter flights: They have to fit the tours in between the scheduled runs."

"There really are lost souls?" Ryan asked.

"So we were told," Iain said. "The tourist runs depart from Victoria Station; the freight elevator over by the Red Star Parcels office. Except some of the time, it isn't."

"Let me get this," Jonathon said. "You go to hell via Victoria Station?"

"It's a very good service," Natasha said. "Your own personal lift operator. Ankle-deep crimson pile carpet, burgundy buttoned-satin lining, and polished brass everywhere."

"It really is hell," Clytemnestra said.

"There's a bar service too," Iain added.

"I don't want to know about the charter flight," Jessica said. "Hurry up and tell us about hell." She and Jonathon seemed to be holding hands—at least—under the table. Jessica's voice was unusually husky.

"Your rep meets you when you step out," Natasha said, irritated by the interruption to her flow of theatre. "He gives you your Safe Conducts, which you are not to remove under any circumstances, and tells you the secret Word of Summoning, should something unforeseen go wrong and you need him in a hurry."

"Safe Conducts?" Hugh asked.

"Part of the holiday contract," Iain said. "It identifies you as a visitor, grants you access to all parts of the hell you've chosen; ensures nothing can be done to you against your will; you suffer no harm or damage from any environments or devices, such as hellfire, infernal cold, eternal screaming, noxious fumes and so on; while you receive full benefits of the damned, like not needing to eat, sleep, drink or any other annoying biological necessity. In addition, it guarantees that whatever situation you find yourself in, you will be returned to the elevator by check-out time."

"Tell me about bloody hell!" Jessica shrieked in frustration.

"The one we'd booked into was called Ahenobarbos," Iain said.

"Also known as the Citadel of Eternal Pain," Natasha added.

"I can't speak for the Citadel," Iain continued. "All we got to see were corridors. Nothing but corridors. Bloody gray corridors, one after the other, with no doors and no windows."

"Corridors, with people in them," Natasha said, adding theatrically,

"Or things that used to be people." Every un-oaked Southeast Australian Chardonnay froze midway to lips. "It is a place of pain, a pain that transcends physical agony into an altered state of consciousness. So the Ahenobarbs—that's what the inmates call themselves—told us."

"It was all rather Clive Barker," Iain said. "All black leather and mutilation. Personally, I found it a bit crass. Tasteless. For instance, the first Ahenobarb we run into is this fat man—and I'm talking seriously fat, mondo blimpo fat—who's, like, hooked into this frame on wheels by his fat. There are these big metal staples driven right into the blubber, hooked to chains that stretch it out into nasty big peaks. All over his body: belly, thighs, cheeks, chins. Couldn't make out a word the poor bastard was trying to tell us, he was pulled that tight. And that wheeled cube frame he was hooked into took up most of the corridor. Luckily, it had a squeaky castor so we could hear it coming several corridors off and avoid getting pinned against the walls by several tons of flab."

"We kept bumping into eviscerated women," Natasha said. "All over the bloody place. You'd turn a corner, and there'd be another one. Same Goth roller-and-tray white makeup, black lipstick, wearing these ludicrous leather corset-things with rings and hooks all over them, with their intestines pulled out and fastened to these eyelets and rings with wire. It was quite a relief, I'm telling you, to meet the ones who'd had their windpipes pulled out through their throats as well; at least they didn't prattle on about pain and the transcendent knowledge of the Lord of Torments. It got to the stage where we'd see one coming and say, 'Oh, for fuck's *sake*…'"

"One poor sod, I remember, had had his penis cut in half," Iain said. "Lengthways." All the men winced. "And they'd shoved this barbed metal plate between the halves and then bolted them together again." The men winced again, more so. "It wasn't the pain he minded so much, he told us, it was that he couldn't play a quick solo on the pork guitar without cutting his fingers off. And he told me there wasn't a lot else to do down there."

"What did they do to the man's penis, Mum?" Seven-year-old Keanu and five-year-old Poppy had arrived in the kitchen. Moppet-haired Poppy could barely rest her chin on the table. Something to do with atmospheric pollutants, the growth specialists had said. Nanny Bernie lingered in the utility-room door with a basket of washing, giving her employers her I-know-all-your-secrets look. She was going. Definitely. When Natasha and Iain found the courage to fire her.

"Go on, Natasha, answer Canoe," Clytemnestra said. She had never made any secret that she thought Keanu a stupid name.

"You know quite well it's pronounced Kee-*ah*-nu, Clittie," Natasha replied, using the detested university nickname that Clytemnestra had never succeeded in killing.

"What's clittie, Mummy?" Poppy asked.

Nanny Bernie was summoned dramatically and told to make sure that the children stayed in the playroom during Sunday lunch, please. The talk returned to the hell, and to this really nice man Iain and Natasha had met, except that he was half-skinned.

"When I say 'half-skinned,' I don't mean top half, or bottom half, or left or right," Natasha said. "I mean all over, in strips, from the top of his head to the soles of his feet."

Maya looked disgusted. Jonathon and Jessica seemed to be enjoying it, or maybe it had been the bit about the man with his penis cut in half.

"Actually, he was a pretty okay guy," Iain said. "They'd all been worshippers of pain, before; they reckoned that through it they could share the mind and will of the Lord of Torments himself, on his throne of glowing, spiked iron at the heart of the Citadel of Eternal Pain."

"I thought it made quite a lot of sense," Natasha said. "More than the Mormons."

"The problem is that it wore off after a century or two," Iain went on. "The nerve endings deadened, they got used to it, and it stopped working for them. They found they were really crass-looking people in these endless gray corridors, who couldn't get out, and that they were always going to be this way. Some of them were pretty depressed about that, especially because the new arrivals, most of whom seemed to be devotees of horror novels, were still having visions and revelations and hallucinations, channeling with the Lord of Torments himself. Though Charlie—that was what we called the guy who was half-peeled; his real name was something in Hittite we couldn't pronounce—told us that the mind of the Lord of Torments was pretty pathetic really, just constant anger about being sealed up in his Citadel of Eternal Pain by the Omnipotence Himself, with no one to take it out on but the Ahenobarbs. Pretty petty-minded, actually. A lifetime of faithful devotion, and what did they end up with? Peanut-butter-and-jelly man, and scrap iron up your dick. Except that it was hell, I'd say it was a wee bit of a disappointment. Certainly wouldn't go back."

"Not voluntarily," Ryan said. He was surprised when everyone laughed.

"Tiramisu, anyone?" Natasha whirled the cocoa-dusted desert onto the stripped pine table.

Speaking of hell, Hugh asked if anyone had heard from Richard lately. Iain said he'd phoned to say he was coming to the lunch but hadn't turned up, which was hardly surprising; divorce wasn't something you got over in a couple of weeks, or even a couple of months, and it took time to get back into socializing again, no matter how supportive your friends had been through the whole healing process. Which wasn't helped by the Child Support Agency shafting him with an outrageous assessment while his job was under threat—white-collars were going to the wall all over the country now that the information economy jobs were moving down the net to the Philippines and South America. And if the job was under threat, the apartment was too, just as he was settling into it; the mortgage companies were getting ratty, with property prices sliding once again into negative equity. Natasha took the tiramisu round again to lighten the mood, and Jonathon and Jessica told everyone about the enclaving scheme in their development and how safe they would feel with walls and gates and security cameras and dogs and night-watchmen, and a good night's sleep was well worth two hundred a month. Really. Hugh opined that it was only a question of time before the police were armed and routine patrol work would be sold off to security companies. Private police forces were inevitable, which were really no different from armed civilian posses and vigilantes, except legally sanctioned, but if it stopped drug-crazed youth gangs, then it was No Bad Thing. Really. Everyone had horror stories of people they knew who had been burgled mugged raped assaulted by drug-crazed youth gangs, but before they could tell them Nanny Bernie came in with Keanu and Poppy to borrow the tazer stun-gun because they were going down to the hire shop to look for the latest Battle Cats TM video.

Richard was at the next lunch at Hugh and Clytemnestra's. This was because he was staying with Hugh and Clytemnestra. A twelve-year-old in Manila was doing his job at a ninetieth of his pay. Rather than await the court action for possession, he had dropped the keys to his apartment through the loan society's door. They blacklisted him, of course, and bad-mouthed him to twenty other credit-reference agencies. He turned up on Natasha and Iain's doorstep with a suitcase and a quarter of a mile of classical CDs folded into ten Hamley's bags. Natasha and Iain were in the middle of the fraught preliminaries to firing Nanny

Bernie and sent him round to Hugh and Clittie, who happened to need a house-sitter that weekend as they were going to hell.

"Exactly like you said, guys," Clittie said, peering past the Ghanaian twisted-wire candleholder at Natasha and Iain at the other end of the American white-oak Shaker dining table. "Harrow, Victoria Station, everything. And the red plush interior was *ecstatically* kitsch. Natasha, could you stop Canoe from playing with that, please? It's Vietnamese."

"But after that, it was totally different," Hugh said. He was exceedingly mellow on single-vineyard Rioja.

"Quite civilized, really," Clittie continued, seeing that New Nanny Claire had rescued the woven lemon-grass lampshade. "Though the decor was inspirationally vulgar. Positively *orgasmic* with glitz and gilt. Pure Las Vegas Caesar's Palace. Pillars and mirrors everywhere."

"Hell," Jessica said, firmly.

"Of course. Sorry. Anyway, the rep showed us into this enormous domed room, all mirrors and pillars and little gilded demons—well, you don't want to know about that. But everyone was in evening dress—except for Amanda, she'd been a yoga teacher and was in something stretchy, which was probably the best the poor kid could afford. I'd wondered when Mr. Conway told us to dress formal."

Richard laughed. He had the kind of laugh that could kill any social context instantly.

"And when you looked, the door had disappeared," he said. "I know this one. Pure Jean-Paul Sartre. *In Camera*. Hell is other people. Sealed in a room, no way out, ever, with the people you hate most in all the world."

"Actually," Clytemnestra said, "they were rather fun. Victor excepted—he'd been a second-string tenor back in the Fifties and had really never escaped the Golden Age of Variety. He would keep regaling us with these tedious stories about acts and comics and hoofers who, truth be told, just wouldn't make it onto television these days, thank God."

"Hell," Richard said, too darkly for the amount of single-vineyard Rioja he had drunk.

"We got on really well with Julia," Clytemnestra said. "She'd been an interior designer too; it was such fun, swapping ideas and hints and horror stories about other people's homes. And Amanda showed us a really good relaxation technique for when everything feels just too ghastly for words, Richard."

The glance got tangled in the Ghanaian twisted-wire candleholder.

"It really does work," Hugh said. His beard had filled in. He had the look now, though none of the Sundays had commissioned a review from him in a month. "I had great chats with Neville about old movies—he was an accountant in his former life; it is hell, after all—but he was a complete Hitchcock buff. Argued for hours over the relative merits of *Vertigo* and *The Birds* as the ultimate expression of The Master's technique. Talk? We did nothing but. You can't imagine how nice it is to go somewhere people are glad to meet you."

"New face in hell," Richard said. "Movie buff."

"Julia was telling me it's all changed tremendously since the tours started," Clittie said. "Now there's someone new to talk to every other day, it seems. Hardly like hell at all, apart from the fact they can't get out. Natasha, could you get Nanny Claire to… Too late. Oh well."

Poppy had pulled out the CD loading drawer and was pressing chocolatey lips to *Orthodox Chant from the Choir of St. Barbara, Minsk.*

"Actually," Hugh said, by now mellow to the point of falling off the Shaker chair, "we enjoyed it so much we're thinking of going back to meet them all again next weekend."

They didn't. The next trip to hell was Ryan and Maya's. They enjoyed it immensely and wanted to tell all the people gathered around their glass-topped wicker table about it, but the conversation refused to veer hellward and orbited stubbornly around Richard. He was in the garden pointing out shrubs and plants to Keanu and Poppy, who paid absolutely no attention. Taking the opportunity, everyone in the endangered-wood conservatory talked about him. He had pushed the Channel Tunnel link and negative equity and Islington's asymptotic crime figures and the collapse of Lloyd's Insurance and the consequent aftershocks bringing down the loose material in the financial markets into poor also-rans.

"It was the last straw," Clittie said. "I mean, we couldn't have debt collectors and bailiffs coming to the door. I could see them watching in number twenty-six. He had to go. Really."

Everyone agreed, passing around the Initially Uninspiring *Jeunes Vignes* That Warranted Reassessment after a couple of bottles.

Richard was now living in his car. He parked it in a different place each night and slept in the backseat in a sleeping bag. Most nights he would be woken by a policeman tapping the muzzle of his assault rifle on the window and telling him to fuck off before he did him for vagrancy. He would drive around the block until the police had gone, and then sleep until daybreak. The police had grown wise to this, and now waited for him to come back. So did the car criminals. Three days ago they had tapped the muzzles of their assault rifles on the window and forced Richard to hand over his stereo, his ten Hamley's bags of classical CDs, his shoes, his spare wheel, and all his cards. The police caught them the first time they tried to use the cards. There were more flags and banners across the data net on Richard's cards than Notting Hill at carnival time.

"If the repo men ever catch up with him, it's the cardboard box under the South Bank Center," Iain said.

"It's a terrifyingly thin line," Maya said. "One slip, one thing goes wrong, and it all falls down."

"We all fall down," Ryan said, not in comedy mode. At that moment Richard returned with Keanu and Poppy.

"Look what Poppy's got!" Keanu declared.

Beaming, Poppy held out a dried white dog turd. Natasha screeched something sounded like 'toxoplasmosis' and rushed the children to the newly installed downstairs bathroom. Ryan thought it was now an opportune time to tell everyone about hell.

"It was hilarious," he said. "Like a Carry-On movie. A truly English cock-up. Carry On Burning."

"Except no one was," Maya said.

"They've privatized it," Ryan announced. "Just like the prison service. Same company, in fact. Unit Five Securities."

"Do they lose as many inmates?" Hugh asked.

"They do. They're having terrible trouble with the new computer system. While we were there a good dozen must have been sent back to limbo or judgment, or ended up with the wrong punishment."

"Who installed it?" Richard asked.

"Computech Services, after an evaluation by Warlock Clinton Petrie; you know, the ones who advised on the National Health sell-off."

Richard laughed. Once again, it silenced everyone.

"Bloody accountants all over the place, even in hell."

"I don't see how they can make a profit," Jonathon said.

"The previous management team contracted to provide Unit Five with worldly power and wealth. They've got it to burn."

"Which explains why their shares lost fifty points yesterday," Richard said gleefully. "Can't trust the Prince of Lies to keep his end of the contract." The others had become aware of Richard's body odor and were discreetly drawing their wrought-iron chairs away.

"But what was it like?" Jessica asked eagerly. Hugh and Clytemnestra's existential hell had been a disappointment. She wanted flames. She wanted chains. She wanted whips, and bare flesh, and lots of screaming.

"Well, the flight in was really spectacular," Maya said. Ryan had his bottle of Turkish *raki* out. As usual no one but him took any, and he only to show off. It gave him hideous heartburn. "It's the classic seven concentric circles of hell; like a pit, understand?" She mimed with her hands. No one understood. "Except some of the upper ones have been closed down—resource targeting and cost-effectiveness maximization. They want to establish centers of excellence in the lower, more profitable levels. The elevator takes you down the center of the pit, right into the top of the brass dome of Pandemonium that covers the city of Dis. Of course, they've made some changes, gone for a more corporate look—pot plants, new carpeting, themed shopping and souvenir areas. I shudder to think what the corporate hospitality bill must be."

"It all looks very organized," Ryan continued. "But, like everything that gets corporatized, underneath it's all crap. It's falling apart. They take you around the circles in these glass tour buses—they're damned-powered, would you believe? a couple of dozen people chained to treadmills down below—but the vale of Treachery, where people who were couples in life take turns to torture each other, a millennium each, was closed for training; and the Chasm of Unending Flame was out because Unit Five were in dispute over renegotiating the contract for the supply of brimstone."

"I still don't know what brimstone is," Hugh said.

"There was the odd flogging, and a pretty spectacular flaying, and a woman having molten lead pumped up her ass, and quite a lot of people imprisoned between stalagmites and stalactites, but an awful lot was closed for refurbishing."

"We did see the Simoniacal priests," Maya said. "But Gog and Magog and the Creatures That Dwell in Eternal Gloom were being re-themed."

"No roaring and wailing and gnashing of teeth?" Jonathon asked.

"Er, no. But we did bring you back a couple of things from the gift shop, didn't we, Maya?"

"Some really nice chains—certified to have bound the Goat with Ten Thousand Names—and a scourge."

"The scourge's provenance is a bit dodgy," Ryan said. "If it was the actual one that whipped the Scarlet Woman of Uz naked around the Cloister of Eternal Penitence, frankly, I'm the Pope. I've seen it; they've got armies of the damned, pulled off the racks and out of the spiked cages, down in factories turning the things out by the thousand. Still, you might have some fun with it, Jonathon. It's a bit of a laugh, really."

Natasha returned from the new bathroom with Keanu and Poppy. Poppy smelled of disinfectant and her hands looked scrubbed and red.

"What was that I missed about the Scarlet Woman and the Cloister of Eternal Penitence?" Natasha asked.

"Ryan and Maya were telling us about hell," Richard said, deciding he would have some of the Turkish *raki* this once. "Sounds just like Islington."

Richard was not there when Jonathon and Jessica threw a lunch to celebrate their weekend in hell. Richard was in a psychiatric bed in St. Botolph's Charity Hospital. He had been found that bed after waiting in FeelWell Healthcare Trust's Accident and Emergency department for sixteen hours while managers and social workers passed him from one to the other. He spent those sixteen hours on a trolley, dripping from the pressure bandages around his wrists, while shift after shift of receptionists asked him his medical insurance number and when he said he didn't have one, told him he could sign up with the FeelWell's in-house plan payable by direct debit from his bank account. He was dripping blood because he had tried to slit his wrists with the top of a can of cat food he had poked out of a bin. He had tried to slit his wrists after the security guards at Jonathon and Jessica's enclaved development kicked the shit out of him because they knew that the Mulcaheys would never have a friend who looked like *that*, in shoes like *those*, with no *car*, and quite frankly, *smelling*, so he was obviously a freeloader from Cardboard City who, if not committing a crime, was about to commit a crime, and thus deserved a good kicking either way. Richard had come to Merry Hill Lodge to get away from the old tramp under Waterloo Bridge who took his money, crept into his cardboard bash and fucked him up the ass twice a night. One night, a shower and a shave, was all he had wanted. Now he was in the only available psychiatric bed in St. Botolph's Charity ward, and Monday he was coming out because someone else needed it. Correction. He was being *cared for in the community*.

Some things were just too gross to be topics of conversation around

Jonathon and Jessica's wrought-iron table on the patio with its view over the immature Leylandii cypress hedge of all the other patios of Merry Hill Lodge. The second round of imported beer had been passed around from the tin bath full of slushy ice. Newest Nanny Colette had Keanu and Poppy off to see the latest Disney, so Jonathon and Jessica could talk adults-to-adults about the Hell of Endless Bondage.

"We're thinking of suing," Jonathon said.

"We're very angry about this," Jessica said. "Fuming. It was nothing like the brochure. Not remotely. Surely that contravenes the Trades Descriptions Act or counts as gross misrepresentation or something, Ryan?"

"I mean, it all began so well," Jonathon said. "When they fitted us with the rubber suits—God knows how they got the sizes right, or where they got them from, but then I suppose God isn't the right one to invoke is he?—anyway, we thought, aye, aye, this could be rather fun."

"They had to put the Safe Conducts on the outside," Jessica said. "By the time they fitted the masks and the gags, all you could see were eyeballs."

"Total enclosure." Jonathon said. "And it got even better in the next chamber. That was where they fitted you into the cages. Well, they called them cages, but they were more like sets of medieval stocks; lots of manacles and clamps and iron bands. Like something from the very best issue you ever read of *Sadie Stern's Monthly*."

"You mean, you get *Sadie Stern's Monthly*?" Clytemnestra asked.

"You mean, you read *Sadie Stern's Monthly*?" Ryan asked.

Jonathon brushed the questions aside.

"You lie on your back, with your legs up and your ankles clamped to an iron spreader bar, with your wrists shackled between your ankles to the same bar. Get the picture?"

The Sunday Lunchers raised their eyebrows.

"Grotesque," Natasha said.

"Spikes everywhere," Jessica added brightly. "And metal bands around your body and head. Can't move a muscle."

"Where's the problem?" Iain asked, helping himself to another beer.

"After the demons push you in your cage through the iron Satan's-mouth gate," Jessica said, "you shoot up and down through the dark for a while—sort of like Space Mountain in Eurodisney...."

"In rubber," Ryan said. "Maybe if it had been in rubber the place wouldn't have bellied up."

Jessica was undaunted.

"Anyway, after a bit of that, you shoot out into this gray light, and winged demons with big spanners take hold of your cage and fly you into position. And that's where the problem starts."

"You see, this hell is millions—probably billions—of identical cages, all bolted together," Jonathon said. "Each with a lost soul clamped inside, unable to move, unable to speak, able only to see those on either side and above. And every few seconds, the demons bolt on a new one."

"This hell seems to require a potentially infinite number of iron cages and latex bondage suits," Ryan mused.

"Better than our mail order company," Jessica agreed. "It would be pretty awful if you were one of the inside ones; fortunately, we were right on the outside—tourists get the best views—and we could see that all these billions of identical cages went together to make up a much bigger one. A huge cage: it must have been thousands of miles across."

"And like the smaller cages, there was a figure imprisoned inside this enormous cage made up of all the smaller cages," Jonathon said.

"Satan?" Maya suggested.

"In a very big rubber suit?" Ryan ventured.

"Don't be silly," Jessica said. "Where would they get one that size?"

"What did he look like?" Maya asked. "Satan?"

"We'd been put in a good position to see," Jonathon said. "We were on the spreader bar, just to the left of his right hand—which looked about the size of Wiltshire, so we could see right along him. It was a bit hard to make out facial features: He was lying on his back and he was very foreshortened by distance—it must have been several hundred miles, at least—but what I could see, he looked very, very pissed off. No hair, of course. And a kind of dark-red color all over. No surprise, really."

"Good body though," Jessica added. "He must have worked out. Amazing how he's held on to the muscle tone, the length of time he's been there."

"How long had he been there?" Hugh asked.

"Well, we couldn't really be sure, hell being outside time and all that, but I reckon it was probably a couple of thousand years. Less than a million. Not enough time to have lost the pissed-off expression."

"So, what is the problem?" Ryan asked. "Sounds like paradise for you guys. Why do you want your money back?"

"Because it was bloody boring," Jessica said. "All you did was lie on your back in this sweaty rubber suit, couldn't move, couldn't talk, couldn't even make eye contact with anyone."

"And lie there, and lie there, and lie there," Jonathon said. "With it never ending. A million billion years lying there in your cage, and you haven't even started. Do that ten times, a hundred times, a million, a trillion times, and you are still no nearer the end. You haven't even begun to begin. If we were bored after a couple of hours and couldn't wait to get out, what must it be like for those poor bastards who aren't tourists and have to stay there?"

"Best kind of hells, the ones where eternity really counts," Iain said.

"What did you do?" Natasha asked.

"Slept mostly," Jessica answered. "Looked at the view."

"I don't see how you have a case for complaint," Ryan said. "Hell of Endless Bondage you wanted, Hell of Endless Bondage you got. You must have had some good ideas out of it, surely, you guys?"

"Well, we have been in contact with a sheet-metal worker," Jessica said.

It was beer time again, and the conversation drifted to the impossibility of finding reliable workmen, in sheet metal or any other medium, and how they thought they could charge the money they did for what they did, which was symptomatic of the country as a whole, it was all going down the toilet, and wasn't it *scary* about the animal rights activists claiming they had infected supermarket meat with anthrax, far scarier than the meningitis outbreaks in Islington's primary schools, wasn't it funny how the government minister on the television fed the supermarket steak to his children but you didn't see him eating it himself.

In all the beer-lubricated talk on the patio of 19 Merry Hill Lodge no one mentioned Richard and where he would go when St. Botolph's Charity Hospital reassigned his bed to another who had fallen off the thin, high line.

He told the rep what he had told the elevator, which was what he told Mr. Conway in the office above the shopping mall in Harrow when he had asked the same question. Yes, he knew. Yes, he was sure. Yes, he knew what he was doing.

"We do have to warn you of the consequences, Mr. Albright," the rep said. "As you can imagine, we don't sell many packages of this kind."

"I'm surprised you sell any," Richard said.

"A few," the rep answered, smiling gently.

"Is that the way in?" Richard asked.

"It is. You can still go back if you want."

Richard looked at the gate of ivory fangs in the wall of pitted, hairy flesh.

"You don't sell your wedding ring—the one thing of value you have left, that links you to everything you've had taken from you—if you want to go back."

"I understand. Before you go through the gate, Mr. Albright, might I ask you why?" the rep said. "I've asked the same question of all the other one-way tickets, and I still can't understand why you prefer an eternity of hell to the world above."

"You have answered your own question," Richard said. "In this hell, you know where you are, what you are, and you are secure knowing that nothing is going to change, nothing is going to surprise you, nothing is going to demand that you cope when you have no inner resources left, or damage you more than it is already damaging you. Things in hell will always be exactly as they are, and in time, you get used to that. You may even get to enjoy it. And that, compared to what I've come from, isn't hell at all. More like heaven."

"Does the never-endingness not frighten you?" the rep asked.

"Like everything else, you cope with it one day at a time," Richard said. "Have I answered you? Can I go in now?"

"Never be too eager to pass through the gates of hell."

"I feel like I'm passing out of the gates of hell. Where do I leave my clothes?"

"Just here, by the gate. There will be someone to meet you on the other side and take you to your place." The rep watched Richard undress and pile his grime-stiff, stinking clothes by the gate's bottom right back molar. A twitch in the gate's grimace distracted Richard; when he looked back, his clothes had disappeared.

"You won't ever have a use for them again," the rep said. "I suppose this is one of the better ones. Are you quite decided?"

"I am utterly decided," Richard said.

"Well, you have been warned," the rep said quietly. "Go figure."

The gate opened into a yawn. Richard stepped between the dripping molars and passed through. On the far side a demonette in a micro skirt and roller boots was waiting for him.

"Mr. Albright?"

"Yes." Richard studied the place that awaited him. The photograph in the brochure had caught it pretty well: the endless plain of dun grass under the white, sunless sky; the tall, fleshy excrescences of the demon-lovers, each with a human pumping and humping within its embrace. Much worse hells than this. Paradise, to some.

"One-way ticket?" The demonette looked puzzled. Puzzlement was a pucker between her rather fetching golden horns.

"That's correct."

"Come with me, please."

The grass was soft beneath Richard's bare feet. There was a warmth in the sunless white sky. The brochure hadn't talked much about the climate, but it probably never rained here, or got cold. He would be comfortable at least. He studied the damned as he passed, each copulating in blind ecstasy with their demon lovers. Men, women, held in the things' arms and claspers in a variety of positions and postures, some extremely acrobatic. Were they allowed to change, or were you put into one in which you had to remain? You could get used to it, Richard thought. The brochure had said that the demon lovers took away all consciousness but the sensations of sex. Endless intercourse, untroubled by thought, care, emotion or the awareness of where you were, what you were doing, how long you would be doing it.

He could live with that.

"This is yours, Mr. Albright," the demonette said.

Richard looked long at the thing he would be fucking for eternity. It looked a bit like an oven-ready chicken and a bit like an orchid made of rump steak and a bit like a rotting sheep. Its arms and claspers were open to receive him. Its fleshy, dripping orifice was pulsing in anticipation. He could sense its pheromones stealing down his spine to caress his penis.

"Miriam," he said. "I will call you Miriam."

"What?" the demonette asked.

"My ex-wife," Richard said. He stepped forward. Flesh closed around his flesh. He felt himself swell, and then consciousness melted away in the need to thrust and thrust and thrust.

"Miriam!" he shouted. "Miriam Miriam Miriam!"

At least it wasn't Islington.

Get on Board the D Train

by Gary Gygax

It was tough being a small-time hustler in Chicago these days. Most of the people with money had too much savvy now. From Rush Street to Old Town and all along the Gold Coast—even into the newly developing "upscale neighborhoods," they were alert for scams, and that made slim pickings. The working marks with money had followed the middle class out to the 'burbs. So why didn't Denny Donaldson pack up and move too? Simple, really. A cheap chiseler stands out in a suburb, even a big 'burb. The dozens of communities were no substitute for the massive anonymity of the big city. Only a place as big and corrupt as Chicago served to hide him. Oh, sure, Denny had thought about changing metropolises. New York? Too much first-class competition. Los Angeles? No way. It was worse than the Windy City. Miami was Hispanic. Detroit, Pittsburgh, Philly, all the rest would be a step down. He was what he was, and so he made the best of it.

"Mornin', Reverend Ike."

Denny had to pause. Part of his image, of course. The gray twilight of late November made Wilson Avenue seem grimier than usual. The redneck who had sent the sarcastic greeting was leaning against the front of a bar. Despite the chill, he wore only a baggy sports coat over his stained T-shirt. Fiddle music accompanying a nasal voice drifted out from the saloon, perfectly in harmony with the stench of stale beer and cheap bourbon that hedged its entrance. "The Lord's work demands that this shepherd tend a flock of night creatures, Willie B.," responded the clerically clad Denny Donaldson. "Morning, indeed, and a good one to you. See you at the midnight prayer meeting?"

Willie B. spat, then chuckled. "Hell no! I'll buy you an honest drink,

'Reverend,' but I sure as shit won't drop no money into yor collection plate."

"Don't blaspheme. The collection is for the Lord, sinner!"

"Haw!" Willie B. had no education, but he was schooled in the streets and knew a grifter when he saw one. He was third-generation North Side hillbilly. "You can blow that right out yor ass. Ain't fleecin' me like you skin all them dummies that believe yor a man o' God."

Denny clamped his jaws tight to keep from spitting out a few choice phrases regarding Willie's parentage, eating habits and sexual practices. "Unbelievers, those lacking any faith, can be saved, Brother," he managed to grate from between clenched teeth. "The temple's door is always open—even to the likes of you."

"Unbeliever? Shore thing. You…"

Denny was moving on by then, so whatever the fellow was now shouting at him was lost to his ears in the noise of an L train grinding to a halt at the station platform above. *Maybe there is a god,* he thought. Denny, currently going under the name of the Reverend Isaiah, Pastor of the Temple of Salvation, hurried west. Soon he turned a corner and was at the rundown storefront that he had rented and converted into the temple. Even a supposed holy place had to be well secured in Uptown. It took him almost a minute to get all the locks undone, to open the establishment for business.

He switched on the lights, wincing at the shabby appearance of the "temple." Paint flaking from dirty walls, a filthy carpet, battered folding chairs. "Not even enough money for a decent pulpit," Denny muttered aloud as he surveyed his establishment. Fleece, hell. He'd gladly skin the bastards if he could. Trouble was, the people in this neighborhood were hardly able to afford to live in poverty. That left precious little for him to skim off. Still, a lot of sharp operators before him had gotten filthy rich in the phony religion business. He, Denny Donaldson, should at least be able to make a comfortable livelihood from it. Only, he wasn't. There were plenty of folks in his "congregation." Because he was sufficiently slick to con the basically good and credulous, the temple's income kept him alive, even bought him some luxuries—mainly liquor, dope and an occasional hooker, the latter only when he couldn't find a young female in the congregation he could—or dared—seduce. One had to be careful around rednecks. They tended to take the law into their own hands when it came to their womenfolk.

They were bad-asses around here, for sure. He had to be careful. Not as careful as around the black or Latin drug pushers. Denny would have preferred dealing dope, but everywhere in the city he could hope to do that, there were vicious gang members who'd kill a competitor without a thought. Pimping was much the same. He couldn't make the cut, so to speak, when it came to that. No hope for any of the really big-time action. There wasn't much in the way of non-violent crime he could get into, being what he was, so he had to settle for this racket.

"Crap. This is too much like work." With that, Denny stalked to the back and entered his office sanctum. The room at the rear was small, boasting a teetering table and chair that had come with the place. He'd added a rickety bookcase and a collection of religious magazines and books he'd managed to scrounge and steal from various places. He laughed aloud when he recalled boosting the big Bible. It was seeing it at an antiques show that gave him the idea to get into the preaching business, sort of. Just why he had the sudden urge to have such a book, Denny didn't know. He simply couldn't resist the urge. A match into a stack of packing boxes, the confusion of the alarm, and "helping" to save valuables from the flames. Piece of cake. Once away with it the rest had followed automatically. He would become a revival preacher and make his living from the sweat of others, so to speak.

Then Denny grimaced. He'd have to read it. Real religion was not Denny's strong point, but since getting into this scam he'd had to learn a lot of Scripture. The process was a pain, but his sermon had to be a real scorcher. Hell-fire and brimstone for sure, and all that everlasting punishment awaiting those who didn't cheerfully give all their worldly possessions to him so as to save their souls. The chair creaked as he sat on its worn seat. The table rocked as he shifted the heavy Bible to consult its concordance. "Let's see.... Rich, money and giving—which of these frigging scriptures mention those things?" With like mumblings, Denny went to work to ready his pep-talk for tonight.

"A fire in your bones?" the woman said.

Denny nearly jumped out of his skin. "Jesus H. Christ!"

"Is the H in that name for Holy?"

"You scared the sh—stuffing out of me, ah...." He trailed off as he got a better look at her. Even the dim light from the single lamp on the table was sufficient to show his unexpected visitor was beautiful and built. "Ummm... Sister? What's this about a fire?"

She smiled back provocatively, no trace of resentment evident as Denny stripped her with his gaze, leering as he did so. "Forget the sister. Just call me Lil, Reverend Ike. I've come to help you in your work. I was alluding to something in the Bible when I spoke of fire. Forget it. You don't call yourself Jeremiah after all."

Her last words really confused him. What Denny really wanted to know was how in hell she'd gotten into his office without him hearing her. There were bells, and a mat with a buzzer too. Even if he'd somehow forgotten to lock the front door, she should have made plenty of noise to alert him when she came in. He shot a quick glance behind him as he arose. The steel rear door was barred and locked. Then he looked at her again and decided he didn't care how she'd managed to surprise him. It was worth it. "Sister… Lil. A great pleasure to make your acquaintance—especially since there's no fire. You say you've—"

"Come to help you in your mission."

"This isn't a mission, my dear. The Temple of Salvation is a church, a place of Biblical teaching and truth. According to the Holy Writings, only a man is allowed to preach."

She smiled again. It was something between reassurance and seduction. "Oh, don't worry about that. I know this isn't a mission, and I can quote the Scriptures. Becoming an active participant in your… work isn't what I meant. I'm here to help *you* in a much more personal way."

Denny swallowed hard. "My work. You are? Why?" In his confusion he couldn't keep the last question back. Her dress and style said "money and breeding." This was no local bimbo, but the proverbial high-class dame. Maybe she was slumming, a rich bitch feeling guilt for the cash her daddy made and handed out too easily to her. He appraised her in light of that thought, rejected it. Something in her eyes said she was no bleeding heart. In fact, it made Denny uneasy to meet her gaze, so he slid his eyes down to her chest instead. Much better.

"You'd be surprised to know just where your name is known, Reverend Ike. The things you have done here have had a far-reaching impact."

"They have? I mean, of course. It's just… astonishing to me that my efforts to, ah, turn the lost sheep around here back to the Lord could possibly be known anywhere else. Are you from the North Shore? Zion?"

Her laugh was both sweet and icy at once. It gave him chills. "Oh yes, a few important ones have noticed. But no, I'm from quite a ways from here. I made a special trip to meet you in person."

Denny Donaldson was immediately alert. "You're a cop or a reporter!"

"No. I am neither. I know most of the police officials in this city. None are in the least interested in you, Denny—Reverend Isaiah. The media isn't concerned at all either. Take me at my word. It's just me and you."

He was close to her, and without warning grabbed and shook her. "Bullshit! You even know my real first name. Tell me the truth, or else!"

Instead of shrinking back or struggling, the beautiful woman named Lil pressed against him when he manhandled her. "Ooo! I love rough treatment," she purred in his ear. Then she bit the lobe, hard but not so hard as to draw blood.

Denny was instantly excited. A heady perfume filled his nostrils, and her soft but firm body moving against his own was almost more than he could bear. "Gimme your purse," he said in a thickened and savage voice as he thrust Lil to a safe distance. "If you're lying…."

She shrugged, handed over the little clutch bag. Denny took it and shook out the contents. Nothing but a few cosmetic items and some bills. He picked up the money, fanned out several hundred in fifties. "You could get killed around here for this much bread."

"I won't."

"Where's your ID, *Lil?*"

Without answering, she sat on the table, putting her arms back to brace herself thus and incidentally accentuating her breasts. "Who needs stinking identification?" Lil said, then laughed her eerie laugh. "It's no wonder you're struggling along in this dump instead of enjoying the good life you deserve, Denny. You're a chicken at heart."

The truth in her words made him rage, and when Denny was angry, he struck out. After slapping Lil he grabbed and mauled her. Again the beautiful woman's only response was to encourage him. He took her hurriedly there on the makeshift desk, brutally using the act to demean her even as it satisfied his lust, slaked his growing fear.

"That was very good, Denny. What I'd hoped for from you," Lil said with sincerity as he was zipping up his fly. "Now that's over, are you ready for the rest?"

"I got all I need from you, bitch."

"A few bucks and a quickie? Come on! I came here because I want you to get what you really deserve—the big time, so to speak."

Denny flopped into his chair. "Get the fuck out of here and don't come back. I gotta sermon to prepare."

"A couple of hundred thousand interest you?'

He looked up at her still sitting there on the table before him. "You must be a nut case."

Lil didn't change expression. "Evanston, 'Reverend Ike.' There's a perfect mark there. Just hop a train to Howard Street, walk a couple of blocks and pay your respects."

"How much did you say?"

"Half a million."

Denny nearly choked. So much! Impossible. "I don't kill for cash—and I don't do robberies or burglaries either, sweetie," he added with as much sarcasm as he could muster. What was her angle? It bothered him that he couldn't look directly into her eyes. Something about Lil was frightening, even after raping her as he had done.

"You didn't rape me, Denny. I decided to have you."

That made him shrink back, blood draining from his head so as to make it spin a little. She'd read his mind! Naw. Denny knew his face betrayed too much of his thoughts when he was not on guard. She had only seen his look of satisfaction when he recalled sticking it to her. "Tell that to your crotch."

"Sure. It knows too. But we're not talking murder or anything else except spreading the gospel, Rev. You are now a preacher-man, aren't you?"

"One with a midnight revival and prayer meeting to get ready for. Get out of here with your bullshit."

"I'm giving it to you straight. Why not just screw the congregation like you did me? You know that what you're doing here is all a lie anyway, and the take is piss-poor besides."

Denny jumped up, made as if to hit her again. Lil just looked at him, and he sank back.

"That's much better. Forget this penny-ante business. Listen. With the money you'll get from this simple deal, you can clear out and retire."

"Okay, smart-ass. Half a mil, you said. Let's pretend I believe you. Just what do I have to do, and how do I get the dough? No crap; the real details."

For the first time since she'd appeared in his place Lil seemed serious. No more sexy poses or smiles. All business. "Here's the address. You get there tonight before ten. The old man who lives there will be expecting someone to call. You will be the one who does. Show up with that Bible," and she pointed to the one Denny had open, "and he'll let you right in."

"That's a heavy sonofabitch to haul around," he interjected.

"It's impressive, old, has a history you know nothing about. That one, understand?!"

"Yah." Her eyes were boring into him, and his inclination to take one of the small Bibles he'd swiped from here and there slipped into nothingness. "I can lug that for a lot of cash."

"You'll do more than lug it, Rev, you'll read from it. Now pay attention. He'll ask you a lot of questions, but don't answer any of them. Just say you are come to share prophecy. That's important. You must say exactly those words, *share prophecy*. Then look solemn and keep your eyes down, on the book. Whatever you do, don't look at him, never meet his eyes."

With a little shudder Denny nodded agreement. He didn't want to look into Lil's either. "And...?"

"He'll take you into his study, ask to examine the Bible. Let him do so. Then he will say something to the effect that sharing the Gospel is the path to salvation. That's your cue. You'll open the book and read. I want you to read three passages—no more, no less."

Denny Donaldson wasn't anybody's fool. "And then he gives me a bag of gold because I did so well? Why am I talking to you? Listening to this—"

"Asshole!" she spat. That wasn't nearly as stunning as the sudden pain caused by her slim white fingers pressing on his shoulder at the collarbone. One must have pinched a nerve, for terrible pain shot through his chest. He gasped, nearly fainted. The torment was momentary. Lil released her hold. "That's better. You said you'd listen. I just made you a man of your word, Denny—Reverend Isaiah, rather. You *must* be in character for this."

"Right," he managed to gasp. She remained standing, too close. Denny couldn't move away, didn't dare to try to beat her as he longed to. He considered the switch-blade stiletto he carried, rejected the thought immediately. Lil was frightening. How could a skinny broad have such strength?

"If you knew, you'd just shit," she said in a teasing and sultry tone. "Don't flinch, and pay attention. After you've read to him our friend will be in... a state of a transcendent sort, shall we say?"

He screwed up his courage. "Meaning?"

"He'll be knocked out. Unconscious. Transported, in a way. There's a cabinet behind the desk in the study. The key will be in his vest pocket. He won't object when you get it, unlock the cabinet, and take out what's there."

"So I'm going to rob this guy after all."

Lil shook her head. "On the contrary. You'll be recovering property he stole. That is absolute truth. Open the cabinet, take the silver box inside, and get out. Do that immediately. One last thing. The most important of all. The silver box will be sealed. Don't break the seal. Don't open the box. Don't look at what's inside the box."

"That's three last things. What about the money?"

"I'm coming to that. Leave the house, go back to the Howard Street station. Get on the first southbound car that comes along. I'll join you after it goes underground, and I'll have the money. You give me the silver box for the cash. And don't worry about how I'll know which train you're on. I'll know."

He didn't doubt it. A thousand questions seemed to be buzzing around in his brain, but he didn't dare to focus on any of them, let alone articulate the foremost one. Instead, Denny picked up the paper from the table, stared at the address, then at the three Scripture references that were written below, which he was to read. He didn't recognize any of them. Funny… His contemplation of the matter was broken by noise, pounding. Looking up, Denny was startled to find himself alone. Lil wasn't there, gone as silently as she'd come. That was a relief. That there were several people attempting to get inside the so-called temple dawned on him next. That meant the door was locked.

"Damned bitch probably locked it behind her," Denny reassured himself as he got up hastily. "So long, suckers," he breathed as he unbarred the rear entrance and departed. He left the lights on and the door wide open. Maybe some bum could find something worth taking in the place. He sure as hell didn't want any of it anymore. A half-million for sure. Maybe more if he played his cards right. A million, even two, maybe, would make for a lot better retirement than a measly five hundred thou! Despite all that had occurred, Denny was grinning, even whistling, as he made his way to the flea-bag hotel where he rented a kitchenette apartment. Under the current circumstances he was glad that the store didn't have running water and a toilet. He'd cursed that when he first rented it, regretting the expense of having to have a separate pad to live in. Now it gave him the slack he needed.

He went up the three flights of stairs to his place, entered hurriedly, and got his battered carry-on bag out of the tiny closet. It was his only luggage. Into it went the big Bible. Nothing else. None of the few possessions he had here were worth taking. His emergency cash went into his front pocket. Only a few bucks, anyway. Then he flushed his stash down the john. Too risky to carry or leave. Besides, there was plenty of great stuff in Rio, they said. Denny paused to check his appearance in the mirror. "I look like shit," he allowed upon seeing his pale, haggard face. "Just the way a real evangelist should look when going forth to preach to the wayward." He wondered if the rather old-fashioned backward collar and worn black suit were too much. "Screw it. It'll have to do." He'd found the suit at a local Salvation Army shop, but the shirt was almost new, for he had had to buy it to complete his imposture.

A check of his watch, about the only expensive thing Denny owned, showed that it was now half-past nine. The timing was close. He paused only to lock the door. No sense in advertising his absence. If there was trouble from this, the colder his trail the better Denny's chances of not being traced. He hastened down the steps, going quickly but quietly, with racing heart. A cloud of oppressive energy seemed to hover over him, but Denny kept his focus on the payoff. The thought of all that money kept him going, allowed him to keep the weight of fear from weakening his resolve into feeble inaction.

The alley served to hide his exodus from the tenement. By chance, he saw nobody who knew him on the short stretch of Wilson he had to cover to get to the elevated station. He had a token, so it was easy to go through the turnstile and make it up to the platform without delay. Once there, he stood in the shadows between the platform lights, and soon a Howard Street train rumbled around the curve in the tracks to the south and screeched to a halt. Denny went through the doors into the glaring light of the dirty car, took a seat at the very front, looking ahead. Nobody else could see his face thus.

Wilson to Howard wasn't a long ride, and it was north- not southbound. Despite this, a couple of young hoods boarded the train at Argyle and decided that Denny might be fair game. Sitting alone and dressed as he was in clerical garb, these two thought they had some easy pickings. "How about some spare change, parson?"

Denny ignored the arrogant voice.

"Hey, dummy, he talkin' to you!" the first young thug's companion said, with implied threat heavy in his tone as he moved to get a look at the supposed pigeon.

Just as the fellow came close, Denny spun and snarled, "Don't let the suit fool you, mofo! I'd as soon kill you as have to look at you. Get your asses out of here. Go hassle some chump in another car."

"Okay, man, easy! We weren't dissing you. Jes' wanted some—" The leader got a look at Denny's eyes, cut his whining short, and walked off. It was better to see if there was indeed someone else to coerce or threaten to get some bread. No sense risking trouble with a man like that, a bad dude with a crazy look. No way.

At Howard Street the CTA train ended its run where Chicago's northern limit was reached and reversed course to make the long run to the south end of the elevated train system. The Windy City side of the street was alive, the Evanston side darker and a lot more subdued. Denny went across to the shadows, then walked briskly despite the heavy bag. It was chilly, and the address he sought was several blocks distant. In five minutes he found it: an old brownstone mansion showing faint lights behind window shades and drawn drapes. "Not a minute to spare. Perfect timing," he murmured as he peered at his wrist and saw in the faint illumination of the entrance light that the big hand was between the 1 and the 2 of 12. Ten o'clock sharp!

The building oozed wealth. Not many of its kind were kept as single-family residences any longer. A few on North State, along the upper lake shore, and… "Goddamn, Denny-boy. You have finally fallen into something good," he whispered aloud. "Let's make this a *three*-million-buck swap!" As he spoke thus to himself, Denny pressed the bell, and he heard a distant chiming sound.

It took at least a full minute for a response. It was all he could do to refrain from hitting the button impatiently during that wait, but somehow Donaldson refrained. "Be cool and refined," he kept telling himself. "Act the part of a solid man of the cloth!" There was a peephole in the big door, and someone could be watching. At last there came the sound of locks opening. The door swung inward. A small, distinguished-looking man of uncertain age stood there in the warm light. Perhaps as young as his seventies, or maybe nearing a hundred years, Denny couldn't tell. He was appropriately attired, considering the place in which he resided. Denny hadn't thought anyone wore striped trousers and a smoking jacket these days.

"Good evening, sir. What is it you want?"

Without a pause, Denny launched into his well-prepared spiel. "And a good evening to you, sir. I have come to share prophecy." Few words required, but as he said that Denny raised the flight bag, held it before him and tilted his head so as to direct the old man's attention to its weight and implied contents. It worked like a charm, as Lil had assured him it would.

"I see. Then you may enter, sir. Please come this way."

Breathing a sigh of relief, Denny entered. The big foyer was done in Victorian, a whole lot of what had to be original art nouveau. Denny had a chance to give it a quick appraisal as the old man shut and secured the door, then led him out of the entry hall, through a parlor stuffed with a mix of the older style with the straighter lines of art deco furnishings. Amongst his other nefarious dealings, Denny had tried his hand at antiques peddling—along with some abortive forgeries, All too quickly the old man led him into another cluttered room, this one lined with bookshelves.

"My study, sir. Please be seated. You are?"

"Reverend Isaiah," Denny responded smoothly, but without looking up. Instead he busied himself opening the bag, removing the book from inside and settling down into the wide armchair his host had indicated for him.

The old man looked Denny over. His gaze seemed sharp and penetrating. "May I examine the work from which you wish to read?"

"Certainly, sir, certainly." With as much of a flourish as could be managed Denny moved the tome from his lap to place it in the old man's hands. "It is heavy, sir," he warned as he did so.

Despite his apparent years and frail stature, the fellow managed the big book easily. He took it, placed it on a stand on his desk so that the lamp there allowed bright light to fall upon it. "A most unusual Bible. I don't recognize it. It must be a rare and valuable edition!" he exclaimed as he opened it with great care, stared at its frontispiece. Then the old man went on, examining various portions. "Seventeenth-century from the look of it, and in perfect condition too. Such a Bible is worth a great deal of money… Reverend Isaiah."

"All works of Gospel are precious, more valuable than silver and gold, sir," Denny uttered piously.

"Yes. Of course. So now, as prescribed, you must commence." He turned the stand so that the book faced Denny. With relief evident on his lined countenance, the old man leaned back in his leather chair, wiping his face absently with a hand. "The Ritual is trying, but necessary." His bright green eyes were incongruous in his old face. They fixed on Denny as he said that.

Denny ducked from that stare, hastily bending forward as if eager to fulfill his task. He was, in fact, in a hurry to get it over with, but Denny also recalled vividly the warning given to him by the frightening Lil. He would not meet the old fellow's green eyes no matter what. Denny cleared his throat. "Yes. Sharing prophecy is necessary."

"How many verses will you read, Reverend Isaiah?" There was a sudden edge to the old man's voice. He was suspicious.

"Three, sir. Exactly three. No more, no less."

"Very well. Read."

Without raising his head, Denny moved his eyes up to steal a glance at the old man. He was sitting straight, arms resting on those of his maroon leather chair, eyelids lowered, almost shut. He looked like someone about to be examined by a dentist. Denny hastily shifted his gaze back to the big book. He couldn't remember which verses he was supposed to read! Near panic, he surreptitiously began searching for the scrap of paper.

"Is there something wrong?"

Denny began turning pages hurriedly. "Not at all, not at all. I was merely… taking a moment to say a silent prayer before beginning."

Again the old man relaxed. "Pardon. That is fitting—prudent under the circumstances, I must add. It is just that time is so critical, but you know that, do you not?"

"That is why I have come to you," Denny replied with a strained voice.

"Do not allow my nervousness to affect you, good pastor!" the old fellow cautioned with real concern. "A mistake could damn both of us."

Damn? What was this ancient fart talking about? Religious crazies were the goofiest of all, that was certain. "Do not be alarmed, sir. I shall perform my task without flaw. Now then, let me begin…."

"Do."

Denny had said that when his groping fingers had come into contact with the crumpled scrap of paper. He was about to palm it and sneak a peek to refresh his suddenly failed memory when he found that ploy unnecessary. Merely touching the note sent a jolt to his brain. Without conscious volition, his hand turned the pages, past the illuminated title, *Bel El Nergal'ush*, to a place near the front portion.

"*Nimrod*, chapter two, verse six."

"Wha—"

"*And I will look up to the heavens, not to see glory, but to send an arrow into the eye that watcheth from there.*"

"No! I beseech you!"

A thumb riffled to the midportion of the work. His voice was deep and booming as he read, "*The Book of Erishkigal*, chapter four, verse six: *None who oppose darkness will be hidden from us, though they seem to avoid retribution for a time.*"

"For the love of God and all that is Holy, stop!"

Even if he had wanted to, Denny would not have been able to comply with that imploring request. A vast inner power filled him now, and it drove him on as a rider would a galloping stallion. The thrill of the release of power made Denny feel as if he were a mile wide and twice as tall. Even the thought of the money he was soon to have couldn't match this euphoria. It was better than any drug he'd ever dropped, snorted, smoked or spiked. Somewhere in the back of his mind, he made a vow to retain the book and read it as often as he could. What a high! His mind was racing, and various parts were functioning quite independently. There was no stopping him now. His hands kept moving as if separate entities. The pages turned, and he was at the back of the book.

"*Obfuscation*, chapter nine, verse six. *Then will be loosed the demons of Tiamat, and Kingu will send forth his fiends to reap revenge on all who sought to destroy her.*"

A gargling sound came from the old man. Denny dared to look at him now that he'd completed his reading. The green eyes were open but had no light, only a vacant stare. Breath still came from the narrow chest, but the drool slipping from the corner of the open mouth told Denny that the geezer was in no shape to do anything for a while—maybe permanently. "What the hell was so shattering about that?" he wondered aloud as he stared at the barely breathing form. "Well, old fart, you've lived too long anyway, if you ask me. Too damned fancy, too. Now, let's see where you keep that key Lil mentioned."

Denny had spotted the cabinet he'd been told was in the place. It was against the wall behind the old man's chair. Without hesitation Denny searched the jacket pockets, finding the key in the right-hand one. Before opening the chest he paused to put on gloves, then checked the desk drawers. "A professor, eh?" he muttered as he went through the papers and miscellany of personal effects contained in the desk. "Must have been a big shot at the local U once. All those letters after your name, but I'll bet you inherited this place. Ah, gotcha! Sure enough. A tin box filled with money." Denny slipped a thick sheaf of big bills into his inside pocket and replaced the box. There were a dozen little things immediately catching his fancy. Denny was tempted to lift them, but restrained his impulse with ease. The power was fading, but a lot lingered. "The cash isn't traceable, but the tortoiseshell stuff and all the other small goodies are. I'll keep my eyes on the prize, as the Good Book says."

It took only a moment to open the cabinet. Despite its commodious size, there was only one item locked inside. "Just like you said, Lil," Denny continued talking aloud to himself as he grabbed the small silver coffer centered squarely on the cabinet's middle shelf. He relocked the chest, examined the container he held. "Antique. No, not just antique, really old. Ancient. Something that belongs in a museum for sure. Heavy, and look at the ugly bastards decorating the lid. This is worth a fortune by itself. What the hell's inside?" He shook it. There was only a slight shifting of the contents. The silver box was either padded, or whatever it held was well wrapped.

He stood motionless for a moment, mentally debating. Then he set his jaw in determination. This was no place to linger. The sooner he was gone the better. The old man was still breathing shallowly, but Denny's appraising eye told him that it was odds-on the decrepit sack would kick off before the sun rose. To be seen here, especially with the silver box, would be tantamount to conviction and hard time in Joliet. *Get going, then check the contents.*

"What the f—" Denny was stunned. The huge old Bible—no, it wasn't really a Bible at all, he realized as he looked in dismay at the empty stand. "The book is something else…. A sort of wolf in sheep's clothing. Where in hell could it have disappeared to?!" As he spat that under his breath he checked the floor, all around the desk, beside and under the chairs. No book. "Goddamnitall! This could…" He searched frantically a second time, then stopped, stood still, drew a deep, shuddering breath. "Think."

Of course there was no logical explanation for the disappearance. The old man was out, hadn't moved. Books don't have legs, can't stroll away. Nobody else was there to remove it. It had simply vanished. The last of the rush of energy was draining away, but as it left, him Denny understood. The book had volition of its own. The power that had infused him had come from it, and with the force it had moved itself to, to… wherever it belonged, he supposed. That had to be it. Given this likelihood, things were less complicated than before.

Galvanized into action, Denny grabbed the battered flight bag, stuffed the silver box inside, zipped the case closed. He glanced around to make sure he'd left nothing, then strode through the parlor, into the foyer, and listened. No sound from anywhere else in the mansion. He put his eye to the peephole in the front door. The distorted view of the street was reassuring. A lone car moving past. No pedestrians in sight. He checked the wall, saw a long panel of old-fashioned push-button switches, two different from the others. He jabbed a gloved finger twice in succession to make them match the others. The hall went dark, and when he peered out there was no front light on anymore. He fumbled, opening the lock, then slipped outside, closing the door quietly, making sure the safety lock caught.

He was around the corner and away in seconds, his walk fast but not hurried, like someone walking to keep warm or with urgent business to tend to, not fleeing a crime scene. On Howard Street again he laughed aloud softly. That had been as much fun as his first petty theft or big score. More fun actually, because he hadn't really broken any laws at all. Well, aside from pilfering the old fart's dough, he hadn't. Who the devil could say that Denny had done something wrong in reading from a book? What a book, too. Wishing it hadn't disappeared, regretting that he hadn't immediately tried to secure it, Denny made his way upstairs to catch an L south. The money he'd soon have would take care of everything except the rush he'd had from reading the book. He had planned on a lot more of it. Now he'd have to buy shit to get a lesser high. "Man! If I could sell that, I'd have more money than all the Colombian kingpins put together."

"Were you speaking to me, Father?"

Startled, Denny realized he'd spoken the last aloud. The inquiry came from the tired-looking woman in the change booth of the station. "Nothing, nothing at all. Just recalling a verse from the Good Book."

The woman wasn't really interested, had looked away before he finished his excuse. "Sure. Have a nice night, Father."

Denny didn't respond at all. He took the stairs two at a time as soon as he was out of her sight. It wasn't late, not much past eleven, but the platform was deserted. There was a single car standing ready for passengers, its doors open. "Take the first train you can, she said, and so I am." He hurried inside, this time taking the rearmost seat. As soon as he could, he'd get rid of the parson's get-up. For now he disposed of the backward collar, first making sure nobody was there to see it. Then, as the doors shut and the car started south, he unbuttoned a couple of buttons to complete the transformation.

Something didn't seem right. Denny looked around. The car was empty save for himself. He put a hand against the window so as to shield the glare, peering out at the buildings. The L was loafing along the track at a slow speed, especially for this time of night. By the time they got to the Morse Avenue station, he was nervous. They passed it without a pause, then rolled through the Loyola stop, too. "Son of a bitch! She's rigged the damn car as an express—only a damned slow one," he said loudly to the emptiness. Denny peered at the train designator to see if it was an A or B. The reversed letter he saw was neither. "What the hell is a D train?" There was no one to answer his query, and Denny had no idea of his own. He got up, walked to the motorman's cubicle. The shade was only partially drawn. He crouched down and looked inside. "What the hell?" he exclaimed loudly again. There was nobody there. The car was running on its own, without benefit of a driver.

After several minutes of futile pounding and trying to force the door, Denny gave up. "She wants this box I've got, has rigged this whole thing somehow, so she isn't about to engineer a crash to kill me. Her precious silver box would get smashed in a wreck." Saying that to himself relaxed Denny. It also made him think about the contents of the strange and ancient coffer with its demonic contingent prancing and leering on the lid.

"You screw with my head, Lil, you gotta expect me to do the same to you." He plopped down in the nearest seat, unzipped the flight bag. There was the silver object, its lustrous metal gleaming softly in the harsh light of the elevated train carriage, the dark underlying tarnish of ages fighting off the modern neon with ease. "This would be a beautiful work of art if it wasn't for you ugly fuckers," Denny observed as he held it close and looked at the lid. "Now where's the seal?"

It took a moment for him to realize that it wasn't a hinged container at all. The box was a combination affair. The outer part was a sort of sleeve. There was a tray or another box inside it. Where it was supposed to slide out had been closed with something like solder, though. The strip went all around the bottom end of the coffer, broad and thick, with some sort of writing engraved in it. He tipped it and looked at it closely. "Looks a lot like the writing on synagogues. This a Hebe artifact or..." His gaze fastened on a circular piece set into the solder. It looked like an iron coin about half the size of a dime. On it was a sign like the Star of David enclosed in a double circle, with more tiny characters set between the circles. "Yep. That's Jewish for sure. Must be how to open it up."

His hand was shaking a little, but greed was stronger than fear. Denny grasped the protruding disc and pried it loose with his fingernails. It came away easily enough. The sealing metal came with it, and sound, also. Or did it? Was there a moaning like the rush of wind through a crack? The high-pitched giggling he thought came with it was imagination, the sound of the wheels on the steel rails beneath him. Denny tossed the freed seal into his bag, worked the inner part of the case out of its surrounding box. The oblong revealed was indeed a sort of drawer. It had no top, just a linen sack. That was tied shut, but Denny's eager fingers managed to undo the ties in a jiffy. As he worked at it, he could feel something like a statuette beneath the thick cloth. "Heavy, maybe gold, and covered with jewels, I'll bet. That's why you didn't want me to open this sucker up!"

He was disappointed when the contents were free of the linen. It was a statue, all right. One at least as old as the silver box, older even, and it was much, much uglier than the figures that decorated the coffer's top. "Fry my ass if you isn't the goddamnest piece of hideous sculpture ever made. Who in hell would give a half-mil for this?!" He looked away from the figure in disgust. It was a misshapen man-thing, with six wings and a vulture-like face. It had hawk-claw hands and feet, and looked evil. He didn't care if it was the oldest figurine ever made by man, nobody would pay that much money for a piece of ugly shit like that. Looking at it hurt his eyes, made him want to puke. Denny shoved it hurriedly back into its covering, replaced the linen bag back into the tray, slid that back into the sleeve, and then did his best to force the sealing strip back into place. It fit, but loosely. "I'll tell her that it must have gotten jarred loose in transit," he told himself as he zipped up his carry-on. He reconsidered. Lil wouldn't buy that. She'd do something. Denny realized he was scared of her, scared to death. Better to forget getting her payoff.

Maybe he could sell the silver box and the hideous statuette inside to a museum, a private collector. Even if he couldn't, so what? The old man's cash was enough to get him away from the city. Places like New Orleans, Philadelphia and Seattle didn't seem so bad anymore. Denny realized he'd somehow gotten into something he couldn't control, a very dangerous something. Time to bail. Fast! Wishing he had had the guts to stick his shiv into her, Denny's mind kept returning to Lil. Everything about her was wrong, as wrong as this freakin' L that was running by itself. He *had* to get out and away. Claustrophobia and a sort of panic swept over him.

Where was he along the route? It was familiar to him, of course, the elevated artery he was now rolling along on. A glance showed him the car was nearing Wilson. Would it stop? No. At its own stately pace, the lone car rolled through the station. There were a half-dozen people on the platform. Not one bothered to glance at its passage despite the fact that Denny was now pounding at the window and yelling at the top of his voice.

Denny ran to the front of the car again, saw nothing but green lights on the track ahead. It was plain that this car had a clear path for as long as Lil wanted. He looked around in desperation. He was trapped. He could force open a door, no problem, but to jump out the car at even twenty-five miles per hour would be certain death. On one side was a sheer drop, while limb-breaking ties and third rails waited on the inner one. What to do? What to do? "Got it!" He was now shouting to bolster his courage, to retain his sanity. "Pull the emergency brake, you fool!" As he screamed this order to himself, Denny rushed over and grabbed the red switch.

When he yanked it down, there was no immediate result. His guts turned to water, and he was on the verge of collapse at that moment. Then the car began to slow. "Oh yes, oh yes, oh YES!" When it came to a halt he could get out and run like hell along the narrow way between the tracks, get to a place where—

His exaltation dissipated slowly, was replaced with a creeping horror. The car was stopping at a station, but there was no platform between Wilson and the Sheridan Road stop. He ran to the nearer doors, looked out. What he saw made him reel back. The place looked rotten, decayed and unreal. The sign said Buena. "Christ!" From somewhere in his now-fervid brain, Denny dredged up a piece of local history. "They tore this station out half a century ago. I must be crazy!" But he couldn't be crazy. There were passengers in sight, a file of people marching up the stairs and coming toward the car to board it. "I'm out of here when those doors open," he grated, then hunched close to the exit and got ready to shoulder his way through on a dead run.

The car halted, but the doors did not fold inward in invitation. Crouched as he was, he could not help looking out at the spectral platform and its growing throng of waiting boarders. Each one walked slowly and stiffly. All were cadaverous. The nearest were merely mummy-like; those trailing were in worse stages of decomposition. At the tail end of them were skeletal figures clad in rotten rags.

It was then he vomited. The spewed contents of his stomach fountained onto the glass, ran down the metal door, pooled on the floor. Denny turned, choking, fought to open the opposite doors, those away from this station-that-didn't-exist. They wouldn't budge. His mind denied it all, of course, even as he saw what lay beyond the raised tracks to the west. The old Buena station had been near the midpoint of the expanse of Graceland Cemetery, the burial ground of many of the most rich and famous of Chicago's citizens, a vast space filled with elaborate mausoleums as well as ordinary graves. A lone light by the railroad tracks below that paralleled the elevated ones he was upon revealed the high wall of red bricks that hedged the cemetery. It also illuminated the small gate there. From it shuffled a figure, then another. Denny saw the latter shut the gate before following the line of similar forms moving east to where the station had been.

"Please, God, help me!"

There was no response. The lone car designated by a D remained stationary. Its doors were shut fast. The only outside movement was from the throng waiting to board. Each passing minute the crowd grew, compacting slowly with a jostling and swaying motion but without sound. Inside the carriage there was quite the opposite. Denny ran backward and forward, raving and screaming at the top of his lungs. His hands were bloody from beating on the glass, fingernails, too, from vain attempts to force an exit. At the moment when his mind was ready to snap, where all sanity would forever be lost, he made a recovery.

"You are Denny Donaldson. You are Denny Donaldson. This can't be happening!" Somehow the litany he was chanting saved him. He stopped shrieking, ceased his useless, panicked motion. With a few deep breaths and a moment with his eyes closed, he summoned every last ounce of his inner reserves. "Now, Denny, deal with it." He opened his eyes, looked. The crowd of what looked like zombies was still there, waiting with mindless patience to join him in the car.

"Okay. There are walking corpses out there on a station platform that doesn't exist. So what?! What's happening is something that dirty bitch has trumped up. She won't get away with it." As he reassured himself somewhat thus, Denny was struck by a similarity. His reading to the old man had sent the codger into a coma. "So now you think you'll scare me to death too, is that it, Lil? Well, it won't work!" He dug out his switchblade, then grabbed up the flight bag from under the seat he'd vacated what seemed an age ago. Thus prepared, Denny set his back in the angle between the front door of the car and the motorman's cubicle. "Come and get me, you rotten bunch of corpses," he snarled in challenge.

As if in answer to that, the doors on the platform side of the car clunked open. A wave of the foulest stench rolled in, and after it came the waiting passengers. They walked with jerky and uncertain steps, but nevertheless they came, moving left and right, filling the nearer seats, coming closer and closer with a hideously slow and inexorable advance. They were many, so many that they would fill the whole space to capacity.

That such things as he saw coming toward him might come close, might touch him, was unthinkable to Denny. The knife was useless, he realized. This was no gang of actors. "My God, my God!" he mumbled as the weapon fell from his nerveless fingers. What could he do? Again, Denny's inner reserve came to the fore. He had the answer, had had it all along!

Desperately he worked to get the flight bag open. The zipper stuck after moving only a couple of inches. Bloody fingers worked into the small space and, with utmost effort, Denny pulled his hands in opposite directions as he stared at the oncoming horrors. Before him was what had once been a tall man, now a putrid thing with long and matted hair, shreds of skin peeling from it, somber burial attire besmirched from its corruption. The hollow openings where its eyeballs had rotted were black, but pinpoints of purple-white luminescence glittered from within. Those ghastly gleams seemed to be fastened upon him.

The terror evoked by that sight gave Denny the strength of a mad man. The zipper tore free. He seized the silver coffer with one hand, then hurled the bag at the corpse with his left. It struck hard, actually sending the zombie-like thing reeling back a pace. But the crowd behind it was there to stop such retreat, to press it forward as they themselves advanced. The slight pause was all Denny needed. The broken seal fell free, the drawer slid from the protecting sleeve, and then he had the hideous little figurine in his hands.

"There!" Denny screamed as he ripped the linen covering away from what it had shielded. "The precious statue. Maybe you haven't eyes, but you can see—know what it is." He brandished the figure before him. The corpses near to him stopped coming closer. Even though those outside the car kept forcing their way on board, it was as if there was a barrier around Denny, an invisible wall that extended for an arm's length. "Gotcha!" he caroled with hysterical triumph.

Denny lunged at the gruesome thing nearest to him, the tall cadaver which he had initially driven back with the bag. Maybe he could clear the car of them! The lunge turned to recoil as the force rebounded to affect him. Denny was tossed back into the corner in which he had huddled, the wind driven from him. As he gasped and regained his breath, the last of the crowd of corpses boarded the car. The one stopped in the remains of Denny's puke took not the slightest notice of the stuff as it stood shoulder-to-shoulder with the rest. Standing room only, and a lurch and swaying which gradually ceased as the D train left the phantom station and rolled on south.

After some time had passed, Denny Donaldson recovered sufficiently to think again. He cursed Lil, whatever gods there might be, the rotting things filling the carriage, even himself as a fool. Yet all the while he clutched the vile little statue. It was his last hope. A hasty glance over his right shoulder showed that the tracks ahead sloped downward. They were about to make the transition from elevated to subway train. With a shuddering worse than any that the jolting progress of the car could have made, Denny understood the symbolism of that. The dark opening ahead yawned like the gates of hell.

"NO!" he shouted.

There came not the slightest response from the corpses, save that their empty eye sockets seemed to stare at him. In his mind he heard the old man's desperate plea when Denny had read from the cursed book. Tears ran down his cheeks—tears for Denny Donaldson's fate.

A croaking sound came from the lanky corpse with the fiery points in its skull. "Damn you!" Denny spat at it.

"Damn *you!*" it rattled from a rotten interior. Then it croaked its mirthless chuckling sound again. If it had had lips remaining, it would have smiled. "Your greed has consigned us to abomination, but you're coming along for the ride."

Sound echoed and roared through the car. It drowned out any further whisperings from the dead thing. They had passed into the tunnels beneath Chicago and were now proceeding southwards in the subway. Denny tried once again to open the foremost door. They would certainly stop somewhere down here, and if he could— What he saw then ended the forlorn thought. It wasn't a subway tunnel ahead. It was an ever-steepening decline that moved the car at breakneck speed toward the bowels of the earth. Denny screamed his throat raw as he saw that, and the demons that stood along the way leered as they watched. Finally he snapped, and darkness came over him.

"Time to wake up, Denny." The sweet voice was full of laughter and mockery. Perfumed cruelty.

Denny shut his eyes tighter, tried to return to unconsciousness. Every fiber of his body denied what had happened, what was…

"Useless. Stand!"

His eyes opened involuntarily, and he stood. Lil was there, looking evilly beautiful. No rotting bodies, no demons, just her. Maybe it had all been hallucinations, like really potent LSD or something she had somehow slipped him. "Listen. So I screwed up a little, opened the box when I shouldn't have. I'll forget the money you promised and we'll call it a wash."

"On the contrary, Denny. You didn't screw up at all. Everything you did was just right, what we wanted."

"Whatdoyoumean? You gotta—"

"Silence!" she commanded. Denny's tongue swelled to fill his mouth, nearly suffocating him, until he remembered to breathe through his nose.

Lil observed the process with amusement. “I mean that I knew you were a liar, cheat and chiseler. You were supposed to break the seal, because none of us could. Now it’s done, and we are in control again.”

“Control? What the hell does a goddamned box and an ugly statue have to do with control?”

“I’ll humor you because it’s fun for me, Denny. The book that wasn’t a Bible is a weapon against good. It’s hidden now, but in time some agent of the enemy will find it, bind it, and then begin to seek out our power foci and negate them likewise.”

Denny was lost. “I don’t get what you’re saying.”

Lil frowned. “This is no longer amusing. The old man you did in was a guardian of one of evil’s most potent symbols. You freed it by breaking the wards sealing it from us, loosing its power. “

“But the zombies?”

She laughed in glee. “Yes, my special touch. Sort of combining pleasure with business. They are some of those who thought they’d cheat us of their bargains, Denny. Do you believe it? They once thought themselves safe and their souls uncollected!” She laughed again. “I thought they’d be good company for you as you rode the D train here to deliver the demonic key to me. I’m so sorry you didn’t enjoy their company….”

In his mind Denny saw the shuffling line of corpses, souls rejoined to mortal remains, heading into some distant hell to suffer torments barely imaginable. “Damn me,” he whispered as he recalled what the zombie had said to him. Then he dropped to his knees, begging: “Anything, anything, Lil. Just don’t send me down with those corpses.”

Her lovely lips writhed into a scornful smile. “You want a reprieve?”

“Yes! Please. Give me a break, and I’m your slave!”

“Done. I was observing you on the train, and I think it was fitting. You’ll drive the D train—whatever form it might take—until we’ve collected all of the damned.”

Denny wavered, fell prostrate. Weeping, he stammered, “No, not that! I can’t spend forever cooped up with rotting things….”

“Don’t worry, Denny. In a decade or two the job will be over, and *then* you can join your passengers.”

He ranted, screamed, tried to attack her. No use. Lil was gone, and he was in the driver’s seat of a bus. The wracking pain in his feet came from the nails that held them to the floor, and the barbed wire fastening his hands to the steering wheel tormented him with each movement he was forced to make. A spiked safety belt completed his confinement and torture. The bus was rolling slowly through the streets of New York and dark forms were being drawn toward it.

As the vehicle stopped, one of these damned clambered aboard. "I want to be the first to congratulate you on your new job," it said. "Ten years will pass quickly, Reverend, won't they? Eh, heh, heh!"

Denny couldn't reply, because Lil had sewn his mouth shut so he could breathe only through his nose.

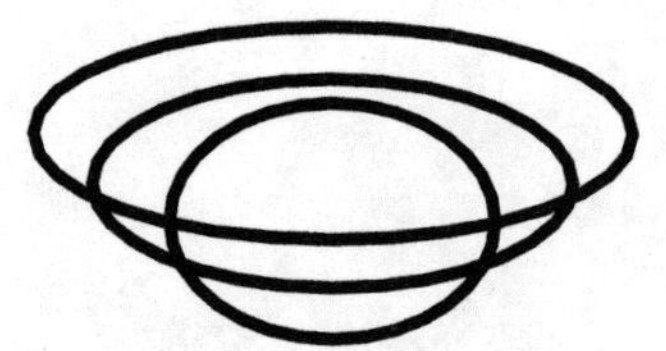

EPIPHANY

by Rick R. Reed

I

They were on their way home from their honeymoon. They were tired and wished they didn't have to rely on public transportation. As it was, they had to take the train from O'Hare all the way to downtown Chicago, switch from the blue line to the red line, then head north to their stop at Granville. It was a long ride, made longer by having to lug along their bags. And then there were the people! Bess usually thought the more colorful passengers charming in their own bizarre slice-of-urban-life way. Tonight they were merely tiresome.

First there was the woman on the blue line. Bess had snuggled against Ryan, her eyes burning with the need for sleep, his large bulk a comforting warmth. Ryan had slid his arm around her and, if things could have continued in this vein, the dark pressing in against the windows, the rumble of the train, Bess might have made the trip contented. But somewhere along the way a woman with a throaty, cigarette-scarred voice had boarded. Bess had heard her at first only in dim aural periphery; Bess had assumed she was talking to a friend.

But the woman's voice grew louder, and soon other conversations on the train ceased. Passengers turned in their seats. Bess disengaged herself from the warmth of her new husband, sat up straight and rubbed her eyes.

She could not wait to get home.

"You with your Swedish bakery cookies and your Christmas trees. Can't get a fuckin' straight answer out of one of ya!" The woman shrieked, standing.

Bess wondered if the woman was ranting at someone only she could see or if she was directing her tirade at the entire car.

"You're supporting a hundred of them!" The woman sneered. "And

I hope it breaks your goddamn financial back! I *sincerely* hope so."

Just before Bess and Ryan reached their stop, the woman exited. She marched through the subway station in her dirty pink down coat, an Aldi shopping bag in one hand. Her face was pinched, of an indeterminate age.

Bess clutched her husband's arm. "That could be me some day. Could you stand it?"

Ryan smirked, lips curling in a lopsided grin. Blue eyes probed, searching, as always, for the glimmer of truth behind her sense of humor. He stroked her hair. "As long as it didn't break my goddamn financial back."

Bess laughed as the conductor called out their stop. "Halfway home," she said.

The subway was filled with people. The air was damp with years of underground mildew. Even the cold air that wafted in above them was wet with snow.

Everywhere there was noise. Boomboxes, snatches of conversation, laughter. At one end of the station, a black man with a Bible in his hand warned that those who hadn't been saved were "on a journey to a place where you will burn forever and ever." At the other end of the station a fat woman at a keyboard sang "Between the Devil and the Deep Blue Sea."

They had to go downstairs and through the tunnel that ran between Dearborn Street and State Street to make the connection that would take them home.

A Rastafarian with years-old dreadlocks and raggedy clothes stood midway through the tunnel, pounding out a tribal beat on a bongo drum. He accompanied himself with a high-pitched tuneless whistle that reverberated off the tile walls, like a woman screaming.

Before him a large black woman in a navy blue ski parka shouted, "Yeah!" and danced in front of the man, twirling, arms in the air.

Past the drummer and his ecstatic dancer, a biker-jacket-clad man sat Indian style on the floor, arms upraised. "Get close to Lucifer!" he cried, repeating the phrase over and over, a litany.

As Bess and Ryan hurried by him, he shortened his cries to: "Lucifer! Lucifer! Lucifer!"

"This is a dream, isn't it?" Bess nudged Ryan as they neared the steps. "This is just too weird. I'm going to wake up and we'll be back in Florida, right?"

"I wish."

At least the ride home was uneventful. Nothing but the late rush-hour crowd heading north, bleary-eyed bored faces staring out of windows as the landscape sped by.

Bess wondered if she and Ryan would ever look like the other passengers, locked in lives of complacency and routine. And then she glanced over at Ryan, his face a pale profile against a backdrop of lakefront high-rises, shadowed by the brim of his navy-blue corduroy baseball cap. How could she ever tire of that childlike face, those blue eyes that were always alive with questions, the full lips so quick to twist into a grin or a pout?

She laid her head on his shoulder and closed her eyes. No, she would never tire of Ryan. And she would make sure he would never tire of her.

"Granville. Granville is the next stop on this northbound Howard train."

Bess roused herself.

"C'mon," Ryan whispered. "We better get ourselves up to the door."

Night pressed in around them. Their building was just a block to the east and a block to the north, and Bess couldn't wait to travel the short distance. A quick dinner—a salad, some soup maybe—and then she and Ryan could light a few candles and crowd into the bathtub together.

Their honeymoon wasn't over until tomorrow.

They rounded the corner off Granville and started up Kenmore. Ryan must have seen him first. Bess, intent on getting to the red-brick six-flat on the corner of Rosemont, had become oblivious to her surroundings. Because she was holding on to Ryan's arm, she felt him stiffen.

He stopped.

"Up there," he said softly, not moving his lips.

Bess looked north, where Ryan had indicated. All she saw was a campus building of Loyola University at the end of the street and apartment buildings, lined in orderly rows, on either side of Kenmore. Later, she would admit to herself that she had been in a hurry and, in her haste, hadn't wanted to see anything other than her front door.

Later, she would wish she had listened to Ryan and not talked him out of his sudden apprehension.

In fact, she would go over the next few minutes again and again, in detail, wishing they had done something as simple as crossing the street, or walked up Sheridan and come east on Rosemont, arriving at their building with only a few minutes lost.

But no matter how often she replayed events, there was nothing she could ever do to change them.

Bess looked again. The shadows grew dimmer and she saw, a couple of buildings ahead, the cause of her husband's fear.

Near the opening of a parking garage, a man stood perfectly still. He wasn't doing anything. He wasn't en route to another destination. He was not smoking a cigarette. He was not staring up at the night sky, searching in vain for a star not obliterated by the lights of the city.

It was his stillness that was, at first, the most disconcerting. January in Chicago was not a time to be standing about outdoors. With the wind off Lake Michigan, just two blocks away, the temperature was well below zero.

But the man didn't move. His arms hung at his sides. He stared forward.

And then Bess realized the second disturbing thing about the stranger: He was wearing a mask. As her eyes grew more accustomed to the darkness and the figure before her, she realized he was not wearing a ski mask, which would have been unusual, but relatively ordinary. This man was wearing some sort of leather hood. Even from where she stood, she could discern the jagged zipper across the mouth.

He *was* creepy… but they were almost home, and Bess had seen her share of strange people that evening. And all of those strange people had had one trait in common: They were harmless.

"C'mon." Bess took a step forward and tugged on her husband's hand. "We're almost home."

"Let's just go around the block. I don't like that guy."

Bess rolled her eyes. "Ryan! You're a big guy. He's just another weirdo. If you were going to be afraid of someone, you should have been afraid of that 'Lucifer' character."

"Just around the block. Just to be safe."

A gust of wind whistled across the tops of the buildings, chilling them with its painful frigidity. A few more steps, really, just a few more, and they would be in the vestibule of their building. Warmth, light.

"Look. I'll protect you."

Ryan shook his head. "Don't be ridiculous." He hoisted the bigger of their two suitcases up on his shoulder. "Let's go."

Why hadn't they gone around the block? Why?

As they passed the man with the mask, he was silent. If he had bayed at the moon or shouted, it would have been more comforting. But he said nothing, remaining motionless.

His eyes, the only exposed part of him, watched as they passed.

And then he was behind them.

Bess' throat suddenly constricted. She wanted to drop the bag she was carrying and run, heading for the safety of her building, protected behind a locked door.

But she couldn't run. That would be panic. She would look preposterous.

She and Ryan *did* quicken their pace. Bess glanced over at Ryan, looking out of the corner of her eye for reassurance.

But she got none. The fear was naked on his face: His eyes glistened and he breathed quickly through his mouth.

Why was it everything seemed to slow? Why did everything suddenly become cloaked in the leaden movement of nightmare? The whole ordeal took only seconds, and yet it seemed they couldn't move, as if their veins were filled with a substance heavier than blood.

He was behind her. Bess didn't have a chance to scream. His arm around her neck, yanking hard enough to make her gasp for the cold air which had suddenly vanished.

His other arm extended toward Ryan, glint of the switchblade blue-silver in the moonlight.

Her feet, kicking, scraped along the pavement as he dragged her into the parking garage.

Ryan stood helpless and confused for only a second. Then he dropped the suitcase and hurried after them, dancing away from the knife, pleading, "Hey man, you've got to let her go. Don't do this."

Ryan turned his head, bleating into the darkness. "Help!"

And then the shadows gathered around her. The parking garage smelled of stale air and exhaust fumes. The man's weight was an unbearable warmth at her back.

His arm squeezed down hard against her, propelling her backward, arms pinwheeling to break her fall, doing no good. The hard, oil-stained floor rose up to slam against the back of her head, jarring, causing tiny flecks of silver light to dance before her eyes. Her teeth dug into her tongue. She didn't realize it until a moment later, when her mouth filled with the coppery warmth of her blood and the pain that rose up, beastly and undeniable.

The man turned to Ryan, unzipping the mask. His voice emerged, a croak: "Beat it, man! I'm not gonna hurt her. Not unless you stick around."

And then Ryan lunged.

That was all it took. That one movement of violence and aggression merged with their attacker's fear and resulted in disaster.

Why hadn't she done more? Why did something so pivotal have to take only a few seconds? Why hadn't there been time to think?

The switchblade did not glint in the darkness, gave no warning of its malicious intent. Their attacker plunged it into Ryan's throat with sureness and rage, stopping the world for just an instant.

And then he was gone… running, running, switchblade still in hand. Later, they would discover the brown stains that trailed behind him, blood dripping from the knife.

And Bess was alone with Ryan, who said nothing more, who only gasped a time or two and then was dead.

Everywhere around her there were people: people in high-rises, warm yellow lights against the black sky, people in cars rushing by, people coming in and out of bars and discount stores less than a block away on Granville. Everywhere, people—and not one of them heard her screaming.

II

Bess was alone. Four months had passed. Snow had melted, giving way to gray skies and thunderstorms, which suited Bess fine. But now spring was at the door, impatient, already making its colorful entrance.

Outside Bess' second-story window stood a redbud tree, its impressionist buds of lavender mocking her. The forsythia bush did the same; Bess couldn't bear the vibrant yellow when she made a rare emergence from her front door.

So she tried to stay inside. It wasn't that hard to do. She had no appetite; when she absolutely had to eat, she could usually find a cracker in the pantry or a can of soup. She had long ago disconnected the phone. Even the mail no longer got to her: When she remembered to remove it from her mailbox, she simply added it to the white snowdrift of paper inside her front door.

When she looked in the mirror, a sallow woman gazed back with listless eyes. After Ryan had died, she had stood in front of the mirror and cut her wavy, whiskey-colored hair close to her scalp. After all, who was there to look good for now? What did she care?

The rent was unpaid. The calls from her boss and co-workers at the educational publishing house where she had once worked as an editor had ceased. Soon, Bess thought, she would find herself evicted. Perhaps she would go and live in the subway.

Most days, Bess did nothing more than sit on the couch in the living room, watching the quality of light as it changed from morning brightness to the lengthening shadows of dusk.

She wondered why she didn't just kill herself and get it over with. Something held her back… perhaps a sense of unfinished business.

There had to be something more.

This afternoon, the air and light from outside had been even more irritating than usual. In the past, on a day such as this, she and Ryan would have mounted their mountain bikes and headed to the lakefront trails that wound all the way south of downtown. She would ride behind him, "drafting," caught up in the force of his powerful pedaling, watching his blond curls blow back in the wind, feeling the cool of the air suspended over the blue-green water and anticipating a time when they would stop, set their bikes on the grass and lie side by side, watching other bikers, runners and roller-bladers speed by.

Today's sunshine and warmth were cruel. Didn't they understand how she felt? Couldn't the children outside—the boys playing Frisbee, the girls with their jump ropes—realize how grating their loud voices were?

The buzzer sounding in the little apartment caused her to cry out. It sounded again, a sharp metallic bark.

She would not answer it. She didn't care who it was.

And then the sound of the glass-fronted door downstairs slamming.

Bess stiffened at the first tentative knock.

"Bess? Honey, are you in there?"

Bess held her breath. Her mother hadn't been over in at least two weeks. The last time, she had insisted on cleaning the place up, cooking her daughter a meal. Bess didn't think she could bear her mother's pained expression as she surveyed the mess of the apartment and the lack of interest her daughter had in life. She couldn't stand those wounded brown eyes as her mother went through the apartment, picking up clothes, throwing away junk mail, sorting through the bills and wiping down sinks and countertops.

The knock came again, louder, a hollow echo. "Bess, please open up. It's Mom. Please… I'm worried about you."

Bess had just begun to breathe normally again when she heard the jingle of keys. *Oh no…*

The air rushed out of the room as her mother fitted the key in the lock. Panicked… a wild animal caught in a trap.

Just as the tumblers clicked, Bess rushed into the bedroom and scurried under the bed. Safety in the darkness, with Ryan's Nikes and the dustballs.

Perhaps she would stay awhile.

Footsteps clicked on hardwood. Sensible, low-heeled pumps. Bess imagined her: salt-and-pepper hair pulled up, dark skirt and a light cardigan with pearl buttons.

"Bess?" The word came out shaky and Bess bit her lip. "Please don't cry, Mother," she whispered. "If you cry, I will be forced to slide out from under here, and I like it here. I like it."

After a while, the door closed, tumblers sounded once more.

Bess slid out. Day's brightness had watered down at last to a dull orange glow. She sneezed and sat on the bed, looking down at her sweat pants covered with dustballs. She slid them off and lay back.

Ryan's baseball cap was on his pillow. Bess lifted it, fingering the wales in the corduroy, biting her lower lip. She had gone back the next day, numb, a zombie, to the parking garage where he had been taken from her. She didn't understand why she would want to return. Perhaps to reassure herself that everything had really happened. Perhaps seeing the bright yellow police-line tape and the chalk outline of her husband's body would make it real.

Or maybe it was just to find the hat she now caressed. It had blown into a corner, or had been propelled there from the scuffle.

However it had gotten there, Bess was grateful it had been she who had found it. Grateful it had not been put in some sterile Ziploc bag by a police-evidence technician.

Bess imagined she could still smell Ryan's hair in the brim of the cap. She held it close, remembering the faint strawberry scent.

And then he was there, in her arms. And she was kissing him and he was gazing down, their eyes locked for an instant before his face found her neck and she felt the cool damp of his tears.

Bess clutched his back, holding on so tightly she was afraid she might hurt him, but also afraid if she let go she would lose him once more.

Then, as quickly as he had come, Ryan was gone, leaving Bess holding a dusty navy-blue corduroy cap and wondering if anything was real.

Inside the cap lay a single strand of blond hair. Bess plucked it out, certain it had never been there before.

III

The next night Bess lay sleepless. Her eyes had long ago grown accustomed to the darkness and the objects in the room: Furniture, discarded clothing, had taken on the shapes of gray hulks, almost alive in the shadows.

Sleep was elusive. She dreaded its coming, even though her eyes cried out for it, even though her muscles ached.

What if Ryan came back as she slept? What assurance would she have he might slip into her dreams? Besides, even if she had such an assurance, Bess wanted more than this ethereal connection.

In spite of her resolve, she found herself drifting. The confines of her bedroom would dissolve, and she would find herself on slippery outcroppings of granite and limestone, where one misstep would send her plummeting into an abyss so deep and black, the darkness rose up, palpable as stone. One wrong step was all it took for Bess' muscles to retract, hurling her back into wakefulness.

It was during one of these fugues that something else brought her back.

"Bess."

A whispered voice.

"Bess."

Again, the voice whispery, dry and empty as a husk, the end of her name a sibilant hiss.

Bess got up on her elbows, searching the silver-gray darkness.

Was it Ryan?

Nails dug into sheets, clawing. What if it was him? She needed to show her love and desire, not terror.

"Bess." Whisper segued into a dry, throaty chuckle.

Bess flattened herself against the headboard, one quivering hand reaching out to switch on the lamp on her night stand.

Light broke into the room, shattering the darkness.

Empty.

Perhaps under the bed? Nightmare images assaulted her. The closet door stood open a few inches, enough to give the banished darkness a shelter, enough to cause Bess to wonder what lurked within.

Ryan's hat was on the pillow, and Bess snatched it up.

She put her feet to the floor, expecting taloned hands, red and sore, to fly out from underneath the bed. The hands would grab her ankles tightly enough to force the blood out; bright rings of white appearing above monstrous fingers.

And Bess would be pulled under the bed and farther down, deeper, until she could no longer breathe.

Until she vanished.

Bess squatted. Under the bed was nothing more horrifying than clumps of gray dust and pairs of shoes, both hers and Ryan's continuing to mingle.

She crept to the closet and swung the door open. The darkness disappeared and Bess was faced with rows of hangers…coats, dresses, blouses.

Yet what was in the back, where the light did not penetrate?

Wasn't there the shape of something? The shape of something stooped, yet human?

Bess' heart stopped; her mouth was dry. With the last of her resolve, she pushed aside the hanging clothes and let in the light.

Ryan hid like a child: stooped, arms gripping himself in an attempt to make himself smaller. He stared at the floor and, when he looked up at Bess, his eyes had an odd clarity, a paleness that almost made them translucent.

He chuckled. And then, mocking himself, whispered, "Bess."

The room, for an instant, lost substance, whirling around. She felt drunk: the same dizziness and nausea. She sat down and placed her head in her hands.

When she looked up, he was squatting beside her. He was naked, and she was shocked to see he was aroused.

"Ryan?" She touched his face. A light stubble covered his oddly cool chin. Bess ran her fingertips over it, marveling in its reality.

"You're really here, aren't you?"

Ryan's response was to lift Bess from the floor and carry her to the bed. He lowered her to the sheets, which were cold and gritty.

Bess lay back, staring into the eyes, trying to forget that these eyes were paler than Ryan's. They were close enough.

She bit the inside of her cheek as he spread himself out on top of her, a blanket of silken cool, conjuring up images of water: blue-green. She gripped his back as he entered her, unable to stop the sharp cry of pain at the ice of his penis as it rammed into her, insistent in a way Ryan would never have been.

Bess tried to accustom herself to the pain and the chill, biting her lip and grasping him so tightly her nails dug into his back, drawing blood.

IV

Morning found her nauseated. The medicine-cabinet mirror threw back a wild-eyed, ashen wraith.

Bess gripped the sink, cool porcelain scant comfort to her racing heart and the blood pounding in her ears. Close to the spigot, she splashed cold water on her face, over and over until it ran in rivers down her body, puddling on the floor.

Then she collapsed in the cold water and wept. Bitter salt tears reddened her eyes, made her gasp. She trembled, clutching herself.

Between her thighs, reddened skin, chapped. Skin frozen, charred.

Late afternoon: Dying rays of wan light cast slants of gray on the hardwood. Outside, a purple sky filtered down to pink, tinged with gold on the horizon. Budding trees blackened in silhouette.

She pictured Ryan coming in the darkness: strong form, broad shoulders, wavy blond hair and stubbly face. Imagined disappointment reflected in ice-blue eyes as his gaze penetrated the darkness, seeking her out.

But it wasn't Ryan! Ryan was dead.

A rustling in the bedroom, fabric hitting the floor, interrupted.

Bess stiffened, mouth suddenly dry. Sweat trickled down her sides.

Standing on legs that felt like water, Bess was unsure which door to head toward.

She took a few steps toward the bedroom, pushed the door, causing it to slide open a little… enough to see him standing there. Half-light revealed his baseball cap, crooked grin below it.

"Bess?" Voice querulous, uncertain.

Bess moved toward him. As she did, the phone rang. She ignored it even as the voice of her mother came through. "Bess? It's Mom. Pick up."

Even as her mother spoke, Bess was surrendering to him, arms enfolding her: swan wings, protective.

As she closed her eyes, breathing in woodsmoke and flame, yet feeling icy chill from his body, she thought, "It doesn't matter."

But it did matter. And as another morning slipped into the apartment, creeping under her eyelids with thin, watery light, Bess knew that, today, she must find a way to climb out.

Her stomach roiled with nausea and hopelessness. Where to turn? A spiritualist? A satanist?

An image rose up and Bess recalled something about the night of Ryan's murder she hadn't thought of since that time. Before her, a young man, scruffy goatee and a chipped tooth, dingy reddish-brown hair topped with a stocking cap, wearing a black leather biker jacket and jeans with the knees ripped out. Bess was amazed at her recall. And even sharper in her memory was the sound of his voice, deeper, older than his appearance, shouting: "Get close to Lucifer! Lucifer! Lucifer!" His arms were upraised… in what? A gesture of supplication?

He was important wasn't he? A precursor of things to come. It had been no accident she had seen him that night. No accident Ryan had been the one who had passed closer to him. Ryan, she now remembered, who had met the man's eyes.

And what eyes! Pale, paler than human. Eyes of a saint, a monster, a devil, an animal.

Eyes just like the Ryan who had come to her in the night.

"Am I going completely insane?" Bess wondered aloud, then laughed. Gazing about the room, she tried to discern if she was seeing things in a different way.

But the room looked the same: Navajo print rug, with tones of forest green and rust, still partially covered the hardwood; carved-oak mirror still stood on the mantel, reflecting her grinning face.

Insanity would be such an easy defense.

If only it were true.

Bess hurried into the bedroom to dress.

V

Doors closed, and the train rumbled away from Fullerton station. Bess sat in the front seat of the first car. This way she could watch as the train descended from the el into the subway tunnel. As the train lumbered forward, the light began to dim above as the el tracks of the Ravenswood line became their rooftop, as they headed underground. Lights lined the subway tunnel, the dark round hole into which she was hurtling.

Over and over, forehead pressed against cold glass, she told herself this was crazy. What assurance did she have that he would even be there?

And if he was, what help could he offer? Would he be able to tell her just how to "get close to Lucifer"? Was that really what she wanted to know?

"Do you know if this train stops at Grand Avenue?"

Bess almost screamed as the female voice, tinged with a Southern accent, came from behind. She hadn't heard anyone sit down.

She turned. Young woman on the seat behind her, tentative smile. Bess wondered how she must appear to the woman, knowing only too well how her cheeks had sunk in, how her eyes had become listless, her hair drab, colorless.

The woman was a contrast. Everything Bess had once been. Slightly plump, reddish cheeks, black hair that tumbled in curls out of a yellow knitted cap. Deep-blue eyes.

"What?"

"Grand and… what is it," the woman consulted a post-it note, "State. Does this train stop there?"

"Yes, I think it does."

"Thank you."

Bess wanted to look away, but couldn't. The woman held an infant, a tiny, blue-wrapped bundle. Squirming. Whimpering.

"Would you mind if I nursed him a little?"

Bess shook her head.

The woman smiled. "Some people, you know, are funny about that." She unbuttoned her blouse and undid a strap on the left cup of her bra. A flash of white skin, brownish-pink nipple, and then the blue bundle covered everything. The woman gazed down at the baby, gently touching its forehead. She smiled.

The train went dark for an instant as it passed over a non-electrified part of rail.

When the lights came back on, the woman was gone.

Bess scanned the car, looking for the royal-blue wool coat, the yellow cap. She knew it was futile. The train had not stopped and there were only a few passengers.

Bess stood and, knowing there hadn't been enough time but seeing her mission out anyway, walked to the back of the car and peered through the window into the next car.

As she expected, Bess saw no trace of the woman.

"North and Clybourn." The train slowed to a stop and Bess reached out to grab a pole to maintain her balance.

The next few stops went by in a blur. Bess couldn't concentrate; at times everything around her dissolved. When she was between stations and the walls of the dark tunnel were hurtling by, she wondered if she would ever emerge again or if, instead of pulling into a station, they would pull into a riot of ghouls milling around, flames the size of buildings, shooting upward to lick a black, starless sky.

Get close to Lucifer.

Trembling, she got out of the car at Jackson. Ahead of her the green rail of the stairway beckoned. The stairway that would take her into the tunnel between the State and Dearborn Street subways.

Nightmare movement. Glue in her veins, soundless crowds passing her in slow motion. Green-railed stairway growing larger and larger as she neared. Bess stopped, breath coming in gasps.

She gripped the green railing: cold and wet, something viscous. Bess snatched her hand away, wiping it on her coat.

She descended.

Sometimes, Bess thought, *you just know things before they happen.* Inexplicable certainty.

She knew he would be there.

Knew before his craggy voice ricocheted off the tile walls and high, arching concrete ceiling.

The tunnel was bright, a place that shouldn't exist. One long concrete floor, the color of dried blood. Dingy white tile trimmed in industrial green. Commuters hurried through and, as each train above expelled them, another rush would come down the stairs, rushing through the tunnel. There was something insect-like in all this movement, making Bess dizzy.

This was a place where nothing lived.

A man, wrapped in a brown wool coat, red stocking cap and dark corduroy pants that defied color, played a saxophone, accompanied by a driving bass beat coming out of a boom box. The sax wailed, broadcasting its song of despair into the tunnel, where it sought escape and found none.

And just down from him, a *déjà vu* postcard, sat the man. Everything about him was the same: leather jacket, jeans, thermal shirt, unlaced army boots. Sitting Indian style on the rough concrete, arms upraised. "Get close to Lucifer!"

Bess thought of turning and running back up the stairs, going home. And realized there was no turning back. A force as relentless as gravity pulled her through the tunnel. Closer, closer.

She stood in front of him, the only person in the crowd rushing by to do so. Their eyes met.

He knew. He expected her.

Bottomless eyes, cloudy glass, pupils suspended in irises that were like colorless jelly. He grinned, revealing a chipped front tooth. Licked his lips.

Bess covered her mouth in horror.

His tongue ended in two points, like a serpent's.

No.

She wanted to rush to him, pry the cracked lips apart and see again for herself, wanting to see a normal human tongue, not this.

"Get close to Lucifer."

A whisper.

Bess squatted beside him. The scent of him set circuits to humming in Bess' brain. Recall: the scent of woodsmoke, embers. Ryan. Or the one masquerading as him.

"What do you know?" Bess searched his eyes for an answer.

"Get close," he hissed.

Bess moved close enough to smell the oiled leather of his jacket, stench of perspiration.

"You wanna get close to the devil, lady? That what you want?" He giggled. "He been waitin' for you, *chère*. Been wantin' you."

"But why?"

"You know why, doncha? You opened the door."

"What door?"

"The door to Hell!" His voice boomed out, deep, sonorous. Commuter eyes on her, burning. She had become one of the crazies she used to gawk at.

"What are you talking about?"

"Our father who art in Hades… he puh-reys on the grieving. The ones who've lost the will. You. Easy prey. You better pray, easy prey. Better pray, prey." He hiccuped out a laugh and Bess recoiled. This thing had soiled her. Was he just crazy, or did he know something? "What do *you* know about my grief?"

"He whispers to me, *chère*. Tells me all about you." He winked.

"What? What are you talking about?" A tiny rodent with razor teeth gnawed from inside her gut, desperate to get out, moving from place to place, biting and clawing.

"I can get you close. What you want, ain't it?" He cocked his head. Eyebrows raised in a leer. "Just take the dark hand, grasp it tight… and you're there. With *him*."

Bess wanted to cry, eyes welling, choked tears back like caustic fumes. Not in front of him. "What are you talking about?"

"The dark hand! Take the dark hand!" He scowled at her, eyes alive with dancing light, tongue whipping out to lick at the air. His arms came up slowly as if being pulled from above. As if he had no control. A marionette.

"Get close to Lucifer!" Voice booming. Thunder.

Bess scrambled to her feet, heart racing. She stumbled down the passage, bumping into the tide of recently discharged passengers, gasping and pushing them out of her way. The tunnel suddenly felt cold, so cold.

The walls were closing in.

"Get close to Ryan!"

No. He hadn't said that. *Had he?*

Dashed up the stairs, up, up, up, stumbling, arms blindly reaching out for purchase. Top of the stairs, dizzy, breathless. Downcast eyes sweeping past. Worse: the gaze of the curious, the concerned.

"Leave me alone!" Bess shouted, weeping.

Rushing to the edge of the platform, Bess gazed into the darkened mouth of the subway tunnel. Twin luminous eyes waited. "Take the dark hand; get close to Ryan," Bess whispered, no air left for her voice. *When the train rumbles into the station, I will throw myself in front of it.*

Take the dark hand….

Was this what she really wanted?

Memory rose up, like an assault, like a gift. A summer morning, early. Outside their window, the sun came up over Lake Michigan, turning the grayish waters deep teal, the gold of the sun catching the foam on the waves, turning it tangerine. A strip of pink on the horizon; the sun a huge, gilded ball just above the water.

Ryan, sleepy-eyed, blond hair in his face. Lips red from kissing, pressure. Bess lay at one end of the bed, watching his mouth move as he sang, off-key and hoarse, "You Are My Sunshine."

Cornball memory stole her breath. Another: Ryan coming to her in the darkness, or what seemed like Ryan, the chill of his body as it spread itself over her. Engulfing.

She took another step forward; toes dangled over the edge of the platform. The train in the station west of her rumbled forward, a monster growling, coming to claim her.

The dark hand.

Get close to Ryan.

So simple just to step off into darkness. The pull irresistible. She took one last look up. Soon, she would be with him again… in Hell, wherever.

It didn't matter.

A flash of blue against the gray of the station. Royal blue. The woman from the train earlier stood at the other end of the tunnel, smiling. Their eyes met, and a curious warmth washed through Beth as the woman's blue-eyed gaze pulled her forward. Bess was unable to draw her eyes away as the woman turned the blue-wrapped bundle in her arms so it was facing Bess.

Although she had taken no steps, the woman seemed closer. Bess could make out details she hadn't before. The brass buttons of her coat. Ruddy hue of her cheeks.

The woman drew back the blue blanket to reveal the baby's face.

Even though it was the face of an infant, Bess recognized it at once: Ryan. The same blond hair, the same lopsided grin.

She shuddered and cried out as a whistle blew.

The train, whistle shrieking and sending up a great rush of air, blew through the station like a banshee, not stopping, racing. Bess stumbled backward from the force of the speeding silver train.

"Attention, passengers, another train is immediately following," a static-cloaked voice boomed from a loudspeaker. "That delayed eastbound train will make Clark and Lake its next stop. Another train is immediately following."

Bess turned back to find the woman, the child with Ryan's face.

But they were gone.

Again, no trace of the royal-blue coat or the swaddled bundle she longed to see.

Bess stepped back from the platform. Even though the woman was gone, Bess tingled still from the curious warmth she had imparted when Bess had locked gazes with her.

She couldn't do it. Couldn't take the proffered dark hand. Something more, she didn't know what, had to be out there.

She would return home on the next train. Return home and begin life anew.

Bess made her way through the station, pausing at the top of the stairs, unsure if she could face the biker-jacket-clad man once more.

But there was a lot she would have to face, and it would take time to rebuild her strength. Facing the stranger would be the first step on the road back.

She descended into the tunnel once more.

Magic lost. Dim, empty corridor, curved ceiling choked with mildew, floor scarred with the passage of many feet. A woman at one end (no royal-blue coat this time) disappeared up the stairs. A blind man sat midway, hunched over his white-tipped cane, cigar box full of chewing gum for sale open on his lap.

Bess hurried through the tunnel, certain the biker-jacketed man would come down the stairs, grinning, forked tongue whipping out, rushing toward her like something from a nightmare.

But there was no one.

Bess climbed the stairs, made her way through the State Street subway station. She wanted to board the front car, where she could sit in the first seat and watch as the train moved from the darkness of the tunnel into day's bright light.

Standing. Waiting. Voices behind her indistinct: a staticky radio, tuning dial being whirled.

Finally: lights at the end of the tunnel. Headlights, not eyes.

Relief as Bess pictured the train moving north, grinding into the station, pneumatic wheeze of doors. Homeward bound.

Bess pawed the back of her neck, aware suddenly of a coolness behind her. The sensation was deeper than the mere damp chill of the subway station. A dark blanket. Shadow eclipsed.

The train rumbled, growing nearer. Bess stepped forward a tiny bit, trying to free herself from the closeness of the stranger behind her.

The dark blanket followed.

Just as the rumbling reached a crescendo, the shadow deepened and darkened behind her.

A frightened cry erupted out of Bess like a hiccup. A desire to turn and run aborted: no time. Sirens erupted inside as she felt the firm pressure of two hands on the small of her back.

And the hoarse voice, screaming, "Get close to Lucifer!" erupting just as the train roared into the station.

And Bess was flying, caught up in screeching, screaming brakes and light so bright it burned her retinas.

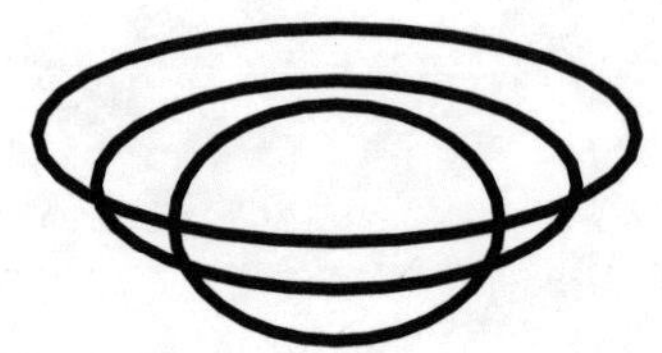

Screams at the Gateway to Fame

by Ray Garton

The young couple was like all the other countless couples that had run together into a smiling, nodding, tale-telling blur in Janine Werner's memory over the years. Except for… something. Something about the couple that Janine had not yet isolated, but she was trying.

Jack and Della Bellinger sat across from Janine and Tom in the booth, four cups of coffee on the table with the small tape recorder in the middle silently capturing their words as they told their story loudly enough to be heard above the clamor of the diner, but not so loud that others could hear.

"We moved into the house last summer," Jack said. "It was perfect, 'cause, y'know, we couldn't afford a lot of money, and it was pretty reasonable."

"Reasonable?" Della interrupted with a smirk. "It was a steal. We couldn't believe it. I mean, the place was just *gorgeous*, and the price was so *low*."

Tom nodded slowly, significantly, and said, "That's very common. Sometimes you get more than you pay for."

"Things were fine at first," Jack continued. "It was real nice, y'know? We'd never lived in such a big place before. Then come October, our little boy, Richie, he started telling us about this man." Jack bowed his head a moment, sipped his coffee.

"Richie said the man was real tall and thin," Della said. "And bald. He wore a black suit. And he'd come into the boys' room in the basement at night and just walk around, looking at things on their dressers, peeking into the closet."

"The boys sleep in the basement?" Tom asked.

"It was their idea," Jack said. "It's real big, a little drafty, but they loved it right off. They even got their own bathroom down there. No shower, but a sink and toilet, y'know."

"Did your other son see this man?" Tom asked.

Jack and Della, both thirty-five, had three children: Richie, seven; Wendy, eleven; and J.J. (for Jack, Jr.), fifteen.

"Oh, well, uh, no," Della said haltingly. "See, J.J. is, uh… kind of a heavy sleeper." She glanced at Jack twice as she spoke.

Janine knew immediately that there was something wrong with their oldest boy, something that troubled them. Something they didn't want to talk about. A violent rebel? A drug problem, perhaps? She picked up nothing specific yet, but knew she would eventually. Perhaps whatever was wrong with J.J. had been the source of that jagged tension, that underslept, wire-taut anxiety Janine had felt when she'd shaken hands with Jack and Della not twenty minutes ago.

It was present in all of them, that anxiety, in every couple she and Tom had ever dealt with. Sometimes only Janine could pick it up; sometimes they wore it on their drawn faces, held it in their baggy eyes. Of course, the cause of that tension never had anything to do with the reason Tom and Janine had been called. It was usually alcoholism or drug abuse, sometimes a woman or a child cowed by the fists of the violent man of the house, sometimes even incest. It was always something, as Janine's mother used to say. But it had nothing to do with Tom, Janine and their work.

It had gnawed at her at first, those families and their dirty, ugly secrets. But that had been decades ago. She was fifty-nine now, and Tom was sixty-eight. Just as they had grown accustomed to a certain daily schedule at home, to watching certain TV programs, to eating certain foods, they had grown accustomed to the peripheral peculiarities of their work.

It would come to Janine eventually, the source of Jack and Della's anxiety. And perhaps she would discover, as well, that one thing that made them different from all the other couples, that single, nagging, ungraspable thing.

"Have *you* seen this man?" Tom asked.

Hesitantly, Jack said, "Yeah. We have. We didn't believe Richie at first. We even punished him for lying to us. Then, one night, I went downstairs to their room to make sure they'd gone to bed and… there he was. Richie was sitting up in bed wide awake, eyes really big. The guy looked right at me. He smiled. Then he went into the floor. Just… sank away into the floor. Like it was quicksand." Jack's hands fumbled nervously around his coffee cup and he glanced at Della darkly.

"After that," Della said, "it's like this gate opened up or something.

I mean, all of a sudden, things started happening. Just strange things at first. Then they got… well, scary."

The waitress came with their orders: cheeseburger and fries for Jack, chef's salad for Della, chicken-salad sandwich and raw vegetables for Janine, and a chicken-fried steak with mashed potatoes and gravy and a tiny, obligatory, green salad for Tom.

Janine looked at Tom's plate sadly. She kept trying to warn him. He'd already had one heart attack, and he was at least a hundred pounds overweight. He was a short, gray-haired man with a belly so large it gave his back fits and had decayed his posture over the years. At five-ten, Janine stood three inches above her husband, not counting the tall bouffant of brown-dyed hair on her head, and with the help of some lucky genes Janine had kept her figure and was only a few pounds heavier than she'd been in high school. But she worried about Tom: He had no genes working in his favor, and he did nothing to take up the slack.

"What kind of things happened, Della?" Janine prompted gently as the four of them began to eat.

"Toys. The kids' toys, um, in the living room, you know how kids leave their toys everywhere. Well, first they started disappearing. I didn't think anything of it, okay? I mean," she shrugged, "kids're always losing their toys, right? Then, uh… Jack lost his job at the factory."

There was an uncomfortable silence then; it was as loud as all the clatter around them.

"Hey, look, I'm a good worker, y'know?" Jack said suddenly. "I mean, I've got problems. Me and Della… we've had some problems. Who doesn't, y'know? But I've always been a good worker, always on time, always the last to leave, always willing to come in when somebody else was sick. Then one morning, I go into work and my boss and four other guys I worked with corner me and say I been makin' these phonecalls to 'em. In the middle of the night. Really foul, obscene calls. They say it was my voice and I even identified myself. I tell 'em, hey, I says, I don't know what the hell they're talkin' about. But they wouldn't listen. I was fired. They practically chased me out."

"The factory's a toll call," Della said quietly. "We checked our phonebill. The calls were there. In the middle of the night. To the numbers of Jack's boss and four coworkers."

"But I swear to *God*, I didn't make them calls!" Jack insisted.

Tom lifted a hand and wagged his thick fingers at Jack. "Don't worry," he said. "We've seen this before. It's okay. We believe you. Right, honey?" He turned to Janine.

"That's right, Tom."

They could have been following a script, so identical were their words to all the other couples they'd dealt with, who were so identical to Jack and Della Bellinger. Except:

Janine was feeling that anxiety again, coming to her from Jack now like the wavering heat off a dying fire. It was real. And unlike everything else about the conversation, it was... *different*. She watched Jack's fidgeting hands, saw him fumble with his wedding ring. Janine saw an identical gold band on Della's finger. Then it struck her. She thought of all the couples they'd met over the years and remembered the crucifixes being worn around necks, the rosaries being caressed during conversation; all of them, every single couple, without fail, clutching their religion in the form of trinkets and icons, there for all to see, to draw attention away from the dark and diseased secrets of their lives.

But Jack and Della carried none of those icons, wore none of that jewelry.

"Are you Catholic?" Janine asked both of them.

Jack shook his head as Della said, "Oh, no."

"Any religion at all?"

Della chuckled nervously. "Not us."

Jack said, "Neither of us come from religious families, and we've just never taken to church-going, tell you the truth."

Janine nodded, trying to hide her surprise. It was a first, and she glanced at Tom, but he did not react to it at all.

"After Jack lost his job," Della went on, "things got really bad. Instead of disappearing, the toys... they started just, um, moving around. On the floor. By themselves. Lots of things in the house moved and were broken. And the voices... the wailing and crying and laughing at night, and other things that, um... well, they're personal, okay? I mean, they're hard to talk about."

Tom cleared his throat and leaned forward as much as his belly would allow. "Are they of a sexual nature?"

"Uh, yeah," Jack said, fidgeting even more, ignoring his burger. "They are. We, uh... well, something came into our bedroom one night. Into our *bed*."

Della said something with her head bowed, staring at her salad, her voice too low for the words to be understood.

"I'm sorry?" Tom said. "You'll have to speak up."

Tom was highstrung, his manner coarse, and he was often thought rude by strangers, even when that was not his intention. Janine nudged him with an elbow, a signal for him to lighten up. Tom smiled and added, "If you don't speak up, dear, the recorder won't catch it."

"It touched me first," Della said. "Something… above the covers. It squeezed my breasts. It even scratched me."

"I saw the scratches," Jack said. "Four of them. Across her left breast. They bled."

"It was a hand," Della added. "Nothing was there, okay? I mean, I couldn't see anything, but… it had four fingers and a thumb. And it squeezed. And pinched. Hard."

"It bruised her. I saw the bruises."

"Honey, do you think—" Della turned to Jack reluctantly, placed a hand on his arm, "—do you think you can tell them what it… did to you? I mean, without breaking down?"

Jack turned away from all of them and stared out the window beside the booth for a long moment. Finally, still gazing out the window, he spoke, voice brittle: "It raped me. One night. I was in bed, lying on my back. It flopped me over. Like I was a rag doll, y'know? Just flopped me over. Onto my stomach. It hurt. I never screamed before in my life, but I did that night. That was the first time it happened. But not the last."

Della put her hand over Jack's and squeezed.

It never failed. In recent years, there was always sodomy involved in every case, whether the victim was male or female. It puzzled Janine, but it delighted Tom, because he thought it did wonders for book sales and sounded great on the talk shows. On the surface, this sounded like every other story of demonic rape she and Tom had heard, but… beneath the surface, things were different. What she felt from Jack was so upsetting that it withered her appetite and she pushed her plate away.

"Then there were the dreams," Della said, still holding Jack's hand. "Horrible nightmares. But I mean *really* vivid, okay? Like they were really happening. Horrible. Every night. Pretty soon, we couldn't sleep. None of us."

"Not even the children?" Tom asked.

"No," Della said. Then she tossed a look at Jack, glanced all around nervously. "Except for J.J. He's… different. He hasn't been bothered by any of this. In fact, he stays away from us. Out of the house. He says we're crazy. See, J.J. is, um… we've been having problems with him. He's been… doing drugs. We've tried everything. Punishing him. Pleading with him. Even turning him in to the police. Nothing works."

Tom closed his eyes and nodded knowingly. "That's not at all uncommon. In every case we've handled where a teenager was involved, there's usually drugs involved."

Janine knew that was true, but this was another first. In every other case, the family tried to hide whatever drug problem existed. Tom and Janine always found out by accident, and the couple always apologized, as if it might damage their credibility, their chances of going on *Jenny Jones*. But never before had anyone revealed the problem during the first meeting.

Tom continued: "We haven't figured out yet whether the drug problems are the cause of the evil presence or the result of it. Maybe we'll be able to pinpoint it in this case."

Janine ignored that; it was the usual prattle Tom had developed over the years, more lines from the nonexistent script they followed while dealing with one ruptured, broken family after another. She ignored it because she was still trying to process the oddities that kept popping up in this particular case: The Bellingers weren't Catholic, or religious at all; they surrendered the information about their son's drug problem; and that… *thing* she kept feeling, especially from Jack, that anxiety, that *fear*. It was not the usual secrets she always felt crawling and writhing around beneath the clean surface of all the other families; it was different, new and disturbing.

Jack and Della went on to tell familiar stories: screaming white faces hovering over them at night in the dark; being awakened in the night by the cries of their two youngest children; taking their young son and daughter into their bed protectively as voices and laughter sounded throughout the house all night long. And one more thing that sounded familiar:

"The man in the black suit," Jack said, "he told my son that the house, the ground beneath the house… well, he said that we were living at… the gateway to Hell."

"You mean, he said your house was the entrance to hell?" Tom asked.

"Something like that. He used the word gates, or gateway. The gateway to hell was open beneath us, something like that."

"All right," Tom said. "I think we've heard enough to know that we're definitely dealing with a hostile supernatural force, most likely demonic. Tell you what. We're gonna go back to our hotel room, get ourselves settled, then we'll come over to your place in about an hour."

Della said, "That sounds fine."

"I hope the hotel's okay," Jack said. "We couldn't afford anything really expensive, but we wanted you to be comfortable."

"Oh, it's fine," Tom assured him, "just fine. Uh, one more thing. Why did you call us? Did you read one of our books or articles? See us on a talk show, maybe?"

Jack shook his head. "We'd never heard of you before."

"Beg pardon?" Tom said, cocking his head.

"Really, we didn't know who you were," Della said. "No offense, but we'd never heard of you till they told us to call you."

"They? They *who?*" Tom asked.

Jack and Della exchanged a long look. Then:

"The voices in the house," Jack said.

"And that man in the black suit," Della said.

"And in our nightmares. They told us in our nightmares."

Della nodded. "Yeah. All of them. They said to call you."

"Tom and Janine Werner," Jack said. "They said your names. It's all we've heard since this whole thing started. Call the Werners, Tom and Janine."

The tape came to its end and the two depressed buttons on the recorder popped up with a quiet but startling *plick*.

Janine had possessed her peculiar talent for as long as she could remember. She was barely five when she'd first put her secret perceptions into words spoken aloud. She'd been sitting on her mother's lap, her head leaning on her mother's breast, and suddenly she'd said, "Mommy, something's growing in your titty." Her mother had found the remark humorous, had treated it as nothing more than the fanciful babbling of a child. But the breast cancer metastasized, made its way from one organ to another, and she was dead in a little over a year. But Janine had known it was there the whole time. She had felt it with her mind, seen it with her feelings. She had *known* it.

It was something that had been with her so long that she thought nothing of it. So when she met Tom, while she was in high school, she thought nothing of the fact that she was attracted to him when all of her peers saw him as a figure of fun. He worked in a fishmarket in the small northern California coastal town in which they lived, and he always smelled of fish, even though she knew (without having any reason to know) that he bathed and washed constantly to get rid of the smell.

She also knew that inside him existed something that drew her to him, a lifespark, an ambition, a consuming but directionless *desire* that made her say yes the first time he asked her out and every time after that. She knew other things about him, too: He'd dropped out of high school years before to go to work and support his ailing mother and little sister after the death of his abusive, drunken father. But Tom told her none of those things until after she'd married him, right after graduating from high school.

Two years after they married, the fishmarket where Tom worked—where everyone came to ask Tom's advice about which fish was freshest and what was the best way to cook it and which wine would best complement it—closed down. No one wanted to go to a fishmarket anymore when they could get everything they needed at a supermarket, and without the unpleasant smell. After that, Tom went from one job to another, none of which was high-paying, and none of which he kept for long. None of them gave him the feeling of belonging that he'd had while working at the fishmarket; everyone in town had known him then, they'd respected him, he'd been *somebody*. But the jobs that followed were not the same, and Tom began to change. He became depressed, sluggish, and that bright light of ambition and desire that had once glowed inside of him began to dim, until it was nearly extinguished.

Janine knew all these things because she felt them from inside of him. And she knew something else. She knew what was *really* wrong with him, but did not know how to approach it because there was really no way she *could* know; Tom knew nothing of her gift yet, and she wasn't sure how to tell him. After all, she had told no one up to that point. No one at all.

Tom started drinking. He'd stay up all night listening to the radio, then doze off around dawn on the sofa, and by the time he felt like job hunting, it was much too late in the day. Sometimes she caught him talking to himself, sniffling. And when Janine got a part-time job at a drugstore soda fountain, he got even worse.

One afternoon, she came home to find Tom shattering dishes in the kitchen and screaming obscenities. He was drunk, but she knew that wasn't the only cause. He didn't even notice when she came into the room.

"You're only *making* your father's prediction come true, Tom!" she cried, and he stoppped, just froze where he stood, both hands holding a plate between them, ready to smash it to the floor. He looked at her with the eyes of a sleepwalker who's been awakened on a street corner, lowered his hands slowly. The plate slipped from his fingers and landed with a dull clap without breaking. He went on staring at her, looking confused.

"You don't have to be the failure he always said you'd be," she said softly. "Not unless you *want* to be. It's up to you. You know I have faith in you, Tom, but you're sick now. You have... an illness. We need to work hard to make you well. Then you can prove your father wrong."

He dropped to his knees then, embraced her legs and sobbed, "How did you know? How did you know?"

After a hot meal, when he was feeling better, she told Tom how she knew about his father, a brutal alcoholic who'd never held a job for more than two weeks, who'd beaten Tom and his mother relentlessly, but Tom especially. Tom the worthless sissy-boy who would never amount to anything. She told Tom how she knew, and that she'd never told anyone before in her entire life. It would be their little secret, just between them.

Although Tom went to the county hospital the next day and checked into the psychiatric ward—all of his own free will and with promises that he would be much better when he came out—he never quite recovered. The doctor gave him some pills upon his release, but Tom threw them away and became furious whenever Janine mentioned them. He said they made him tired, they didn't work, he didn't need them. He was fine, he said. And for a long while, he was. But over the years, the illness returned, because it had never left. It lolled just beneath his personality, behind his smile and his laugh, behind his eyes, underneath his incredible energy and enthusiasm, and occasionally it would bob to the surface like some bloated, purple, grinning corpse coming up from the bottom of a powerful river, and there would be a dark period of anger and silence and insomnia and drinking, and sometimes—not always, but sometimes—a period when Janine would have to go visit her parents or sister to keep from being beaten.

But Tom did manage to prove his father wrong. He'd made something of himself—of *both* of them. And he'd sacrificed their little secret to do it. It wasn't their little secret anymore.

"This is it, honey," Tom said, slipping his coat off as he plowed into the hotel room like a John Deere. He tossed his coat onto the bed and started pacing, back hunched, head lowered like a bull's, this way, that way, fists clenching, unclenching. "Did you hear what they said? They asked for *us*. By *name*!"

Hanging her coat in the closet, Janine admitted to herself that was certainly an interesting twist. She was not surprised by Tom's elation, but she knew it was a lie; of *course* the Bellingers had seen one of their books or articles, or caught them on *Sally Jessy Raphael.* But Tom no longer saw things the way she did.

"Tom, don't you think there's something different about this couple?" Janine asked, making herself a glass of icewater at the sink.

"You're damned right there is. They're gonna get us on the cover of *People* magazine, *that's* what's different about 'em."

"No, not just that business about the spirits asking for us by name. I mean them, the Bellingers themselves. Didn't you notice anything about them that was different from all the others?"

"Nope, 'fraid I didn't, sweetie," he said as he hefted a suitcase onto the bed. It was their prop case, a large Samsonite filled with religious icons, vials of holy water (blessed by a defrocked priest they knew back home), Catholic literature, and Bibles of every size, as well as copies of their books, videotapes of their talk-show appearances, and a scrapbook of newspaper and magazine articles and photographs of "haunted" and "possessed" houses and people they had helped.

"Well, I did. For one thing, they're not Catholic."

"So? That's not a crime. And besides, Evil doesn't care what religion you are or aren't, honey, you know that." He sorted through the contents of the open suitcase carefully.

"Have you ever known a *Protestant* to call us, Tom? *Ever*? Not to mention anyone who has no religion at all?"

He raised his head, cocked it to one side and frowned, as if he'd heard a sound he thought he should be able to identify but could not. "Well, no, not exactly. But," back to work, choosing icons from the case, placing them on the bed, "that doesn't mean anything. Remember that Florida couple?"

Janine remembered the Florida couple, all right. It had been the usual stuff—furniture moving, voices crying in the night, something that looked like blood gurgling up from the sink drains. But the feelings Janine had gotten from the family were *truly* frightening, especially from the teenage girl. Janine told Tom she didn't want to deal with those people, but Tom was quite taken with the case because the house had been a funeral home about eighty years ago and he was sure that would add the kind of color to the story that might get them noticed. So Janine had gone along with it. They'd performed their usual rituals, and minutes after they were done, the family said the house felt different already, and so did they, safer, cleaner, normal again, and they concluded that whatever had been tormenting them was gone, thanks to the Werners.

But Janine knew it was not gone, and she could tell that the silent girl who made eye contact with no one knew it as well. And as she left the house, Janine had given the girl a hug and—

—she got a glimpse of the real evil that lurked within the walls of that house. Daddy. Daddy who had been touching the girl for as long as she could remember, touching and much worse, and when she could take it no longer and knew she was about to go screaming mad, the girl had gone to her priest for help, and the priest had done the same thing, just like Daddy, and somehow Daddy found out and he beat *her* for it and said they would never go to church again and they didn't, and Daddy still came to her room at night and whatever fragile, whole part of her she'd taken with her to the priest was shattered now because she had nothing left, inside or out, only Daddy Daddy Daddy—

—and Janine could not get away from that family fast enough. She'd cried on the plane all the way home, and she'd tried to tell Tom about it, but he wouldn't listen because the story was too good just the way it was, and it became their first successful book, got them on lots of talk shows and was their first book to be made into a movie of the week. But Janine couldn't forget that girl, and months later she'd called the family, just to see how the girl was, because she had a feeling, a bad feeling. The girl had opened her own throat with a box-cutter and had bled to death in her bed. Janine had not hugged a stranger since, and never would again.

Tom went on: "That Florida couple, they weren't Catholic when they called us. They'd left the church, didn't want anything to do with it. 'Course, they didn't mind having some holy water sprinkled around their house once their beds started floating, but technically, they weren't Catholics. So I guess the Bellingers aren't the first, are they?"

"What about their son?" she asked, ignoring his question, swallowing her frustration with a gulp of icewater. "They told us their son has a drug problem."

"Oh, you know these people, honey, *somebody* in the house is *always* doing drugs."

It always amazed her: One moment, he spoke of their work with the fervor of Van Helsing in pursuit of the Prince of Darkness, and the next he sounded as cynical as a veteran carnival barker. Over the years, the cynicism had been giving way slowly to the fervor.

"But they *told* us, Tom. You know they *never* tell us. The Bellingers offered the information."

"So they offered!" he snapped impatiently as he turned to her.

"What's the big deal? What the hell *difference* does it make? This one's got a different angle to it, the demons are actually *asking* for us!"

She nodded, finished her water, then dumped the ice in the sink. She heard him sigh, felt his hands on her shoulders. When she looked into the mirror over the sink, he was looking at her over her shoulder.

"Sorry, honey," he said quietly. "I didn't mean to bark at you like that. It's just that an angle like this... it's really *good.* A house that's the gateway to Hell... well, hey, you know, it could be our gateway to fame. The kind of fame that keeps slipping away from us, the real thing, sweetie."

She forced a smile. It took little effort after all these years. When she turned around, he kissed her. Then they got ready to go see the Bellingers.

Tom's fascination with her talent, when she'd first told him about it, had been comical, almost childlike. She'd found it amusing at first. Until he came across an article in the *National Inquisitor* about a family whose house was haunted. They wanted to move, the article said, but couldn't afford it at the moment, but living in the house had become nightmarish because of the sounds of a baby crying and the angry screams of a woman. Janine caught Tom reading the article over and over to himself, having read it aloud to her three times, and she could sense the idea forming in his mind, could feel it solidifying, until he finally told her what he wanted to do. She'd resisted at first, more adamantly than she would think of resisting today; she'd been young then, and so had her disapproval, young and strong. She reminded him it was their little secret, something private and hidden from the world, but he'd broken her down with his energy, enthusiasm and optimism, then, finally, with his anger and fury. With his illness.

He called the haunted family in Walla Walla, Washington, told them about his wife's psychic powers and offered her help in ridding their house of the offending spirits if they would only pay for travel expenses to and from and put them up in a hotel. Janine was sure Tom would be laughed at and hung up on, but the family accepted almost immediately and arranged for the flight the next day.

The allegedly haunted house was old and had once been very small, but a number of add-ons had been built over the years. When Janine went through the front door, her insides shriveled. She quickly learned that she could see and hear things the others could not, and before long, she felt alone in the house, alone with its spirits. Before the afternoon was half over, Janine had communicated with the restless spirit of the woman who had been the first occupant of the house nearly one hundred years before. The woman's husband had not wanted a child, and when she gave birth to their first—and last—he'd drowned it in the sink. Not much later, she'd tried to kill her cruel husband, but had not been fast enough; he had killed her, the murder had been considered self-defense, and he'd lived a long and prosperous life. The woman's spirit would not rest until her baby had received a proper burial. Janine listened as the woman's distant, hollow voice spoke words the others could not hear, watched the woman's wavering, vaporous face, which the others could not see, as it twisted and bent in expressions of long-suffered pain that Janine could feel but the others could not.

Janine led the others down to the small root cellar and told them to dig up the dirt floor, where they found the scant remains of the infant's skeleton. The police were called, the *National Inquisitor* was back on the story in a heartbeat, and Tom and Janine were the center of attention. The baby's remains were buried in a cemetery, the supernatural activity in the house came to a halt, and the story not only made the cover of the *Inquisitor*, but AP and UPI as well. The tabloid paper hired Tom and Janine as full-time "paranormal investigators," and they were flown to "haunted" houses all around the country to report back to the paper.

The case in Walla Walla remained vivid in Janine's memory because, unlike every single other case they handled, it had been real. There had been a real haunting, a real spirit with a solid reason for its unrest. Everything after that had followed a specific pattern, right up to this particular case, the Bellingers… even though there were differences about the Bellingers that bothered her.

Tom and Janine wrote none of the articles for the *National Inquisitor*; they were all ghosted—Janine used to smile at the pun—just like everything else after that, from their articles for legitimate newspapers and magazines to their nineteen books, the covers of which credited them as the authors.

After four years as "paranormal investigators" for the *Inquisitor*, Tom and Janine had enough of a reputation to leave the paper and go ghost hunting on their own, which they did with some success. Their *Inquisitor* articles were compiled in a book, but they got only a fraction of the profits because the tabloid owned the rights. Tom brooded over that for months and vowed it would never happen again; they would own the rights to everything they did, everything they published. That was one of the reasons they were never able to work with the same ghostwriter twice, because the author was paid a very modest flat fee, no royalties. Along with the books came speaking engagements, first for small clubs and societies interested in the paranormal, later at junior colleges and, still later, universities. They told of their experiences, showed pictures of the houses they'd "cleaned," fielded questions about the behavior of evil spirits and warned their audiences against dabbling in the occult with ouija boards or tarot cards, which could possibly attract harmful supernatural activity. Over time, their audiences grew from six or eight blue-haired women gathered in a parlor to university auditoriums filled with everyone from unshakable believers to cold skeptics.

They made their first talk-show appearance six years after leaving the *Inquisitor*, on the *Merv Griffin Show*, and Merv kept making jokes about their work, getting laughs from the audience. One of the assistant producers had told them before the show that it would be a "light conversation" with a few jokes and some good-natured ribbing, but Tom was not prepared for all that laughter, and Janine was not prepared for his reaction. At first, she saw anger growing in Tom's eyes and feared an outburst right there on Merv's stage, with Steve Lawrence and Edie Gormé sitting to their right. As the laughter continued, Tom's anger was replaced by something akin to childlike pouting, but the sadness in his eyes was as real as tears and Janine thought she actually saw his lower lip quiver a couple of times. As Merv began to wind down for a commercial break, Tom launched into a quiet but impassioned speech about their work. Janine had never heard him speak so eloquently about anything, and Merv and the audience and Steve and Edie all fell silent as stones and listened as Tom told them that there was nothing funny about the work he and Janine did, because the people they worked with were hurting very badly, very deeply, their lives were in chaos because of forces not only beyond their control, but beyond anyone's complete understanding, beyond this *life*, and to laugh at that was to laugh at the pain and misery of innocent people who simply wanted their lives back, people whom Tom and Janine helped to heal, and just before he finished his speech there was a small, quiet break in his voice, a hitch of emotion. Then he bowed his head, and after a pause, the audience began to clap, applauding the compassionate, healing work of Tom and Janine Werner as the band began to play softly and Merv promised his viewers that he would be right back after a word from the people at Woolite. During the commercial, Merv was too busy having his makeup touched up to speak with the guests, but Steve leaned over and said to Tom, "That was beautiful, baby."

It was during Tom's speech on the *Merv Griffin Show* that it had first showed itself—the fact that the line between the fantasy of their work and the reality of it was beginning to fade for Tom. But Janine thought nothing of it at the time, thinking it was just the showman in Tom coming out unexpectedly at the perfect moment. That very week, they received calls from six other talk shows, four regional and two national, and they had to get an agent. Tom used variations of his speech on the other shows; it was never as emotional, but always convincing, and the only time Tom ever mentioned it to Janine was to say that it probably had something to do with the increase in their book sales.

What had once been just between them, their little secret, had become a full-time career. They went from haunted house to haunted house, sold book after book, appeared on one talk show after another, and Janine avoided touching strangers any more than was absolutely necessary. But she kept smiling, and she nodded sagely when people told her and Tom of the horrible things happening in their homes, and she tried not to pay any attention to Tom's little talk-show speech, which he later incorporated into their lectures, because she knew the only thing they were *really* helping people to do was to sweep their twisted secrets, their *real* problems, farther under the rug.

By 1970, business slowed way down. Apparently, people simply were not as interested in ghosts as they used to be. After all, with that party going on in Vietnam and with Nixon in the White House, scares were a penny a gross. But something happened that put their career back on its feet: *The Exorcist*. First the novel, then the movie. Then their phone began to ring at all hours with calls from parents who suspected their children were possessed by demons, from children who suspected their parents were possessed by demons, and from whole families being tormented by demons. Suddenly, ghosts were passé and Satan was the villain of the hour. That was when they had enlisted the help of their defrocked priest friend, Father Bill, who had his own flock of rebel followers who didn't care *what* the Vatican thought of him. Tom and Janine never asked Father Bill why he'd been defrocked, and he never offered the information. And Janine was careful never, ever to touch him, because she did not want to know. They were back in business, more popular than ever, and in the wake of *The Exorcist*, two of their books made the *New York Times* bestseller list, in both hardcover and paperback.

But nothing really changed. As far as Janine was concerned, they had simply recovered from a slump. Some of the words were different—

demons instead of ghosts, which needed to be exorcised instead of released—and Father Bill accompanied them on some of their trips, performing exorcisms, blessing houses. And Janine kept smiling, telling the families of the evil presences she sensed in their homes—but never what she *really* sensed, never what she *really* felt as she walked through their bedrooms and bathrooms and kitchens. She never told Tom, either, because she'd tried before and it hadn't worked, so she just followed the game plan, played by the rules.

Many of the people they dealt with really believed they were being tormented by demons. Some even experienced actual poltergeist activity generated by adolescents in the family (she'd done a great deal of reading on the subject). They were all Catholic and took comfort in their icons, and while exorcising their homes or children or spouses of the minions of Hell, the families often became emotional and wept copiously, and over the years a few people even fainted. But with the exception of that first experience in Walla Walla, what those people really wanted Tom and Janine to do was to put another big, case-hardened steel lock or two on the door behind which they hid their sins. While gathering fodder for their books and lectures and conversations with Merv Griffin and Mike Douglas, and later Jerry Springer and Montel Williams, Tom and Janine were performing a sort of reverse therapy for those families. It wasn't *real* therapy, because that was supposed to heal, to improve, and what they did was the exact opposite. Each family had a big, smelly elephant in the middle of the living room which they ignored, walked around and refused to look at—booze, drugs, beatings, incest, whatever—and Tom and Janine made them feel better by telling them that it wasn't an elephant at all, it was a *demon*, and it was bringing a piece of Hell to their lives through no fault of their own. Tom and Janine threw a Halloween fright wig on the elephant, went through some prayers, maybe had Father Bill sprinkle some holy water on the furniture, wave a cross a few times, say a few things in Latin, and they made the elephant easier for the family to ignore, and much, much harder for outsiders to see. But the elephant remained there between the sofa and the television, shitting and pissing and stinking up the place with foul odors that only the families could smell, and then only if they *let* themselves.

Janine often thought that, although they worked under the titles of "Paranormal Investigators" or "Demonologists" or whatever title might be appropriate at the time, they were really in the insurance business… and they specialized in Elephant Coverage….

DANTE'S

The Bellinger house was modest, simple, with a small yard and even a white picket fence. A few toys lay on the lawn. It was in the kind of old neighborhood in which the houses and yards were not identical to one another, a neighborhood once pristine but now rundown, with oaks and maples twisted and hunched with age, branches bare beneath the cloud-streaked autumn sky.

Jack Bellinger came out onto the porch as Tom and Janine walked up the front path, and greeted them with a weary half-smile as he led them inside. Tom carried a leather duffle bag slung over his right shoulder.

"The kids aren't here," Jack said, closing the door behind him. "Richie and Wendy are visiting friends, and J.J.... well, we told you about J.J. He's out. Somewhere."

Something was moving inside Janine. It had started the moment she walked through the door, as if her intestines were shifting, like a bucket of worms squirming over and around one another in a tight, writhing ball.

Della came into the small, tidy living room, drying her hands on a dishtowel. "We used to keep track of him all the time, but now, with the things that've been going on here... with him being so—"

"You don't have to explain," Tom said, holding up a hand. "We understand, really. Right, honey?"

"Of course we do," Janine said, forcing a smile.

Jack said, "Well, take off your coats, make yourselves comfortable, please."

As they did so, Jack asked, "Anything happen recently?"

"Not today," Della said.

"Have you noticed if things happen more often when the children are around?" Tom asked.

"Funny you should ask," Jack said. "We looked for that, seein' how it was Richie who first... noticed things. But no, things happen when they happen, whether the kids are around or not."

"I just finished brewing some coffee," Della said, slapping the towel over her shoulder. "Can I get you some?"

Tom and Janine both accepted as they seated themselves on the sofa, and told Della how they liked their coffee.

Jack moved toward a recliner, but remained standing, nervous. "I suppose you'll want a tour of the house, right?"

"Not exactly," Tom said. "Please, Jack, sit down, relax. We're not scientists. There's nothing formal about this. It's not like we're from

60 Minutes."

Jack eased into the recliner.

Tom continued: "The way we do things is like this. Before you take us through the house, Janine likes to go through the place by herself, from room to room. Alone, and without anybody telling her anything about the place."

Jack cocked his head, birdlike. "Really? Well, I mean, y'know, that's fine if that's the way you do… whatever you do. But… why?"

"For impressions," Tom answered. "Psychic impressions."

Jack blinked a few times, but said nothing.

"You knew Janine is psychic, didn't you?"

"Oh." Jack chuckled softly. "No, no, like I said, we never heard of you before. We don't know anything about you. Nothing at all, really. We contacted you because the voices told us to."

"Okay, yes, I understand *that*, but, but—"

Janine pressed her knee against Tom's to let him know he was sounding a bit too harsh.

Tom pressed his lips together tightly, smiled, nodded once, licked his lips, and continued in a softer, gentler voice. "What I mean is, you had to look us up, right? I mean, you had to find out something about us before you could contact us, right?"

"Oh, no. The voices gave us your address and phone number." Jack looked apologetic. "Didn't we tell you that over lunch? I thought we did."

Acidic nausea began to ooze between the squirming, viscous tubes inside Janine.

"No, see," Jack continued, "the voices gave us your address and phone number and at first, we didn't know what it meant, y'know? Finally, we called—well, *I* called the number. I figured you'd hang up on me 'cause I didn't know who I was callin'. But when you answered—" he nodded to Janine "—I asked if you were Janine Werner and you said yes, and I just started tellin' you what was happening. So, no, I'm sorry, I didn't know you're psychic, Janine."

Janine suddenly felt an overwhelming urge to scream at the top of her lungs as the flesh over her back rippled like the surface of a disturbed pond, but Della came in holding two mugs of coffee and placed them on the scuffed coffee table.

Della said, "If you want more cream or sugar, just let me know, and I'll fix it. Be right back."

She hurried out and Janine looked at Tom as he lifted his mug to his lips. His brow was etched with deep lightning-bolt lines, all pointing downward in the middle, and his eyes were squinting in that way they did whenever he was worried about something.

Was it finally hitting him? Was it starting to sink in that something was different here? That this was something new, something they'd never dealt with before?

Janine looked away from her husband, lifted her mug of coffee and took a sip, hoping it would quell with a great splash the furious activity going on inside her.

In a moment, Della returned with two more mugs. She handed one to Jack and took hers to the delicate-looking rocking chair that was separated from Jack's recliner by a round-topped wooden lamp-table with two coasters, where each of them placed their mugs.

"I guess I'm coming in on the middle of this, huh?" Della asked, smiling as wearily as Jack had earlier. "So… did I miss anything?"

No one responded for a long moment, and Janine began to get anxious, began to form a response in her mind, even opened her mouth and took a breath to speak. But Tom beat her to it.

Tom repeated what he'd just told Jack.

Della's eyebrows rose and her smile fell away as she turned to Janine. "You're a… a psychic? Really?"

Janine nodded as she took another sip of her coffee, although it was making no difference in her guts.

"Oh," Della said quietly. "I didn't know that. Well, we figured you'd want a tour of the place, okay? If that's how you do it, then go ahead and do it."

Tom turned to Janine and asked, "You feel anything yet, honey?"

Janine took another sip of coffee as thoughts spun and toppled in her mind, and all she could manage was: "I feel… discomfort. That's all. So far."

"All right, honey, well, why don't you just start on your little trip through the house. Take your coffee, if you want. I'll sit here and chat with Jack and Della. You come back and tell us your impressions. When you're ready. Okay, honey?"

Janine stood slowly, as she tried to ignore the wiggly feeling in her knees. She pushed the ends of her mouth up as she said, "Yes, why don't I do that. You three just sit here and talk. I'll be back shortly." And then she left the room, still wearing her stiff, plastic smile.

The fear was everywhere. It was in every room, in every inch of the narrow hall, even in the bathroom. Fear and tension everywhere. Tearing into her like the claws of small rodents. Into her mind, her heart, her flesh.

And something else, everywhere she went in the house, every room, every step. A thick, moist blackness. A diseased molasses. A cancerous syrup. Clinging invisibly to everything, to the furniture, the walls, making her feet stick to the floor, a nightmarish slop that dripped from every surface around her.

Evil. It was evil, that's what it was. It was everywhere and it made her shake so much that she began to spill her coffee, and she finally abandoned the mug on top of the old, battered washing machine in the laundry room, where she encountered the door to the basement. She knew where the door led the moment she laid eyes on it, and she stood there staring at it for the longest of times. The old brass knob made her hand tingle when she touched it, and the old wooden door seemed very heavy when she pulled it open. Beyond the doorway, narrow wooden stairs disappeared into utter blackness.

Janine leaned forward, turning her head to the right, looking for a light switch. It was there. She flipped it. All the steps appeared before her, and a floor, and walls.

Every molecule in her body resisted, but she took the first step. Then the second. And then she was on her way down the stairs, and she was on the concrete floor, and she saw the posters on the wall—a few rock groups, two sexy female TV stars, a couple of comic-book heroes—and the beds, two beds, one made, one not; and two nightstands and two dressers, none matching, cluttered with the things of boyhood, and something else, something, something—

—evil. It moved through every part of her body. It made her hair shift, made her cuticles itch, made her nipples shrivel into hard nubs. She turned around without hesitation and clasped the banister of the staircase with her right hand, ready to make her way back up quickly, when she heard the voice:

"Hello, Mrs. Werner. I'm so happy you could make it." The voice had a big smile in it.

Janine could not move. Her fingers clutched the wooden banister tightly, until her entire hand became numb. She had no control over her body. No matter how loudly her mind screamed at her body, nothing would move.

"We were beginning to think you would never show up," the voice said. It was a gentle voice, low and oh-so-well-modulated, like some radio announcer from a bygone era, a voice that did not fit into today, into now, perfectly smooth and friendly, so as to conceal the pustular, scabrous reality beneath it.

She couldn't even turn her head. That was all she had to do to see where the voice was coming from, just turn her head, although she knew—in her mind, she could *see*—where the voice was coming from, but she could not do it.

The voice continued: "This one isn't for the magazines, Mrs. Werner. Or the lectures. It's not for your talk-show appearances or your books. This one is just for *you*. For you and your husband."

Her hand trembled as she removed it from the banister.

"You seem troubled," the voice said quietly, pleasantly apologetic. "I'm very sorry about that, Mrs. Werner. You have no reason to be troubled right now. There is one thing, though. Your husband is not here. We need both of you to be here."

Her legs trembled beneath her, threatened to send her to the floor in a heap.

"And please do not take this personally, Mrs. Werner. We are simply following orders. We are following orders from… well, a higher office, so to speak."

Her feet managed to move haltingly over the concrete floor in such a way as to turn her body slowly to the right, toward the boys' bedroom, toward the beds and the nightstands and the dressers… and the voice.

"Like your husband and yourself," the voice said, "we are simply doing… what we do. This is our work. You have yours… we have ours. As far as we're concerned, you have been doing wonderful work, absolutely tremendous. For *our* cause. But there are others who… well, you've had some religious training, so… you understand how things work. We have a boss. But, unfortunately, our boss has to answer to Someone Else. That Someone Else… well, His orders are the ones we are now following. You understand, don't you?"

She tried to move faster, but her body seemed to be trapped underwater, and she turned slowly, so very slowly. But she did turn, and she saw him, the source of that voice, standing there between the beds, where he had not been just an eternal moment before, tall and thin in his black suit, spotted with dust and cobwebs, his white shirt beneath the suitcoat spotted with disgusting stains, hoary hands locked before him at the waist, a stick-like, vein-threaded neck seeming to barely hold up his head, which was bald except for a few yellow tufts of hair, with big ears sticking out on the sides and eyes swallowed so deeply in their sockets that they were little more than shadows as his paper-thin lips curled into a smile, nearly splitting his narrow, hollow-cheeked face in half as it revealed long, brown teeth that had no gums. She saw him, but she knew in her heart that he wasn't really there, that if Tom were there he would not be able to see the man, because the man had the substance of a shadow, a flat shape that could not be touched with human fingers, that was real even though it did not *quite* exist.

"Could you please call your husband?" the thing asked.

And Janine screamed. She stumbled backward until she slammed against the wall, screaming and screaming.

She heard movement upstairs, the hurried footsteps and the yammering voices. But the thing between the beds continued to smile at her, standing as if at attention, as if it were the maitre d' of a four-star restaurant greeting a customer, while the concrete floor began to open up. It opened as a mouth opens, dry lips spreading, clinging for a moment in spots, parting, yawning open silently to reveal a darkness that was darker than dark, a blackness that released a draft so cold that Janine felt her scalp shrink and her throat tighten. It was a darkness like no other, a darkness that lived and breathed and hungered.

There was a thunderous sound to Janine's left and she jerked her head to see Tom leading Jack and Della down the stairs, all three of them moving rapidly.

Janine held up a hand at them and forced a smile, trying to control her panic and fear. "No, wait. Just Tom. You two stay upstairs. Please." She wasn't in the mood for the explanations she would have to give them. "Everything's fine, we'll be up in a minute, you just go on, now."

When Jack and Della were gone, Janine's smile collapsed and Tom clutched her arms, speaking to her breathlessly. "Honey, what's wrong, what's the matter?"

She didn't look at Tom. She stared instead at the tall, bony man behind him and the gaping hole in the floor, at the pulsating blackness beneath it. She put her hands on Tom's chest and gasped, "We have to go, Tom. This is n-n-not like the others, not at all, we're in trouble, it's finally happened, everything we've ever done, it-it's all come back on us, Tom, we're—"

He shook her gently, his face dark with worry. "Sweetie, what's wrong, what're you talking about?"

She stopped talking and fought to catch her breath, closed her eyes a moment, then whispered, "Tom, I want you to… turn around very slowly… and tell me what you see."

He turned, but not slowly. His eyes scanned the room, passing right by the tall figure and never even glancing at the hole in the floor. When he looked at her again, his eyes were worried but he wore a gentle smile. "Did you see something? I mean, *really* see something down here?"

Janine watched as the cadaverous man tilted his head back slightly and chuckled.

"You don't see him at all, do you?" she asked, clutching at Tom's shirt.

He glanced over his shoulder one more time, then: "Are you feeling okay, honey? You wanna come back and do this later?"

Then the tall man across the room began to walk toward them, taking long, purposeful strides.

"We have to go, Tom, please, my God, we have to go!" She began tugging on his shirt as she moved toward the stairs, trying to drag him with her, but Tom put his hands on her shoulders and pressed her back against the wall.

"Janine, would you please tell me what's the matter?" he said, rather firmly.

As she watched the grinning figure walk over the large black hole as if it weren't there, her voice became high and ragged: "Tom, upstairs, go upstairs, we've got to go upstairs and get out!"

The man reached out a bony hand as he approached Tom from behind, long fingers curving slightly as he lowered it over Tom's shoulder, and Janine's voice became louder, more frantic, as the hand touched Tom's shoulder and sank into it, disappearing like vapor, and Tom's body stiffened suddenly. His mouth dropped open, eyes bugged, shoulders hunched, and both hands slapped over his massive chest.

"Oh God… oh God," he said, the words barely making it beyond his throat. And then he fell backward, passing through the grinning apparition and hitting the concrete floor with a horrible, thick sound. His chest heaved a couple of times, then he made a rattly gurgling sound… and he became still.

The tall man grinned gumlessly at Janine as she fell to her knees at Tom's side and screamed, "Oh my God, no, no! Tom! *Tom*!"

"Perhaps you should have tried to get him to eat right, maybe exercise," the man said with mock concern. "But then… you prefer not to get involved. Don't you, Janine?"

"Help! Jack, help, please!"

A moment later Jack clattered down the wooden stairs and didn't hesitate to kneel beside Tom and begin administering CPR.

Janine watched as Jack performed mouth-to-mouth, then pumped Tom's chest, back and forth between the two. Every inch of her body grew numb until she could no longer feel herself breathing, and for a moment, she thought she'd stopped. And all the while, standing a few inches away from Tom's head, looking down on it all, was that gaunt, smiling figure. Waiting. For something.

"It's not working," Jack said tremulously, face glistening with perspiration. Over his shoulder, he called, "Della? *Della*!" After a moment: "Dammit, she can't hear me. She was afraid, so she stepped outside. Look, Janine, I want you to stay right here. I'm going to call an ambulance and I'll be back in just a second."

Jack turned and rushed up the stairs noisily as Janine leaned over her husband. She knew the ambulance would never arrive in time, because it was already too late. There was no life left in the fleshy bulk on the floor. She reached down and placed a numb hand over his as her tears began to flow, and for that moment, brief as it was, she forgot all about the figure watching her, until:

"Janine."

She looked up slowly, not wanting to see that face again but unable to ignore that icy voice.

"I finally have the two of you together," he said. "It's time."

Sudden movement caught Janine's attention and she looked around the tall man to see hands. They were reaching up out of the impossibly black hole and grabbing hold of the edge, pulling, struggling. Then faces began to rise above the edge of the hole. Familiar faces. Horribly familiar.

The face that rose above the edge of the hole first was the most familiar, but Janine recognized all of them. They were all naked, the women and children… toddlers and teenagers… even a few wide-eyed little babies, pulling themselves up onto the floor with their tiny, pudgy hands.

It was that first girl—the one from Florida whose father had molested her for years until she went to her priest for help, only to receive the same treatment from him—who got to her feet before the others and looked directly into Janine's eyes.

They said nothing; they did not make a sound as they stood and moved forward, the babies crawling without so much as a whimper, and they were led by that girl from Florida, whose name Janine could not remember, but whose face—and whose pain—had haunted her for years.

Janine could not speak. She could only look silently and in horror from one face to another, faces she recognized from cases she and Tom had handled: women whose husbands had beaten them, children whose fathers had beaten them, or molested them; people who had buried their problems beneath tales of supernatural torment and demonic possession, stories of their children being beaten and sodomized by evil spirits and invisible demons.

They closed in slowly but steadily, with great purpose, the Florida girl stopping at Janine's side and staring down at her with an expressionless face while the others gathered around Tom. They leaned forward silently and clutched his arms and legs, his clothes, his head, and began to drag him toward the black, hungry hole. The only sound was that of Tom's body being moved over the concrete floor.

"No!" Janine finally blurted, standing suddenly. "What are you doing? Leave him alone!"

They ignored her and continued dragging her husband's corpse away from her.

"Wait! What are you doing? Where are you taking him?"

The tall, cadaverous man chuckled as he watched the silent, naked figures, then turned to her, his lips peeling back over his long teeth again. "Surely, Janine, you don't think we're only taking your husband, do you? You see, the higher-ups—and when I say that, I do mean *higher*, and I do mean *up*—have ordered us to take you both."

The women and children, even the babies, had reached the hole, and Tom's head hung limply backward over the edge as they continued pulling him, pulling, slowly tipping him into the blackness.

When Janine spoke, her voice was less than a whisper. It was all she could manage, as if she were in one of those smothering, paralyzing nightmares in which movement and speech are impossible. "What… are you talking… about?"

"Well, Janine, you must admit that you are not without guilt in this particular venture to which you and Tom have devoted your lives, am I correct?"

She felt sick, like she might throw up any second. "Please… no," she breathed.

"Not only have you been the driving force," the man went on in his bone-dry voice, "but you've been turning the other cheek like a good Christian, am I right? Yes, you've been turning that cheek… and with it, a blind eye. To all of it. That's why, unlike your husband, you aren't dead right now, Janine."

She watched helplessly as Tom's body slid into the hole, his feet tipping upward, then disappearing into the pulsing darkness.

The Florida girl took Janine's arm in her hand and tugged. Janine jerked her arm away, but the girl simply took it again, her face dead, completely without expression. She tugged on Janine's arm again, harder this time, as the others—the naked women and children and silent infants who had just thrown Tom into that gaping hole—turned and moved toward her, reaching out their hands for her, taking her hands, her arms and legs, tugging, pulling her toward the hole.

"You're not dead because we wanted to make sure you couldn't ignore this," the man said, "as you've ignored so many other things over the years."

"No," she breathed, over and over again, "no, please, no."

She did not have the strength to fight them, even though they were not forceful. She was simply drained of any resistance. And in a moment, she stood at the edge of that hole, staring down into its endless darkness, and then—

—she was plunging downward with their hands on her, holding her arms, her legs, dragging her down as they tilted and spun through the blackness, spinning, spinning.

Janine wanted to scream, but she could not get the scream outside of her body; it went no farther than her gut, no farther than the inside of her head, where it went on and on and on.

She saw the hole above her as she fell away from it, glimpsed the basement ceiling through it, as it closed like a mouth at the end of a yawn.

And the hands did not let go, big hands, small hands, tiny hands, and she looked to her right to see the Florida girl, still expressionless. But the others… the others…

The women and children were gone. They were no longer even human. Their leathery faces grinned at her around needle-like fangs, and their batlike wings flapped softly as they dragged her down, farther and farther down, into a darkness that became steadily colder, until it was so cold that Janine feared that breathing the air would freeze her lungs and make them break like ice.

She tried to scream, but her voice was gone, as was any strength that had remained in her a moment before.

Farther and farther down….

"I'm telling you, they were here, right *here*, just a few *minutes* ago!"

"Well, they're not here now," the paramedic said to Jack, flatly. He looked angry.

"But they couldn't have *gone* anywhere!"

The second paramedic said, "Look, buddy, do you know how much trouble you can get into for making a call like this? On false pretenses?"

"It wasn't on false pretenses!" Jack insisted, frustrated. "The guy was lying on the floor, *dead*! I tried CPR, but it didn't work!"

"Maybe he got up and went to the hospital himself," the first paramedic said sarcastically.

Jack was too angry to respond.

The two paramedics started back up the stairs.

"Maybe," the second one said, "they were ghosts."

From that moment on, the Bellingers experienced no further supernatural activity in their house, and after a time, they never brought it up again.

— *For Cheri Scotch*

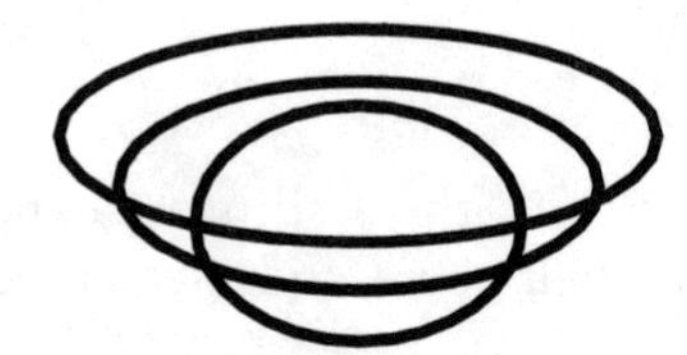

Elegy for a Maestro

by Alexandra Elizabeth Honigsberg

O star that burned so bright and lit the night
with thy dark'ning power, where art thou now
as we lie barr'n, bereft of hope and flight?

Thy staff, once magic's fount, alive somehow,
now dormant sits, awaits some other's call,
as we watch, suff'ring, to revive it now.

The pulsing crowds who flocked to fill thy halls
all clamour for the feats of other gods,
or sigh to thy songs' echoes 'neath stone walls.

Disciples who did lately bow, applaud,
dig corpses 'mongst thy lifetime's legacies
to lay before their massed and hungry hordes.

And thus their empty, fickle fantasies
hunt other pleasures, greater poisons, pains,
whilst thy life's light smashed ego's fallacies.

We touched thy fire's endless, perfect reign,
transformed, ablaze, fancied ourselves angels
but scattered, fallen on the sun-scorched plain.

Thy blinding brilliance, midwife to a spell
which resurrected other masters' songs,
condemned faint-hearted creations to Hell.

Perfection and debauchery our throng
did embrace, judgment Art's alone to make,
'til Fate did fell thee with Death's mighty gong.

Yet standing still, no dream, pow'r to forsake,
thou didst hold, defiant, unto the last,
beyond the gnawing of thy soul to slake.

And birthed a world, the greatest spell to cast,
dispersed the darkness, composed life's anthem,
so we, thy children, hold it fast.

Above It All

by Robert J. Sawyer

Rhymes with fear.

The words echoed in Colonel Paul Rackham's head as he floated in *Discovery*'s airlock, the bulky Manned Maneuvering Unit clamped to his back. Air was being pumped out; cold vacuum was forming around him.

Rhymes with fear.

He should have said no, should have let McGovern or one of the others take the spacewalk instead. But Houston had suggested that Rackham do it, and to demur he'd have needed to state a reason.

Just a dead body, he told himself. Nothing to be afraid of.

There was a time when a military man couldn't have avoided seeing death—but Rackham had just been finishing high school during Desert Storm. Sure, as a test pilot, he'd watched colleagues die in crashes, but he'd never actually seen the bodies. And when his mother passed on, she'd had a closed casket. His choice, that, made without hesitation the moment the funeral director had asked him—his father, still in a nursing home, had been in no condition to make the arrangements.

Rackham was wearing liquid-cooling long johns beneath his spacesuit, tubes circulating water around him to remove excess body heat. He shuddered, and the tubes moved in unison, like a hundred serpents writhing.

He checked the barometer, saw that the lock's pressure had dropped below 0.2 psi—just a trace of atmosphere left. He closed his eyes for a moment, trying to calm himself, then reached out a gloved hand and turned the actuator that opened the outer circular hatch. "I'm leaving the airlock," he said. He was wearing the standard "Snoopy Ears" communications carrier, which covered most of his head beneath the space helmet. Two thin microphones protruded in front of his mouth.

"Copy that, Paul," said McGovern, up in the shuttle's cockpit. "Good luck."

Rackham pushed the left MMU armrest control forward. Puffs of nitrogen propelled him out into the cargo bay. The long space doors that normally formed the bay's roof were already open, and overhead he saw Earth in all its blue-and-white glory. He adjusted his pitch with his right hand control, then began rising up. As soon as he'd cleared the top of the cargo bay, the Russian space station *Mir* was visible, hanging a hundred meters away, a giant metal crucifix. Rackham brought his hand up to cross himself.

"I have *Mir* in sight," he said, fighting to keep his voice calm. "I'm going over."

Rackham remembered when the station had gone up, twenty years ago, in 1986. He first saw its name in his hometown newspaper, the Omaha *World Herald*. *Mir*, the Russian word for peace—as if peace had had anything to do with its being built. Reagan had been hemorrhaging money into the Strategic Defense Initiative back then. If the Cold War had turned hot, the high ground would be in orbit.

Even then, even in grade eight, Rackham had been dying to go into space. No price was too much. "Whatever it takes," he'd told Dave—his sometimes friend, sometimes rival—over lunch. "One of these days, I'll be floating right by that damned *Mir*. Give the Russians the finger." He'd pronounced *Mir* as if it rhymed with *sir*.

Dave had looked at him for a moment, as if he were crazy. Then, dismissing all of it except the way Paul had spoken, he smiled a patronizing smile and said, "It's *meer*, actually. Rhymes with fear."

Rhymes with fear.

Paul's gaze was still fixed on the giant cross, spikes of sunlight glinting off it. He shut his eyes and let the nitrogen exhaust push against the small of his back, propelling him into the darkness.

"I've got a scalpel," said the voice over the speaker at mission control in Kaliningrad. "I'm going to do it."

Flight controller Dimitri Kovalevsky leaned into his mike. "You're making a mistake, Yuri. You don't want to go through with this." He glanced at the two large wall monitors. The one showing *Mir*'s orbital plot was normal; the other, which usually showed the view inside the space station, was black. "Why don't you turn on your cameras and let us see you?"

The speaker crackled with static. "You know as well as I do that the cameras can't be turned off. That's our way, isn't it? Still—even after the reforms—cameras with no off switches."

"He's probably put bags or gloves over the lenses," said Metchnikoff, the engineer seated at the console next to Kovalevsky's.

"It's not worth it, Yuri," said Kovalevsky into the mike, while nodding acknowledgement at Metchnikoff. "You want to come on home? Climb into the *Soyuz* and come on down. I've got a team here working on the re-entry parameters."

"*Nyet*," said Yuri. "It won't let me leave."

"What won't let you leave?"

"I've got a knife," repeated Yuri, ignoring Kovalevsky's question. "I'm going to do it."

Kovalevsky slammed the mike's off switch. "Dammit, I'm no expert on this. Where's that bloody psychologist?"

"She's on her way," said Pasternak, the scrawny orbital-dynamics officer. "Another fifteen minutes, tops."

Kovalevsky opened the mike again. "Yuri, are you still there?"

No response.

"Yuri?"

"They took the food," said the voice over the radio, sounding even farther away than he really was, "right out of my mouth."

Kovalevsky exhaled noisily. It had been an international embarrassment the first time it had happened. Back in 1994, an unmanned *Progress* rocket had been launched to bring food up to the two cosmonauts then aboard *Mir*. But when it docked with the station, those cosmonauts had found its cargo hold empty—looted by ground-support technicians desperate to feed their own starving families. The same thing had happened again just a few weeks ago. This time the thieves had been even more clever—they'd replaced the stolen food with sacks full of dirt to avoid any difference in the rocket's pre-launch weight.

"We got food to you eventually," said Kovalevsky.

"Oh, yes," said Yuri. "We reached in, grabbed the food back—just like we always do."

"I know things haven't been going well," said Kovalevsky, "but—"

"I'm all alone up here," said Yuri. He was quiet for a time, but then he lowered his voice conspiratorially. "Except I discover I'm not alone."

Kovalevsky tried to dissuade the cosmonaut from his delusion. "That's right, Yuri—we're here. We're always here for you. Look down, and you'll see us."

"No," said Yuri. "No—I've done enough of that. It's time. I'm going to do it."

Kovalevsky covered the mike and spoke desperately. "What do I say to him? Suggestions? Anyone? Dammit, what do I say?"

"I'm doing it," said Yuri's voice. There was a grunting sound. "A stream of red globules... floating in the air. Red—that was our color, wasn't it? What did the Americans call us? The Red Menace. Better dead than Red.... But they're no better, really. They wanted it just as badly."

Kovalevsky leaned forward. "Apply pressure to the cut, Yuri. We can still save you. *Come on, Yuri*—you don't want to die! Yuri!"

Up ahead, *Mir* was growing to fill Rackham's view. The vertical shaft of the crucifix consisted of the *Soyuz* that had brought Yuri to the space station sixteen months ago, the multiport docking adapter, the core habitat and the Kvant-1 science module, with a green *Progress* cargo transport docked to its aft end.

The two arms of the cross stuck out of the docking adapter. To the left was the Kvant-2 biological research center, which contained the EVA airlock through which Rackham would enter. To the right was the Kristall space-production lab. Kristall had a docking port that a properly equipped American shuttle could hook up to—but *Discovery* wasn't properly equipped; the *Mir* adapter collar was housed aboard *Atlantis*, which wasn't scheduled to fly again for three months.

Rackham's heart continued to race. He wanted to swing around, return to the shuttle. Perhaps he could claim nausea. That was reason enough to abort an EVA; vomiting into a space helmet in zero-g was a sure way to choke to death.

But he couldn't go back. He'd fought to get up here, clawed, competed, cheated, left his parents behind in that nursing home. He'd never married, never had kids, never found time for anything but *this*. He couldn't turn around—not now, not here.

Rackham had to fly around to the Kvant-2's backside to reach the EVA hatch. Doing so gave him a clear view of *Discovery*. He saw it from the rear, its three large and two small engine cones looking back at him like a spider's cluster of eyes.

He cycled through the space station's airlock. The main lights were dark inside the biology module, but some violet-white fluorescents were on over a bed of plants. Shoots were growing in strange, circular patterns in the microgravity. Rackham disengaged the Manned Maneuvering Unit and left it floating near the airlock, like a small refrigerator with arms. Just as the Russians had promised, a large pressure bag was clipped to the wall next to Yuri's own empty spacesuit. Rackham wouldn't be able to get the body, now undoubtedly stiff with rigor mortis, into the suit, but it would fit easily into the pressure bag, used for emergency equipment transfers.

Mir's interior was like everything in the Russian space program—rough, metallic, ramshackle, looking more like a Victorian steamworks than space-age technology. Heart thundering in his ears, he pushed his way down Kvant-2's long axis toward the central docking adapter to which all the other parts of the station were attached.

Countless small objects floated around the cabin. He reached out with his gloved hand and swept a few up in his palm. They were six or seven millimeters across and wrinkled like dried peas. But their color was a dark rusty brown.

Droplets of dried blood. *Jesus Christ*. Rackham let go of them, but they continued to float in midair in front of him. He used the back of his glove to flick them away, and continued on deeper into the station.

"*Discovery*, this is Houston."

"Rackham here, Houston. Go ahead."

"We—ah—have an errand for you to run."

Rackham chuckled. "Your wish is our command, Houston."

"We've had a request from the Russians. They, ah, ask that you swing by *Mir* for a pickup."

Rackham turned to his right and looked at McGovern, the pilot. McGovern was already consulting a computer display. He gave Rackham a thumbs-up signal.

"Can do," said Rackham into his mike. "What sort of pickup?"

"It's a body."

"Say again, Houston."

"A body. A dead body."

"My God. Was there an accident?"

"No accident, *Discovery*. Yuri Vereshchagin has killed himself."

"Killed..."

"That's right. The Russians can't afford to send another manned mission up to get him." A pause. "Yuri was one of us. Let's bring him back where he belongs."

Rackham squeezed through the docking adapter and made a right turn, heading down into *Mir*'s core habitat. It was dark except for a few glowing LEDs, a shaft of earthlight coming in through one window, and one of sunlight coming in through the other. Rackham found the light switch, and turned it on. The interior lit up, revealing cylindrical beige walls. Looking down the module's thirteen-meter length, he could see the main control console with two strap-in chairs in front of it, storage lockers, the exercise bicycle, the dining table, the closet-like sleeping compartments, and, at the far end, the round door leading into Kvant-1, where Yuri's body was supposedly floating.

He pushed off the wall and headed down the chamber. It widened out near the eating table. He noticed that the ceiling there had writing on it. Rackham looked at the cameras, one fore, one aft, both covered over with spacesuit gloves, and realized that, even if they were uncovered, that part of the ceiling was perpetually out of their view. Each person who had visited the station had apparently written his or her name there in bold Magic Marker strokes: Romanenko, Leveykin, Viktorenko, Krikalev, dozens more. Foreign astronauts names' appeared, too, in Chinese characters, and Arabic, and English.

But Yuri Vereshchagin's name was nowhere to be seen. Perhaps the custom was to sign off just before leaving the station. Rackham easily found the Magic Marker, held in place on the bulkhead with Velcro. His Cyrillic wasn't very good—he had to copy certain letters carefully from the samples already on the walls—but he soon had Vereshchagin's name printed neatly across the ceiling.

Rackham thought about writing his own name, too. He touched the marker to the curving metal, but stopped, pulling the pen back, leaving only a black dot where it had made contact. Vereshchagin's name *should* be here—a reminder that he had existed. Rackham remembered all the old photographs that came to light after the fall of the Soviet Union: the original versions, before those who had fallen out of favor had been airbrushed out. Surely no cosmonaut would ever remove Vereshchagin's name, but there was no need to remind those who might come later that an American had stopped by to bring his body home.

The dried spheres of blood were more numerous in here. They bounced off Rackham's faceplate with little pinging sounds as he continued down the core module through the circular hatch into Kvant-1.

Yuri's body was indeed there, floating in a semi-fetal position. His skin was as white as candle wax, bled dry. He'd obviously rotated slowly as his opened wrist had emptied out—there was a ring of dark-brown blood stains all around the circumference of the science module. Many pieces of equipment also had blood splatters on them where drops had impacted before they'd desiccated. Rackham could taste his lunch at the back of his throat. He desperately fought it down.

And yet he couldn't take his eyes off Yuri. A corpse, a body without a soul in it. It was mesmerizing, terrifying, revolting. The very face of death.

He'd met Yuri once, in passing, years ago at an IAU conference in Montreal. Rackham had never known anyone before who had committed suicide. How could Yuri have killed himself? Sure, his country was in ruins. But billions of—of rubles had been spent building this station and getting him up here. Didn't he understand how special that made him? How, quite literally, he was above it all?

As he drifted closer, Rackham saw that Yuri's eyes were open. The pupils were dilated to their maximum extent, and a pale gray film had spread over the orbs. Rackham thought that the decent thing to do would be to reach over and close the eyes. His gloves had textured rubber fingertips, to allow as much feedback as possible without compromising his suit's thermal insulation, but even if he could work up the nerve, he didn't trust them for something as delicate as moving eyelids.

His breathing was growing calmer. He was facing death—facing it directly. He regretted now not having seen his mother one last time, and—

There was something here. Something else, inside Kvant-1 with him. He grabbed hold of a projection from the bulkhead and wheeled around. He couldn't see it. Couldn't hear any sound conducted through the helmet of his suit. But he felt its presence, knew it was there.

There was no way to get out; Kvant-1's rear docking port was blocked by the *Progress* ferry, and the exit to the core module was blocked by the invisible presence.

Get a grip on yourself, Rackham thought. *There's nothing here*. But there was. He could feel it. "What do you want?" he said, a quaver in his tones.

"Say again, Paul." McGovern's voice, over the headset.

Rackham reached down, switched his suit radio from VOX to OFF. "What do you want?" he said again.

There was no answer. He waved his arms, batting around hundreds of dried drops of blood. They flew all over the cabin—except for an area, up ahead, the size of a man. In that area, they deflected before reaching the walls. Something *was* there—something unseen. Paul's stomach contracted. He felt panic about to overtake him, when—

A hand on his shoulder, barely detectable through the bulky suit.

His heart jumped, and he swung around. He'd been floating backward, moving away from the unseen presence, and had bumped into the corpse. He stopped dead—revolted by the prospect of touching the body again, terrified of moving in the other direction toward whatever was up ahead.

But he had to get out—somebody else could come back for Yuri. He'd find some way to explain it all later, but for now he had to escape. He grabbed hold of a handle on the wall and pushed off the bulkhead, trying to fly past the presence up ahead. He made it through into the core module. But something cold as space reached out and stopped him directly in front of the small window that looked down on the planet.

Look below, said a voice in Rackham's head. *What do you see?*

He looked outside, saw the planet of his birth. "Africa."

Millions of children starving to death.

Rackham moved his head left and right. "Not my fault."

The view changed, faster than any orbital mechanics would allow. *Look below,* said the voice again. *What do you see?*

"China."

A billion people living without freedom.

"Nothing I can do."

Again, the world spun. *Look below.*

"The west coast of America. There's San Francisco."

The plague is everywhere, but nowhere is it worse than there.

"Someday they'll find a cure."

What else do you see?

"Los Angeles."

The inner city. Slums. Poverty. They haven't abandoned hope, those who live there.... Hope has abandoned them.

"They can get out. They just need help."

Whose help? Where will the money come from?

"I don't know."

Don't you? Look below.

"No."

Look. Your eyes have been closed too long. Open them. What do you see?

"Russia. Ah, now—Russia! Free! We defeated the Evil Empire. We defeated the Communist menace."

The people are starving.

"But they're free."

They have nothing to eat. Twice now they've taken food destined for this station.

"I read about that. Terrible, unthinkable. Like committing murder."

To take food from the mouths of the hungry. It is like committing murder, isn't it?

"Yes. No. No, wait—that's not what I meant."

Isn't it? The people need food.

"No. The space program provides jobs. And don't forget the spinoffs—advanced plastics and pharmaceuticals and… and…"

Microwave ovens.

"Yes, and—"

And dehydrated ice cream.

"No, important stuff. Medical equipment. And all kinds of new electronic devices."

That's why you go into space, then? To make life better on Earth?

"Yes. Yes. Exactly."

Look below.

"No. No, dammit, I won't."

Yuri looked below.

"Yuri was a cosmonaut—a Russian. Maybe—maybe Russia shouldn't be spending all this money on space. But I'm an American. My country is rich."

Los Angeles, said the voice that wasn't a voice. *San Francisco. And don't forget New York. Slums, plague, a populace at war with itself.*

Rackham felt his gloved fists clenching. He ground his teeth. "Damn you!"

Or you.

He closed his eyes, tried to think. Any price, he'd said—and now it was time to pay. For the good of everyone, he'd said—but the road was always paved with good intentions.

Starvation. Enslavement. Poverty. War.

He couldn't go back to *Discovery*—he had no choice in the matter. It wouldn't let him leave. But he'd be damned if he'd end up like Yuri, bait for yet another spacefarer.

He slipped into the control station just below the entrance portal that led from the docking adapter. He looked at the cameras fore and aft, the bulky white gloves covering them like beckoning hands. An ending, yes—and with the coffin closed. He scanned the controls, consulted the onboard computer, made his preparations. He couldn't see the entity, couldn't see its grin—but he knew they both were there.

"—in the hell, Paul?" McGovern's voice, as Rackham turned his suit radio back on. "Why are you firing the ACS jets?"

"It—it must be a malfunction," Rackham said, his finger still firmly on the red activation switch.

"Then get out of there. Get out before the delta-V gets too high. We can still pick you up if you get out now."

"I can't get out," said Rackham. "The—the way to the EVA airlock is blocked."

"Then get into the *Soyuz* and cast off. God's sake, man, you're accelerating down toward the atmosphere."

"I—I don't know how to fly a *Soyuz*."

"We'll get Kaliningrad to talk you through the separation sequence."

"No—no, that won't work."

"Sure it will. We can bring the *Soyuz* descent capsule into our cargo bay, if need be—but hurry, man, hurry!"

"Goodbye, Charlie."

"What do you mean, goodbye? Jesus Christ, Paul—"

Rackham's brow was slick with sweat. "Goodbye."

The temperature continued to rise. Rackham reached down and undogged his helmet, the abrupt increase in air pressure hurting his ears. He lifted the great fishbowl off his head, letting it fly across the cabin. He then took off the Snoopy-eared headset array. It undulated up and away, a fabric bat in the shaft of earthlight, ending up pinned by acceleration to the ceiling.

Paint started peeling off the walls, and the plastic piping had a soft, unfocused look to it. The air was so hot it hurt to breathe. Yuri's body was heating up, too. The smell from that direction was overpowering.

Rackham was close to one of the circular windows. Earth had swollen hugely beneath him. He couldn't make out the geography for all the clouds—was that China or Africa, America or Russia below? It was all a blur. And all the same.

An orange glow began licking at the port as paint on the station's hull burned up in the mesosphere. The water in the reticulum of tubes running over his body soon began to boil.

Flames were everywhere now. Atmospheric turbulence was tearing the station apart. The winglike solar panels flapped away, crisping into nothingness. Rackham felt his own flesh blistering.

The roar from outside the station was like a billion screams. Screams of the starving. Screams of the poor. Screams of the shackled. Through the port, he saw the Kristall module sheer cleanly off the docking adapter and go tumbling away.

Look below, the voice had said. *Look below.*

And he had.

Into space, at any price.

Into space—above it all.

The station disintegrated around him, metal shimmering and tearing away. Soon nothing was left except the flames. And they never stopped.

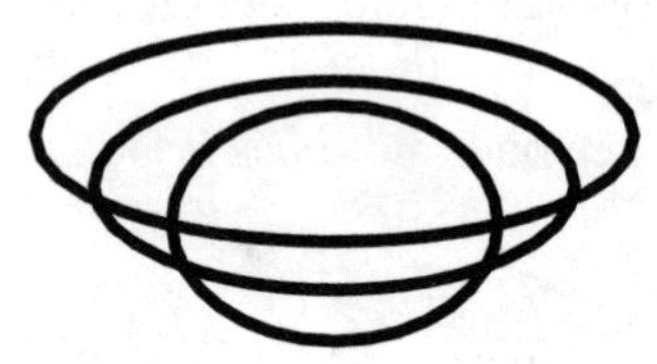

DANTE'S

THE BURDENS

by Steve Rasnic Tem

"Stiffen your back; then it won't hurt so much."

His father used to say that before giving him a whipping, one of the vicious ones, with the leather beltstrap flying all over buttocks and thighs and back like frantic, heavy wings. As the beating proceeded, he would be aware mostly of the wings, and imagine a great prehistoric bird attacking him, sinking its beak into the flesh covering his spine, attempting—in fact—to eat him. Later it would occur to him that that was a special thing—they called it a "vision" in the Bible, and he imagined that the vision gave him an extra strength that ordinary people didn't have. It made him special. He could bear more than most.

In the Bible people had visions of heaven and visions of hell. He had both, but he couldn't always tell the difference between the two.

"Stiffen your back; then it won't hurt so much."

Those words, repeated again and again before the whipping—strange how his father always said them so gently, so softly, and with what seemed to be such regret. The strange thing was he never could decide if that was good advice or not, if it really made it hurt less or if it was a trick his father played on him, actually designed to increase the pain. Or maybe his father had been trying to teach him a particular sort of posture to take toward circumstances: the stiffened back, the spine that refused to be bent, much less broken. Those words were still the most gentle words his father ever said to him. But with all that regret, his father never softened the blows, never held back. His father saw those blows as his duty, his burden.

And now, each night in bed, the words came back to him, soft and insinuating. Now that he had his own family.

He couldn't see well in the darkened bedroom, and he found it difficult to reach his arms out to touch Linda on her half of the bed. His head was too heavy. His arms were pressed so firmly into the mattress he could not lift them. Some nights he thought he might smother. Some nights he thought he might die without the comfort of his wife's embrace.

Embraces. Difficult for him even during the daylight hours, with his back so stiff, his torso so rigid. There was imagined pain when he forced himself to bend his arms for an embrace. Such strong arms, too, in most other ways. By day they moved pianos, sofas, credenzas, entire bedroom suites from warehouse or showroom to various homes in the metropolitan area. He'd been at it a long time. Had to keep at it, with the kids growing up so fast, eating so much. He didn't understand how you kept a family going—he didn't like to think about it. If you thought too much about it you couldn't do it. Like swimming—if you really thought about how you were doing it, you might sink. He just kept working, moving the heavy loads with back and two good arms, and they kept giving him the money.

He was sure that his wife knew better, but he never could bring himself to talk to her about it.

Two good, strong arms. Just like his father—he remembered the old man as all back and arms. Enormous back and enormous arms. He could live by those alone. Well-equipped for any burden.

The ticking of the clock was muffled, his ears were pressed so firmly into mattress and pillow. Earlier in the evening his hearing was always much more acute, but as the hours ticked on the old gravity took over, and he slowly began to sink into his own bed, as into a sensory-deprivation chamber. He wished he couldn't hear the clock at all. The muffled ticking was a constant reminder of his burden.

Two good arms. Stiffen the back. You can carry a real load then, boy, a helluva load.

As he got older, the stiffness in his back had become much more pronounced. He was particularly aware of it when he was just walking, not trying to carry anything. The back was like a board—it made the hips feel much too loose, the legs irritating the joints when he moved. He'd want his entire body to stiffen, to become immobile. Then maybe the pain would go away.

The dark shifted on his shoulders; a shadow leaned out over his head, as if to try to see the expression on his face, see how he was handling the weight. The heaviness settled over his back, increasing, and he had to stiffen it, stiffen it real good this time because he could feel the back muscles protesting, squirming on his thin frame. His father always said he was built too small to do most kinds of work.

The back stiffened, and the muscles stilled. He could feel the dark hanging over him, pushing him farther into the bed. He tried once again to lift an arm and reach out for Linda, but the arm would not budge. It adhered resolutely to the mattress, as if it were finally lost to him.

He never dreamed anymore. All his thoughts had been drawn up into the darkness overhead.

Sometimes—when he didn't fight it, when the back stiffened as if of its own accord and there was no pain to speak of because of that—sometimes his rigidity during the long nights was actually enjoyable. As if he were a bridge over a dark stream. He could hear, or imagined that he could hear, every sound along the stream beneath his span, even the flies threading the cattails, and nearby, his wife's blood pumping slowly into secret places. Traveling from an island downstream, the sound of his two children dreaming of their futures echoed against his brick.

And his vision at those times—he could see dark animals at the banks, and black flowers with gigantic blooms. He saw things which might have been demons, or angels, if there was a difference. He wasn't sure. The fish leapt greedily beneath his shadow, snapping at the flies crawling across his belly.

His back spasmed; the muscles writhed as if trying to escape his shoulder blades. It had never been this bad before. He could sense the dark shadows leaning forward and back, trying to catch him by surprise, making it almost impossible for his back to adjust to the enormous, shifting weight. Like wings flapping, pounding, attempting to take off into the night with him.

He sank farther into the mattress, and was suddenly afraid he would no longer be able to breathe. The weight put a claw into his heart, and he began to choke.

Panicked, he began to push upward. Using those two good arms. The back began to rock, the muscles to split before he knew what was happening. He thought of the bird and its scratching as the shadowy things began to scatter out of his flesh. For the first time he could turn his face to look up into the dark.

To see his wife staring down at him, her feet well-planted in his flesh, her eyes widening as she realized what was happening. His two children clutched her, and above them was his father, and his grandfather, his great-grandfather and all the other tired, frightened faces, too numerous to count.

They were too exhausted to scream when the entire structure toppled. But just before his ears stopped working, he could hear them, and himself, weeping.

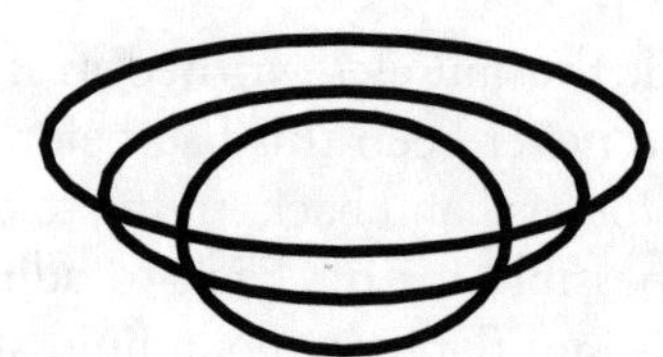

DANTE'S

A Taste of Heaven

by James Lovegrove

Mephistophilis:

Think'st thou that I that saw the face of God
And tasted the eternal joys of heaven,
Am not tormented with ten thousand hells
In being deprived of everlasting bliss?

—Marlowe, *The Tragical History of Doctor Faustus*

Harold hadn't been down to the shelter for several weeks. I asked about him, asked anyone that I knew to be a friend of his if they'd seen him, and got only shaken heads and frowns in reply. "Think he might've gone up north," was one suggestion, but I knew Harold: With winter approaching, the last direction he would be heading in was northward. London, for all its faults, at least had the advantage of being a few degrees warmer than Manchester or Newcastle, and once winter set in Harold stayed here usually until the first buds appeared on the trees. More to the point, he never left the city for long. A week or two, three at the most, and then, his wanderlust satisfied, his footsteps would turn toward the capital again, London a Saturn whose heavy gravitational pull he could not escape.

No, there was definitely something wrong, and once I had begun to fear the worst, every little symptom of poor health that Harold had exhibited the last time I'd seen him took on a new and sinister significance. That cough of his—it had been getting worse, hadn't it? Had been turning bronchial, definitely. And the sore on his forehead—just a lesion? Or a sarcoma? God, I'd lost count of the number of times I'd heard about one of the shelter regulars turning his or her toes up overnight, for no reason other than that the unending hardships of the vagrant lifestyle had finally taken their toll. Harold had been in no worse shape than most of them, but that didn't mean he couldn't still be lying undiscovered beneath a shambles of newsprint in an alley somewhere, clenched in a fetal knot of death.

I missed him, and though I didn't give up hope that he might still be alive, quietly, privately, I began to mourn him. Of all the strange and mad and sad and extraordinary human beings who passed through the doors of the shelter, Harold was perhaps the most remarkable. In his time, before answering the call of the road, he had been a fireman, a trawlerman, a professor of linguistics at a minor provincial university, war correspondent for a French magazine and campaign manager for a Colombian presidential candidate; he had worked as a missionary in Zaire and also enjoyed a career as a petty criminal back here at home; he had fitted curtains, carpets and men's suits, had sold double-glazing, life insurance and Jesus door-to-door, and had earned an Olympic Bronze for pistol-shooting, a gold disc for a song he co-wrote that was made popular by Marti Wilde in the sixties, and the respect of a number of peers of the realm for his sound advice on the preservation of British wetlands (his suggestions had led to a bill being passed in Parliament). And these were just the achievements I knew about. Harold darkly hinted that there were more, and that he had done some things so shady, so hush-hush, that if he told me what they were he would have to kill me. He said that he had run errands for people so nebulously important and powerful that even politicians in the highest echelons of government didn't know they existed, and that his eyes had passed over official documents the contents of which were so alarming they would have turned my hair white. He said this in that calm, cultured voice of his that only served to reinforce the impression that he was truly *au fait* with the secret workings of the world, the unseen cogs that turned the hands on the clockface of everything that ordinary people perceived.

He was, of course, lying his arse off. Everybody knew that. Even I, who have the word "gullible" stamped across my forehead, had ceased to believe anything Harold told me after the first couple of fables I had fallen for. Harold lived to lie. It was his craft, his art, his true vocation. He did not do it idly or maliciously, to start gossip or spread a rumor or destroy a reputation. He lied the way you or I might collect records or read books. It was his recreation. It took him out of himself. It cleared his head of mind-junk, spring-cleaned the attics of his brain. It was a diversion, an entertainment, a stage act. Harold didn't expect anyone to believe his stories, but he told them anyway, and out of politeness or admiration or a weird kind of gratitude no one turned around to him and said, "Shut your mouth, Harold, I can't breathe for the stink." Once you'd been seduced by a tale of his—and Harold was always careful to hook a new listener with one of his more plausible lines—you couldn't help but admire the eloquence and unselfconscious audacity with which he wove his webs of untruth, and wonder at the lengths he would go to in order to keep you, and himself, amused. Nothing in Harold's imaginary world could be proved. Nothing, equally, could be disproved, so it was foolish to try to reason or argue with him. Any objection would only be met with a bigger lie, and if you persisted in protesting, claiming that what he was telling you contradicted another story he had told you earlier or else was blatantly impossible, his tales would just grow taller and taller and taller until he had built a wall of mendacity so high it could not be scaled, and you gave up exhausted. Resistance was futile. It was easier simply to accept what Harold said at face value and, if you were in the mood, perhaps let drop a well-chosen question that would encourage him to yet more outrageous flights of fancy. And maybe, just maybe, if you got lucky, this lifelong liar might trip himself up and accidentally find himself telling the truth. You never know.

I've always thought that Harold would have made a fine novelist or playwright. He had the vocabulary for it, the skill with language. He spoke the way most people write, in well-formed, thought-through sentences, which made it all the more logical for me to suggest, as I did once, that he set the story of his life down on paper (by which I meant compose a work of fiction). Harold's reply was uncharacteristically straightforward and self-effacing: "What would be the point, Mark? If I wrote it down, who would believe it?"

And now he was gone, or so it seemed. As the days shortened and the trees shed and the sky turned hazy like a cataracted eye, and still Harold did not show, the hope that I had been nurturing like the last ember in a grate gradually dwindled and cooled. Every evening, having left the office and arrived at the shelter in time to help with the dinner shift, I would walk slowly along the rows of tables, checking each bearded face I saw, smiling if its owner caught my eye and offered a greeting, but smiling without any joy or conviction. And then, as I served out food to the shuffling, murmuring queue, each face would come under scrutiny again. Harold might, after all, have shaved his beard. He might have got rid of—far more likely, lost—the battered, greasy homburg that never left his head, even on hot days. He might even have had to part company with his army-surplus greatcoat. But however he looked, I would have recognized him instantly had he shambled up to me, plate outstretched, to receive his helping of mashed potato. You do not easily forget the face of a friend.

Finally, I became so concerned that I called the police, though I knew they would tell me that there was about as much chance of tracking down a missing vagrant as there was of finding a lost sock at a launderette. Which they did, albeit somewhat more tactfully. I gave them a description of Harold and a list of his known haunts, and was assured that an eye would be kept out for him. This was the best I could hope for, but it didn't prevent me from feeling aggrieved and frustrated. Vivian, the shelter supervisor, sympathized but pointed out that someone like Harold, who had fallen through a hole in the net of society, would always be in danger of slipping out of sight altogether. "These people have already, to a certain degree, disappeared," she said, raising a wise eyebrow. "There's little to stop them taking a last little hop-skip-and-jump to the left and vanishing completely."

I didn't understand precisely what she meant, but I accepted the basic truth of the statement. In desperation, I pinned my home and office phone numbers to the shelter noticeboard, with a request to the other volunteers to get in touch with me, no matter what time of day or night, should Harold turn up. And winter deepened, and a rare December snow came down in thick flurries and left London with an ankle-deep coating of sooty slush, and Christmas came and went, and a New Year crawled over the horizon filled with the promise of much the same as last year, and January turned bitter, and the last spark of hope that Harold might still be alive winked out, and I learned to live with the fact that I would never see him again.

Then one morning, around about four o'clock, the phone rang, and the voice of one of the damned croaked my name.

The tiny portion of my brain that never goes to sleep knew who it was straight away, but the bit that thinks it does the thinking needed longer to place the identity of the caller, so, playing for time, I muttered something about the ungodliness of the hour and told whoever it was that he had better have a bloody good reason for waking me up. There was a long silence at the other end of the line, but even though I thought the connection had been cut, something prevented me from putting down the receiver. Then the voice spoke again. It sounded as though each word was being forged only with great effort and pain.

"I saw your note on the board. I must speak with you."

My conscious brain finally engaged gear with my subconscious. "Harold? Jesus, is that you, Harold?"

"It is."

"Well, I mean… What's happened? Where have you been? Are you all right? No, okay, listen, you're at the shelter, right? I'll be right over. Man, I really thought I was never going to hear from you again. Wow. Okay, Harold, stay put. I'll be right there."

"Listen," Harold said and, from the effort of concentrating so much energy into the command, left himself speechless again. There was breathing—sore, labored breathing—and then the pips went. I shouted at Harold to give me the number of the pay-phone so that I could call him back, but he managed to insert a coin in time. "This is how it is, Mark," he said. "I'm not at the shelter now. I've been there and I got your number there, but I didn't stay long—I didn't want anyone seeing me. I'm coming round to call on you at your place. I need the address."

"Okay." I gave it to him and said I'd have a hot cup of tea waiting for him when he arrived.

Either he didn't hear or he didn't care. "I'll be about an hour," he said, and hung up.

After a shower and a shave, neither of them particularly satisfying, I sat down in front of the television. All that was on was an Indian film. The hour passed slowly, with me drifting again and again toward the threshold of sleep and just managing to snap myself awake each time, with the result that my impressions of the film were a bewildering, fragmented chaos of blue gods, portly heroes in polyester shirts, and sinuously dancing women. At last the doorbell rang. I switched off the television, lit the gas beneath the kettle, and buzzed Harold up, leaving the flat door ajar. The concrete staircase that served all the flats in the building was uncarpeted, and Harold's slow, shuffling footfalls echoed all the way up. When he reached the landing outside my door he hesitated, pondering, breathing hard, and then, with a feeble knock, he entered.

Nothing could have prepared me for the profound change that had come over him. It wasn't just that he had lost weight, more weight than a man in his situation could afford to lose. Nor was it the unkempt straggliness of his hair and beard, which he was normally at pains to keep brushed and trimmed and tidy. It wasn't that his once-pristine greatcoat was mud-stained and had a number of torn seams, or that frostbite had left three of his fingertips black, shriveled and hard. It wasn't even the way he walked, stooped over where once he had carried himself with dignified erectness, bent as though bearing an invisible boulder on his back. It was his eyes that shocked me the most. While the rest of him had been somehow *lessened*, his eyes were larger and wider than I remembered them, and stared, crazy-veined, with a despairing emptiness from oyster-gray sockets. They looked without seeing, and when they finally found me standing by the stove in the small kitchen area of the living room, it took them awhile to focus on me and make sense of me.

Forcing on a smile, I pretended that there was nothing different about him. "Hey, man, how're you doing? It's good to see you. I'm glad you're alive."

His reply was dragged up from a moss-encrusted well of misery: "*I'm* not."

Without saying another word he plodded over to the living-room window and, with some effort, drew back the curtains. The street was misty, the milky air tinged orange by the streetlights, the houses opposite blank-windowed and cold-shouldering. It was the dead hour of the night, when the pavements belong to cats and foxes, when no cars disturb the stillness and you can almost hear the burn of the neon bulbs in their glass casings. Harold gazed out for a long time. It was almost as if he couldn't bear, or didn't dare, to take his eyes off the city for a second. The kettle burped steam and I made us tea, and it was only when I nudged Harold on the shoulder with a full mug that he turned away from the window and, with a nod of thanks, accepted the mug, made his way over to the armchair and settled down. I took to the sofa, and in the eerie small-hours quiet we sat without talking and sipped without tasting. The pain that had been clearly audible in Harold's last remark kept me from asking him anything. Though I burned to know what had happened to him, and though I was deeply concerned about the state of both his physical and his mental health, I recognized I would have to wait for him to speak; the only way he was going to give up any information was by volunteering it. And while I hated myself for even giving them headroom, the words "cancer" and "AIDS" did flit across my mind. What else but a terminal illness could so ravage a man, suck so much of the juice out of him, make a husk of him in such a short space of time?

"You want to know where I've been, don't you?" Harold said at last, haltingly, like a man treading barefoot over sharp stones. "Gone all this time—must be dead, right? Sometimes, you know, I think I am dead. I *feel* dead, that's for sure. If this isn't how it feels to be dead, I don't know what does."

"I was worried. We all were, all of us at the shelter. You'd never been away for so long before."

Harold didn't seem to care that someone cared. "I'm going to tell you something now, Mark, and you'd better listen, because I'm never going to tell another living soul. I'm not even sure I should be telling you."

"If it's a matter of national security," I joked, "perhaps I shouldn't be—"

"This is real." From beneath the brim of his homburg Harold fixed me with his eyes: Briefly they gained a luster, though it was not the pleasant, twinkling light that accompanied his forays into falsehood—this was a mean light, bitter in its brightness, harsh and hard. "This is something that actually happened to me, and I'm telling you because I have to tell someone. Because I'll go mad if I don't. I regret, for your sake, that it has to be you, but of all the people I know, you're the one I trust most to remember and believe. Everyone else will think I'm making it up. Everyone else will think this is just another of Harold's stories."

It was the first time I'd heard him even come close to admitting that the tales he told about himself, the tales he maintained in the face of all opposition were true, were lies. While it didn't amount to an outright confession, it was near enough to one to make me sit up and pay attention, which was perhaps what Harold had intended.

"You know me, Mark," he continued. "I've been wandering London for a fair old number of years now. I think I know this city pretty well. As well as a husband knows the body of his wife, you might say. There's not a street I haven't been down, not a square inch of pavement in the Greater London area that hasn't seen the soles of my feet. I've worn parts of this city away with walking. It's worn parts of me away in return. I really thought there was nothing new in it, nothing that could surprise me. It turns out I was mistaken.

"It happened last October. Nice, wasn't it, October? Mild, mellow, calm. Trees putting on their autumn firework display. Lovely weather to be out in, all the more lovely because you know it's not going to last. Well, I'd strayed into the suburbs, south of the river. Down Balham way. There's a couple of churches round there that open their crypts at night to let us sleep in them. One of them has a health-care place attached to it, you can get seen by a doctor almost straight away, and I'd had a cough that had been bothering me for weeks, you probably remember. The doctor said it was nothing serious and gave me some antibiotics for it, and I left the health-care place feeling pretty good about myself, the way you do when you're ill and you've just been to see the doctor and he's given you something that you *know* is going to make you well again. I'd got a meal inside me, too, from one of those charity vans that do the rounds. Soup and sandwiches: God's way of saying, 'Cheer up, old fellow, things aren't so bad.' And I'd picked up a pair of trainers from a skip—these trainers I've got on here—and they happened to fit me just right. Air-cushioned soles, nearly new. That put a spring in my step, all right. So I had just about every creature comfort you could think of, nothing whatsoever to complain about. I wonder if that had something…? No, never mind. I'll just tell you the story straight. It hurts too much to think too hard about it.

"London lives. You know that, don't you? Perhaps you don't. It's true of every big city, of course, but it's something you're only aware of if you know that city well, and the way to get to know a city well is not to travel across it by bus or tube, not to drive around it in a car, but to walk through it. That's when you're moving at its own pace, do you see? Contrary to popular opinion, there's nothing fast about cities. The people who live in them may rush around all the time, but cities themselves grow and change so slowly, it's hard to see it happening. It's like mold forming, like a rising-damp stain spreading across a patch of wallpaper. A building goes up, a building comes down, and most of the time we're whizzing by too quickly to notice. Haven't you ever found yourself strolling down a street you know well, only to be caught up short because a house you didn't even realize was being demolished has gone? Whish! Like a conjuror has magicked it away. And I'm sure there have been times when you've stumbled across a brand new block of flats or a brand new shopping center and, when you stop to think about it for a moment, you realize you've been passing that site every day and not once did you spot even one piece of scaffolding. Shops are changing hands all the time, aren't they? Facades get repainted. Black brickwork gets sandblasted clean. And all this goes on around you, and yet only occasionally—usually when you're out on foot—does it ever strike you that the city is constantly renewing and reshaping itself, that it's not just a great mass of brick and stone that sits there moldering and decaying, that the place you live in is something that breathes, pulses, has a heartbeat, may even have some dim kind of sentience."

Here Harold paused, giving me an opportunity to take in what he had been saying so far and prepare myself for what was coming, which, judging by the ironic purse of his lips, was going to be harder still to swallow. I don't think he appreciated how immune I had become to his fictions and fabrications. Neither his savagely altered appearance nor his insistence that this story, of all his stories, was true gave me any reason to suspect that I wasn't just being spun another yarn. I'd decided to hear him out because I thought it would be good for him to get whatever was plaguing him off his chest and hoped that this unburdening would be a stepping stone to getting at the real problem, the real reason why he looked and spoke like a soul in torment. I'd also decided that, when he was done, I would bundle him into a taxi and get him to a hospital; even if his spirit was beyond repair, his body could be mended.

Harold drew a deep breath and sent it hissing out through his nostrils. "I was coming up through Streatham when it happened. At first I didn't know what was going on. I felt it all around me, like something vast and unseen turning over in its sleep, but I'd no idea what it was. The sky rumbled like a jet was passing overhead, though one wasn't, and the air turned a different color, darkening several shades. The street I was walking down was busy, full of midmorning shoppers and pedestrians, and for a few seconds, while this 'shift' was taking place, while the city twitched and stirred and scratched its nose, everyone paused and looked up and around and at each other like there was something they were supposed to be communicating, some thought, some vital piece of information they were supposed to be sharing. And then the rumble faded and the light brightened and, the moment past, everyone dropped their heads again and carried on with their lives. A few children, for no apparent reason, started crying. A dog that was barking fell silent. That was it. Nothing else was different. Yet I knew—*I* knew—that things had changed. Ever so slightly, but perceptibly. And I started walking again, warily now, glancing around me in every direction, hoping to find what was new about the city, what London had done to itself.

"It didn't take long. I hadn't gone more than half a mile when I came across a street I didn't recognize. I said I knew London as well as a husband knows his wife, didn't I?"

"'Knows the body of his wife,' were your precise words."

"Right. Well, imagine you discovered a mole—no, a tattoo, an old, faded tattoo on your wife's right buttock that wasn't there before, couldn't have been there or else you'd have noticed."

My bachelor status made it difficult to empathize with the metaphor, but dutifully I made the imaginative leap. "Okay."

"Same thing," said Harold. "What I found was a street that I would be willing to swear on the Bible, the Talmud *and* the Koran hadn't existed before that odd moment, that 'shift,' occurred. Leading off a road I'd been down dozens of times before: a new, perfectly ordinary-looking, perhaps somewhat seedy little street. One that appeared to have been there for ages, for as long as all the other streets around it, at least a century, perhaps longer, but a new street all the same.

"Well, what would *you* have done? You'd have investigated, wouldn't you? And that's what I did. I wasn't scared. I was curious, and part of that curiosity was fear, but not enough of it was fear to make me turn and walk away, which I should have done. Things would have been so much better if I'd simply turned and walked away. But then, we don't do that when we're confronted with a mystery, do we? And it was also a challenge. A stretch of road I'd never been down before, a virgin piece of the city just begging for me to trample all over it—how could I resist? Me, who's known London so intimately for so long? How could I not walk down those fresh pavements and make my knowledge complete?

"The most peculiar thing about that street was, it felt and smelled and sounded just like any other street. Radios were playing, and there were cars parked along the curbs and net curtains in the windows of the houses, and people had done different things to their houses, stone-clad them, pebbledashed them, had paved over their front gardens, made little glades out of their front gardens, or not bothered at all with their front gardens and let the weeds grow up and the low front walls crumble and sag. Lives had been lived there on that street. Children had been born, old people had died. Dogs had filled the gutters with their droppings. The street had a history—and yet, less than a quarter of an hour ago, it hadn't existed.

"And that wasn't all. At the end I came to a pair of huge wrought-iron gates, topped with spikes, wide open. And beyond them was the park.

"I couldn't tell how large the park was when I first stepped through the gates. It was as big as I could see, it stretched in every direction to the horizon, but there were trees and low hills that made it hard to make out exactly how far it extended. It was larger than Hyde Park, that's for sure. Larger, maybe, than Richmond Park. But I wasn't wondering about that at the time. Certainly that was at the back of my mind, but what I was really thinking about was how this place couldn't possibly fit into the map of London I have etched in my head. There wasn't room for it in the network of densely packed suburban streets in that area. For that park to exist, thousands of houses would have to have been shunted aside, acres of built-up land would have to have been leveled and planted. It was a municipal impossibility. But there it was. I was standing within its perimeter, my feet resting on a solid asphalt path, and I was inhaling the damp, sweet, autumn aroma of its trees and grass, and I was staring at its flower beds and its small, swelling hills and its neatly clipped bushes and hedgerows, and I wasn't dreaming and I wasn't hallucinating—I hadn't had a drop of alcohol all week. It was all perfectly real, perfectly there. I couldn't have created a whole park out of nothing. No one's imagination is that good.

"I must have stood there like a zombie for the best part of twenty minutes. People were strolling past me, giving me curious looks—questioning, not wary. A jogger almost ran into me, checking his watch. He apologized and carried on panting along the path. A dog veered away from its owner to sniff at my shoes, tail wagging, and then got dragged back by a tug on the lead, and its owner, a pretty young girl, gave me a brilliant smile and said sorry. She wasn't scared or suspicious. She simply smiled and said sorry, and I said there was no reason to apologize, and she smiled again and carried on her way. Some pigeons strutted over to me and pecked expectantly at the ground around my feet. And then the sun came out.

"It had been overcast all morning, not cold, just gray, but the clouds had been threatening to part for an hour or so, and now at last they did, and the sunlight came down like a blessing and suddenly everything was aglow. The trees were no longer weighed down with yellow leaves, they were dripping with great, gleaming flakes of gold. The breeze had been nagging and chilly and a little unpleasant, and now, suddenly, it was warm and wild and playful. It was amazing, the way the clouds rolled away across the sky and left everything below bright and sparkling. Like a TV advert for floor polish, you know what I'm talking about? One wipe of your mop and your linoleum is gleaming. Only on a giant scale. I didn't take my hat off, of course."

"Of course." Harold never removed his homburg outdoors, and seldom indoors. He had worn it ever since the day he had been struck by lightning in the Sudan (yeah, right). He believed the hat protected him from being hit again, and so far no one could deny that as a talisman it had been an unqualified success.

"That was what finally got my feet moving," he continued, "that sweep of sunshine. It was an invitation. 'Come on,' it said, 'come and explore.' So I did. Any sane man would have done the same."

Harold took a swig of lukewarm tea and set the mug down on the coffee table. For the first time since arriving at my flat, he smiled. It was a half-hearted smile, a tenth-generation photocopy of the real thing.

"What can I say about that park? It seemed to have been designed with one thing in mind, and that was to please the human eye. The shapes of the flower beds, the shrubs and the roses that still were still blooming even in October, the patterns made by the hedgerows, everything just so. Where you expected to see a tree, there was a tree. Where you expected a pathway to turn or fork or intersect with another, so it did. The lawns were immaculate, clipped to an inch, rolled, and springy underfoot, the perfect resilience, and where a path cut through there was a clean division, a ridge of sheared-off earth the color and texture of chocolate cake. And whichever way you looked there was always something to catch your eye: a little Roman garden, a privet maze, a cupola perched on a low hill, a small windowless Georgian house at the end of an avenue of cypresses that was there not to be lived in but because it looked right, a wooden bandstand straight out of an American town square circa 1958, painted blue and cream.... Did I mention a maze?"

"You did."

"I stood for a while at the entrance and watched people go in and out, hearing exasperated cries and peals of laughter coming from inside. No one got lost for long. Everyone who went in emerged after about ten minutes, grinning and satisfied, saying that the maze was just the right difficulty, puzzling but not perplexing. I didn't try it myself. There was too much else to see.

"There was a boating pond where a dozen amateur admirals—young and old, from eight to eighty, the boys as intense as grown men, the grown men as blithe as boys—were sending their precious craft on perilous voyages across an Atlantic twenty yards wide. Destroyers and ducks were engaged on maneuvers side by side. Hopes were pinned on the whims of the wind to bring sailing yachts safely back to shore. A lone submarine glided underwater, popping up every so often and surprising everyone.

"And there was a playground, a playground like you only ever dreamed about when you were a child. There were swings, there were roundabouts, there were slides and seesaws, and best of all there was a climbing frame as big as a house, a sprawling fantasy of ladders and portholes and turrets and fireman's poles, its various sections joined together by wooden suspension bridges hanging from knotted ropes. To the children clambering all over it, it was Sherwood Forest, the *Marie Celeste*, Fort Apache and the Death Star all rolled into one, and they were having so much fun, I had to fight the urge to join them. And do you know what? In any other park in the country, if I'd stood for as long as I did watching those children, at least one of the adults present would have come up and asked me to leave, if not threatened to call the police.

But in that park the mothers and fathers and nannies and au pairs just smiled up at me from the benches that surrounded the playground, understanding that I was simply sharing their delight at seeing children at play.

"Not far away there was an ice cream van. I didn't have much change on me, and it wasn't what you might call a blistering-hot day, but right then I could think of nothing nicer, nothing that would cap my mood better, than a vanilla cone with a Flake in it. I joined the queue, and, can you believe it, they were giving the stuff away. A promotional offer, the young man in the van called it. A new brand, apparently. I don't think I need to tell you how much sweeter that ice cream tasted for being free.

"I took my cone to a bench on a rise just above the playground and gazed out across the park, licking slowly, savoring, nibbling the Flake to make it last. I looked for houses, but there were none. Their rooftops were hidden by trees. I couldn't even see a tower block. There was just park whichever way you looked. Park to the north, park to the south, park in every direction. There were bright green tennis courts, and men and women in clean white sports clothes running backward and forward, and the yellow balls arcing over the nets. There were three teenage boys tossing a frisbee to each other, and with them a red setter that rushed to and fro and every so often leapt up and snatched the frisbee from the air in its teeth and wouldn't give it back without a long, grinning, growling tug-of-war. There were young couples wandering hand in hand, pausing now and then for a lingering kiss. There were other young couples lolling on blankets on the grass, legs entwined. There was even an elderly couple behaving like a young couple—moving a little more slowly, to be sure, but taking more time over their kisses, too.

"At no point during that long, happy, sunlit afternoon did I ask myself if this was possible, if a place like this could really exist. Exactly the question you're asking now, Mark, with your eyes. What you must realize is that I wanted it so badly to *be* possible that I wasn't going to let a little thing like common sense get in the way. So a vast park had appeared where a park could not possibly be—so what? Sitting there with the sun on my face, a free ice cream in my belly and a view of dozens of happy people in front of me, why would I want to muddy the illusion with questions?

"I stayed there all afternoon, heavy with contentment, the kind of contentment I haven't felt since I was a very small child. A peace that, to coin a phrase, passed all understanding. A sense that the world and I had come to terms with each other, shaken hands and declared a truce. And the sun rolled down and shadows fell, and gradually people began to gather up their belongings and move off. One by one the tennis courts emptied of the clean-white-clothed players. The young couples suddenly found a purpose after a day's dawdling and hurried off to the pictures or a pub or a bedroom somewhere. Supremacy over the boating pond was given back to the ducks. The ice cream van whirred away along the pathways, headlights on against the clustering dusk, tinkling a mournful tune. The climbing frame was abandoned. Beside it the swings swayed vacantly to and fro. And finally, when there was no one else in sight and I felt like the only person left alive in the entire world, I hauled myself to my feet, stretched the cricks out of my spine, and set off down the hill in the direction of the gates. Everything was hushed, that twilight a sacred hour. The only sound I could hear was my own reluctant, dragging footsteps. Had it been summer I might have thought about spending the night there, perhaps on the very bench on which I'd been sitting all day, but what with my cough and the dreadful dampness of autumn nights, I thought it would be best if I found somewhere indoors, one of those crypts perhaps. And I could always come back to the park tomorrow, couldn't I? I could keep coming back as often as I wanted.

"There seemed to be only one way in or out of the park, and that was the way I'd come in, through those gates. And now, as darkness was beginning to fall, one of them was shut and there was someone standing by the other. A plain-faced man in uniform. A park-keeper. He had on a cap and a courteous smile.

"'Last one out, eh, sir?' he said to me. Someone in uniform calling *me* 'sir'!

"'Am I?' I replied, glancing around. I really thought there would be others like me, stragglers unwilling to leave. No one. 'I'm sorry. I was enjoying myself so much, I entirely lost track of the time.'

"And the park-keeper said, 'That's all right, sir. We deserve a little enjoyment in our lives, don't we? One day of happiness to make up for all the other miserable ones.'

"I told him he couldn't be righter, thanked him for the use of his park and said I'd be coming back soon. It was too wonderful a place not to revisit. And he just smiled again, a little sadly I think, and ushered me through the gate and closed it behind me with a heavy, ringing clang and wished me good night and strode away. I was halfway down the street when I realized I had forgotten to ask him the name of the park, but by then it was too late. I looked back, and he was nowhere to be seen.

"I slept well that night. The crypt was warm—once a hundred or so bodies had heated it up—and a mattress makes all the difference, doesn't it? A mattress and the memory of a day so strange and delightful you can hardly believe it happened.

"And then, near dawn, I woke to the sound of the 'shift' taking place again. A great groaning, far off, like the bellow of a dinosaur in pain. A grating noise like a huge stone being rolled across a cavern entrance. And up and down the length of the crypt sleeping people stirred and moaned and rolled over, as though they were all sharing a bad dream. I lay there for a moment frozen in horror, then leapt out of bed and threw on my hat and coat—of course I'd kept my new shoes on in bed; amongst even beggars there's precious little honor—and I sprinted out of there filled with a panic I couldn't explain, a sense of foreboding, of abrupt and irredeemable loss. I dashed through the dawn streets like a madman, driven by fear and the need to know, and finally I reached the street from which the other street, the street that had come from nowhere, led off. Gasping for breath, I staggered down it to where the junction with the other street had been. But I knew, even before I got there, that…"

I completed the sentence he couldn't finish himself: "That it was gone."

"As though it had never been there," he sighed. "The street was gone, the houses were gone, the iron gates were gone, the park was gone. What had been unearthed by that first shift of the city had been buried again, packed neatly away back where it came from, like a toy no longer wanted."

He paused there, as if unable to contemplate the magnitude of his loss.

"I don't understand the hows or the whys of it," he said eventually. "Perhaps the street and the park belong to a London we don't normally see, a secret London that exists alongside the city we know, a second London, a ghostly twin that's made up of all our hopes and dreams and longings of what this city should be like, and sometimes the two, for some reason, overlap and you can move from one to the other. I don't know. Or perhaps everyone, once in their lives, is allowed a glimpse of how things *should* be. Perhaps that's what the park-keeper was telling me when he said that everybody deserved a day of happiness to make up for all the miserable ones. Perhaps he meant that we should never forget that true contentment is possible and, whatever our circumstances, we should keep striving to achieve it. I don't know. And what about those people? Who were they? Were they Londoners who, like me, had strayed into the park by accident? Or did they belong there? That might explain the cheerfulness I had seen everywhere, the fact that they were part of the park itself, living embodiments of the delight of every spring, summer or autumn day anyone had ever spent in a city park. The ones I'd exchanged words with—the jogger, the dog-owner, people in the queue for ice creams—had all been kind and gracious and generous with their time. They hadn't shied away from me like most people do, worried that I'm going to ask them for money and that they won't know how to respond. These well-dressed, smiling human beings had without exception treated me as an equal. Much like you do, Mark. You don't know what that means to a gentleman in my position. No, no, I don't know who they were or how they got there. All I know is this: I've been searching for that park ever since. For four months I've been roaming London in a state of shock. I've hardly slept, I've hardly eaten, I've hardly communicated with anyone—I've talked more this past half-hour than I have in the entire past four months. I've just walked and walked and walked, gradually coming to look like a cartoon parody of a tramp, and hoping constantly, with the desperation of a fool, that somehow I'd find a way back to the park, or another park like it, another pocket of perfection in an otherwise ruined world.

"At times I think I've been close. Once or twice I've heard a distant rumbling, but so far away, too far away to be sure that it wasn't just a bus revving in the next street or a tube-train thundering beneath my feet. Once or twice I've detected a change in the quality of the light, but how can I know for certain it wasn't just a cloud passing in front of the sun or my eyes playing tricks on me? I can't. I can't be sure of anything except that the park was real, that the peace I felt there was real, and that I will never stop looking until I find both that park and that peace again.

"What do you call it, Mark, when you get a taste of heaven and realize that nothing will ever be that sweet again?"

"Growing up? Growing old?" I hazarded.

Harold lowered his gaze to look at his cracked, frostbitten hands. "I call it Hell," he said, simply.

There wasn't much else to be said. The alarm clock trilled in the bedroom, slowly winding down to silence. Outside, the street had become marginally brighter, and every so often a car swished past. Lights were on in some of the windows opposite. London and its inhabitants were gearing themselves up for another day.

"Harold," I offered tentatively, "how about I take you to a doctor? Get you looked at?"

"What's the point?" he said, after a moment of actually looking like he was considering it.

"The point is, frankly, you're in awful shape, and in my opinion if you're not careful and you carry on the way you have been, you're going to do yourself irreparable harm."

"And in *my* opinion I think I should be going now." So saying, Harold rose stiffly to his feet.

"Harold," I said, "you're mad."

"Mark, I wish I were," he replied, and turned to go.

I didn't stop him. I know I should have, but really, what could I have done? Manhandled him down the stairs and wrestled him into a taxi? Knocked him unconscious with a candlestick and called for an ambulance? I had no right to force Harold to do anything he didn't want to do. Or so I justified it to myself then, and have been justifying it ever since. The fact is that I watched Harold shuffle out of the flat and listened to him make his way painfully down the stairs and didn't lift a finger to prevent him because right at that moment I hated him. I hated him for having sat there in my armchair and manufactured a story of utter preposterousness—possibly the most ludicrous and pointless story he had ever told, not to mention the hardest to disprove—rather than simply own up to the truth. What the truth was I had no idea (I fear he actually had contracted a terminal illness), but whatever the real reason for Harold's physical and spiritual deterioration, I hated him for not having the courage to share it with me. Until then his stories had been a source of amusement and wry pleasure, but that morning I saw Harold clearly for the first time, saw him for the pathetic, deluded, degraded man he was, a man so vain and yet so devoid of self-esteem that he felt he had to lie to make himself interesting.

And I'll tell you this, too. I have never seen Harold since that morning, which is getting on for half a year ago now. Neither has anyone else, and it seems to all intents and purposes that he has vanished off the face of the earth. And while an ungenerous part of me thinks good riddance, another, kinder part hopes that, wherever Harold is, he has found his park again.

In the meantime, whenever I'm walking around London, I find myself half-listening out for what Harold called a "shift"; a faint, far-off rumble that will mean that the city has in some way reconfigured itself to show another facet briefly to the world, revealing the truth behind the facade—or the facade behind the truth (Harold would have known the difference). And for all my cynicism, for all my skepticism, I find myself hoping that, in this one instance, Harold was on the level.

Well, you never know.

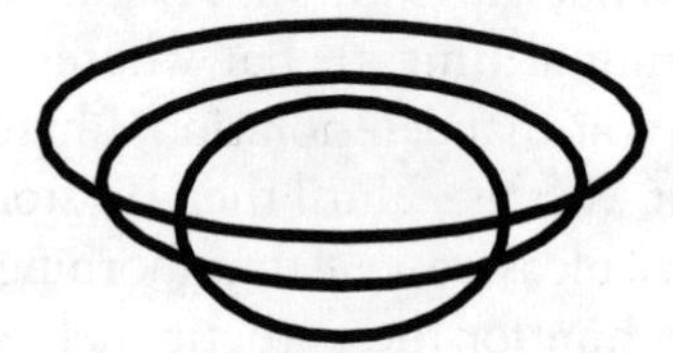

DANTE'S

F E R R Y M A N

by Doug Murray

DAY ONE, 9 A.M.

The mayor of New York sat back in his seat, preparing himself for the day ahead. *It's gonna be a killer*, he thought. *Damn Teamsters!* He shook his head. *I've got to relax—get myself under control!* He turned to look out at his city. It was a nice day. The sun was actually visible over the eastern skyline, warm light pouring down, filling the street in front of him. *Nice morning*. The mayor saw a major pothole just in front of him, picked out by the early shadows. *Great! Better do something about that*. He grunted as the car bumped through it. *Maybe tomorrow...*

Traffic was moving well; the limo glided past block after block of... *Odd, there are an awful lot of people out there*. He pursed his lips, worried. *Are those new homeless shelters full already?*

He shook his head. *I hope not! There's no money for any more*. The mayor sighed. *And no damn way to raise more, either*. He turned away from their stares, pulling out his notes for today's meeting. *Not if I want to stay mayor*.

The limo rolled past a street corner full of faces. *And God help me, I do*.

George smiled as he walked down the street. Yesterday's job had been *perfect*! On time, on target—everything by the book. George's smile grew wider. Best of all, it had been the *last* job. Now there was nobody left in his way. He had it all.

George checked the fit of his suit. He'd go legitimate now. Let the younger guys pull the jobs. It was time for him to sit back and rake it in.

The distinctive front of the Club, his new headquarters, appeared a half-block ahead. George squinted. There seemed to be an awful lot of people there. Had something gone wrong after all? But no, they weren't cops, none of them had uniforms. George slowed down, missing a stride; there was something *familiar* about those figures....

George thought about turning around. *No!* He squared his shoulders and strode forward, forcing confidence into his step. *I'm the boss now! The Don! The Capo!* He started to whistle jauntily. *Let those bums get out of my way!* He approached the Club, confident in his power.

And froze in his tracks. *That's Big Willie. And Louie, and Crazy Mike...*

Then a movement in the shadows caught his eye.

No. It can't be him. He's dead! I killed him myself!

Of course, all the others were dead too....

The mayor's concentration was broken when the limo made the final turn into the City Hall parking lot. *Already!* He looked at his watch. *Five minutes early! Miracles* do *happen!* He stuffed his notes back into the briefcase. Let the Teamsters come; for once, he was ready for them. He straightened his tie as the door opened. Always assuming that there were no surprises.

The mayor fell back into his chair, stunned. "You can't be serious!"

Timmons nodded, putting a new sheaf of papers down in front of his boss. "I'm afraid I am."

The mayor leaned forward, hand stopping just short of the documents. "And my meeting with the Teamsters?"

"Canceled." Timmons chuckled sardonically. "Apparently they have problems of their own."

The mayor closed his hands around the damning papers. "I'll just bet!"

"I don't care who he is!" Charlie McLean didn't lose his temper often, but today was shaping up as something special. "Get him out!" He glared at the figure sitting behind his desk. "Now!"

Herman Senercia looked at his boss, noted the color rising up the other man's neck and realized he had to do something.

Problem was, he didn't know what he could do.

"But, Boss," Herman decided to try an appeal to reason. "It was *his* chair too—he was never really voted out…."

McLean's color grew deeper. Dangerously dark. Herman changed his tone, softened it, made it as plaintive as he could. "Besides, there's no way I *can* move him." Herman reached for the seated figure. "I can't even touch him!"

"Damn!" McLean watched his aide's hand slide through his predecessor. "You're right!"

"They have *who* in their office?" The mayor was shocked. This couldn't be happening.

Timmons looked at his papers. "Jimmy Hoffa, sir. Seems he won't get out of McLean's chair."

"Jimmy Hoffa, back from the grave." The mayor leaned back, rotating his chair to look out the window. *Or the forty-yard line at the Meadowlands!*

Timmons pulled a few papers out of his folder. "We have a few problems of our own."

The mayor looked at the figures Timmons presented and sighed. "Yes, I can see that. How many of these walking dead are there?"

Timmons dug into his file. "It's too early to say, sir. I can tell you that they're not walking dead. They're not… solid."

The mayor stared at him. "Not solid?"

Timmons pulled out some more papers, along with a pile of photos. "No sir. They're insubstantial."

"Like ghosts?"

"Or," Timmons shrugged, "if you prefer a more classical reference, shades."

"Okay." The mayor slammed the file down onto his desk. It was time to go to work. "Let's find out why this is happening then maybe we can figure a way to stop it."

Timmons pulled out a steno pad, ready to take notes.

The mayor stood up and started to pace. "First, get the police working on this."

"They already are, sir."

The mayor nodded. "Good." He paused for a moment of thought. "They'll need some specialists. Talk to the cardinal."

Timmons started to write. "How about the chief rabbi?"

The mayor nodded. "Good idea." He ran a finger across his jaw. "You'd better get some of the brains at Columbia on it too. They may be able to come up with something."

Timmons closed his book and headed for the door. "Right away, sir."

"And Simmons..."

The aide stopped, turning to his boss. "That's *Timmons*, sir."

The mayor waved a hand. "Whatever." He returned to his chair. "Bring me some aspirins. I've got a whale of a headache."

Timmons nodded. "Right away, sir."

The door closed. *Jeez,* the mayor closed his eyes. *As if the Teamsters weren't bad enough.* He looked at the pile of papers on his desk. *Now I've got to deal with the dead!* He grimaced. *What comes next?*

He shook his head. *No, I take that back.* He sat back down at his desk. *I don't think I want to know.*

DAY TWO

Wesley Skipp sighed as he settled into the seat of his car. *At last,* he thought. *It's over.* He'd always hated funerals. Messy things, slow as molasses. Filled with people trying to act sad. He grinned. And every one of them with something better to do.

He certainly had better things to do. Things he'd waited—he shook his head—ten years, for! *Now it's time for Wesley to play.* He grinned, putting his feet up on the facing seat of the limo. *She's gone now!* The grin widened. *And I've got it all! The house, the car...*

Wesley stretched. *And all that lovely money!* The car started up, heading out of the cemetery. *It's gonna be Easy Street from here on.*

Wesley woke from a light, pleasant doze when the car finally turned into the driveway. There was someone on the stoop. *Now who...?* He sat up, looking at the figure waving at him. *No! It can't be!* A sob escaped his lips. *I just buried you!* The sob bubbled out, became a scream as his mother, smiling beatifically, walked *through* the door of the limousine and sat down beside him.

"Sharon?" the mayor roared. "You're telling me this is all the work of somebody named Sharon?!"

"That's *Charon*, sir. With a C." Timmons motioned toward the other man in the room. "At least, that's what Dr. Milner tells me."

The mayor's eyes drilled into the other man. "Are you sure of this, Doctor?"

Milner adjusted his glasses slightly, a practiced movement that gave him an instant to choose his words. "Reasonably sure. At least, the appearance of the shades fits well with classical descriptions. As you may know, Homer and Virgil both spoke of…"

"Please!" The mayor interrupted just as Milner dropped into lecture mode. "I don't have time for all that." He waved at the pile of papers on his desk. "I'm getting *buried* under paperwork from all these… what did you call them? Shadows?"

"Shades." Milner moistened his tongue, ready to start again. "Spirits of the dead."

"Whatever." The mayor leaned toward the professor. "I need to know what they're doing here…." He motioned to Timmons. "And what I have to do to get rid of them!" The aide produced a large sheet of paper, which the mayor signed. "This is a blanket authorization. Find out what this Charon wants." He handed the paper to Milner. "Do it quickly."

DAY FIVE

"I got it!" Jimmy Davis put his glove up, carefully shading his eyes from the sun. Just a little farther and…

Roger Maris, Ty Cobb and Johnny Lewis all flashed into sight, each of them diving for the ball. "No!" Davis yelled. "*I* got it!" The ball whizzed through Maris' glove, whistled through Cobb's chest… and hit Davis in the face. Blood spurted from his nose as the ball fell harmlessly to earth.

Davis cursed, wiped the worst of the blood away, and scrambled to try to pick up the ball from between the hands and feet of the dozens of outfielders converging on the scene. Behind him, the crowd roared as scores of baserunners scurried around the bases. *What the hell am I doing?* Davis stood up. *They ain't paying me enough for this*. He let the shades scramble for the untouchable ball and headed for the clubhouse. *This ain't baseball!* He looked back at the crowded field. *I don't know what it is*. He ducked inside, heading for the shower. *I hope it ain't too crowded!*

"He wants what?"

Milner cleaned his glasses, taking his time, ignoring the mayor's growing anger. After one last, appraising glance, he put them back on and turned to the official. "He wants his due."

"His due! For what?"

Milner snorted. "It's obvious, Mr. Mayor, that you haven't read any of the material I gave your assistant." He glared at Timmons, standing silently in the corner. "And you haven't been properly briefed."

The mayor waved his hands, his own anger gone now. He'd dealt with academics before. He knew he'd have to mollify the professor if the other man was going to tell him what he needed to know. "Okay, Professor Miller…"

"That's *Milner*!"

"Whatever." The mayor sat back and smiled. His best re-election smile. "I haven't read any of the books you brought. Suppose you tell me what I need to know."

Milner nodded, already reinspecting his glasses. Sure of his audience now, he put them back on and began. "To begin with, Charon is a ferryman…."

The mayor rocked back in his chair. "Oh my God! A Teamster!"

Milner nodded. "Yes, I guess you could call him that. It is his task to convey the dead across the River Styx, which, oddly enough, runs directly under New York City."

"Figures." The mayor sighed.

Milner glared at the second interruption, noted the mayor's gesture of apology, and continued. "Charon takes the shades of the dead across that river, delivering them to the underworld, where they are destined to spend the rest of eternity."

"Obviously, he's not doing his job."

Milner sighed. "That's our fault. We've broken the pact."

The mayor leaned forward. "We had a *contract* with this…" he glanced at Milner, "Charon?"

Milner's glare would have melted an underclassman. "Of course we had a contract with him! For millennia!" Milner stood and started to pace. "Surely you've seen movies or read books in which coins were placed on the eyes of the dead?"

The mayor's eyes went thoughtful. "Yeah, I've seen that."

Milner stopped to readjust his glasses. "Well, those were meant as payment for the ferryman. Now, however…"

The mayor leapt from his chair and began pacing also. "Now people are too cheap to leave the coins."

"Precisely." Milner beamed his approval.

"Okay." The mayor stood up. "So we owe him some money." He turned toward the window. "How much?"

"I asked him about that…."

"And?"

"He told me…" Milner hesitated. "He told me that the time-honored fee is two gold pieces per passenger."

"Gold pieces?!"

"He was quite specific about that."

"He would be—the bastard's a goddamned *Teamster!*" The mayor threw himself back into his chair, pulling out a pad. "Okay, how much gold are we talking about?"

"Well, according to *his* figures, we owe him for about one hundred million passages."

The mayor went stiff, shock spreading through his body. "One hundred million gold pieces?"

Milner raised two fingers. "Two."

"Two hundred million…"

Timmons cleared his throat. "I took the liberty of checking the exchange, and my calculations indicate that such a payment would come to about eighty trillion dollars at today's rate."

The mayor's eyes went wide. "Eighty trillion…"

Milner adjusted his glasses one last time. "Of course, there is a possible alternative."

Hope sprang into the mayor's eyes. "Anything!"

The professor nodded. "I suspected you might say that, so I suggested the following arrangement…."

DAY SEVEN

Father Andrew sighed as he surveyed the crowd on Fifth Avenue. *Just like the St. Patrick's Day Parade*, he thought. *And all moving downtown.* He watched them stream by. *The mayor must've worked something out. Things are going back to normal.* Too bad. For a time there, it had been standing room only in the church. The priest shook his head. *Of course, most of those had* already *gone to their reward.* He still didn't know how the cardinal was going to handle all this. No heaven or hell, just an underworld. *Who would've guessed the Greeks got it right?* He sighed again, and walked down the aisle. He had candles to light.

The mayor rocked back in his chair, enjoying the sunlight streaming in through his window. "Well, Timmons, we got off easy on that one!"

"Indeed we did, sir!"

"Imagine! All that Sharon—"

"*Charon*, sir."

"Whatever. All he wanted was a bigger boat! And us with all those ferryboats out on the river."

"The people in Staten Island aren't happy, sir."

The mayor turned toward the window. "Screw them! It was either give up one of their boats or bankrupt the whole…" There was a disturbance below. The mayor leaned forward; there were an awful lot of people outside. "Timmons, there's something going on down there; could you…" He turned as the door banged open. "Milner!"

The professor strode in, face red with anger. "You two-faced political hack! I do my best to help you—act as your intermediary—give my word! And all the while…"

The mayor's hands moved, trying to placate the irate scholar. "Wait a minute! What's going on? What's the problem?"

Milner stood up to his full height and motioned to his side. "You lied to us both! And now you're going to explain why—in person! Charon…"

The mayor's eyes widened as a new figure entered the room. A tall man, covered by a long cloak of some dirty brown cloth. "Mr. Sharon, I presume…."

"That's *Charon*, you dolt!" Milner's face was redder than ever.

"Sorry." The mayor resorted to his re-election smile. "What can I do for you, Mr. Charon?"

"*Why didn't you tell me the truth?*"

The mayor froze for a moment, stunned by both the question and the voice that spoke it. Then his wits returned. Anyone who had been to the Bronx could handle a voice like that. "The truth, sir?"

"*About the rules in your world.*"

"Rules?" The mayor turned to Milner, baffled. "What rules is he talking about?"

Milner leaned forward, hissing at the mayor. "The problem is all your goddamned labor contracts!"

"That's right!" A new voice came from the doorway. "And old Charon understands the sanctity of a contract!"

The mayor whirled. "McLean!"

Charlie McLean grinned at the mayor. "Yep, it's me all right." He gestured to his right. "And my new adviser."

The mayor goggled as the shade of Jimmy Hoffa bowed sardonically to him. "But he's dead!"

"So?" Charlie let himself drop into one of the office chairs. "What's your point?"

The mayor waved that off. "Forget about that. What's going on here?"

Charlie grinned. The grin of a shark that smells blood. "Simple." He gestured outside. "Moving that ferry of yours is a Teamster's job." He nodded to Charon. "And, under the terms of our contract, it's much too big to be handled by just one," he put his arm over Charon's shoulder, "of our brothers."

The mayor let his head fall into his hands. He should have known this wasn't going to be so easy. Damn Teamsters! Old *and* new!

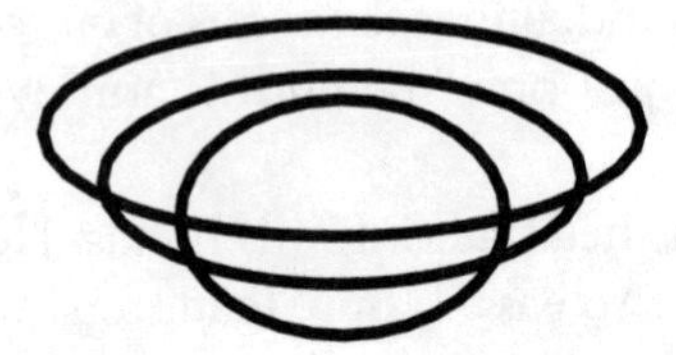

DANTE'S

Return to Gehenna

by Storm Constantine

She didn't know how she'd caught the awareness. Perhaps she'd walked through an infected area one night when she'd been drunk, and hadn't felt its presence. Or it could have been coughed onto her by someone. Maybe. Perhaps its spore had impregnated itself into a piece of paper she'd handled at work. She hated work. Wouldn't it have come for her there? Work was hell.

It was hard to pinpoint exactly when the awareness had started, and whether the incident that occurred on the dead-skied Tuesday had actually been the first or not, but it was the first that Lucy could remember.

"Hell is not a place, it is a state of mind." So said Dolores, who occupied the desk opposite Lucy's. Lucy had just kicked herself backward across the floor on her swivel chair, announcing, "This place is hell." Her work bored her rigid; the company sold insurance.

Dolores, with her long pink nails which Lucy suspected were false, liked work. She had double chins and a strangely slow tongue that reminded Lucy of a parrot's. It was pointed and narrow, and peered out without speed to lick the sticky parts of envelopes like a questing, blind worm. Dolores disapproved of what she saw as Lucy's lazy temperament and streak of rebellion. Everyone had to work, so why not do your best? To help fulfill this urge, Dolores made copious cups of tea for the boss —a mangy nonentity, who smelled salty—and grovelled before the boss' wife whenever she called into the office. The boss' wife was vague and always seemed slightly surprised, unnerved by the obsequious Dolores. Lucy could not imagine that all of these drab people had a life beyond the office walls.

Lucy hated Dolores' smug piety more than she hated the job; but if she didn't get on with the woman, life there would be unendurable, since there were only the two of them and the boss didn't count. She also suspected that Dolores was quite capable of losing her her job if she felt riled enough, but fortunately the woman made an effort to excel at being kind. Dolores was just too good; perhaps it was why she looked so poisoned and bloated.

"You make life so hard for yourself," Dolores said. She was filled to the brim with platitudes and sayings that advised on how to exist nicely and properly. Niceness and properness were concepts that filled Lucy with dread. She felt she had somehow been cut adrift from the life she was supposed to have had and become marooned here, eking out a living in a nine-to-five job that barely paid for her small apartment. It wasn't as if she could get a better job, with her lack of qualifications. Sometimes she wished she'd done something with herself at school, or perhaps later; but in her early twenties, all she'd wanted to do was party. Now, on the cusp of thirty, all her wild friends had turned suspiciously into people who wanted children and normality. Somehow, without Lucy noticing, they had acquired degrees, or training that ended in certificates. They had deceived her; they were not the people she'd believed them to be. If they did come out for an evening, they talked about what their kids did, or joked about wallpaper. Lucy's horror had reached its height when she'd spotted a set of golf clubs in the boot of a car belonging to a man who had once sold drugs in the shadowed corner of the local student bar and whose hair had been long. Lucy's old friends were all sailing away from her, and she could only wave sadly at their departure. Recently, she had half-heartedly made newer, younger friends, who were happy to go out whenever they could afford it, but they seemed shallow in comparison to the memories of her youth; they had no opinions and no fire. They were too interested in money.

"I've woken up in the wrong life," Lucy told Dolores. "But I can't remember when it happened."

Dolores smiled in gentle disbelief and shook her head. "Really, Lucy, I think you enjoy being miserable. You're an attractive girl. What's the matter with you?"

"I'm not a *girl*," Lucy said, slouching backward in her seat like a relaxing puppet, arms hanging down to either side. "If I were, it might not be so bad. I'd have time to change things." She could see from Dolores' quick, bright glance that the woman was longing to tell her to sit up straight.

"Have you done the filing?" she said instead.

It was dark at five o'clock when Lucy left the office, leaving Dolores to fuss around (unpaid) for an extra fifteen minutes before locking up. Outside, the air was cold and damp with invisible rain, and sound seemed muted. Soon the nights would be drawing out; Lucy looked forward to spring. This year, the winter seemed to have been going on forever. In the mornings, she hated leaving for work in the dark, and then having to come home in it again at night. Lucy preferred heat, raging heat, and blistering light. Was it feasible to emigrate to a warmer country when she had no money and no training?

Lucy hurried to the bus stop, intent only on getting home, where she could shut out the night. Just as she was rounding the corner, she saw the bus coming toward her, having already drawn away from the stop.

"Damn!" She threw up her arms and waved frantically at the driver, but he ignored her. Greenish faces peered down at her in mild curiosity through the passengers' windows.

"Damn!" Lucy glanced at her watch. Since when had the bus been early? It was supposed to leave at ten past five, and she could see it was still only five past. Usually she had to stand there waiting, getting progressively more annoyed. Living on the outskirts of town as she did, she wouldn't be able to catch another direct-route bus for at least half an hour. Half an hour of standing in the depressing drizzle of a late January evening. She didn't have enough money for a cab: It was too near the end of the month when her bank account tended to dry up, or rather her overdraft did. She considered approaching a cash dispenser in the hope of invoking money, but knew her prospects of success were bleak, and it would take her at least five minutes to reach the machine in the square. She might as well walk home. If she walked briskly, it would take only twenty-five minutes.

Her shoes weren't made for walking; they leaked. Lucy cursed the fact she had forgotten about that before she'd started off. As she walked, it seemed the dreary town shimmered in a mist, but the effect was not beautiful. Cars and buses hissed along the main road, throwing up dirty spray. People hurried along with their heads down through the garish gouts of radiance thrown out by shop-fronts. The puddles of light on the ground seemed muzzy at the edges, as if Lucy's vision were blurring. She blinked, clearing her eyes. *Perhaps I am crying*, she thought, subsequently wondering why she felt so numb.

She turned into the narrow street, Victoria Terrace, which provided a short-cut back to Carlisle Avenue, where she lived. Normally she would take the long way around, as the terrace led to silent, dim-lit areas, where her heart would beat faster and her ears strain to detect threatening sounds. Tonight she assured herself that, at this time of day, there could be little danger, and there wasn't. The danger came from inside her.

Lucy knew the area well. On the boss's birthday, she and Dolores would accompany him to one of the many small Chinese restaurants that lined the street, where he would pay magnanimously for a very mediocre meal. Farther down was the sandwich shop where Lucy went to buy her lunch. Acknowledging the landmarks of restaurant and shop, Lucy considered that her life had become narrow, and its horizons were contracting all the time. Atoms of herself must be left on this street that she traversed so regularly. When she died, her ghost might haunt it.

Reaching the end of Victoria Terrace, Lucy turned left. The streetlights here were few and far between, and high, narrow, three-storied terraced houses of gray stone huddled together on either side of the road.

Lucy hesitated at the corner. She had walked down this street hundreds of times before, yet this time, on this cold, dark Tuesday, it was not the same. Normally Lucy would see a row of terraced cottages —once cream, now soot-drenched—on one side of the road, and on the other, a line of shops, most of which were boarded up and abandoned, with litter on their porches. This street of tall, gray houses she had never seen before.

I have been day-dreaming, she reasoned. *I have taken a wrong turn.* Looking back up Victoria Terrace, she realized the thought itself was folly. The only intersection was halfway up, and she could see it from where she stood.

Lucy's first instinct was to retreat, take the long way home, even return to the main road and wait for a bus, because this couldn't be happening. She must have gone mad, but in a moment of total disorientation she found herself wondering if the street had always looked this way, and it was her memory that was faulty. Now that she thought about it, could she really swear the street had been lined with shops and dirty-cream houses? Perhaps she was thinking of another street.

But I have never been here before....

The scene before her was utterly still; no lights burned in the tall, crowded buildings. At the far end of the road a massive edifice reared up, like an ancient factory or a prison. Its severe outline spoke of despair.

Without thinking, Lucy began to walk up the center of the road. Looking up, she could see the sky was no more than a narrow, gray-orange band between the looming roofs. She did not feel afraid, only rather insubstantial, as if she too could blink out of existence at any time.

Her feet made a dull sound upon the tarmac, and the sounds of traffic seemed to fade away. *I should turn back*, Lucy thought. *Where am I going?* She thought she could hear faint music, lively and staccato, but when she strained to hear it properly, it died away. Perhaps the sound existed only in her mind.

The huge building at the end of street was growing larger before her. It might be a mental institution or a temple to a dark god. No, it was a factory. People toiled there.

A movement on the road ahead of her caught her attention. She saw what appeared to be a thin skein of smoke twisting in the air, close to the ground. As she approached, this perplexity resolved itself into a crumpled piece of paper, fretted by ground-level breezes. Closer still, and Lucy saw, with surprised disbelief, that the paper was in fact a fifty-pound note. After looking around herself to check for owners of the note, and finding none, she picked it up.

Strangely enough, the note was dry. Someone must have dropped it very recently. Lucy looked up. Perhaps it had fallen from an open window, or even from an aircraft. She had heard of how human waste, and even dogs, had been known to plummet from the sky to splatter unsuspecting victims below. She did not object to being the victim of such a relatively large amount of money.

A noise now caught her attention, and she moved her perception from the magical note to the side of the road. Dim, crimson beams of light spilled from an open doorway, illuminating the wet sidewalk. The door apparently led into a bar of some kind; above its lintel a bottle shaped from pink neon tubes glowed and buzzed, two cocktail glasses winking in and out of existence beside it. Lucy was sure that moments earlier there had been no crimson light, no neon display and no bar. She smiled to herself as a foolish thought came to her: It was almost as if finding the money had somehow prompted the doorway to spring into being. Didn't she crave excitement in her life? What further nudging did she need? Lucy approached the open doorway, the money still held in her hand.

Inside, the bar was very dark, its air filled with what sounded like live, jazzy piano music, although she could see no piano. Its decor was shabby but somehow alluring; shredding red plush and pink and red lamp-light. At first glance, she could perceive no patrons other than herself. There was a smell of stale beer and tobacco smoke, beneath which lurked an odor of hamburger and onions. Lucy approached the bar itself, although there did not appear to be anyone on duty there. A tall, oblong spill of yellow light, which interrupted the gleaming shelves and mirrors behind the bar, indicated an open doorway, which perhaps led to a kitchen. Lucy leaned on the polished counter. She could buy anything she fancied; the thought of a whole bottle of wine was attractive. Then she could sit at one of the shadowy tables, alone with a bottle and a glass, kick off her wet shoes and drink for an hour or so. Normally Lucy would not feel comfortable doing any such thing, but she felt she had somehow stepped into an enchanted pocket of time and space, and the opportunity should not be wasted.

As a woman came through from the brightly lit area, it seemed a shadow was conjured into being at the end of the bar. Lucy could see now that she was not the only patron, for a thin-faced man in a heavy, dark coat sat hunch-shouldered on a stool, half-turned toward her. He did not look up, but stared into a tumbler of amber liquid around which he had cupped his hands, although his fingers did not touch the glass. The bartender, who wore a bright red blouse of shiny material, came to stand in front of Lucy. Lucy looked up at her. The woman had a tired face, yet her eyes were unusually bright, almost as if a more vivacious creature were trapped within the listless flesh. "A bottle of wine, house red will do," said Lucy.

"We don't serve wine." The woman's mouth barely moved, although her eyes darted quickly to left and right; it seemed to be a tic.

"Beer?"

"No beer."

Lucy peered past the woman at the shelves behind her. They were filled with a startling array of weirdly shaped bottles, which all looked as if they contained liqueurs. "What do you recommend?" Lucy asked. She did not recognize the names on any of the bottles: Ogerond, Betwixtit, Tegammera.

The woman shrugged. "What's your favorite color?"

"Black," Lucy responded, to be awkward.

Without changing her expression, the woman reached behind herself and produced a tall, dark bottle. From this, she measured a small amount of what appeared to be black ink into a glass that resembled a miniature champagne flute. "Two pounds."

"I've only this. Sorry." Lucy handed over the fifty-pound note, eyeing the strange little glass before her with caution.

The woman took the note from her, but did not hold it up to the light for inspection, as most people would. She sniffed it. Perhaps there were many ways to check for forgeries.

While the bartender busied herself with sorting out change at the till, Lucy lifted the little glass and sniffed its contents "What is this?" It smelled highly alcoholic and faintly of coffee, but also of molasses, and perhaps spoiled milk.

"A drop of black, as you asked for." The woman handed her a bundle of notes and coins.

Lucy did not bother to check her change. She stuffed it all into her bag. "But what's it called?"

"Axings," replied the woman. She went back toward the oblong of yellow light and was swallowed by it.

At this point, Lucy considered that she might actually be dreaming and would soon be awoken by her alarm clock, nagging her into another pointless day's boredom at the office. She knew it was possible to be aware that you were dreaming while you were doing it. If that was so, she would enjoy it. Anything was possible, surely, in a dream? She took a sip from the tiny glass. It was difficult. She felt like Alice in Wonderland: a giant of a girl trying to drink from a doll's glass. Perhaps the liquid in it *was* ink. The liquor stung her tongue, but its taste was that of fear of the dark, of untraveled roads, of seduction. Astonished, Lucy put down the glass. How could such things have tastes? "Surreal!" she said aloud.

"A distillation of feeling." The voice came from farther down the bar, from the mouth of the thin-faced man.

Lucy looked at him. He was handsome in a gaunt sort of way. "What?"

He raised his glass to her. "Curiosity or fear?" The words sounded like a toast.

Lucy suddenly became uneasy. She felt the bar had filled up behind her, for she could sense pressing bodies, but when she looked around, it was still empty. Nervously, she took another sip of the drink, bracing herself against the strange sensations its taste conjured in her mind. She felt the thin-faced man's scrutiny, the oppression of invisible bodies behind her. Whatever she looked at appeared stretched, as if it might break apart at any time. She glanced down at the diminutive glass held in the fingers of her left hand. It seemed she had made no impression on the contents. *I must not finish what I started....*

Not knowing why she had thought that, Lucy found herself at the door. She could not remember having walked away from the bar. Looking back once as she stepped out into the night, she saw the bartender had come back into the room and was standing next to the thin-faced man.

Both of them were looking at her with expressionless faces. Her glass stood where she had left it, only something small and scurrying seemed to be moving swiftly away from it. Lucy went out into the street.

She felt disoriented, not frightened but confused, and staggered down the street for a few yards. *Where am I going? I should go back the way I came*. Her head was swimming. As she looked up, the world spun before her eyes. *Can I be drunk from one sip of the black?* Her vision cleared, and when it did, she fell back against the wall of a house behind her.

The street appeared as it always had: drab little cottages, once clean, now soot-drenched; a row of worn-out shops. The sound of traffic murmured distantly from the main road, hidden by a huddle of decaying buildings. She heard a siren and the hoot of an angry horn.

"No!" Nausea came suddenly, and she had to double up to vomit onto the sidewalk. It looked like blood; black in the streetlight, but immediately after the spasm had passed, she felt better, normal.

At home, she turned on all the lights and emptied the contents of her bag onto the tiny Formica-topped table in her kitchenette. A tide of paper scraps came out. Lucy pawed through it with shaking fingers. Receipts, faded with age and like felt to the touch for being kept in the bottom of a coat pocket; an extortionate electricity bill addressed to "the occupier" at an address she didn't know; a letter from a bank advising of an abused overdraft facility, written to "whomever it may concern"; an eviction order for non-payment of rent. A catalog of tears and woe—financial distress in all its forms—but anonymous; evidence only of universal, urban misery. Lucy stared at this drift of cruelty for over a minute, the fingers of one hand pressed against her mouth. Then she began to laugh. *Fairy gold; of course…*

The following day, when Lucy arrived at work, Dolores remarked upon her appearance, which she said was "peaky." Lucy considered, for a moment, telling her colleague about what had happened last night on the way home, but then remembered she had enjoyed discomforting Dolores a few weeks previously by describing her eventful drug-taking experiments of some years back. It was easy to imagine Dolores's private inferences, if not her overt responses, to Lucy's story. Perhaps acid flashback *had* been the cause of the episode. It was comforting now to think that.

At lunchtime, Lucy slouched through a slicing rain to investigate the street of transformation. By day, it was its mundane self: A thin, lank-haired woman came out of one of the houses with a push-chair; one of the few active shops remaining had a stock of exotic vegetable produce displayed outside its window. Lucy went to stand in the road. For a few moments, she closed her eyes, willing some bizarre image to manifest before her. When she looked upon the world once more, it seemed the scene before her shimmered, as if another place existed there, waiting to be focused upon, brought into being. Lucy blinked. A headache was starting. She had tried too hard to recapture a dream. It hadn't happened.

Nothing too remarkable occurred for several days after that, although in retrospect Lucy did wonder whether she'd just missed the awareness when it crept across her. Then, one lunchtime, as she strolled along the main street looking into shop windows, she suddenly had the distinct impression she was walking through a movie set, that nothing she saw was real, but a facade. It seemed she only had to half-close her eyes to become aware of something beneath the skin of the city: another place at once more exotic, yet decayed. Her flesh shuddered in a thrill of anticipation, excitement and fear. There was something she wanted so badly, yet she had no name for it. Merely the thought of its existence filled her with an unexpected hope. A noise swooped toward her like a wind, a great whine, a buzzing, trailing a jet-stream of suffocating perfume, redolent of vanilla and ashes. Lucy gasped and threw back her head, trembling and vulnerable.

The feeling soon passed, and, collecting herself, Lucy noticed that several passersby were taking a wide detour around her and pointedly looking in a direction other than hers. She wondered whether she was starting to experience some mild form of epileptic seizure. Could there be some weird condition of the brain that caused sensory hallucinations? Thoughts of making an appointment with her doctor began to form in her mind, but before she could make any firm decision, a man walked close by her, brushing her arm with his coat. Lucy opened her mouth to complain—he had plenty of room to pass without jostling her, after all —but when she saw him, no sound came out of her. It was the man she had seen in the red-lit bar several nights before.

Their eyes met.

He did not slow his pace, yet they seemed to be within close proximity for several seconds. He said, "Curiosity or fear?" And then he was gone, swallowed by the lunch-time crowds.

Something is happening to me, Lucy thought, and for a while she dared to hope that it was something that could show her the door to the life she had misplaced somehow, the life she was supposed to live.

Back at the office, the weird sensations pulsed in and out of her awareness. At one point, sitting opposite Dolores as they drank tea during their break, Lucy felt she possessed tunnel vision, and that only the area in her line of sight appeared normal. If she could but turn her head quickly enough, she would see the room that existed beneath, or alongside, the office that was so familiar to her. She sensed it was a darker place of crumbling decadence, its appointments baroque. Dolores herself would be seen as she really was: a large, colorfully-plumed bird with limited intelligence but able to be trained to perform certain routines.

"Are you all right?" Dolores asked, her face creased in concern. "Are you eating properly, Lucy? Do you sleep enough?" She laughed in mild censure. "I'm sure you spend too much time burning the candle at both ends."

"I burn my candles from the middle," Lucy answered.

Dolores shook her head. "You should look after yourself. None of us is getting any younger."

Lucy was not disposed to thank Dolores for that reminder.

From then on, the awareness came upon Lucy more frequently. It could strike at any time, in any place, teasing her because it did not reveal any secrets, only hint that they were there. Sometimes, when she was out in the open, she thought she caught glimpses of the thin-faced man, although he did not speak to her again. Once, she tried to follow him, but without success. Several times, desperate for answers, or a conclusion, she walked home the short way, hoping that one evening she would come across the tall, gray buildings again, but the narrow street at the end of Victoria Terrace appeared as it always had. She got the impression that the special conditions that had allowed the "other place" to materialize had moved on to somewhere else in the city, like a cloud. She would just have to find it.

During these weeks, Lucy confided in no one about what was

happening to her. She stopped going out with friends, but spent her nights either sitting in her apartment willing the awareness to steal across her, or else walking the streets, searching for an area of magic. She soon realized that concerted effort provided the least success. It seemed that only when she wasn't thinking of the awareness would it come upon her, and then, because she now hungered for it, with annoying brevity. She noticed, without experiencing any particular emotion, that none of her friends had bothered to call her to discover why she had dropped out of circulation. Obviously she meant little to them, but this did not surprise her. She felt little for them in return. No one was concerned about her but for Dolores, whose concern she could well do without.

As March tried vainly to transform the dirty streets of the city, Lucy's boss and his wife celebrated their silver wedding anniversary. Wanting to share their happiness and provide a treat for their two employees, the couple offered to take Lucy and Dolores out for a meal on Friday night. In the office, Dolores agonized about a suitable present, which she felt she and Lucy should buy for the couple. Lucy, disinterested, donated ten pounds, which she could tell Dolores didn't think was enough. Neither could she be bothered to discuss what should be bought. "I'll leave it up to you," she told Dolores, who would probably top up the fund to at least forty pounds with her own cash.

"They're very good to us," Dolores said, her voice full of hurt disappointment. No doubt she often wished she had a colleague more like herself.

Lucy experienced a pang, which began as a warm kind of feeling but quickly hardened to resentment. "They keep you comfortably on your perch," she said, "but you could be flying free."

Dolores stared owlishly at Lucy, clearly attempting to decipher this cryptic statement. Lucy saw her *truly* then. She was not a bird, but certainly bird-like, dressed in disintegrating rags of red, yellow and blue, her hands scaled like the claws of an eagle, her face drooping with pendulous jowls that were very similar to the wattles on a chicken. Lucy stared at Dolores, who had now dropped her attention back to what lay on her desk. The desk itself was different: an ancient, carved table, covered in leather-bound ledgers and dusty glass candlesticks coated with thick wads of colorless stale wax. Long, yellow flames burned steadily up from the mess. Lucy lifted her eyes. Around her, the office had transformed from beige-and-cream tidiness to a high, cavernous room of gray and brown. It was enormous—Lucy could not see its nether end —and filled with huge, shadowy, metal machinery. She was sure these machines were the photocopier, computers, printers and coffee machine, all evolved from some kind of alternative technology which was massive where modern technology was small. The scene before her was horrifying and beautiful, alien and endless. Tilting back her head, she could see that, far above, cracked sky-lights provided a dim illumination, augmented only by the sputtering candle-light. The ancient panes were occluded by the dust and grime of centuries. Lucy became aware that, beyond the office walls, there was a thumping sound, as of vast machinery churning and grinding.

The boss came out of his office, which was now a yellow-paned booth reached by a flight of wooden steps. He looked like a corpse, clad in a robe of rotting brown sacking, his hands bound with flaking bandages. Lucy stood up and walked slowly across the room. She saw a small window frame covered by fraying brown fabric, which she lifted with one hand. Outside, a limitless horizon of unfamiliar buildings reared up in Gothic spires, or spread low in curling labyrinths. Dominating all was the huge, dark factory she had seen near the phantom bar. Tiny figures moved in and out of it in regular lines and sometimes an orange glow would ignite behind its myriad windows. Steam issued from rusting conduits in its walls, while behind it roiled a yellow-black sky, punctuated by the reaching limbs of metal cranes so gigantic they disappeared into dirty cloud. Lucy's eyes ached for the scene before her. She wanted to drink it all in.

Only when she had opened the window, to let in the unsmelled odors of the true city, did she realize Dolores had her hand upon her arm and was repeating her name. Time and space jerked, with a feeling like a cricked neck, sudden and sharp. The awareness had gone.

"What were you doing?" Dolores sounded panicked.

Lucy shook her head. "I saw something."

"That was obvious!"

"Take the rest of the day off," said her boss, clearly discomforted by what he perceived as women's strange behavior, perhaps connected to hormones.

"No," Lucy said. "I'm fine."

Friday evening, Lucy dressed with care, faintly depressed that this riskless gathering was going to be the highlight of her month. Her apartment, she felt, was a bubble of normality within a plasmic mass of uncertainty outside. Soon she would enter into it, step out into the dark and potential.

As she'd anticipated, her walk to the appointed restaurant was surreal. Sometimes it seemed as if there were more than two realities pulsing in and out of her perception, but none of them gained a hold. Realities overlapped. Along the normal city street, a troupe of women dressed in black feathers stalked, wearing grimacing masks, their hands sheathed in scales of dull metal. A shining dark vehicle streaked by like an instrument of torture, barbed and sickled. Lucy saw an old woman, dressed in a sensible camel-hair coat and flat brown shoes, gazing into the window of a shop where a naked, shaven-headed boy pirouetted on a plinth. His limbs were oiled and gleaming in a ruddy light, his chest and arms laced with cuts that leaked a dark liquid which did not look exactly like blood. Lucy laughed out loud at this particular tableau, which caused the old woman to glance around in fear. The shop before her sold tasteless clothes—Lucy could see that now—and the window display was only of stiff, tired mannequins from an earlier age that gestured blindly at one another in the dark.

As she strolled, almost drunkenly, toward her destination, Lucy realized her life had become interesting again. She might be going mad, and this indeed seemed the most likely explanation, but if so, she welcomed it. Anything was better than the non-life she had slipped into. Perhaps this acceptance was part of the madness, and soon she'd be found, mindless and drooling, lost to the "other place" that tantalized her senses. She tried to imagine how Dolores and the boss would cope if this should happen at work. She'd be carted off to the funny farm. *And would that mean that, one day, she'd wake up in a bare white room, cured of her delusions and thus sentenced to eternal tedium in a world she had grown to despise?* The thought of that frightened her more than anything her mind might be doing to her now. She had to learn to control her episodes of awareness, or hide them. Incidents like that which had occurred in the office today must not be repeated. If the awareness came to her, no one must know it but herself.

The meal, surprisingly, took place entirely in the realm of the ordinary. Lucy, though deprived of weird sensations, felt utterly dislocated from her companions. Strangely, this made her feel unexpectedly warm toward them. Her boss and his wife were absurdly happy celebrating this anniversary of perpetual dullness. Their innocence and ignorance touched Lucy's soul. And sad Dolores, manless and childless, caring so much about others when no one was prepared to care about her.

After the meal, Dolores suggested that she and Lucy might share a cab home, even though they lived fairly widely apart. Lucy, however, liked to walk everywhere nowadays. The awareness never came to her in cabs or on buses. She could see the disappointment in Dolores's face as she refused the invitation: The woman did not want the evening to finish. For Lucy, it was yet to begin.

Out on the street, she somehow guessed that tonight something was scheduled to happen. Desperate for revelation, she forgot about going home, and ventured down any narrow, dark street that yawned before her. Instinctively, she sensed that these places were the most likely gateways to the "other place": among the trashcans, beneath fire escapes where desperate measures had been taken in lives devoid of all hope. Walking down unfamiliar alleys where the buildings pressed close together in damp darkness, it would be difficult to tell when she crossed over. She must not strain for it. She must just walk.

She heard the music first: jangly piano. Then the red light spilled across her shoes, and she looked up. There was the bar almost directly beside her. Victory crashed through her body in a hot wave. She virtually ran into the building, determined to ensnare it in her senses before it vanished.

Inside, the bar was full of people, and Lucy realized it was not the same one she had stumbled across the first time. This place was more brightly lit, and less shabby. Huge fans turned slowly in the low ceiling, carving the smoky air into amorphous lumps that caught the light—red and green—and became twisting, vaporous creatures, alive only for a minute. Bloody light glinted off crystal and gold; the carpet beneath her feet was like red velvet. The clientele all looked as if they were on their way to somewhere else. All wore coats and drank rapidly from glasses of every shape and size, talking animatedly, making sharp, thrusting gestures with their hands. Lucy was slightly disappointed that they all appeared so ordinary. She would have expected to see a collection of people like those you'd find in a fetish club: leather and straps and spikes. But then, she reasoned, such fads and fashions were the trimmings of her own hated city. Here, it would have to be different. When she looked more closely at the people around her, she realized they were not ordinary at all, but the difference was in their eyes and in their movements: a sense of danger and threat and promise.

I am home, Lucy thought, and then, *Am I home?*

She walked up to the bar and a thin, sallow-skinned girl in a black halter-neck dress came to take her order.

"Do you have wine?" Lucy asked.

The girl shook her head, and behind her Lucy saw an array of ornate bottles come sharply into focus, dream bottles that had perhaps not existed a moment before.

"Give me something red," she said.

The girl said nothing, but swung away to plunge her arms in among the sparkling bottles, delving for something too far back to be reached.

Lucy looked around herself. For a moment, she thought she saw Dolores sitting on a stool a short distance away from her, then realized it was only a very similar woman: large and fading, with her hair tumbling out of confinement around her neck and shoulders. Dolores' hair, Lucy realized, was created to tumble, but she always pinned it up severely so that it had to strain to escape. Perhaps this stranger *was* Dolores, but a Dolores who had never allowed herself to exist. The woman before her sensed Lucy's attention and directed a smile at her. Something in the expression, which was not exactly predatory, but very akin to it, made Lucy shudder and turn away.

The bartender was putting a glass down before her—a small globe of crystal on a twisted stem, its bowl blistered with vitreous crusts of gold and green.

"How much?" Lucy asked.

The girl jerked her head. "Paid for. By him."

Lucy glanced down the bar and saw the thin-faced man raise his glass to her. Two coils of long, black hair framed his face. He was grinning. She knew then that she had to go to him. It was time, at least, for that.

"Thank you for the drink," she said.

"Taste it." His voice was low, and balanced on the edge of laughter.

Lucy was afraid it would taste of blood, but it didn't, not entirely. This was a taste of ecstasy, of passion, of intense hatred, a road accident, a field of burning poppies. "Different," she said, and waited for him to respond with the words, "Curiosity or fear?" but he didn't.

"You were waiting for the taste," he said.

"Tell me," Lucy said. "I need to know where I am." She felt he knew she was a stranger to this reality, a visitor.

The man shrugged. "There are many junctions."

"That is not an answer." She sighed, fixed him with a stare. "I wonder whether, one day, I'll be able to stay here and not go back."

Again, a shrug. "That is your choice."

"Who are you?"

He smiled more widely, showing very white teeth. "A catcher of dreams. And you?"

"Perhaps a spinner of dreams." She laughed uneasily. "This is all so weird. I can't believe I'm accepting it."

"*Are* you accepting it?"

Lucy looked into his face. It was like looking down a long tunnel. "Yes. Anything is better than nothing." She paused. "Were you waiting for me?"

He put his head on one side. "I have suspicions about you, that's all. A hunch. There's no pressure."

"I want to see this world," Lucy said. "I don't want to hover on the edge. I want to be in it. I know that it exists." She faltered. "I don't want to go back."

"Why not?"

"My life is hell back there. It is nothing. I might as well be dead."

The man raised his brows. "Oh!" He turned toward the bar, signaled the skinny girl, before glancing back at Lucy. "Another drink?"

"I haven't finished this one yet," Lucy said, and then realized that she had. "Oh, all right."

He put a glass into her hand, and this one was the size of a normal wine-glass and filled with a rich green liquid. When she tasted it, summer fields soared over her like a wave. It was an innocent drink and tinged only faintly with the fever heat of tortured jealousy.

The Dream-Catcher led her out of the bar, onto a terrace at the back of the building. Here, the city spread before them, an impossible jumble of tormented shapes and sounds and smells. Lucy breathed it all in, through every pore. It was ugly, yet entrancing; a fantasy world where anything was possible. The people here would not be dull or obsessed with trivia. She sensed they all led dangerous lives, were tragic and fey, cruel and mysterious. Like the man beside her. She looked at him.

"Tell me I'm not mad," she said.

"You're not mad." He leaned upon the rusting railings, which were entwined with the dead stalks of a plant that looked like the bodies of desiccated serpents. Fragile, withered blooms rustled like paper among the fibrous coils. "One day you became aware of the worlds beyond the narrow imagination of the ordinary, that's all."

She sensed he could tell her much more, but perhaps she had to ask the right questions to invoke the information. "But why me? I'm not that imaginative. Does this happen to many people?"

The Dream-Catcher looked at her askance. "Only the hungry," he answered, "the *very* hungry."

Lucy turned around and leaned back against the railings, her arms spread out to either side. "I feel like I'm being given a second chance." She shook her head. "I really don't think I could bear to go back. That is… only if I can't come here again."

"You come here often," the Dream-Catcher said. "You see this world all the time."

Lucy shook her head. "I see *glimpses* of it. That's not enough. I want more. I want to meet people, talk to them. I want to explore every corner. Just an evening a week would do. I could put up with my ordinary life then, I'm sure." She didn't know whether the Dream-Catcher was a powerful figure in this world, but she suspected he had the ability to grant her request if he wanted to. What must she do to convince him? She asked him this.

"You do not have to convince me of anything," he replied, "but you do have to be sure, for once you decide, there is no going back. You cannot exist wholly in two worlds. You have become aware of this one, and the gate is open, but you are just sampling the place at the moment."

Lucy uttered a scornful laugh. "I have nothing to go back for. My life is empty. Here…" she gestured widely to encompass her surroundings. "Here, there is life and adventure and purpose."

"How do you know that?"

Shrugging, she turned away, feeling embarrassed. "Okay, I got carried away. But you just have no idea what my life has become." She glanced at him. "Then again, maybe you do."

He shook his head. "I do not know you," he said. "There are far too many people to know."

"Are you happy here?" Lucy asked him sharply.

He smiled. "There is a color for happiness, and it resides in a pearly bottle. It may be drunk. There are an infinite number of colors."

"I think I want to go back now," Lucy said.

"So much for exploring."

She gave him an arch glance. "I only need to think."

Everyone had moved on; the bar was empty but for the skinny girl, who was wiping the counter with a rag in lazy, circular movements. She did not look up as Lucy passed her. A clock was ticking loudly and the music was silenced. *Do I want to leave?* Lucy wondered. When she stepped outside, it was probable she'd walk back into her mundane life. What if she couldn't find the gateway again? Did she really need to think? There was no fear inside her. She wasn't really sure why she was hesitating over the decision. Tomorrow being Saturday, she'd have to go to the supermarket and stock up on her meager supplies. Then she'd spend the evening walking around again, perhaps without success, looking for a way into this other world, a place where she could hold onto it. What was the point in that?

She walked back out onto the terrace, half-expecting the Dream-Catcher to have vanished, but he hadn't. He was still leaning against the rail, staring out over the city.

"I've made up my mind," Lucy said. "What do I do?"

He turned around slowly. "Are you sure?"

She walked toward him and rested her forearms upon the rail. Out there she heard the echoes of screaming, and a gout of flame spurted up, followed by muffled thunder. There were gunshots, and the crack of leather against flesh. There was hysterical music and crazy laughter. Below, on the street, a young, pale girl danced by in the arms of a tall, dark man. They were followed by a grotesque child banging a tambourine, and a monkey in a waistcoat strewing petals from a little basket. Behind them, soaring high, was the great dark building Lucy had thought was a factory. She could see now that it was a palace. Enormous black statues of winged men flanked its yawning, dark entrance. Fire burned within, flickering behind panes of crystal.

Lucy surveyed this scene for a few moments, then said, "I am sure."

The Dream-Catcher nodded. Now, he wasn't smiling, and appeared tense. Was he afraid she'd change her mind again? "Then take off your coat, for you are home."

It was only a light overcoat, insubstantial against the winter chill of the streets she knew and wanted to forget; a garment bought cheap in a sale because she could afford nothing better. Lucy undid the buttons and, with a feeling of abhorrence, wriggled out of the coat, letting it fall to the ground. As she did so, it seemed something larger than a mere garment fell from her shoulders. She felt taller, and already the tide of memory was turning, reeling in the life of Lucy, going back and back, to the time she had entered the gray world of the mundane. The Dream-Catcher handed her a glass. This was filled with a purple liquid. When she tasted it, it was the essence of kings.

"Well?" said the Dream-Catcher.

Slowly, Lucy felt herself settling into a persona who had been sleeping. It felt slightly uncomfortable and unused, but familiar. Not all of what she had experienced was clear yet, but she knew what the Dream-Catcher wanted to hear. "I was right," she said. "But I had to see for myself. They claim to avoid the unspeakable, yet in their greed and ignorance, they have created all the worst possible forms of what they perceive as hell." She shook her head, smiled quizzically. "Famine, slaughter—they are some of the faces—but there are others too, the gray faces of conformity and dead minds and hearts. It is bizarre, but the process must work in reverse now. Hell's torments are torments no longer. In that world, I have seen people attempting to emulate the extremes of the inferno in an attempt to escape the horror of their predicament, which is nullity. They have created a void for themselves. It is terrible." She reached out for the Dream-Catcher with one long, sinuous, bronze-skinned arm. How beautiful her flesh felt to her soul. He nestled to her side, and she kissed him. "Dark angel, I have missed you!" she said.

"Welcome home," said the Dream-Catcher.

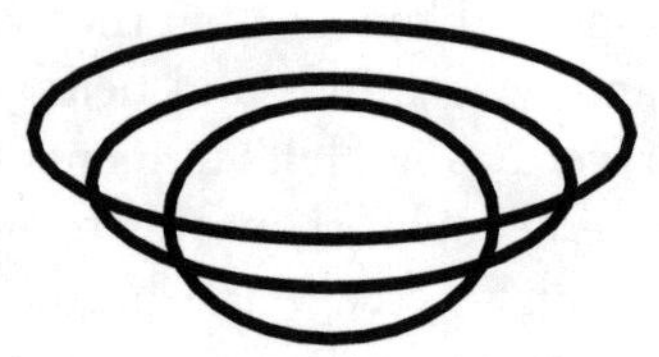

DARK SOCIETY

by Brian Aldiss

...for though he left this World not many Days past, yet every hour you know largely addeth to that dark Society; and considering the incessant Mortality of Mankind, you cannot conceive that there dieth in the whole Earth so few as a thousand an Hour....

—Sir Thomas Browne

People in their millions, dead and unobliging.

Marching the clouded streets, trying still to articulate the miseries that had constricted their previous phase of existence. Trying to articulate what had no tongue. To recapture something...

An undersized military computer op in Aldershot tapped an unimportant juridical decision into the Internet, addressing it to a distant army outpost in a hostile country. Like the mycelia of fungus, progressing unseen underground in a mass of branching filaments as if imbued with consciousness, so the web of the Internet system spread unseen across the globe, utilizing even insignificant army ops in its blind quest for additional sustenance—and in so doing awakening ancient chthonian Forces to a resentment of the new technology which, in its blind, semi-autonomous drive for domination, threatened the Forces' nutrient substrata deep in the planetary expanses of human awareness. The little op, signing over to the next shift, while those concealed forces were already—in a way that took no heed of time or human reason—moving, moving to re-establish themselves in the non-astronomical universe, checked with the clock and betook himself to the nearest chipper.

The battalion had commandeered an old manor house for the duration of the campaign. Other ranks were housed in huts in the grounds, well inside the fortified perimeter. Only officers were comfortably housed in the big old house.

Year by year they were destroying the mansion, pulling down the oak paneling for fires, using the library for an indoor shooting gallery, misusing anything vulnerable.

The colonel damped the audio on his power box and turned to his adjutant.

"You heard most of that, Julian? Division sitrep from Aldershot. Verdict of the court martial just in. They've found Corporal Cleat mentally unstable, unfit to stand trial."

"Dismissed the service?"

"Exactly. Just as well. Saves any publicity. See to his discharge papers, will you?"

The adjutant stalked toward the door and called the orderly sergeant.

The colonel went over to the wood fire burning in the grate and warmed his behind. He stared out of the tall window at the manor grounds. A morning haze limited visibility to about two hundred yards. Everything looked peaceful enough. A group of soldiers in fatigues were strengthening the security fence. The tall trees of the drive were in themselves a reassurance of stability. Yet it never did to forget that this was enemy territory.

He failed to understand the case of Corporal Cleat. Certainly the man was strange. It happened that the colonel knew the Cleat family. The Cleats had made a great deal of money in the early eighties, trading in a chain of electronic stores, which they had sold off at great profit to a German company. Cleat should have become an officer; instead, he had chosen to serve in the ranks.

Some quarrel with his father, silly bugger. Very English habit. Went and married a Jewish girl. Of course, Vivian Cleat, the father, had been a bit of a tight-arse and no mistake. Got himself knighted, for all that.

It was useless to try to understand other people. The army's concern was with ordering people, getting them organized, not understanding them. Order was everything, when you thought about it.

All the same, Corporal Cleat had been guilty. The whole battalion knew that. Division had handled the matter well, for once; the less publicity the better at a rather tricky time. Discharge Cleat and forget about the whole business. Get on with the damned war.

"Julian?"

"Yessir?"

"What did you make of Corporal Cleat? Arrogant little bugger, would you say? Headstrong?"

"Couldn't say, sir. Wrote poetry, so I'm informed."

"Better get in touch with his wife. Lay on transport for her to meet Cleat and get the man off our hands. Goodbye to bad rubbish."

"Sir, the wife died while Cleat was in the glasshouse. Eunice Rosemary Cleat, age twenty-nine. You may recall her father was a herpetologist at Kew. Lived out near Esher somewhere. A verdict of suicide was brought in."

"On him?"

"On her."

"Oh, bugger. Well, ring Welfare. Get shot of the man. Get him off our hands. Back to England."

He took a passage on a ferry. He huddled in a corner of the passenger deck, arms wrapped around himself, fearful of air and motion and he knew not what. He thumbed a lift which took him all the way to Cheltenham. From there he paid for a seat on a coach to Oxford. He needed money, lodgings. He also needed some form of help. Mental aid. Rehabilitation. He did not know exactly what he wanted. Only that something was wrong, that he was not himself.

He booked into a cheap hotel in the Iffley Road. In the market he sought out a cheap Indian clothing stall where he bought himself a T-shirt, a pair of stone-washed jeans and a heavy-duty Chinese-made shirt. He went to see his bank in Cornmarket. In one of his accounts, a substantial sum of money remained.

He got drunk that night with a friendly mob of young men and women. In the morning he could remember none of their names. He was sick, and left the cheap hotel in a bad temper. As he quit the room, he looked back hastily. Someone or something had caught his eye. He had thought a man was sitting dejectedly on the unmade bed. There was no one. Another delusion.

He went to his old college to see the bursar. It was out-of-term time; behind the worn gray walls of Septuagint, life had congealed like cold mutton gravy. The porter informed him that Mr. Robbins was away for the morning, looking over some property in Wolvercote. He sat in Robbins' office, huddled in a corner, hoping not to be seen. Robbins did not return until 3:30 in the afternoon.

Robbins ordered a pot of tea. "As you know, Ozzie, it's really a storeroom, and has reverted to that use. It's been—what? Four years?"

"Five." Oswald Cleat spoke in a low voice.

"Well, it's a bit awkward." He looked considerably annoyed. "More than a bit, in fact. Look, Ozzie, I have a pile of work to do. I suppose we could put you up at home, just for a—"

"I don't want that. I want my old room back. Want to hide away, out of everyone's sight. Come on, John, you owe me a favor."

Robbins said, calmly pouring Earl Grey into his cup, "I owe you bloody nothing, my friend. It was your father who was the college benefactor. Mary and I have done enough for you as it is. Besides, we know what you've been up to, blotting your service career. To put you up here in college again is to break all the rules. As you know."

"Sod you, then!" He turned away in anger. But as he reached the door, Robbins called him back.

The storeroom under the eaves of Joshua Building looked much as it had done. Light filtered in from one northern skylight. It was a long room, one side of it sloping sharply with the angle of the roof, as if a giant had taken a butcher's knife to it. The place smelt closed, musty with ancient knowledge percolating up from below. He stood staring angrily at a pile of old armchairs for a while. Setting to work dragging them to one side, he found his old bed was still there, and even his old oak chest, which he had had since schooldays. He knelt on the dusty boards and unlocked it. It contained a few possessions. Clothes, books, a Japanese aviator's sword, no drink. An unframed photograph of Eunice wearing a scarf. He slammed the lid down and fell back on the bed.

Holding the photograph up to the light, he studied the colored representation of Eunice's face. Pretty, yes; rather silly, yes. But no more of a fool than he. Love had been a torture, merely emphasizing his own futility. You took more note of a woman than of a man, of course. You expected nothing from your fellow men—or your bloody father. All those signals women put out, unknowingly, designed to grab your attention…

Human physiology and psychology had been cunningly designed for maximum human disquiet, he thought.

Small wonder he had made a miniature hell of his life.

Later he went out into town and got drunk, ascending from Morrell's ales through vodka to a cheap whiskey in a Jerico pub.

Next morning was bad. Shakily, he climbed on the bed to stare out of the skylight. The world seemed to have been drained of color overnight. The slate roofs of Septuagint shone with damp. Beyond, slate roofs of other distant colleges, an entire landscape of slate and tile, with fearful abysses between sharp-peaked hills.

After a while, he gathered himself together, put on his shoes, and went along the attic corridor before descending the three flights of Number Twelve staircase. The stone steps were worn from centuries of students who had been installed in rooms here, each in a little cell with an oak door, to sop up what learning they could. The wooden paneling on the walls was kicked and scuffed. *How like prison*, he thought.

Down in the inner quad, he looked about him bemusedly. The Fellows Hall stood to one side. On impulse, he crossed the flagstones and went in. The hall was built in a Perpendicular style, with tall windows and heavy linen-fold panels. Between the windows hung solemn portraits of past benefactors. His father's portrait had been removed from near the end of the line; in its stead hung the portrait of a Japanese man in gown and mortar board, gazing serenely through his spectacles.

A scout had been polishing silver trophies in one corner of the room. He came forward now to ask, with a mixture of obsequiousness and sharpness which Cleat remembered in college servants, "Can I help you, sir? This is the Fellows' Hall."

"Where's the portrait of Sir Vivian Cleat which used to hang here?"

"This is Mr. Yashimoto, sir. One of our recent benefactors."

"I know it's Mr. Yashimoto. I'm asking you about another eminent benefactor, Vivian Cleat. It used to hang here. Where is it?"

"I expect it's gone, sir."

"Where, man? Where's it gone?"

The scout was tall and thin and dry of countenance. As if to squeeze one last drop of moisture from his face, he frowned and said, "There's the Buttery, sir. Some of our less important worthies were moved there last Hilary Term, as I recall."

Outside the Buttery, he ran into Homer Jenkins, a one-time friend who held the Hughenden Chair in Human Relations. Jenkins had been a sportsman in his time, a rowing blue, and retained a slim figure into his sixties; a Leander scarf was draped around his neck. Jenkins agreed blithely that Cleat's father's portrait now hung by the bar.

"Why isn't it with the other college benefactors?"

"You don't really want me to answer that, dear boy?" Uttered with a smile and head slightly on one side. Cleat remembered the Oxford style.

"Not greatly."

"Very wise. If I may say so, it's a surprise to see you about here again."

"Thanks so much." As he turned on his heel, the Hughenden professor called, "Hard lines about Eunice, Ozzie, dear boy!"

He bought a bowl of soup in a Pizza Piazza, feeling ill, telling himself he was no longer in prison. But the narrative of his life had in some way been mislaid and something like an intestinal rumbling told him that there was within himself a part of him he would never know again. *Unseen, the cancer stops to lick chops and then again devours....*

A teenage girl drifted into the wine bar and said, "Oh, there you are. I thought I might find you." She was studying Jurisprudence at Lady Margaret Hall, she said, and finding it all a bit of a bore. But daddy was a judge, and so... She sighed and laughed simultaneously.

As she talked, he realized she had been one of a group of students of the previous night. He had taken no notice of her that he could recall.

"I could tell you were a follower of Chomsky," she said, laughing.

"I believe in nothing." To himself he thought, sickly, *But I must believe in something or other, if only I could get at it.*

"You look, well, ghastly today, if you don't mind my saying so. But then, you're a poet, aren't you? You were spouting Seamus Heeley last night."

"It's Heaney, Seamus Heaney, so I'm led to believe. Do you want a drink?"

"You're a poet and a criminal, so you said!" Laughingly, she clutched his arm.

He did not want her, did not want her company, but there she stood, new-minted, eager, unenslaved, springlike, waifish, agog for life.

"Want to come back to my dreadful dump for coffee?"

"How dreadful?" Still half-laughing, teasing, bright, curious, trusting, yet with a little something like guile born for a relationship such as this.

"*Historically* dreadful."

"Okay. Coffee and research. Nothing more."

Later, he told himself she had wanted something more. Half-wanted at least, or she would never have made her way before him in her brief skirt, upward round the labyrinthine coils of Staircase Twelve to that lumber room, or have fallen, when she gained the top, panting and laughing with open mouth—pristine as the inside of a tulip—on the dusty bed. He had not meant to rush her. Not meant that at all.

Well, she was a sporting young lady, perhaps aware afterward that she had unconsciously enticed him, an older, world-stained man with a smell of incarceration yet about him, and had departed without indecent haste, still with a kind of smile, a smile now more like a sneer, toward safety or ruination as character dictated. Degraded, defeated, possibly, but full of a spirit—he forced himself to hope—which would not admit to that defeat. Not like Eunice.

"Whatever drives us to these things…" he said, half-aloud, but did not complete the sentence, aware of his treachery even to himself.

Near at hand, a relay clicked.

The sky darkened over Oxford. The rain came down again as if the hydrological cycle were working out a new means of replenishing the Thames from an untapped level of the troposphere. It washed against the lumber-room windows with antediluvian splendor.

He stirred himself toward evening and ventured farther into the recesses of the room. There he discovered a crate full of his old books and videos. Pulling it out, he found, hiding farther in the gloom, a box containing his old computer.

Without particularly conscious volition, he carried the Power Paq from its box and plugged it into the mains. He dusted off the monitor screen with his sock. LCDs winked at him.

He pushed in a CD protruding like a square tongue, and rifled the keys with his fingers. He had forgotten how to operate the thing.

A leering face came on, moving into close-up from a red distance. He managed to remove it and eject the disc, whereupon a slight whirring started and a sheet of A4 paper began extruding from the fax slot. He regarded it in nervous surprise as it floated to the floor. He switched off the computer.

In a minute, he picked up the message and sat on the bed to read it. The sender of the fax addressed him by his first name. The text was only partly comprehensible:

Oz as was Oz,

If I say I know where you are. Physical action. Its low comedy mark us, but such. It is such. Where there are no placed no place no position at all as regarding baker's shops.

Or to say only to say or to say all the more the more there is to say like stamens on the pyrocanthus. Is yours also? Also an ingredient. I hope it comes through. Trying.

Clear the street. Clearer in the street. The crooked way. I mean the clear the path from. You and I. Forever its.

The existence. Can you speak of existence of what does not existence. I clear nonexistence. I nonexist. Speak.

Speak me. New street no clear street clear communicate. Slow. Difficulty.

Past tense.

Eunice

"Bloody nonsense," he said, screwing up the paper, determined not to show himself he was disturbed by the mere fact of the message. A haunted computer? Rubbish, balls, idiocy. Someone was trying to make a fool of him; one of the fellows of the college, most likely.

A peremptory knock at the door.

"Come."

Homer Jenkins entered the lumber room, catching Cleat standing there in the middle of the room. Cleat threw the ball of paper at him. Jenkins caught it neatly.

"Evenings are closing in."

"The rain should clear."

"At least it's mild. Don't you need a light in here?"

Polite North European noises. Jenkins came to the point. "A young woman has invaded the porter's lodge with a complaint against you. Sexual molestation, that kind of thing. I am quite able to deal with young women of her kind, but I must warn you the bursar says that if there is such an occurrence again, we shall have to rethink your position, doubtless to your detriment."

Cleat stood his ground.

"That study of yours on the Spanish Civil War, Homer. Have you completed it yet? Is it published, or are you still stuck on that bit where Franco became Governor of the Canary Islands?"

Jenkins was fully Cleat's equal when it came to standing one's ground. The Jenkins family had enjoyed wealth for several generations, ever since the days of Jenkins' Irresistible Flea Powder (no longer mentioned by the newer generations), and owned rolling acres on the Somerset border. This background made Homer Jenkins confident when it came to standing his own ground. He did it, moreover, with a kind of smile and an outward thrust of the chin.

In a calm voice, he said, "Ozzie, you received some recognition as a poet before you served your stretch in clink, and of course the college welcomed your success, minor though it was. We attempted to overlook your other proclivities *vis à vis* your father's endowment to Septuagint. However, if you wish to get back on your feet again, and if possible restore your reputation, you must be advised that the college's benevolence extends only so far. Retribution is never pleasant."

Turning with calm dignity, he made for the door.

"You sound like Hamlet's father!" Cleat shouted. Jenkins did not turn back.

He woke on the following morning to a faint click, audible even above the sound of rain on the roof just over his bed. Another note was emerging from the fax.

Oz was,

O Im getting the it of hanging hang of it. Soon soon hobnails on streets I speak you ordinary. Difficulty. Garble garble other physical laws. Lores

Follow me ill repeat it follow.

Follow dont keep still. Still love you still.

Eunice

He sat with the flimsy paper in his hand, thinking about his late wife. A fragment of a poem came to his head.

Being among the men taken captive
The men the enemy humiliated
The men who cursed themselves
The men whose beloved women had
Preceded them to hell

He began to conjure up a long poem where a man, captive like himself, suffered all to be reunited with a dead wife, even if it entailed a descent into hell itself. He thrilled to the vision. Perhaps he could write again. Words and phrases jostled in his mind like prisoners seeking release.

This time, he did not screw up the message. Without necessarily giving it credence, he nevertheless felt belief of some kind stir within him—a remarkable phenomenon in itself.

Yes, yes, he would write and confound them all. He still had—whatever he once had. Except Eunice. For her he felt an unexpected longing, but he set it aside under the prompting to write. He rummaged about in his chest, but found no suitable writing materials. A journey down to the nearest stationer was indicated. An image swam before his eyes, not of his dead wife, but of a mint, unblemished pack of white A4 copy paper.

Locking the door of his room behind him, he stood for a moment in the gloom of the landing. Waves of uncertainty overcame him like a personalized nausea. Was he any good as a poet? He had been no good as a soldier. Or a son. Or even as a husband.

He would bloody well show the likes of Homer Jenkins, if he had to go through hell to do so. But the gloom, the airlessness of this top landing was oppressive....

He went slowly down the first flight of stairs. The rain was falling even more heavily now, making an intense drumming. The farther down the stairs he went, the darker it became.

Pausing at one landing, he peered out of a slit-like window into the quad below. So heavy was the downpour, it was hard to distinguish anything clearly, beyond walls of stone inset with blind windows. A flash of lightning came, to reveal a fleeing figure far below, carrying what looked like a plate—it could not be a halo!—over his head. Another flash. Cleat had a momentary impression that the whole college was sinking, sliding down intact into the clayey soils of Oxford, where bones of gigantic reptiles lay yet undiscovered.

Sighing, he continued downward.

A little fat man, fortyish and sallow, with rain dripping from hair and blunt face, bumped into Cleat at the next stairwell.

"What a soaker, eh? They told me you were back, Ozzie," he said, without any great display of delight. "There's one of your metaphysical poems I've always rather liked. The one about, oh, you know—how does it go?"

Cleat did not recognize the man. "Sorry, it's been—"

"Something about First Causes. Ashes and strawberries, I seem to remember. You see, the way we scientists look at it is that before the Big Bang, the *ylem* existed nowhere. It had nowhere to exist *in*. At all at all, as our Irish friends are purported to say. The elementary particles released in the initial—you understand that *explosion* is hardly an adequate word —perhaps you poets can come up with a better one—*ylem's* a good one —the initial bang included in that bargain bundle both time and space. So that in that first one-hundredth of a second—"

His eyes blurred with intellectual excitement. A small bubble of spit formed on his lower lip like a new universe coming into being. He had begun to wave his arms, when Cleat protested that he did not want to be drawn into a discussion at that moment.

"Of course not," said the scientist, laughing and clutching Cleat's shirt so that he would not escape. "Mind you, we all feel the same."

"We don't. We couldn't possibly."

"We do, we cannot grasp that initial concept of nothingness, of a place without dimensions of space or time. So *nothingy* that even nothing cannot exist." He laughed in a panting sort of way, like an intelligent bull terrier. "The concept frightens hell out of me—such a no-place must be either bliss or perpetual torment. It is the task of science to make clear what previously was—"

Cleat cried out that he had an appointment below, but the grip on his shirt did not slacken.

"Where science appears to meet religion. This timeless, spaceless space—the pre-*ylem* universe, so to speak—bears more than a superficial resemblance to Heaven, the old Christian myth. Heaven may still be around, permeated, of course, by fossil radiation—"

The scientist interupted himself by bursting into laughter, pressing his face nearer to Cleat's.

"—Or of course—you'll appreciate this, Ozzie, being a poet—equally, *Hell!* 'This is Hell, nor are we out of it,' as Shakespeare immortally puts it."

"*Marlowe!*" screamed Cleat. Tearing himself away from the other's grasp, he rushed off down the next flight of steps.

"Tut, of course, Marlowe…" said the scientist, standing alone and lonely on the stair. "Marlowe. Must remember."

He mopped his streaming brow with a used tissue.

But it was getting so dark. The noise grew louder. The stairs turned about anti-clockwise in tortuous lapidity, and with them went his grip on reality. It was a relief when the steps terminated and he came to a broader space, marked at each end by archways, beyond which dim lanterns glowed in the darkness.

He was slightly puzzled. Somehow, he seemed to have overshot ground level. The clamminess of the air certainly indicated he was underground, lost in the ample cellarage of Septuagint. He remembered the cellarage of old; here, no dusty racks of bottles were to be seen. The halitus of his breath hung in the air, slow to disperse.

Going forward hesitantly, he passed under one of the arches into a cobbled space, where more steps presented themselves. He looked up.

Everything was hard to make out. He could not determine whether rock or stone or sky was overhead. No rain fell. He found it uncanny that the downpour could have cut off. Something prompted him not to call out. There was nothing for it but to go forward.

His mood was glum. Not for the first time, he was on bad terms with himself. Why was it he could not establish friendly relationships with others? Why be so unpleasant to the fat scientist—Neil Someone, could it have been?—who was, when all was said and done, no more eccentric than many other dons in the University of Oxford?

Oxford? This could not be Oxford, or even Cowley! He plodded on until, uncertain of his whereabouts, he paused. Immediately, a figure—Cleat could not tell if it was male or female—was passing by, gray of aspect and clad in a long gown.

"Have you seen a stationer near here?"

The figure paused, tweaked up his cheeks in the genesis of a smile, then strode on. As Cleat started off again, the figure vanished—there, then not there.

"Shit and *ylem*, very peculiar," he said to himself, hiding a distinct sense of unease from himself. Vanished, completely vanished, like one of Neil Someone's elementary particles...

The steps broadened, became shallow, petered out into cobbles. On either side stood what passed, he supposed, for houses; they contained no signs of life. It was all very old-fashioned in an artificial way, like a nineteenth-century representation of sixteenth-century Nuremberg.

He continued uncertainly, to descend once more until he came to a wide space which he mentally termed the Square. Here he halted.

As soon as he stopped, the surroundings began moving. He took a pace back in startlement: Everything stopped. He stopped: Buildings, roadways, broke into uneasy movement. He took another pace: Everything stopped. He stopped again: Everything he could see, the dim and watercolor environs about him, launched into movement again. A sort of forward but circular movement.

An image came to him of a crab, the crab who believes that everyone but he walks sideways.

This relativity of movement was the least of it. For when he walked, not only was the universe stilled, but it was empty of people (people?). But when he stood still, not only did the universe begin its crabwise shuffle, but it became the stage for a bustling crowd of people (people?).

Cleat thought longingly of his safe army prison cell.

Remaining stockstill, he attempted to single out faces in the crowd. To his mortal eyes, how dead and unobliging they were! Jostle they certainly did, pushing past him and past each other, not hurriedly but merely because there seemed so little room: although, with the constant movement of streets and thoroughfares, the various ways seemed to be expanding at a steady rate to accommodate them. Their clothes lacked color and variety. It was hard to distinguish male from female. Their contours, their faces, their body language, were somehow blurred. He found by experiment that, by keeping his head rigid and allowing his eyes to slide out of focus, he could in fact make out individual faces: man, woman, young, old, dark, light, occidental, oriental, long-haired, short-haired, bearded or otherwise, mustached or otherwise, tall, thin, stocky, fat, upright or stooped. Yet—what was wrong with his retina?—all alike without expression; not merely without expression, but seemingly without the facility to conjure up expressions. Abstracts of faces.

Surrounding him on all sides was an immense dark society, who appeared neither alive nor dead. And this society was proceeding this way and that, entirely without ambition or objective.

They seemed like phantasms.

They jostled by Cleat until he could stand the tension no more. As he began to run, as he first tensed his leg muscles for flight, the vast, homogeneous crowd vanished, was gone in an instant, leaving him isolated in a motionless street.

"There must be a scientific explanation," he said. The only one that occurred to him was that he was suffering a kind of terminal delusion. He shook his head violently, trying to think himself back into the familiar old expanding universe of hurtling velocities to which he was accustomed. But this present cloudy world remained, obeying its own variant set of physical laws.

What had Eunice's second message said? Wasn't that something about other physical laws?

A cold horror gripped him, drying his throat, chilling his skin.

Bracing himself to proceed, he told himself that, whatever was happening, he deserved what he got.

He walked and walked, to emerge at last before a different kind of building; an attempt, he thought, at some kind of a… well, town hall? It conformed to no order of architecture he knew, being built of a spongy material, with elaborate flights of steps leading to no visible doorway, with balconies to which no access was visible, with towering columns supporting no visible roofing, with a portico under which no one could walk. It was preposterous, impossible, and imposing.

He stopped in some wonderment—though wonderment was a quality of which he was rapidly being drained.

As soon as he stopped, the universe was set in motion and the enormous building bore down on him like an ocean liner on a helpless swimmer.

He remained rooted to the spot and thus found himself entering the great structure.

A brighter light than he had hitherto encountered in the cloudy world illuminated the inside of the hall. He was at a loss to think where it came from.

Scattered about the floor were huge piles of belongings, extremely tatterdemalion in aspect. Cloudy personages were picking through the heaps. Everything moved with that unsettling crabwise movement, as if caught in the whirlpool of a spiral nebula.

If he stood stockstill, he could see what was happening. He found he could relax his auditory nerve much like his optical one, and so could hear sounds for the first time. The voices of the personages drifted to him, high and squeaky, as if they had inhaled helium. They seemed to be exclaiming with delight as they disinterred items from the various heaps.

He moved forward to see more closely. Everything vanished. He halted. It all returned. *No, I don't want this;* but when he shook his head involuntarily, the building became no more than an echoing, empty place, moving with the stealth of a cat.

The various piles consisted of curious old belongings. Mountains of old suitcases, many battered and worn as if humanly exhausted from a long, sad journey. Stacks and stacks of footwear of all kinds: lace-up boots, ladies' slippers, clodhoppers, children's patent-leather shoes, bedroom slippers, brogues, shoes for this, shoes for that, worn or new, shoes enough to walk to Mars and back by themselves. Eyeglasses in almost as large a glassy heap: pince-nez, hornrims, monocles, all the rest of them. Clothes: countless rags of every description, indescribable, towering up toward the roof. And—no, yes—hair! Hair by the ton, glossy black, lily white, all shades in between, hair of humans, curled and bobbed and straight, some scalps with pigtails, their ribbons still trailing. Teeth, too, the most terrible pile of all: molars, wisdoms, dog teeth, eye teeth, even milk teeth, some with flesh adhering to their forked roots.

They vanished. Instinctively, Cleat had moved, shaken by an agonizing sense of recognition.

He fell to the ground, remaining kneeling. The dreadful interior came back.

Now he saw more clearly, by unfocusing his eyes, the people who picked over the sordid array. They merely reclaimed what had once been theirs, what remained rightfully theirs.

He saw women—yes, that's it, bald women of all ages—reclaiming their hair, trying it on, being made whole again.

Many others of the dark society stood by, applauding, as the seekers were made whole.

Then he thought he saw Eunice.

Of course, she had Jewish blood in her veins. Here in this terrible place you might find her, among the wronged, the disinherited, the slaughtered.

He crouched where he was, not daring to move in case she vanished. Was it she? A watercolor version of the Eunice he had once loved?

Something like tears moved upward through his being, a gigantic remorse for mankind. He cried her name.

Everything vanished except the great, empty hall, unmoving as fate.

He froze, and she was approaching him! She held out a hand in recognition.

Even as he reached for it, she vanished.

When he froze into stillness, she and all about her faded back into being.

"We can never be together," she said, and her voice carried a distant and forlorn note, like an owl's cry above sodden woodland. "For one of us is of the dead and one is not, my Ozzie dearest!"

She kept fading in and out as he tried to reply.

She knelt beside him, resting a hand on his shoulder. They remained like that in silence, heads close together, the man, the woman. He learned to speak with almost no lip movement.

"I don't understand."

"I never understood…. But my messages reached you. You have come! Oh, you have come! Even here you have come! How brave you are…."

At her whispered words, a little warmth kindled within him: so he had after all some virtue, something on which to build in future, whatever that future was to be…. He stared into her eyes but saw no response there, indeed found a difficulty in appreciating them as eyes.

Brokenly, he said, "Eunice, if it is you in any way, I'm *sorry*—just deeply and unremittingly sorry. For everything. I'm living in a hell of my own. I came to say that, to tell you that, to follow you down into Gehenna."

It seemed she regarded him steadily. He knew she saw him not as once she had, but now as a kind of thing, an anomaly in whatever served here as a variant on the space-time continuum.

"All these..." As he almost gestured, the enormous sordid piles wavered towards invisibility. "What are they doing *now*? It's... I mean, the Holocaust, it's all so long ago. So *long*..."

She was disinclined to answer until he prompted her, when her being swam and almost disintegrated before his eyes.

"There is no *now* here, no *long ago*. Can you understand that? It's not like that here. Those time indicators are arbitrary rules in your... whatever—dimensions? Here, they have no meaning."

"Oh God..." He moaned, covering his eyes against an overpowering sense of loss.

When he peeped between his fingers, the building was again in motion. He remained rigid—thinking, if there's no *now* here, neither is there a proper *here*—and passed through the walls into a kind of space that was not a space. He thought he had lost Eunice, but the general movement carried her close again, still kneeling toward him.

She was speaking, explaining, as if to her there had been no sense of absence.

"Nor is there any name, once passionately spoken but long forgotten in your time-afflicted sphere, which is not tenanted here. All, even the most maligned, must join this vast society, increasing its number day by day." Was she singing? Was he hearing aright in his state of profound disturbance? Was it even possible they communicated at all? "The myriads who have left no memorial behind, and those whose reputations linger through what you term *ages*—all find their place...."

Her voice faded as he moved imploringly, hoping for a more human word. If he could get her back... But the thought dislocated as again the great hall was empty and still, filled only with an immense silence as austere as death itself.

Again he was forced to crouch, immobile, until the semblances of habitation and her smudgy presence re-entered the cloudy world.

The shade of Eunice continued to talk, perhaps unaware that anything had happened—or maybe that he had vanished from her variety of sight.

"King Harold is here, removing the arrow from his eye; Socrates, recovered from his hemlock; whole armies freed of their wounds; the Bogomils, back again; Robespierre undecapitated; Archbishop Cranmer and his brave speech absolved from the flames; Julius Caesar, unstabbed; Cleopatra herself, unharmed by asps, as I by my father's cobra.... You must learn, Ozzie...."

As she droned on with her long, long list, as if she had forever to specify a myriad individuals—*and so she has*, he thought in dismay—he could only ask himself, over and over, *how do I get back to Oxford, how can I ever get back to Septuagint, with or without this phantasm of my love?*

"...Magdeburg, Mohacs, Lepanto, Stalingrad, Kosovo, Saipan, Kohima, Agincourt, Austerlitz, Okinawa, Somme, Geok-Depe, the Boyne, Crecy..."

And will this shade assist me?

He broke into her litany.

Scarcely moving his lips, he asked, "Eunice, Eunice, my poor ghost, I fear you. I fear everything hereabouts. I knew Hell would be dreadful, but not that it would be at all like this. How can I return with you to the real world? Tell me, please."

The hall was still marvelously in movement, as though its substance was music rather than stone. Now she was more distant from him, and her reply, dreadful as it was, came thin and piping, watery as bird song, so that at first he could hardly believe he had heard her correctly.

"No, no, my precious. You are mistaken, as you always have been."

"Yes, yes, but—"

"This is *Heaven* we are in. Hell is where you came from, my precious one, Hell with all its punishing physical conditions! This is Heaven."

He collapsed motionless on his face, and once again the great hall with all its restitutions went about its grand harmonic movements.

Office Space

by Richard Lee Byers

When Crandall's eyes snap open, he's lying, cold and stiff, on the hard linoleum floor. Uncomfortable as he is, he knows from experience that he'd feel even more miserable had he tried to sleep in the swivel chair. Like all the other objects in the sparsely furnished office, or the entire tower for that matter, it's misshapen. The casters don't roll, and the seat slopes down slightly from right to left. The latter defect plays hell with his back.

Wincing and squinting at the bright morning sunshine streaming through the row of windows, he clambers to his feet and stumbles into the lavatory. After urinating, he turns on the faucet. Though the building looks modern and new, the pipes groan and rattle as if it were a decrepit tenement. Eventually grayish water spatters from the tap. When the spurts change to a steady flow, he lowers his head and drinks. The water is lukewarm, with a mineral tang, and has an oily texture that leaves a film on his tongue. As he gulps it down, his stomach aches.

He wonders if he should risk washing. In his former life he was fastidiously clean, and he hates being dirty now. But sometimes when he bathes himself he breaks out in a fiery rash. He assumes that chemicals in the water irritate his skin. Eventually he decides to forego washing for now. Perhaps tomorrow he'll scrub his face and hands.

As he shuffles back into the office proper, he realizes that he's a little hungry. He looks around to see if any stony, tasteless doughnuts or danishes have appeared. (Pastry comes, *if* it comes, first thing in the morning; the deli sandwiches, with sliced gray meat like scraps of cardboard, at noon.) But no food is in sight.

He could walk down to the lopsided, melted-looking vending machines by the elevators and get a candy bar or a bag of chips. Fortunately, as he discovered some time ago (weeks, months, surely not years) when he ran out of change, he doesn't need coins to make the machines dispense their contents. But the thought of leaving the office frightens him, particularly when he knows that it's time he was on the job. It would be better to do some work now and worry about eating later.

So he sits down behind the desk and inspects the stacks of paper. The pages are exchanged when he's asleep, a fact he wouldn't know if he hadn't once taken pains, folding certain sheets and arranging them in a particular pattern, to find out. Because he can't read the documents. Like the characters on the telephone buttons, the letters comprising the lines of print are meaningless squiggles.

Nevertheless, he has to hold the pages before his eyes and *pretend* to read them. That's the greater part of his job. Once upon a time, early in his captivity, he'd decided that he wouldn't really do it. He'd merely sit at the desk, and when a Gray Guard (or *the* Gray Guard—never having seen two together, he still doesn't truly know if there are more than one) came to check on him, he'd grab a sheet and pretend to study it until the creature went away again. The scheme didn't work. After a day, a Guard gave him a beating with its nightstick. Somehow it knew he was slacking off.

After forty-five minutes, the phone rings, or rather, emits a harsh bray of a buzz. Startled, Crandall jerks in his chair. Answering the phone is the other part of his job, and he loathes it even more than staring at the incomprehensible papers. Trembling, he swallows, and picks up the receiver. The instrument is a little too heavy, and feels greasy. "Hello," he says.

An incoherent croaking grates into his ear. It may be the voice of a Gray Guard, but he suspects not. The monsters are always mute in his presence. Indeed, they look as if they may not even be able to open their mouths. They taught him what was expected of him with gestures, and corporal punishment.

The Croaker never pauses for a reply, but Crandall is supposed to talk to it anyway. Not knowing what response it desires (he suspects, none in particular), he says what he often says: "I think you can understand me, and that you could really communicate with me if you tried. Please, tell me what you want. Are you studying me? If you'd just *talk* to me, I could tell you everything you want to know."

He stops for a moment, giving the Croaker a chance to make a coherent response, but it just grinds wordlessly on. "Listen to me," Crandall continues. "You'd better let me go. There are people who've missed me, and contacted the authorities. The police are looking for me. Someday they're going to find me, and throw you in jail." Countless repetitions have robbed the threat of any passion or conviction.

The Croaker rasps on for ten more seconds, then hangs up. Crandall does the same. (Fleetingly he recalls how, on his first day in the office, he tried repeatedly to access an outside line and 911, but the inhuman voice answered every time.) Hoping that the creature won't call again today, he returns to his paperwork.

After a while, the task becomes more interesting. A suspicion and a thrill of excitement flower in his mind. The alien characters on the sheets *do* have meaning, and he's on the verge of deciphering it through some extraordinary leap of intuition. And when he can finally read the pages, when at last he understands the messages his captors have composed for him, surely they'll reward him with his freedom!

But eventually the sense of imminent comprehension fades away. With a dull throb of disappointment, he recalls that he's had the optimistic feeling many times before, and it's never come to anything. He tries to make himself stare at the next paper, but his eyes sting, and the squiggles blur. His mind cringes from the prospect of further work.

Fortunately, the Gray Guards allow him to take breaks, if he doesn't abuse the privilege. He twists in the swivel chair and gazes out the window. From here on the sixteenth floor he can't see the street, but he can make out the blue-green expanse of the Hillsborough River, the silvery minarets of the University of Tampa, and some of the neighboring skyscrapers.

(On the first day of his imprisonment, after he tried and failed to phone the authorities, he hit on the idea of plastering papers to the windows using water for glue, forming giant letters spelling out the word HELP. Since *he* could see people in the nearby buildings, it stood to reason that one of them would spot his message and contact the police. It took him three days to accept that for some reason—conceivably his windows are made of one-way glass—the plan wasn't going to work, and then he had flew into a frenzy, battering the panes with the swivel chair, not stopping until his hands were raw and cramped, his arms rubbery with weakness, and exhaustion had transformed his rage into despair. Even knowing it was futile, he tried to smash a window on four subsequent occasions, also, but he hasn't experienced that particular kind of violent anger in quite a while. He feels as if he's forgotten how.)

The sun is bright, the sky blue, and he wonders if it's hot outside. Probably. The office, which is generally either too hot or too cold, is warm and stuffy at the moment. A pigeon swoops through his field of vision, and he fantasizes that he can force one of the windows open just wide enough to place crumbs on the ledge outside. The white bird keeps returning to eat them, and becomes a sort of pet.

He tries to think only of trivialities, to avoid agonizing over his situation. But gradually, perhaps because he's hungry, or because he has already been forced to listen to the Croaker today, his mind starts picking away at the mysteries of his imprisonment.

He wishes that he at least knew how he came to the office. He *believes* that, after working late in another tower, he cut through a dark alley on the way to his Jetta. Someone, perhaps a Gray Guard, sneaked up behind him and hit him over the head. He passed out, and woke up here. But recently the memory has begun to seem untrustworthy, too clichéd and melodramatic, like a scene from a movie. He's starting to wonder if his old job, in which he also spent the majority of his time shuffling papers and talking on the phone, simply *became* this job when he wasn't looking. Or maybe he died and went to Hell, and the living city outside the windows is only a mirage. That would explain why his captors are monsters.

Or perhaps (he doesn't know why he keeps coming back to this notion, but it sticks in his mind) he's trapped in a skyscraper that has awakened to conscious life. He once read in the *Tribune* that downtown Tampa is full of unrented office space, and yet, for some reason, investors keep putting up new buildings. What if one of the structures wasn't content to stand empty? What if it could create furniture and food of a sort, and servants to kidnap some poor white-collar worker to help it fulfill what it conceived to be its purpose?

Crandall grimaces. It's a crazy idea. All his ideas are crazy now. Maybe he himself is insane, locked in a sanitarium somewhere, and none of this is happening. Or perhaps the noxious food, and water for that matter, are poisoning him, and scrambling his brain in the process.

He deliberates for several minutes before taking out his wallet and the photo of his wife and daughter. His hesitation doesn't stem from concern that viewing the picture will sadden him, although it always does. Rather, it's due to a persistent fear that someday he'll look and the photo will be gone, or he won't be able to remember his loved ones' names.

After he's studied the snapshot for a while, teary-eyed, a pang of anxiety rouses him from his contemplation. Glancing at his watch, he sees that it's 12:15, that he turned toward the windows half an hour ago. If he wants to avoid a beating, it's time to get back to work.

But then his stomach churns, and he realizes that he's *quite* hungry now. Peering about, he sees that no grease-spotted white paper bags or Styrofoam food containers have appeared. Evidently his captors don't intend to send lunch to the office today.

That being the case, surely they won't begrudge Crandall two more minutes for a trip to the vending machines, especially if he eats and examines his papers at the same time. Struggling to quash a pang of trepidation, he rises, goes to the door, and peeks out. Since no Gray Guards are in sight, he starts down the hall.

No doubt because the lengthy corridor has no windows, the rectangular light fixtures in the ceiling are always on. They shed a dim, grayish glow more like the sheen of some phosphorescent fungus than ordinary fluorescent illumination. As he skulks toward the vending machines, Crandall remembers his early explorations. Prowling through the tower, he found one empty office and passage after another. Whenever he tried to venture below the sixth floor or above the twentieth, via the stairs or one of the lurching, groaning elevators, a Gray Guard intercepted him and beat him. (Since the building is twenty-five stories tall, he infers that the idea was to keep him at least five floors away from both the ground and the roof.) If he didn't try to climb or descend too far, his captors sometimes permitted him to wander, provided that he did it in the evening, after the workday was through. But on other occasions a Guard came after him and punished him anyway. Eventually he decided it would be best to stick close to the office. It wasn't as if his roaming around was accomplishing anything. Ultimately, it only made him feel lonelier.

Beyond the elevators, the door at the far end of the hall—the entrance to the stairwell—begins to open.

Crandall doesn't think that he's broken his captors' rules (unless they've *changed* the rules, which, though it hasn't happened yet, is always a terrifying possibility) but even so, he has no intention of coming face-to-face with a Gray Guard if he can avoid it. He pivots, poised to scurry back to his office, and then, from the corner of his eye, glimpses the door swinging wider and a head sticking through. A *pale* head, with yellow, curly *hair*.

Crandall freezes in shock. Obviously nearly as surprised as he is, the young woman in the doorway goggles at him, then runs toward him. As she approaches, he feels certain that this encounter is a dream, that in a moment he'll awaken on the office floor.

The blond woman appears to be in her twenties. Her hands and pretty, freckled face are cut and bruised. She's wearing a gold necklace, an engagement ring, a white silk blouse and a red business suit. Her clothes are rumpled, blood-spattered, and smell of sweat, though they're in far better shape than his own.

She grips Crandall's forearms as if she doesn't believe that *he's* real, either, and needs to touch him to convince herself. Peering up into his face, she jabbers, "My god! Your scars, that beard! How long have you been here?"

It's hard to answer. He feels as if his brain has locked up on him. "I don't know," he manages at last.

"Who are they? *What* are they? What are they doing to us?"

"I don't know. How can you be here?" Even as he asks, he realizes the answer. The Gray Guards installed her in the skyscraper after he stopped leaving his own floor. That's why he hasn't seen her before.

"They grabbed me in a parking garage two nights ago," she replies. "I'm trying to sneak out. Tell me about them! How do they keep catching me?"

A stab of alarm pierces the incredulous daze in Crandall's head. The blond woman is behaving the way he did when he first arrived, making the same mistakes, and will surely reap the same reward. Judging from her abrasions and contusions, a Gray Guard has beaten her at least once already. And now that he's met her, Crandall fears that if she persists in trying to escape, their captors will regard him as her collaborator, and resume punishing him as well.

"You can't get away," he says. "In fact, you should hurry back to your office right now, before a Guard comes for you. Tell me what floor you're on, and I'll try to visit you tonight." As abruptly as it burst into his mind, his apprehension gives way to feverish excitement. "You can tell me all about yourself, and I'll tell you all about me! It won't be nearly as bad here, if we can keep each other company. Maybe they'd even let us work in the *same* office—"

Still gripping his arms, she gives him a shake, and, startled, he falls silent. "What's the matter with you?" she cries. "There *has* to be a way out, and we have to find it!"

"I tried," he says. "It isn't there. But as long as you keep looking, they'll keep hurting you."

Grimacing, she releases him. "You poor guy. I promise I'll send help." As she turns toward the door at the end of the hall, it opens, and a Gray Guard shambles through.

The creature is the size and roughly the shape of a big man. Its bald, slate-colored head is disproportionately small, neckless and perfectly round, with rudimentary features that look as if they were scraped and pinched out of modeling clay. One arm, the one with the nightstick, is apishly long, and its right knee is situated six inches higher than its left. It wears a rent-a-cop uniform as poorly made as the furniture in Crandall's office.

The woman gasps, whirls, and sprints in the opposite direction. Its club upraised, the Gray Guard lumbers after her. Despite its mismatched legs, once it builds up speed the creature can lurch along faster than any human being.

Shuddering, squinching his eyes shut, Crandall cringes against the wall. He hopes that his fellow prisoner will at least make it out the door at the other end of the corridor, or around the corner beside it, before the Guard catches up with her. He dreads the thought of watching her being beaten nearly as much as the prospect of being punished himself.

And then, almost against his will, a thought pops into his head: For all he knows, *there's only one Gray Guard.* And if there is only one, and the view from the windows isn't a lie, then maybe, if he delays the creature charging toward him, the woman *can* get away.

For a moment he wonders if he dares to act on this dangerous notion. Then he realizes that he's already decided, and is dashing back toward his office. Defiance, after all this time, feels as surreal as stumbling across a fellow human being. He prays that the Gray Guard will assume that he's fleeing from it in terror.

He reaches his office a few strides ahead of the monster, darts inside, and grabs the swivel chair. Scrambling back to the doorway, he gets there just as the Guard plunges into view. He bellows and slams the base of the chair into the creature, driving it against the wall. Up close, the Guard smells like spoiled hamburger.

Crandall's never landed such a solid blow on one of his captors before. Strong and agile as the monsters are, he could never have managed it if he hadn't caught it by surprise. Exulting, he tries to pull the chair back for another strike. But the Guard grabs it, rips it out of his hands, and flings it aside. The seat bangs down on the floor eight feet away.

The Guard swings up its billy club. Crandall tries to lift his arms to ward it off, but he's too slow. The weapon cracks down on his skull.

A thunderbolt of pain blasts down the length of his body. His knees buckle, dumping him on the floor. The Gray Guard pivots to resume the pursuit.

Crandall knows he hasn't delayed it long enough to allow the stranger to escape. Though spastic with pain, he makes himself scuttle forward and grab its ankle, just as it begins to take a stride. Thrown off balance, the Gray Guard falls.

Crandall tries to haul himself on top of it. He means to wrestle with it and hold it down. But it wrenches itself away from him and leaps back to its feet.

The prisoner understands that he *still* hasn't bought the blond woman sufficient time. He tries to scramble up, so he can keep fighting, but suddenly his limbs won't obey him. At that moment, he despises himself for his failure.

But then he sees that the Gray Guard isn't rushing on after the blonde. Instead it's looming over him with club upraised. Though no one could tell from its crude, immobile features, evidently his resistance has enraged it, so much so that it's forgotten about the chase. For a moment, the mere realization that he's upset it fills Crandall with triumph. He'd laugh if he could catch his breath. Then the Guard begins to batter him.

Crandall wakes to an excruciating throb in the top of his head. A second later, similar pains jab up and down the length of his body. He tries to open his eyes, and discovers that he has to *pry* them open. A coating of dried blood has glued them shut.

When he does manage to look around, he finds that he has double vision. He's sprawled on his office floor, and the swivel chair is lying on its side several feet away. Outside the windows, the sky is black. The towers of Tampa shine, bathed in floodlight.

At first he can't remember what happened, why he received a beating after many weeks of successfully avoiding one. Then, abruptly, he visualizes the blond stranger's frightened but determined face, and an instant later the entire incident comes back to him.

If she escaped, she'll send help! She promised *she would!* Much as it hurts his injured frame to move, Crandall is suddenly too excited to stay on the floor. Grunting, he lurches up, limps to the office door and pulls it open.

The corridor is empty, nor does he hear sound anywhere in the building. No cops are advancing on the office to rescue him.

Reluctantly he recalls that he met the woman between noon and one. If she escaped at all, she did it hours ago. She's already had plenty of time to contact the police.

Snarling, Crandall rejects the obvious conclusion. For all he knows, his fellow captive *did* get away, but ran into complications afterward. Maybe the cops are refusing to enter the building until they can obtain a search warrant. At any rate, he *refuses* to give up on her.

Generally speaking, he feels more comfortable with the door closed, even though it doesn't keep out the Gray Guards. But he leaves it open now, and turns on every dim lamp in the room. When the authorities arrive (and they *will*) the illumination spilling into the hallway will guide them to him.

He hauls the swivel chair upright and sits down to wait for deliverance. His eyelids keep drooping, and he pops them open wide. His chin nods toward his chest, and he jerks himself upright. His injured body craves rest, but he refuses to sleep now, when the end of his suffering is at hand.

Except that it doesn't end. And finally, when the sky turns gray and red, his hope crumbles.

He sobs, and images of suicide flood his mind. He could hang himself with his belt, throw himself down the stairs and break his neck, smash his skull against the corner of his desk, starve himself—

With immense effort, he pushes the alarming, tempting thoughts away, insisting to himself that, despite his disappointment, he's better off now than he was twenty-four hours ago. He has a companion! He'll locate her office this evening. Maybe together, they *can* find a way to escape!

After focusing resolutely on such thoughts, he feels somewhat less distraught. When he notices the cardboard box that has materialized atop the green metal file cabinet, he decides that—his sore mouth, loose teeth and queasiness notwithstanding—he wants to eat.

He hobbles to the carton and finds danishes inside. Knowing that, despite any variations in their appearance, they'll all taste the same, he grabs one at random and takes a bite.

To his surprise, the stringy consistency, if not the lack of flavor, differs from that of any food his captors have provided before. Puzzled, he pulls the danish back from his mouth and peers into the semicircular bite mark. The pastry is laced with strands of golden hair.

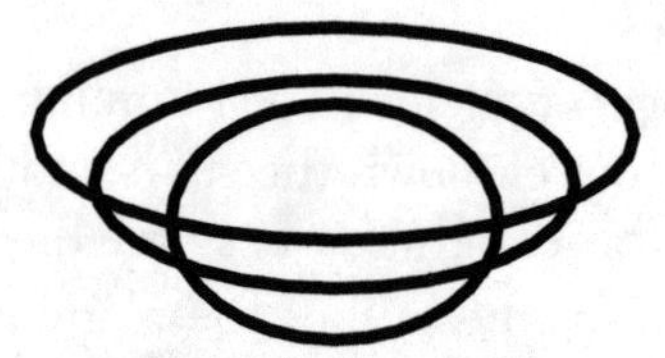

DANTE'S

Among The Handlers

OR,

The Mark 16 Hands On Assembly of Jesus Risen, Formerly Snake-O-Rama

by Michael Bishop

And He said to them, "Go into all the world and preach the gospel to every creature.... And these signs will follow those who believe: In My name they will cast out demons; they will speak with new tongues; they will take up serpents; and if they drink anything deadly, it will by no means hurt them; they will lay hands on the sick, and they will recover."

—*Mark* 16: 15, 17-18

Men in soiled workclothes occupied the cracked red leather booths. Some pointed at their cronies with wrist-twisted forks. Two or three ate alone, a folded newspaper at hand or a scowl of wary dragged-out blankness protecting or maybe legitimating their aloneness. None of them any longer took heed of the smells saturating Deaton's Bar-B-Q: scalded grease, boiled collards, sauce-drowned pork. And the sinuous anglings of the sandyhaired kid waiting their tables drew the notice of only one or two.

Becknell, a hulking thirty-two-year-old in a filthy ballcap, said: So how you like a peckerwood that lifts up snakes handlin yore vittles?

His boothmate, Greg Maharry, said: You mean Pilcher?

Course I mean him. Anyways, it aint my idea of telligent ressraunt policy.

Criminy, Maharry said, who're you to bellyache bout young Pilcher's cleanliness?

Who am I? Becknell squinted at Maharry.

You spend most days up to yore butt in axle grease.

So?

I reckon Hoke knows as well as you to wersh his hands.

Mebbe. But grease's clean gainst them slitherin canebrakes thet Sixteener bunch of his favors.

You ever lifted a snake? I bet you never.

Think I aint got the sand? Greg, thet's—

Hoke Pilcher eased around the honeycombed divider from the kitchen with his tray aloft. Becknell, bigger than Maharry by a head, released a long sibilant breath while Maharry gave Hoke a queasy smile. Hoke lowered the tray to waistheight so that he could remove to the table the loaded barbecue platters, two sweaty amber longnecks, and two heavyweight mugs bearing icy white fur from Mr. Deaton's walk-in freezer. Holding the tray against the table edge, Hoke began to rearrange the items on it for easier transfer.

Mr. Becknell, he said, I aint been to an assembly out to Frye's Mill Road in moren a month.

Becknell said: You blong to thet bunch, don't you?

Yessir. But I've never lifted a snake there. He wanted to add, Either, but swallowed the impulse.

How come you not to've?

No anointin's ever come on me. So far I've mostly just shouted and raised my hands. Waitin and prayin, I guess. Hoke reached the longnecks onto the table, then the mugs with their dire chiseled coldness.

Becknell said: My golly. Yo're a Mark Sixteener thout the balls to do what you say you blieve.

Leave him go, Albert, Maharry said.

Why?

Minit ago you was blastin him for bein a Jesus Only. Now yo're chewin on him for the contrary.

Thet's where yo're flat wrong, Greg.

Okay. Tell me how.

I'm chewin on him for claimin one thing then actin somethin allover yellowbelly else.

Hoke set Maharry's hubcapsized pork platter in front of him and shifted the tray to unload Becknell's wheel of shrimp and chicken, with onion rings and hot slaw around them for pungent garnish.

Becknell said: And if you really blong to thet bunch, whyn hell don't you go to their services?

It's sorter complicated, Mr. Becknell.

You aint turned heathen?

Nosir. I'm tryin—

A heathen's shore as Judas lost, but a Mark Sixteener thet acts like what he sez mebbe has a chanst. Mebbe.

Hoke felt his grip loosen and the tray tilt. Becknell's chicken, scarletbrown in its breathtaking sauce, slid down his mattress-striped overall bib along with an avalanche of slaw and shrimp pellets. The onion rings flipped ceilingward and dropped about Becknell and Maharry like mudcaked nematodes. A longneck toppled. A razorthin tide of beer sluiced across the table and off it into Becknell's lap. He roared and jumped, catching a falling onion ring on one ear and nearly upsetting Maharry's bottle. Maharry grabbed it in a trembling fist and held it down. Hoke's tray, which had hit the floor, rattled from edge to edge.

My cryin cripes! Becknell said. You summabitch!

It was an accydent, Maharry said. Go easy now.

Using the towel on his belt, Hoke picked chicken and slaw off Becknell. He righted the fallen longneck, daubed at the beer, and turned this way and that between the unbroken platter under the table and the reverberating plastic tray. His boss, Mr. Deaton, burst into the diningroom with so many wrinkles on his forehead's pale dome that Hoke could not help thinking of a wadded pile of linen outside a unit of the Beulah Fork Motel. Deaton, stooped from working under the greaseguard that hooded his stove, unfolded to full height.

Hoke, what you done now?

Ruint my clothes, Becknell said. Ruint my meal. Stole my peace of mind.

It wasn't apurpose, Maharry said.

Thet's the second spill you've had today, Deaton said. The second.

See, Maharry said. He didn't mean it personal.

Albert, Deaton said, I'll bring you replacement eats in ten minutes. He thought about that. No, seven.

Free?

Awright. Spruce up in the ressroom. I'll pay for either yore drycleanin or a new pair of overalls. He turned to Hoke. Criminy, boy. My Lord.

My mind's gone off, Mr. Deaton. I cain't focus.

S thet right? Well. I cain't afford to keep you till you git it right. Ast Maltilda Jack to pay you off.

I'm fired?

Yore word, not mine. Just git yore money and beat it on out of here.

Sir, I need this job.

Mebbe you can git you somethin out to the sawmill.

I done ast.

Ast again. Now git. Have mercy.

Hoke tossed the filthy sodden towel onto the table, amazed that the disaster had scarcely dirtied his hands, much less his clothes. He strode through Deaton's Bar-B-Q under the mirthful or slipeyed gazes of maybe a dozen other customers and wrenched back the frontdoor.

From airconditioning to pitiless summer swelter. Hoke hiked straight across Deaton's parkinglot, filched a cigarette from his shirtpocket. The sky pulsed so starwebbed that the neon sign winking Bar-B-Q, Bar-B-Q, could neither sponge those stars away nor make Beulah Fork's maindrag look like anything other than a gaudy podunk road.

Hoke lit up. Smoke curled past his eyes, settled in lazy helices into his lungs.

Thirty minutes later, still afoot, Hoke stopped on the edge of Twyla Glanton's place, a clearing off Frye's Mill Road. He registered the insult of the jacked-up candyapple-red pickup with chromium rollbars parked alongside the deck of Twyla's doublewide. The truck belonged to Johnny Mark Carnes, a deacon in the Mark 16 Hands On Assembly of Jesus Risen, a congregation whose tumbledown stone meeting center lay farther along this blacktopped strip. Like Albert Becknell, Carnes had ten years and maybe forty pounds on Hoke.

Almost aloud, Hoke said: Pox on yore hide, Carnes. Then waded through fragrant redclover and sticky Queen Anne's lace toward the deck. He felt gut-knotted in a way reminiscent of the cramps after a dose of paregoric. What did he plan to do? No clear notion. None.

His tennis shoes carried him up the treated plank steps of Twyla's deck, anyway, and before he could compute the likely outcome of this showdown, his fist began to pound the flimsy aluminum stormdoor over the cheap wooden one that was supposed to keep Twyla Glanton safe from burglars, conartists, and escaped murderers out here in the honeysuckle-drenched boonies of Hothlepoya County. Yeah.

Carnes himself opened the door, then stood in it like the sentry that Hoke would have hoped for, except that Hoke wanted someone else in the role and took no pleasure in any detail of Carnes' manifestation there but the fact that he still had his britches on. Unless of course…

Pilcher, Carnes said. Kinda late to come callin on a lady, aint it?

You've just said so.

I been here a while. Somethin we can do you for?

Even with the light behind him, Carnes presented a handsome silhouette: narrowheaded, wideshouldered, almost oaken in the stolidity of his planting. Actually, the light's fanning from behind improved his looks, dropping a darkness over his sunken piggy eyes and also the waffleironlike acne scars below and off to one side of his bottom lip.

Could I just talk to Twyla a minit, Johnny Mark?

From somewhere in the doublewide's livingroom, Tywla said: Let him in.

Some folks you let em in, it's nigh-on the War tween the States to git em out again. Carnes stood stockstill, unmoving as a capsized tractor.

Twyla appeared behind him. Her look surprised Hoke. She wore a swallowing purple sweatshirt, luminous green and purple windsuit pants with a band of Navajo brocade down each leg, and pennyloafers. Her sorrel hair had a mahogany nimbus from the backglow, and strands floated about her teased-out helmet like charged spidersilk. Hoke, looking past Carnes at Twyla, felt the pilotlight in his gut igniting, warming him from that point outward.

A pearl onion of sweat pipped out on his forehead.

Never before had he seen a Mark Sixteener woman in any garb but anklelength skirts or dresses. Certainly not Twyla, whose daddy had lifted serpents, and who called out His name at every assembly, and who, at Li'l People Day Care in Beulah Fork, had a steady job, where she so staunchly refused to wear jeans that she often got the other workers' goat. Hoke, though, had given her a private pledge of fidelity.

He said: Colby Deaton fired me tonight.

The jerk, Twyla said. Babes, I'm so sorry.

Tough way for a guy to git him some sympathy, Carnes said.

We've missed you out to church, Twyla said. You orter not stopped comin cuz of me. I'm still yore friend.

Thet aint it, Carnes said. He's afraid to come.

Not of snakes, though. I wunst saw him grab a pygmyrattler with a stick and a gloved hand.

No, not of snakes, Carnes said. Thisere wiseboy's scairt of me. Cause I'm even more pyzon than they are.

Wadn't afraid to come up here with yore showoffy truck out front. Or to knock on Twyla's door.

Yall stop yore headbuttin! Twyla pushed Carnes aside and the stormdoor out. She laid a cool hand on Hoke's shoulder, bridging him into the doublewide, beckoning him out of the dark to either self-extinguishment or redemption—if these options did not, in fact, mesh or cancel. Go on home, babes. Sleep on it. Tomorry's got to have a perter face.

I'm footsore, Twyla. Bout wore out.

I'll wear you out, Carnes said.

What you'll do, Johnny Mark, is none of the sort.

Then praytell what?

Yo're gonna carry him home. In yore truck.

Play chauffeur for puley Mr. Pilcher here? Dream on.

No dream to it. And do it now. S bout time for me to turn in anyways.

So Hoke sat hugging the passengerside door of the jacked-up candyapple-red truck as Carnes accelerated through the woods and flung back under his tires long humming stretches of asphalt. Possum eyes caught fire in the headlamps. An owl stooped in cascades through a picketing of trees, and a fieldmouse, or a rabbit, or some other fourlegged hider in the leafmulch was rolled to its back and taloned insensate.

Past this kill, through some roadside cane that loblollies deeper in overtowered, a quartet of ghostly deer—two does, two fawns—made Carnes brake. The deer negotiated a quicksilver singlefile crossing. The truck fishtailed heartstoppingly and squealed to juddering rest on the shoulder in time for Hoke to watch the flags on the deer's rumps bounce into the pines' mazy sanctuary.

Carnes muttered, strangled the steeringwheel, exhaled hard.

Nice job, Hoke said.

Don't talk to me. Carnes took an audible breath.

We could've died if we'd hit just one of em. Hoke spoke the truth. In this part of Hothlepoya County deer on the road comprised an often deadly, yearround hazard. Hoke knew—had known—a highschool girl cut to ribbons by a buck attempting to leap the hood of her boyfriend's car. The buck had landed on the hood and, asprawl there, struggled to free itself from the windshield glass, one bloody leg kicking repeatedly through the glittery hole.

Don't compliment me, Pilcher. Ever.

Awright. I won't.

You aint got the right to tell me nothin. Cept mebbe yo're a sorry excuse for a Sixteener.

Hold it a minit.

And mebbe not even thet. Speak when spoken to. Otherwise, hush it the hell up.

Who made you God?

Carnes pointed a finger, holding its tip less than a wasp's body from Hoke's nose and staring down it like a man sighting a rifle.

I did speak to you, pissant, but I didn't ast you a blessed thing. He dropped the point.

Hoke wanted to say, Up yores, but leaned back against his door instead, shrinking from the despisal in Carnes' face. Who would know or care if Carnes killed him out here on this road, then rolled his body into the cane? Twyla. Thank God for Twyla Glanton.

And thank God Carnes didn't have a row of snakeboxes in the bed of his truck or, even worse, a solitary crate here in the passengerside footwell. Hoke could imagine sitting over an irritated pitviper—copperhead, rattler, whatever—with one foot to either side of the box, the rotting vegetable smell of its scales rising alien and humid to gag him, its heartshaped head searching for a way out. Meantime, though, he had Johnny Mark Carnes less than a yard away, still wired from their close call with the deer, still palpably resentful of Hoke's presence in his truckcab.

Whym I drivin you home, pissant?

Hoke set his teeth and stared.

I ast you a question. You can answer. You better.

Twyla told you to.

Ast me to. Nobody tells me to do anythin, Pilcher, least of all a outtake from the flank of Adam.

Hoke thought a moment. Then he said: You got no bidnus movin in on her. I had my eye on her first. From all the way back in school, even.

I beg yore pardon.

You heard me.

Losers weepers, huh?

I love her, Johnny Mark.

God loves her. You just got yore hormones in high gear.

I spose you got yores set on idle?

You wisht. Look, pissant, what can you give the lady but puppydog looks and a fat double handful of air?

Somethin thet counts.

Deaton canned you tonight from yore waitressin. You live in a verbital cave.

It's not a cave. Don't say waitressing. Men do it too.

Yore mama died of a lack o faith drinkin strychnine.

No, Hoke said. The Spirit went off her cause strife had fallen mongst the people. She had faith aplenty.

And yore daddy hightailed it to who knows where, Minnesota mebbe. No wonder Twyla took her a second look at you.

Like yo're a prize.

Got me balls enough to uplift serpents to the Lord and make us babies in the marriage bed.

Hoke shut his eyes. Yo're already married.

Not for long. Carnes smiled. Comparisons're hateful, aint they, pissant? Least you've got yore faith, though.

Yes, said Hoke quietly.

Which gives you a family in Jesus. Protection from slings and arrows, snakebites and poison. Right?

Right.

So come on to meetin this Friday. Forgit Twyla's migrated affections. Us Mark Sixteeners want you mongst us. Where else you got to go, Pilcher?

Nowhere.

Aint thet the truth. So come on Friday. I got someone you need to meet there.

Like who?

S name's Judas, Pilcher. He's a longboy. Called for the betrayer cause they aint no trustin when or who he next might bite.

Hoke put his hands on his knees and squeezed. Carnes had him a new diamondback, name of Judas. Well, of course he did. Subtlety had never much appealed to Carnes, else he would have linked with Methodists and driven a white twodoor coupe off a Detroit assemblyline.

Now git out, he said.

Yo're sposed to take me home.

Carried you far as I aim to. You aint but a mile from thet crayfish den of yores anyways. Out.

Hoke got out. Carnes put the boxy truck in gear, flung sod and gravel backing off the shoulder, and shouted out the window after a screechy turnaround: Don't I deserve a nice thanks for totin you this far?

Thank you. Hoke eyed Carnes blankly, then stared away down the blacktop at dwindling taillights and the broken ramparts of pines bracketing it. Shithead, Hoke said, turning to foot it the rest of the way home, morosely aware that he had no idea which of them, Carnes or himself, he had just cursed. Nor did the incessant burring of the cicadas among the cane afford him any clue or solace.

He had never lived in a cave. He lived with Ferlin Rodale, a former schoolmate now doing construction work, in a dugout of bulldozed earth, old automobile tires hardpacked with clay, and plastered-over walls strengthened with empty aluminum softdrink cans. Ferlin had seen such houses on a hitchhiking trip to New Mexico, then brought back to Hothlepoya County—whose director of Department of Community Development had never even heard of such structures—an obsession to build one locally, despite the higher watertable and wetter climate. Anyway, to Hoke's mind, Ferlin's dugout qualified as a house. Even the head of Community Development had allowed as much by issuing Ferlin a building permit even though his tirehouse lay outside every local engineering code. It wasn't finished, though, and wouldn't be for another six to eight months, if that soon, and so Ferlin and Hoke lived in the shell of the place, sleeping in a U-shaped room that faced south under a roof of plywood, black felt, and grimy plastic sheeting.

Mebbe it is a kinda cave, Hoke said, limping home through the woods. Carnes is sorta right, the bastid.

Well, so what? Ferlin had wired it for lights, sunk a well, and laid PVC piping so that both sinks and the cracked and resealed commode had water. Hoke paid fifty dollars a month for a pallet in the lone bedroom and split the electric bill with Ferlin. His own folks had never had so nice a place, only a rented fourroom shack, aboveground, with pebbled green shingles on the walls and a tarpaper roof. If Ferlin's house struck some ornery people as cavelike, well, better a cave than a windbuffeted shanty on lopsided fieldstone pillars. Mama and Daddy Pilcher should've enjoyed such luck—even with the beer cans, bottlecaps, cigarette packages, candywrappers, clamlike fastfood cartons, and other junk littering Ferlin's clayey grounds.

In a footsore trance Hoke shuffled over the murderously potholed drive leading in, a drive lined about its full length with blackberry brambles, dogwoods and pines. He had only starlight and lichenglow to guide him, just those undependable helps and the somewhat less fickle guyings of nightly habit. At length he approached a sycamore, a striated ghost among the scaly conifers, on which Ferlin had hammered up a handlettered placard:

TRESPAsERS !!!—
WE AIM to PLEZE But SHOT to KILL!

Hoke stopped, perplexed. Did that mean him? Ferlin had prepared the sign to secure them solitude, even down to the premeditated detail of its misspellings, working on the already frequently borne-out surmise that the image of a surly cracker with a shotgun would scare off uninvited visitors better than a storebought KEEP OUT notice. Hoke, shambling by, gave the sign a fresh twist out of true and chuckled bitterly.

Half the people in Beulah Fork probably thought that Ferlin and he, not to mention every Mark Sixteener in the county, were ignorant sisterswyving mooncalves. Well, damn them too, along with Carnes.

I know a thing or two the President don't, Hoke said. Or a perfessor up to Athens, even.

Like what? he wondered.

Aloud he said: Like I love Twyla and don't want to die in front of her with a snakefang in my flesh.

This saying stirred Ferlin's dogs, a redbone hound named Sackett and a mongrel terrier named Rag that began barking in echoey relay. They came hurtling through the dark to meet the intruder and possibly to turn him.

Hush, Hoke said. S only me.

Sackett took Hoke's hand in the webbing between thumb and forefinger and led him up the trail, his whole ribby fuselage atremble. Rag pelted along behind, kinking and unkinking like an earthworm on a hot paving stone.

From the dugout—doors wide open, plastic scrolled back to the clocking stars—Hoke heard a breathy female voice singing mournfully from Ferlin's totable CD player. It sang about a blockbusted blonde with a disconnected plug at the Last Chance Texaco. Ferlin sang along, overriding the soft female voice, his screechy upndown falsetto an insult to his dogs, to Hoke, to the very notion of singing.

Thank God the Last Chance Texaco cut was fading, drifting like a car whose driver has nodded asleep. But as Hoke crossed the dugout's threshold, into earthen coolness and the glare of one electric bulb swinging on a tarnished chain, the next song began and Ferlin ignored Hoke's arrival to play airguitar and hoot along with Rickie Lee Jones, albeit out of sync and out of tune, the words in his throat *(Cmon, Cecil, take some money! Cmon, Ceece, take you a ten!)* like cogs mangled and flung from the strident clockwork coming-apart of his lungs and throat. Ferlin wore a jockstrap and flipflops, nothing else, and when he finally looked at Hoke, he checked his wrist, which bore no watch, raised his eyebrows, and kept on screeching, his stance hipcocked, showbizzy and questioning at once. At the end of Rickie Lee's cut, he mouthed, *But, baby, don' dish it ovah if he don' preciate it. . . .*

Then Ferlin turned off the player and came over to Hoke with a look of almost daddyish concern on his freckled hatchet face. Squinting and grinning, he said, Home a mite early, aint you?

Deaton canned me. Hoke told Ferlin the whole story, even the parts about stopping at Twyla's and catching a spooky ride in Johnny Mark Carnes' pickup.

But you don't like Carnes, said Ferlin.

I don't like walkin neither.

You walkt in. I didn't hear nothin stop out on 18.

Hoke crumpled into a lawnchair Ferlin had salvaged from the county landfill. Carnes got him a new snake he's callin Judas, he said. Wants me to make the next service out to the assembly so's I can charm it.

Ferlin whistled, a sound like a mortar shell rainbowing in. You aint handled with em yet, and he wants you to lift a serpent name of Judas right out the gate?

Looks thet way.

S why my religion don't include handlin, less a course it's women. Them I'll handle. Devotedly. Ferlin never attended services anywhere, but to willing females he tithed regularly the selfalleged five inflated to ten percent of himself that at this moment he had pouched in his jockstrap.

Such talk. Eddie Moomaw told me to git a new roommate if I planned to stay on a Sixteener.

Ferlin played airguitar. O *mean Mark Sixteener*, he sang: *Climb outta yore rut!*

Hush thet, Hoke said.

But Ferlin kept singing: *You don't like my wiener, So you show me yore butt!*

Didn't I ast you polite to stop it?

Ferlin threw his airguitar at the wall and paced away from Hoke. You got to watch yore fanny. Some of them Sixteeners'll drag you down for pure selfrighteous spite.

Meanin Johnny Mark Carnes?

Him, ol Moomaw, and anyone else over there thet cain't pray a blessing thout first tearin the world a new a-hole.

The world hates us Mark Sixteeners.

It don't unnerstand yall, Ferlin said. Neither do I.

So I shouldn't go this Friday?

You hear me say thet? I just said to watch yore fanny.

So mebbe I orter go?

Ferlin said: I wouldn't visit thet stonecold snakeranch of yall's thout a direct order from God Hisself.

Groaning, Hoke pulled off his tennis shoes and claystained sweatsocks. His feet sang their relief, his anxiety over his lost job, the more judgmental Mark Sixteeners, and Carnes' new diamondback a smidgen allayed by the night air and his roomy's profane straightforward banter.

Then he said: Ferlin, I have to go.

Nigh-on to hatchling naked, Ferlin squatted over his svelte black CD player. Balancing on the spongy toes of his flipflops he punched up a song about Weasel and the White Boys Cool, his wide chocolate irises reflecting a crimson 9 backward from the control console. Ditchfrogs, a cicada chorus and Ferlin all crooned along with the disc (*Likes it rare but gits it well, A weasel on a shoadohdah flo*), but this time so low and softly that Hoke did not feel slighted. Ferlin had heard him, and as soon as cut number nine ended, and before number ten began, Ferlin said:

What would happen if you didn't?

I'm not rightly shore. The Holy Ghost'd probably go off me for good.

Meanin what?

I'd send my soul to perdition for aye and awways.

Better go then, Ferlin said, knobbing down the volume on cut ten. Hell's a damned serious bidnus and forever's a smart jot longern Monday.

Hoke gave him back a forlorn chuckle.

Answer me one thing: Why would a fella with half a brain and a workin pecker take up a pyzonous snake?

To git Spiritjumped and throughblest totally. You won't never know, Ferlin, till you've gone puppetdancin in Jesus' grace yoreself.

Sounds like really rollickin sex.

S a billion times better.

The expert speaks, Ferlin said. Hothlepoya County's Only Still Cherry Stud.

They's moren one kinda virgin, Hoke said. Not bein married I've never slept with a woman. But not bein sanctified you've never come under the Spirit's caress.

Ooooooo, Ferlin said. Got me. Got me good. He fell over next to his CD player, writhing as if gutshot. When Rickie Lee finished singing about her gang's all going home, leaving her abandoned on a streetcorner, Ferlin stopped thrashing and lay motionless: a rangy unclad departmentstore dummy, flung supine into a junkroom.

Hoke struggled out of the lawnchair. He hobbled over to Ferlin and around the CD player on whose console a red 0 had brilliantly digitized. He nudged Ferlin in the armpit with his toe. When Ferlin persisted in his willful unflinchingness Hoke said, Thanks for the words of wisdom, dead man, and retreated to their U-shaped bedroom to dream of Twyla and climbing knots of sullen upraised snakes.

Ferlin drove Hoke in his customized '54 Ford, a bequeathment from Ferlin's daddy, to the Friday-night meeting of the Mark 16 Hands On Assembly of Jesus Risen farther down Frye's Mill Road, on an island between that road and a twolane branch going who knows where. Ferlin dropped Hoke off near a private cemetery about fifty yards from the church itself, with a nod and a last cry of advice:

Be careful, Pilcher, who you take a rattlesnake from!

Hoke recognized the saying as one of the shibboleths of a wellknown Alabama handler selfbilled the EndTime Evangelist, a big amiable man who preached a foursquare Jesus Only doctrine heavier on redemption than judgment. A year ago he had visited their hall, blessing it with both his message and his serpent handling; and when a longtime Mark Sixteener upbraided an older teenager near the front for wearing a T-shirt printed with the profane logo of a rocknroll band, the evangelist helped avert a nasty dustup, saying:

Leave him go, Brother Eddie. You've got to catch the fish before you can clean em.

Hoke remembered that saying and also the preacher's caution against accepting a pitviper from just anybody. Anyway, even should an anointing drop on him like a garment of spiritwoven armor, Hoke would steer clear of Johnny Mark Carnes. A spirit of deceitfulness and envy in a house of worship could undo even an honest-to-Christ mantling of the Holy Ghost, as his own mama had learned too late to prevent her from dying of a pintjar of strychnine so polluted.

Polluted pyzon? Ferlin had said once, reacting to Hoke's story. Aint thet redundant?

A child of the world would think so, but a Sixteener would know from experience that it wasn't. It wasn't that such petty feelings could defeat God, but rather that the Spirit generally chose not to consort with folks nastily prey to them. If It withdrew when you had fifteen pounds of diamondback looped in your hands, of course, you would probably find beside the point the distinction between a defeated Spirit and just a particular One....

Dented pickups and rattletrap jalopies surrounded the stone church. Years ago—a couple of decades, in fact—it had housed a country grocery and a fillingstation. Then it had closed. It had reopened for three or four summer seasons as a roadside produce market, setting out wicker baskets of peaches, grapes and tomatoes, along with two hulking smokeblackened cauldrons for boiling peanuts. Then the place had closed again. An oil company removed the gaspumps. The owner died, and the owner's family sold out.

A Mark Sixteener from Cottonton, Alabama, purchased the building and turned it into a touristtrap herpetology museum called Snake-O-Rama. This entrepreneur equipped the interior with several long trestletables, furnished the trestletables with three or four glasswalled aquariums apiece, and stocked the aquariums with serpents.

For two bucks (for grownups) or fifty cents (for kids), you could go in and ogle diamondbacks, copperheads, cottonmouths, watermoccasins, pygmyrattlers, timberrattlers, kingsnakes, greensnakes, racers, coralsnakes, gartersnakes, one sleepy boaconstrictor, and, for variety's sake, geckos, chameleons, newts, an aquatic salamander called a hellbender that resembled a knobby strip of bark with legs, and an ugly stuffed gilamonster.

Hoke had visited Snake-O-Rama on an eighthgrade fieldtrip with Mr. Nyeland's science class, the year before he laid out of school for good. But tourist traffic on Frye's Mill Road was light to nonexistent, and the number of subsidized trips from the Hothlepoya County schools fell so dramatically during Snake-O-Rama's second year that the welloff Mark Sixteener who ran the place—most members of the Assembly were collardpoor—arranged to sell the building and land, not including the old family graveyard nextdoor, to a dispossessed offshoot of his church from west of Beulah Fork.

The Pilchers began attending the new Assembly as a family. Hoke's mama died only months later—a death the coroner ruled an accidental poisoning—and his daddy soon thereafter fled such crazy piety. Hoke, though, had hung on, convinced that these handlers, poisondrinkers, and ecstatic babblers were now kin and that one day Jesus would bless him if he lifted up and chanted over a handful of coiling snakes. For the most part, Hoke had found that belief fulfilled in his association with the Sixteeners, especially in his friendships with Twyla, an elderly couple called the Loomises, and the family of the black preacher C.K. Sermons, whose surname jibed so exactly with his calling that even a few in their Assembly wrongly figured it a pulpit alias.

In fact, of all the twentyodd folks who met regularly in the former Snake-O-Rama, only Johnny Mark Carnes and two other men in their thirties, Ron Strock and Eddie Moomaw, had ever shown him anything other than acceptance and aid. Their help had included shoemoney, a Bible, and Sam Loomis' appeal to Colby Deaton to give Hoke a job at Deaton's Bar-B-Q.

The trio of Carnes, Strock, and Moomaw, though, saw him as a pretender, a pain in the buttocks, and, in Carnes' case, a misbegotten rival for Twyla Glanton, even though Carnes already had a wife from whom he had separated over her disenchantment with hazardous church practices and his evergrowing inventory of scaly pets. Eddie Moomaw called Hoke the orphan and, in a service not long after Hoke moved into the tirehouse, rebuked Hoke for living with an unredeemed heathen, taking as his text the prophetic recriminations of *Ezekiel* 16:

Then I wershed you in water; yes, I thoroughly wershed off yore blood, and I anointed you with oil! Moomaw had said, his eyes not on Hoke but instead on a wildeyed portrait of Jesus on the Snake-O-Rama's rear wall.

Amen! said many of the unwary Sixteeners, Hoke included. *Tell it, Brother Eddie!*

Brother Eddie told it, at last bringing his eyes down on the target of his rant: You offered yourself to everyone who passed by, and multiplied yore acts of harlotry!

Amen! Woe to all sinners!

Hoke stayed silent, but his napehair rose.

Yet you were not like a harlot, Moomaw said, because you scorned payment!

Sicm, Brother Eddie! Hie on!

Men make payment to awl harlots, but you made yore payment to awl yore lovers, and hired em to come to you from awl aroun for yore harlotry!

Amen! Go, Brother Eddie! At this point, only Carnes and Ron Strock were seconding Moomaw's quoted accusations. No one else understood the reasons for such condemnation. No one else could follow the argument.

I will bring blood upon you in fury and jealousy! Moomaw said, pointing the whole top half of his body at Hoke, snakily twisting shoulders, neck, and head.

At that point C.K. Sermons rose from his altarchair. His skin the purple of a decaying eggplant, he clapped his enormous hands as if slamming shut a thousandpage book.

I will be quiet n be angry no more, he said. The boy you scold does not deserve such upbraision, Brother Eddie. He goes where he muss to put shelter over his head.

Amen! Twyla said. *Amen!* said the Loomises. *Amen!* said a dozen other Sixteeners.

A course he's a orphan. He's done long since lost his mama n daddy. But didn't Jesus say, I will not leave you orphans, I will come to you?

He said it! Deed He did!

So what if the Pilchers come to us stead of vice versa? So what? They's moren one way fo the body of Jesus to surroun this worl's orphans! Moren one way to stretch comfort to the comfortless!

Amen! Praise God!

Thus rebuked, Eddie Moomaw retreated to his own altarchair grimfaced and blanched, his tongue so thick on the inside of his cheek that its bulge looked like a tumor. And only C.K. Sermons raised snakes heavenward that night. Of course, he had also—alone among the evening's worshipers—tossed back a small mayonnaise jar of strychnine (making a comical pucker at its bitterness), foretold in tongues, and restored Brother Eddie to concord with their fold by exorcising from his body a demon of resentment named Rathcor.

Rathcor! Sermons shouted, one hand hard on Moomaw's chest, the other shoving downward on his head. Rathcor, come ye forth in shame n wretchedness! *Now!*

And Rathcor had departed Moomaw, half its vileness in a sulfurous breeze from Moomaw's mouth and half in a startling report from his backside. These smells had lingered in the stone building, a stench that Hoke recalled as burnt cinnamon, bad eggs, and decomposed pintobeans.

S awright, Sermons told everyone. Just means the demon's done hightailed it. Means Brother Eddie's free.

Brother Eddie had smiled, lifting his hands into cobwebby shadow and praising the Lord. But his hostility toward Hoke, not to say that of Carnes and Strock, never fully evaporated, and Hoke could only wonder if a portion of Rathcor had lodged in the most secret passages of Moomaw's anatomy—his nose, his ears, his anus, his dick—because Hoke could not imagine, from Moomaw's present behavior, that Sermons had cast Rathcor out of him entire.

Greet one another with a holy kiss.
—*Romans* 16:16

The closer Hoke drew to the kudzu-filigreed building the louder grew the buzzing syncopated music leaking through its mortared joins. He heard tambourines, trap drums, an electric guitar, a trumpet. This music, pulsing like strobes in the grimy windows, told him he had arrived late, the service had already begun. The stolid rockwalls and the roof of steeply pitched shakes seemed almost to expand and contract with the singing and its jangly backup, like a jukejoint roadhouse in an old Krazy Kat cartoon.

The people crooned: *Oh, weary soul, the gate is neah. In sin why still abide? Both peace n rest are waiting heah, And you are just outside.*

And a fervent chorus: *Just outside the door, just outside the door, Behold it stands ajar! Just outside the door, just outside the door—So neah n yet so far!*

Hoke halted, clammy with the cold suspicion that through this old gospel hymn the Sixteeners were addressing and jeering his tardiness:

Just outside the door, just outside the door—So neah n yet so far!

Then go on in, he told himself. Walk through the gate and face em like one of their forever own.

He did, pushing in more like a gunslinger entering a saloon than a believer in search of his sweet Jesus Only. The ruckus from the toothache-imparting guitar and trumpet, not to mention the rattle of drums and tambourines, smacked him like a falling wall. The handclapping, pogojumping Mark Sixteeners—men to the left of the pewless sanctuary, women to the right—ladled a soupy nausea into Hoke's gut. Usually, such motionful devotion wired him for most of the fiercest God frequencies, but tonight a fretfulness lay on the people, a catching mood of upset, even derangement.

At the end of Just Outside the Door, Sermons leapt to the altardeck from between his wife, Betty, and their thirteen-year-old daughter, Regina, already a jivy trumpeter. The only black male in the building, Sermons wore a sweated-out Sunday shirt and a bolo tie with a turquoise cross on its ceramic slide. He harangued the sweltering room:

I grew up wi the cutaway eyes n the sad caloomniation o folks who figgered me n my kin just a lucky step up from the monkeys.

We hear you, Brother C.K.!

Caw it bigotry, peoples. Caw it hate or ignorance. Caw it puft-up delusion.

Amen!

Whatever anybody caws it, peoples, it hurt—like stones n flails. Sometimes, Lawd Lawd, it still lays me out, even me, faithful servant to our Risen Jesus thet I long since become in my rebornin.

Glory!

Now the chilrens of this worl done started comin after our own. Mockin, namecawin, greedy to troublemake.

Satan has em, C.K.! Satan!

Lissen what they done to Sister Twyla—to make her move off our Risen Jesus to the dead Christ they socawed churches strive to burry eyebrow deep in works n talk!

Preach it!

They bite like unprayed-over snakes! They want to pyzon the chilrens of the light!

God'll repay!

Sister Twyla, cmon up here! Testify to what the heathen n them lukewarm Christians of Beulah Fork's sitdown churches done to knock back yore faith!

C.K. Sermons reached out a hand, and Twyla, modest in a lightyellow anklelength poplin dress, emerged redeyed from the women. She floated across the floor to the platform. She did not mount it, but pivoted to face everyone with a sweet timid smile. People upfront parted to make her visible to worshipers farther back.

Hoke stood admiring. Three nights ago she'd worn her hair in an unrighteous teased-up globe. Now it hung long, reddish streaks flashing in the sorrel every time she moved her head, a small ivory barrette for ornament. Hoke could tell, though, that she'd had a monster bout with tears: Her eyesockets looked scoured, shiny with knuckling.

Bless yall, she said. Praise God.

Praise God!

Yall notice, please, thet Hoke Pilcher's come in. It'd be good if you men greeted him with a holy kiss, like Paul sez to do, and you womenfolk guv him a sisterly nod.

Hoke felt an abrupt heat climb from his chest and settle in his cheeks. The women to his right nodded or curtsied while in their half of the sanctuary the men milled into ranks to bestow on him the holy kiss spelled out in *Romans* 16. Sermons, Eddie Moomaw and Hugh Bexton leapt down from the altardeck to greet him—mechanically in Moomaw's case, it seemed to Hoke—and Ron Strock and Johnny Mark Carnes used their go-bys to pinch one of Hoke's reddened earlobes or to razz him about the irregularity of Twyla's appeal.

I need to remember this tactic, Carnes said, nudging Hoke's cheek: Big entrance, ten minits late.

Ferlin couldn't git his Ford cranked. I wadn't—

Stifle it, Pilcher, Carnes said. Lady's gonna talk.

Twyla absentmindedly rubbed her palms together. Early Wednesday mornin, she said, I had my car tires slashed and my deck strewn with toy rubber snakes. My trees got toiletpapered and my trailer aigged.

Cry out to God, said Camille Loomis, the Sixteener nearly everyone called Prophetess Camille.

Thet's not all. On Wednesday I went to Li'l People, where I've done worked three years now, and Miss Victoria let me go. Said some of her parents don't want their babies tended to by a known snake handler.

C.K. Sermons said: Christian parents, no doubt.

Sposedly. Anyways, I'm a known handler. Like a known car thief or a known ax murderer.

Yo're a known blessed friend, said Sam Loomis.

I cain't work a minit longer cause I might feed somebody's darlin a bowl of baby rattlers. I might wrap a watermoccasin up in the poor kid's didy.

We'll hep you, said Angela Bexton.

I know yall will. Like Brother C.K. sez, it hurts—this persecution by the world.

Somebody suggested a love offering.

Wait, Twyla said. The world thinks we've gone crazy cause we abide in and by the Word. Thet's what the silly children of this world've come to.

Amen!

But much as I love them little ones I seen to awmost ever day for three years, I love the Word—I love the Lord—more. I won't walk outta the light to satisfy any false Christian I may offend by abidin true.

Praise God!

And as Moses lifted up the serpent in the wilderness, even so must the Son of Man be lifted up.

Amen! Praise God!

Jesus sez thet in the Book. Which is to affirm thet I will lift serpents myself at ever pure anointin.

In His name! Amen!

I will do it to lift up the Word thet is also Jesus Risen, else this brief life will fall out in ashes and I myself blow away like so much outworn dust.

Twyla's speech, carrying news of her persecution and the witness of her resolve, stunned Hoke. He could not move. His embarrassment had drained away, though, and in its place welled pride. His love streamed over and then from Twyla like a flood of rich silt. Others among the Sixteeners did move in response to her testimony, reclaiming their instruments, cranking up a gospel shout, swaying to the acid caterwauling of Ron Strock's guitar and the ripple blasts of young Regina's trumpet, leaping about like stifflegged colts, footstomping and handclapping not in unison but in a great cheerful boil that somehow melded them in faith and triumph. Finally, Hoke absorbed through his pores their backasswards confederating spirit. And then he too began to move.

The bite of the serpent is nothing compared to the bite of your fellow man.
—Charles McGlocklin, the EndTime Evangelist

Later C.K. Sermons leapt again to the altardeck. His wife, Sister Betty, a lightskinned AfricanAmerican with the figure and selfpossession of a teenaged gymnast, broke out a video camera. She shouldered it like an infantryman shouldering a bazooka. Hoke had noticed such cameras at other Jesus Risen services, usually in the hands of local TV crews looking for two or three filler minutes for an 11:00 P.M. news broadcast. The red light on Sister Betty's camera glowed like a coal, or a serpent's eye.

Sister Twyla did no preachin tonight, said Sermons. She testified. You see, I just heard some wayward mumblin bout how womens don't blong up here preachin.

They don't, said Leonard Callender.

Nobody disputes it, said Sermons. I know they got no caw to make mens subject to they preachments n foretellins. And Sister Twyla knows it. Futhamore, nothin like thet's happened here tonight. Yall unnerstand?

Praise God we do!

Good. We got new bidnus to tend to, new praises to lift. And none of it'll go Jesus Risen smooth if they's wrong thinkin or foolish resentments mongst us.

A fiftyish man named Darren DeVore bumped Hoke's shoulder. S mazin to me, he whispered, how we got us a nigger preacherman and female testifiers.

Thet so? said Hoke, stepping away.

My daddy woulda cut the fig off thetere fella and led the uppity women outside to catch some rocks.

Whynt you tell it so everbody can hear you?

I aint my daddy, Brother Hoke. I've changed wi the times. Grinning, he angled off through the other men toward the altar platform.

We need some prayin music, Sermons told the band. We got to pray over these pernicious snakes.

The band struck up a hardrock hymn, Regina Sermons cocking her elbows and blowing out her cheeks like a swampfrog. Twyla, Hoke noticed, had a tambourine. She hipbanged it in proximate time to the hymn's rhythm. Only the women sang:

When Judah played the harlot,
When proud Judah mocked her God,
God stripped her of her garments,
Nor did He spare the rod.

Yet His love was such, O mighty such,
Judah He toiled to save:
He proffered her His Jesus touch,
And with sweet rue forgave.

As the women sang, C.K. Sermons, Eddie Moomaw, and Hugh Bexton prayed over the snakeboxes against the church's rear wall. The boxes showed bright handpainted portraits of Jesus, Mary and the disciples. The men prayed with their eyes shut, hands palm upward at shoulderheight or squeezed into juddering fists at their bellies, their voices either high monotone pleas or low gruff summonses.

Shan-pwei-koloh-toshi-monha-plezia-klek! shouted Prophetess Camille, her head thrown back as if inviting a knife to unhinge it at her wattled throat. *Fehzhka-skraiiii!*

Camille sez they's a demon in here, Sam Loomis told Hoke over the tubthumping music.

A demon? Rathcor?

A betrayer. A worker of hoodoo what'll drag hypocrites and baby blievers straight to hellfire.

Camille turned in a slow circle, her arms hanging down like rusty windowsash weights. *Auvlih-daks-bel-woh-oh-vehm-ah-pih!* she cried. *Neh-hyat-skraiiii!*

Camille sez we got moren one in here! said Loomis. But the betrayer he's done fell to pitdiggin!

Sermons did a solitary congadance from the snakeboxes to the edge of the altardeck with three or four serpents in each hand. He dipped from side to side in an ecstatic crouch as the Jesus Risen band veered into a rave-up of Higher Ground. Eddie Moomaw and Hugh Bexton slid forward to bookend Sermons, the way the thieves on Golgotha had flanked the crucified Jesus, Bexton with canebrakes and pygmyrattlers squirming about his wrists like overboiled spaghetti, Moomaw with only a single snake but that one a silky diamondback of such length that it looped his forearms in countergliding coils.

Hoke knew this snake for Judas even before Carnes took it from Moomaw. Carnes began to handle it in an orgasmic frenzy. He may have even moaned glory in his upright congress with Judas, but the rattle and blare of the Sixteener combo, along with the worshipers' continuing babel, drowned even the loudest utterances of the chief three handlers.

In spite of Prophetess Camille's warning, Hoke could feel a benevolent essence—the Holy Ghost—seeping from overhead and even sideways through the stones into the former Snake-O-Rama. He half expected everyone to sprout plumelike flames from the crowns of their heads, like so many outsized cigarette lighters snapping to radiant point.

It entered Hoke, this Spirit, and, amid the crazy din, he too began to dance, jitterbugging in place, barking praise, reconnecting with his dead mama and his absconded daddy as well as with the raptured majority of the Sixteeners. This was what it was like to open to and be tenanted by the Comforter, Jesus Risen at His ghostliest and most tender.

Yes. It was like a blesséd fit.

Hoke began to stutterstep diagonally through the other happy epileptics, a chess piece on a mission. He could smell the Holy Ghost, Who had now so totally saturated the room that C.K. Sermons and the other handlers pranced about veiled in a haze thick as woodsmoke. The smell was not woodsmoke, though, but cinnamon sourdough and overripe juiceapples, offerings to eat and drink, not to laud. Hoke elbowed through this fragrant haze, seeking its source. He suspected that it had its focus somewhere near C.K. Sermons.

Sermons gave Regina—the band now lacked a trumpetplayer—two snakes; and Regina, more child than woman, lifted them through the layered gauze of the Spirit, to the Spirit, one snake climbing as the other twisted back to flick her pugnose with its quick split tongue. Sister Betty videotaped Regina's performance.

Other Sixteeners began to handle, one man thrusting a snake into his shirt, another tiptoeing over a diamondback as if it were a tightrope, enacting Jesus' promise, Behold, I give you authority to trample on serpents.

Sister Camille fell down ranting. Twyla, Polly DeVore and Angela Bexton knelt beside her with prayercloths and stoppered bottles of oliveoil, dimestore items with which to minister to her as holy paramedics.

Hoke, still dancing, had reached the front, hungry for the boon of a serpent from C.K. Sermons. For the first time since joining the Sixteeners, he knew the Holy Ghost had anointed him to handle, as it had anointed nearly every other person in the church tonight. But Sermons had already distributed his entire allotment of snakes. He stood on the platform with a masonjar of strychnine, praying over it, preparing to drink.

Hoke floated past Sermons and many others... to Eddie Moomaw, who still had three or four living bracelets to hand out. He looked peeved that no one had yet come to relieve him of them. Sister Betty, Hoke noted sidelong, recorded the chaos with her video camera, paying as much heed to him and the other congregants as to her own husband and child.

Then Hoke went flatfooted and reached out to Moomaw, his face helplessly grimacing. He mewled aloud. Moomaw handed him a canebrake, a pinkishbeige timberrattler not quite a yard long, a satinback that winched itself up to his chin, shaking its rattles like maracas.

Hoke was anointed, fearless. Gripping the canebrake with both hands, he inscribed 8s with it in the air before him. He slipped into a floating whiteness where the rattler focused his whole attention and no other material body in the Snake-O-Rama impinged on him at all.

Furiously, the snake continued to rattle warning, but Hoke had surrounded and entered it just as the Spirit had done him, and it would not strike. Hoke knew this with the same kind of bodyborne knowledge that made real to him his possession of ears, elbows, knees, even if he made no effort to touch them. He and the snake shared one spellbound mind. In fact, he felt so loose, so brainfree, that he imagined the serpent an extract from his own person: his spinalcord and brainstem in a sleeve of patterned velvet.

Then something in the immaterial sanctuary of Hoke's trance bumped him. *Bumped* him. Someone in the Hands On Assembly was shouting louder than anyone else, louder even than the scouring racket of the Jesus Only band.

Hoke sensed the soft white pocket of his trance blurring at the edges, breaking down. Forms and voices began to intrude upon him. The timberrattler in his hands separated out of the albino plasma that had sheltered them, taking on the outline and bulk of a realworld menace. Hoke finally understood that the loudest screaming in the room was his own. He clamped his mouth shut, thinning out the sound, and turned to Moomaw to rid himself of the agitated canebrake.

Regina Sermons, still powerfully anointed, stood handling beside him, but even without looking at Hoke, she edged away to allow him to make the transfer.

Eddie Moomaw took the snake from Hoke, smiling mysteriously sidelong. Why the smile? Was he disappointed that Hoke had escaped unbit? sorry that a snake had already come back to him? peeved that no one else had returned one? Hoke shook his head and retreated a step.

C.K. Sermons, holding his masonjar, wiped the back of his hand across his mouth. Good to the last drop! he said. Praise God! He beamed at Sister Betty's camera, spread his arms wide, revolved on the deck like a musicbox figurine.

Hoke decided he had to get some air. He turned to thread his way doorward.

Carnes blocked his path. Welcome back, Pilcher, he said. Here. Have you another....

Judas folded into Hoke's arms like eight feet of burdensome firehose. Hoke had no time to sidestep the handoff. To keep from dropping it he shifted the diamondback and, as he did, saw on Carnes' face a look of combined glee and despisal. More from surprise than fear, Hoke lost his grip. Judas, suddenly alert and coiling, dropped. Hoke went to one knee to catch the snake, managed a partial grab, and found himself eye to yellow eye with Judas. Fear washed through him, a quickacting venom, and he shielded his face with the edge of his hand. The snake struck, spiking him just below the knuckles of his pinkie and his ringfinger, a puncture that toppled him.

Somebody screamed piercingly, and this time the rising sirenlike wail belonged not to him but to Twyla Glanton. Judas crawled over Hoke's fallen body. It bit him again, this time in the upperarm, then rippled over the concrete in a beautiful coiling glide.

Help him! shouted Twyla, arrowing in. Hush thet racket and help him, else he's bound to die!

Not if he's got faith! said Carnes.

The band stopped playing, the prophets stopped babbling, and Sermons, Bexton and Moomaw hopped down from the altardeck to see about Hoke. He could hear the cicadas outside, whirring dryly, the sad bellyaching of ditchfrogs, and the faraway hum and buzz of pickup tires rolling on asphalt and ratcheting over a cattleguard.

Git him a doctor, somebody!

Now, Twyla, if we do thet, Carnes said, aint we sayin the Word's not the Word? Before Twyla could answer, Carnes looked down at Hoke. Boy, you want a doctor?

Nosir. Just some kinda ease. Hoke sprawled, burning where Judas had fanged him.

He'd say thet, Twyla said. Just to fit in better here at th Assembly.

He won't ever fit in better if he truckles to this world's medicine, said Carnes.

Sermons knelt beside Hoke. He don't want a doctor, Sister Twyla, cause he knows from whence comes his hep.

Praise God!

Look here, said Twyla. Thet's a big Judas of a snake. It spiked him twyst. Thet much venom'd drop a buffalo, much less a peakèd skinny boy.

Faith can toss mountains into the sea, Carnes said.

Twyla grimaced. When was the last time yore faith tossed a mountain into the sea?

Kept me safe handlin thatere serpent, Carnes said. S moren anybody can say for Brother Hoke.

Hoke'd done handled, Sermons said. You caught m when the Spirit'd gone off him.

Hugh Bexton returned with Judas around one shoulder like a great drooping epaulette braid. He stood directly over Hoke, and Hoke could see Bexton and the snake looming like paradefloats against the cracked ceiling. Judas seemed to probe about for a baseboard chink or a skylight, a way to escape. Occasionally, though, it coiled the upper portion of its length floorward and flicked its tongue, swimming over Hoke with the airy loveliness of a saltwater eel.

If Brother Hoke dies faithless, said Camille Loomis, he'll go straight to—

—hellfire, Sam Loomis finished for her.

It was told me from on high, said Camille.

What happens to the hoodoo workers here amongst us? Twyla said. Do those betrayers go to hellfire too?

Not till they die, Camille said.

But they laid the hoodoo on Judas and got poor Hoke bit.

Camille sounded sad or embarrassed: No, missy, them hoodoo workers just showed up his weakness.

What garbage, Twyla said. What backasswards crap.

The Loomises looked at each other and backed away. Hoke watched Judas swimming, climbing, loopsliding in dimensionless emptiness. The Loomises' curse—*straight to hellfire*—rang in his head. The faces of those still hovering over him revealed a peculiar range of passions, Twyla's running from cajolery to outrage, Carnes' from amusement to satisfaction. Sermons made a series of increasingly sluggish peacemaking gestures. Judas bobbed down in a slowmotion arc and once again laid its yellow gaze on Hoke.

Somewhere beyond the diamondback's scrutiny glowed a single pulsing red dot.

Hoke thought: I'm going straight to hellfire.

Like Jesus, Hoke rises from himself and strides out of the cooling tomb of his own bones.

He leaves Twyla, Carnes, Moomaw, Sermons, and all the other Sixteeners and ambles into the quiet darkness—no cicadas, no frogs, no trucks—outside the Hands On Assembly of Jesus Risen, formerly Snake-O-Rama. He walks and walks. In less time than it takes to leap a ditch he comes to a steeppitched road lined with blackberry brambles, dogwoods, pines.

A sycamore almost concealed by this other foliage bears a handlettered sign:

TRESPAsERS !!! —
WE AIM to PLEZE But SHOT to KILL!

He has come home to his roommate Ferlin's tirehouse in a hard-to-reach pocket of Hothlepoya County. Neither Sackett nor Rag rushes out to greet him. The house itself blazes like a firebombed tiredump, turbulent coalblack smoke billowing away, climbing into the sky's midnight fade.

The conflagration does not devour the house, but surrounds, dances on, and leaps from it. Pungent smoke skirls ceaselessly from the twoply radials and the halfburied whitewalls. Hoke calmy observes the fire, then cuts painlessly through its pall, and enters the dugout's U-shaped livingroom.

Ferlin! he shouts. You to home?

The interior startles him. It looks like an immense tiled lavatory. The walls glitter like scrubbed kitchen appliances, even if their white enamel faintly reflects the movement of fire and rippling smoke. Although he has no trouble breathing here, he must hike forever—longer than it takes to leap a ditch—to reach the glass cage, a bulletshaped capsule, across from Ferlin's frontdoor.

Hoke rides the capsule down. Flames twist in the glass or clear hardplastic shaping it, flickering from side to side as well as up and down. Beyond these flames the countryside (yes, countryside) looks infinitely hilly. Figures—faceless sticks dwarfed by the buttes and spires in the brickbrown landscape—cower in halfhidden rock niches or flee over plains like fiery icefloes.

Occasionally a longnosed fish, or a mutant parrot, or a parachuting man-of-war drifts past the capsule, each with some raw disfigurement: a gash, an extraneous growth, an unhealthy purpling of its visible membranes. Hoke wants to pull these wounded critters inside the capsule and heal their wounds with hands-on prayer.

Can God dwell in any of these freaks? In any part of this infernal canyon? Hoke thinks so. How could he have trespassed here without help?

In the subbasement the capsule halts. Hoke emerges, and an ordinarylooking man in a chambray shirt and a pair of designer jeans meets him. The man does not speak. His sunglasses lenses betray neither friendliness nor hostility. Hoke discovers his name only because it is stitched in flowing script—JUDAS—over his heartside shirtpocket (if he has a heart). He greets Hoke with a crooked thrifty bow.

This man, this Judas, leads Hoke through a tunnel lit at distant intervals with baseboard lights fashioned to resemble lifesized Old and New World serpents: cobras, mambas, pythons, shieldtails, eggeaters, rattlesnakes, vipers and so on, each of these sinuous devices plugged in at ankleheight and aglow with an icy radiance that both animates and eerily Xrays the shaped light. Hoke can see the skull, vertebrae, and tubelike organs of each makebelieve serpent.

Leading the way, Judas lists to one side or the other of the tunnel, but Hoke walks straight down its middle, trying to ignore the threat implicit in the baseboard lamps. The tunnel—itself a hollow, kinking serpent—goes on and on. Sometimes its twisty floor and curved walls seem to tremble, as if bombs have fallen close to hand.

At length the tunnel opens into a chamber—Hoke regards it as a satanic chapel—with a crooked wingless caduceus where the cross would hang in most decent Protestant churches. Ringing the chamber's squat dome are bleak stainedglass windows whose cames outline serpents in a stew of motifs, all colored in deep brown, indigo, or slumbering purple, with intermittent shards of crimson or yellow to accent the snakes' hooded or bulgingly naked eyes.

In these cames Hoke sees the same kinds of snakes in two dimensions that he saw rendered in the tunnel in three, except that here the serpents are all venomous cobras or pitvipers. The conflagration outside the chamber inflicts a sullen glitter on the dome's glass, but Hoke draws some comfort from it, as he would from a fire on a stone hearth.

Unlike the church on Frye's Mill Road, Judas' antichapel has pews. Three rows of benches face the pulpit, each one covered in snakeskin. Behind the pulpit, a choir loft made of long white bones and ornate ivory knobs faces outward beneath a stainedglass triptych.

With a gesture, Judas urges Hoke to find a place among the pews. Hoke chooses the curved middle pew and sits halfway along its scaly length. Judas mounts to the pulpit, growing two feet in height as he uncoils from a deceptive stoop. For the first time since arriving down here, Hoke can study Judas' face.

It is the machinemolded face of a departmentstore dummy, with just enough play in the blockfoam to permit the creature to smile faintly or to twitch a lip corner. When he removes his sunglasses, he reveals yellow eyes like a diamondback's and his face deforms into the soft triangle of a pitviper's head, with severe dents in the cheeks and a smile that has widened alarmingly. The rest of Judas' body maintains a human cast, and, hands gripping the pulpit's sides, he leans forward to regale Hoke, his lone congregant, with a stemwinding sermon. Outside, bombs or depth charges continue to explode, and Judas responds to the tremblors by rubbernecking his head around and whiteknuckling the lectern that seems to hold him erect. Hoke pays close heed.

Judas' sermon has no words. It issues from the creature's smile as hisses and sighs. Flickers of a doubletipped tongue break the sibilance, and at each pause Judas seems to rethink the next segment of his message. Then, as the crux of his text demands, a quiet or a vigorous hissing resumes, along with more tongueflickers and sighs. Sometimes Judas pounds the lectern or ambles briefly and shakily away from it. Hoke can make no sense of any of it, but Judas' voiceless sermonizing continues without relent. Hoke would like to make a getaway back through the tunnel, but his dead mama taught him never to walk out on a preacher and so he sits longsufferingly in place. Maybe Judas wants to torment him the way Carnes and the handlers tormented their spiritdrugged snakes.

Long into his sermon, a blue film creeps over Judas' eyes, turning them a sickly green. This milky film thickens. As it does, Judas' eyes go from green to seagreen to turquoise to a dreamy cobalt. These cobalt veils blind Judas, but he goes on hissing his wordless rant.

When Hoke thinks he can take no more, Judas stops hissing and rubs his snout with his human hands. The skin over his snout loosens all the way back to his capped eyes. Judas grabs this scaly layer and peels it back. Then the skin on his hands splits, and the new hands beneath these glovelike husks break through to peel away the old skin, including his chambray shirt and designer jeans.

With one reborn hand on the pulpit for support, Judas steps out of this old covering and sets it aside. The husk rocks on its feet like a display mannikin fit only for junking. The new Judas, meanwhile, clings to the pulpit in the guise of a human female: another mannikin, but an animated one for the women's department. With chestnut hair that cascades down and trembles over her shoulders, this female version of Judas picks up her discarded skin by the shoulders, carries it to the choir loft, and places it in one of the five chairs there. The integument of this molt rattles dryly, its snaky head deforming again into something recognizably human, as if its serpentshape had never really taken.

Hoke sits mesmerized. He no longer wants to run, simply to understand. At the lectern again, the female snakeperson goes on changing, her face shrinking and triangulating, her tresses pulling back into her skull and weaving into satiny snakeskin. Looking past her, Hoke sees that the molt in the choir has come to resemble his daddy, who ran out on his mama and him shortly after she had yoked them with the Sixteeners.

You bastid! Hoke shouts at the thing.

Outside, very near, a bomb falls. The explosion rocks the domed chamber, audibly warping the stainedglass in its cames, swaying the pulpit and rattling the hollow imago of his daddy, which totters in its chair. The imago has no eyes, only gaping vents, but it stares at Hoke without love, remorse, or any plea for understanding. It sits, merely sits, teetering whenever ordnance detonates.

The snakeperson at the pulpit ignores Hoke's daddy and launches into another harangue—a hissyfit, Hoke thinks—that expands and expands. Usually Hoke's bladder, given the length of these speeches, would expand too, threatening rupture and flood, but here in Ferlin's subbasement his bladder has lots of stretch and he too much endurance.

At last, though, the second Judas' eyes grow a milky film and a second shedding occurs, revealing a new snakeperson and leaving behind a female husk that the third version of Hoke's guide places in the choir loft next to his daddy. The face of this shell takes on the features of his mama, while the third snaky preacher begins a brandnew tirade.

Hoke nods. At length, a third molt puts a fresh male husk in the loft with his folks. This tedious process occurs twice more. By the end of the diamondback's fifth hissyfit, every seat in the choir is occupied. The choir now comprises five false human beings whom Hoke sees as wicked likenesses of his daddy, his mama, Johnny Mark Carnes, Twyla Glanton and Ferlin Rodale. They rustle to their feet, and the sixth Judas sheds its preacherly garments to join them in the loft as an immense coiled rattler.

How can they sing an anthem when they have no voices? Why does the sixth Judas lace her long anatomy among the other five betrayers, then raise her triangular head above the zombie face of Johnny Mark Carnes?

Ulo-shan-pwei-koloh-ehlo-scraiiii! says the sixth Judas in a female voice familiar to Hoke. *Neh-hyat-kolotosh-mona-ho!* Her split tongue flits among these syllables like a hummingbird sampling morningglory blossoms. Then, on her warning rattle, the choir, once mute, joins her in pealing out a hymn that Hoke well knows:

O for a thousand tongues to sing....

Hands pressed against him, their warm palms on his chest, upperarms, forehead. One pair had a viselike grip on his temples, flattening his ears and struggling to touch fingertips behind his head.

Here he comes, a voice said. Glory.

Bring m out, Jesus. Bring m on out.

Hoke let the faces surrounding him clarify in the glare of a ceilinglamp. As his pupils narrowed, even the darker faces among the four took on definition. He recognized Twyla Glanton and then every member of the Sermons family.

Praise God.

Twyla's face came toward him, and she placed one ear less than an inch from his lips. Say again, she said. Her sorrel hair touched his face.

Lift him from the pit n set him upright midst us, said C.K. Sermons. Bless his ever goin forth n comin home.

Say again, Twyla said again.

Hoke tried—no sound, but his lips quirked.

Looky there, said Regina Sermons. He be smilin.

Hoke stayed with the Sermonses the next three days. They prayed with and over him, often laying on hands. They fed him unsalted rice, applesauce, bananas, and tea made of chamomile flowers, passionflower leaves, and crushed rosebuds. With no other medical attention but this food and prayer ("Antivenin is the antichrist and doctors are its antifaith disciples," Carnes had liked to say), Hoke recovered quickly.

On Sunday morning, the Sermonses held an outdoor service on the decks of the splitlevel gazebo in their backyard. No one brought snakes into it, although Hoke knew that the Sermonses kept a dozen or more in crates along the rear of their double garage. Twyla, Ferlin Rodale, and Sam and Camille Loomis (who had forgiven Twyla her words at the Friday-night snakehandling service) attended this informal gathering. Oddly, though, no other member of the congregation showed up, and Hoke began to suspect that something more dire than his own rattlerbites had disrupted Friday's worship.

The Sermonses refused to talk about such matters while his body went about healing itself. When not praying or reading the Bible with him, they gave him his space, including free run of their house and grounds.

Their brick house sat on an acre off White Cow Creek Road, ten miles west of Beulah Fork. It appeared to have been lifted from a hightone suburban subdivision and set down again in the sharecropper boonies. It had three bedrooms, a study, and a den with a hightech entertainment center: largescreen TV and VCR combo, multideck stereophonic CD soundsystem, and, because none of the Mark Sixteeners were teetotalers, a wellsupplied wetbar. The Sermonses could afford such a place because C.K. sold insurance as well as preached, and Betty worked a deskjob in the Hothlepoya County Health Department, even if her job struck Hoke as peculiarly at odds with the noninterventionist doctrines of their Hands On Assembly.

On Monday evening, Twyla, Ferlin, and the Loomises came for another call. This time, though, C.K. herded everyone into the den to watch the videotape that Betty had shot three evenings earlier. Hoke understood that C.K. had organized the gathering as a small party in honor of his recovery. If it had any other purpose, beyond showing off Betty's skills as a camerawoman, he could not have named it.

This past Friday a true anointin came on Brother Hoke, C.K. said. Yall watch n see.

Somebody had wound the tape exactly to the point at which Eddie Moomaw passed Hoke a timberrattler. The tape showed Hoke handling, there among the other Sixteeners. The hopping and stutterstepping of the worshipers, the clangy music, the scary inscrutability of the snakes —everything on the tape united to make Hoke see himself and his friends as part of an outlandish spectacle, separate somehow from their everyday selves. He recognized himself, and he didn't. He recognized Twyla and the Sermonses, and he didn't. Betty's tape tweaked the familiar old church and the ordinary folks inside it into a gaudy circus tent, with jugglers, acrobats and clowns.

My Lord, Ferlin said.

You know you'da loved to been there, Twyla said.

F yall think this's gonna work on me like a recruitin film, yall just don't know Ferlin Rodale.

Where is it? Hoke said. I don't see it.

Betty Sermons leaned over and patted his forearm. Where's what, baby?

The Spirit, Hoke said. Thet night it was so thick in there you coulda bottled it.

It don't tape, Betty said. Never has.

Hush, Prophetess Camille said. This's where Brother Hoke passes his serpent on back to Eddie Moomaw.

Hoke watched himself hand off the timberrattler. Then he watched C.K. take a hearty swig of poison and Carnes explode into view to unload an even bigger snake on the video image of himself. On the Sermonses' largescreen, Hoke accepted and then almost dropped the diamondback.

Yall're flakier than a deadman's dandruff, Ferlin said.

From a threestage recliner, Sam Loomis leveled a hard gaze on Ferlin. Who taught you yore manners, young man?

Beg yore pardon, sir. I've just never liked snakes.

They've awways spoken well of you, Twyla said.

The videotape continued to unspool, flickering and jumping in testimony to Betty's active camera technique.

Here comes the bites! Regina said.

Hoke flinched. So did Ferlin, who looked off at the framed underwriter certificates on the wall. Hoke kept watching and soon saw himself sprawled on the concrete floor, surrounded by Twyla, the Loomises, Sermons, Moomaw, Bexton, and two bigeyed little boys—the Strock twins—who had wriggled free of their mama's restraining arms to hunker next to Hoke and gawk at him in cheerful expectation of his demise.

Brats, thought Hoke.

Aloud he said: This's where I died. Then walked home to Ferlin's. And rode a elevator straight to hell.

Except, of course, the largescreen showed no sequence of events like that at all. Instead they saw Judas writhing above Hoke in Hugh Bexton's arms, and Twyla saying, *What backasswards crap*, and the Loomises moving stiffly out of view. Then the screen showed a dozen worshipers milling, smoke rolling over the floor from beneath the altardeck, a painted churchwindow shattering, and a fractured brick tumbling end over end on the concrete.

Sermons and the others raised their heads to register the broken-out window. Smoke began to rise through the church from baseboards, closets, windowsills, and the junkrooms behind the altar. The pictures of the outbreaking fire careened even more madly than Betty's earlier shots. Folks scrambled to flee the building. A sound like the amplified crumpling of Styrofoam dominated the audio; shouts, children crying, and the slamming of car and pickup doors echoed in the background.

C.K., Darren DeVore, Leonard Callender, and Ron Strock—there to shoo away his twins as much as to assist Hoke—picked Hoke up and hustled him in a hammockcarry to the door. Other men crated up and rescued their snakes, sometimes appearing to put their decorated boxes and the creatures inside them before their own wives and kids. The tape's last poorly exposed shots included a pan from the church's burning facade to the gleaming asphalt road going past it.

What was thet all about? Hoke said.

A fire got goin in the dry kudzu behind the church, Twyla said. It burnt us out, comin through the back.

How? Why?

Somebody done set it, C.K. Sermons said. A enemy like unto them cropburners in the gospels.

Only part standin today is walls, Betty said.

Twyla allowed that the fire could have started from a flungaway cigarette, but that C.K.'s investigation on Saturday morning did make it look that somebody had piled dry brush and maybe even two or three wheelbarrows of waste lumber, ends and pieces, against the church's rear wall. Then the sleazes had soaked the piles with kerosene, covered them with kudzu leaves and evergreen branches, and sneaked up during the snakehandling to drag the brush away and light the kindling.

Why'd anybody try to kill yall? Ferlin said. Yall're in a damnfool hurry to do it yoreselves.

Rathcor had his claws in it, said Camille. And whilst them snakes were out, I bet you cash money thet Carnes, Moomaw and DeVore awl played divil's innkeeper.

You don't know thet, Twyla said.

She sez it she's nigh-on certain, Sam Loomis said.

Plus it looks like Carnes's done skedaddled outta thisere county, C.K. said.

Hoke cavecrawled into himself. The Mark Sixteeners had lost their meetinghall, Johnny Mark Carnes had vamoosed without a faretheewell, and a disagreement of fierce consequence had split the Assembly—Eddie Moomaw and his cronies arguing that the fire bespoke a judgment for allowing a descendant of Ham to preach and handle snakes amongst them; the Loomises, Twyla, and their friends adamant that Moomaw had laid a vile scapegoatment on the Sermonses for reasons having less to do with theology than with low blood, covetousness, and whitetrash pride. There had been no full Mark Sixteener fellowship on Sunday morning not merely because their church had burnt, but because a schism along skewed racial and maybe even economic lines had cleft the Assembly.

Why'd Johnny Mark run? Hoke said.

I tracked him, Betty Sermons said. Taped his ever step wi thet big Judas snake of his. He figgered if you died, we'd put it out to Sheriff Ott thet he murdered you.

Then the bigger fool he, C.K. said. Law aint gonna squash no Sixteener for killin a Sixteener.

Why not? Regina said.

Same reason it aint like to vestigate our church fire as a arson, said C.K. dyspeptically, as if the strychnine he'd drunk had soured his stomach.

Or look too hard at the mischief out my way, said Twyla.

Rewind, said Regina.

Mam? said C.K. Sermons.

Rewind. Show me playin wi them ol snakes again.

Betty Sermons rewound the tape, and everyone watched Regina handle her rattlers again. Then the TV rescreened Hoke's work with the canebrake. Was that Hoke Pilcher? he wondered. Yes, but Hoke Pilcher under a throughblest anointing. In spite of everything else—snakebite, hellfire, schism—the sight of this miracle poured a tart joy into him, and Hoke perched before it, utterly rapt, oblivious to his surroundings.

That autumn Twyla Glanton moved from Hothlepoya County to Cottonton, Alabama. There she found a job as assistant city clerk and joined a small offshoot of the Hands On Assembly of Jesus Risen. In early October Hoke got Ferlin to drive him to Cottonton to see her, but Twyla had begun to date a surveyor in the Alabama highway department, and Hoke's visit brought down embarrassment on everyone but Ferlin.

Johnny Mark Carnes, according to Eddie Moomaw, had opened an upholstery shop near Waycross. In this shop, he recovered easychairs, divans, carseats, footstools, threestage recliners, and a variety of other items from pewcushions to the padded lids of jewelryboxes. Occasionally, according to Moomaw, he used snakeskin, for which reason he made frequent unauthorized jaunts into the Okefenokee Swamp.

The Mark Sixteeners in Hothlepoya County remained divided. The Moomaw faction held brush arbor services on New Loyd Hill until the first frost in October. The Sermons family met with the Loomises, the Callenders, and the Bextons in either their garage or the splitdeck gazebo in their backyard, depending on the weather. Both groups suffered snakebites over these weeks, but no one died. Neither faction attracted anyone new to its meetings except the occasional media reporter and GBI agents in scruffy but futile disguise.

Hoke attended the services of neither group. He had gone to hell in a disorienting feverdream, but the conflicts among the local Sixteeners, especially in the absence of Twyla, had tormented him a thousand times worse than either his snakebite or his resultant delirious trip to the sheol tucked away under Ferlin Rodale's tirehouse. Why attend services if a spirit of feud and persnicketiness held the real Spirit at bay? Hell had nothing on a holeful of serpents or an assembly of quarrelsome believers. Hoke would gladly risk eternal judgment if he could avoid the latter two kinds of snakes.

Aside from spiritual issues and Twyla's leavetaking, Hoke's biggest worry was putting money in his pockets. Ferlin forgave him rent shortfalls and overdue payments for the electric bill, but Hoke cringed to impose and even in his exile from Deaton's Bar-B-Q often ventured into Beulah Fork to prune shrubbery, cut grass, sweep parkinglots, or carry out groceries. Sometimes he went with Ferlin on roofing or carpentry jobs, earning his hire by toting shingles, bracing ladders, and sorting nails into the pockets of canvas aprons.

In December, Colby Deaton rehired him to bus tables, wash dishes, and run errands, and Hoke stayed with this job—despite the ragging of halfwit good ol boys like Albert Becknell—until early March, when he quit to begin a new line of work, catching and selling poisonous snakes.

A Japanese tuliptree had flowered in the wilderness among dogwoods and redbuds still under winter's spell. Hoke stopped with his crokersack to marvel at it. The tuliptree had set out its pink blossoms on whitespotted grey limbs altogether bare of leaves. These flowers danced like ballerinas against the naked boughs. Another coldsnap, no matter how brief, would kill the flowers; a violent rainstorm would knock them to the leafmulch, and no one would ever guess that they had bloomed.

At the base of an uglier tree nearby—Hoke took it for a blighted elm—a timberrattler slithered languidly up into the day from a hole down among the tree's roots. Hoke had come for just this event, the emergence of a congregation of snakes from their hibernating place. Because it was still early, he could expect more snakes to follow this one to the surface. Dens in which to pass safely an entire winter commanded allegiance, and snakes that had successfully hibernated returned to them fall after fall. Many serpents slept coiled together in the same den, moccasins with cottonmouths, diamondbacks with canebrakes, an immobile scrum of pitvipers in coldblooded wintersleep. And this first rattler, Hoke knew, signaled like a robin the coming of even more of its kind.

In his lowcut tennis shoes he crept up to the elm, seized the canebrake behind its head, and quickly bagged it. Then he crouched and waited. This strategy brought results. In an hour, with the latewinter sun steadily climbing to the south, he caught four more snakes, bagging them as efficiently as he had the first.

Even this small early haul promised a decent payoff. He could get ten dollars a snake from some of the Sixteeners and possibly as much as fifty if he captured a rattler longer than six feet. Snakes died over the winter, or escaped, or emerged from their crates bent like fishhooks from clumsy handling. Conscientious handlers would replace and retire their injured snakes. That turnover meant a career of sorts, if Ferlin would allow him to breed members of like species inside or near the tirehouse. And Sam Loomis had told Hoke of a research center in Atlanta that bought pitvipers for their venom, yet another likely customer and income source.

Hoke caught three more emerging snakes, and then there was a lull. Well, fine. All work and no lolligagging made Hoke a dull dude. His gaze wandered to the tuliptree again and to the pink chalicelike blossoms fluttering in it—pretty, so pretty. Then Hoke started. A human figure sat in an upper crook of the tuliptree, balanced there as shakily as an egg on an upended coffeecup. The figure shifted, and Hoke recognized her as his dead mama, Jillrae Evans Pilcher. He stood up.

Good to see you again, Hoke.

You too, Hoke told his mama. He meant it.

What day is it, honey?

Sunday, he said.

Well. You orter have yore tail over to the Sermonses then, shouldn't you?

Hoke explained about Rathcor and Carnes and Judas and the schism that had come to the Mark Sixteeners in the aftermath of the fire at the former Snake-O-Rama. He explained why he would never encounter the Holy Spirit among either of the church's contending factions and how attending the services of one or the other turned him into an angry uptight nitpicker, a heathen nearlybout. God, he said, would more likely happen to him here in the woods.

My me, said Jillrae Pilcher. The classic copout.

Mama, I cain't do everthin the same blest way you would.

Look quick, she said. They's more comin.

Hoke looked. A halfdozen pitvipers had boiled up through the tunnel from their den. They burst forth into the dappled noon in a slithery tangle. Hoke chuckled to see them, but made no sudden grab to catch one. He glanced back at the tuliptree, his awkwardly perched mama, and the pink blossoms stark against the reawakening woods. His mama faded a little, but because he held his glance, the pink grew lovelier, the sunlight crisper, and the separate trees beyond the tuliptree both more distinct and more mysterious, a pleasant contradiction. Then a snake raced over Hoke's instep. He had no need to look away from the tuliptree at the escaping serpents because their touch told him nearly everything and the woods into which he continued to peer told him the rest.

What is it? said his mama, clinging to the forking branches over her head.

Hoke smiled and blew her a kiss.

The woods behind the tuliptree filled with a haze like a cottony pollen, and this haze drifted through the dogwoods, redbuds, and conifer pillars until it hung from every limb of every tree within a hundredfoot radius of Hoke's dying elm. The awakening snakes boiled out into the haze. Hoke knelt and picked up pitviper after pitviper, two or three to each hand. Standing again, he handled them in the enabling white currents of the drifting pollen grains. His mama, looking on, faded toward invisibility. Hoke lifted a handful of serpents to her in heartfelt farewell. The woods rang with a shout, his own, and the haze pivoting around Hoke's blight elm either drifted or burned away.

Ferlin burst into the clearing.

My God, he said. Way you uz yellin, I figgered somebody'd done kilt you.

No, said Hoke, bagging the snakes in his hands. I'm just out here laudin God.

Alone? said Ferlin, closing the distance between them.

Only takes two or three, said Hoke.

Not countin them divilish snakes there, who's yore second, Pilcher?

Hoke gestured at the tuliptree, realizing as he did that Ferlin was unlikely to have seen his mama stranded amid its blazing pink flowers. He set his crokersack down and dropped a friendly arm over Ferlin's shoulder.

How bout you? he said.

[Author's note: I owe a significant debt to Dennis Covington's *Salvation on Sand Mountain: Snake Handling and Redemption in Southern Appalachia* for much of the background of this story. Charles McGlocklin, the End-Time Evangelist, whom I quote three times from Covington's book, is a real person, but all the other characters and situations are imaginary; resemblances to real human beings, living or dead, or to actual situations in the histories of real snakehandling congregations are entirely coincidental.]

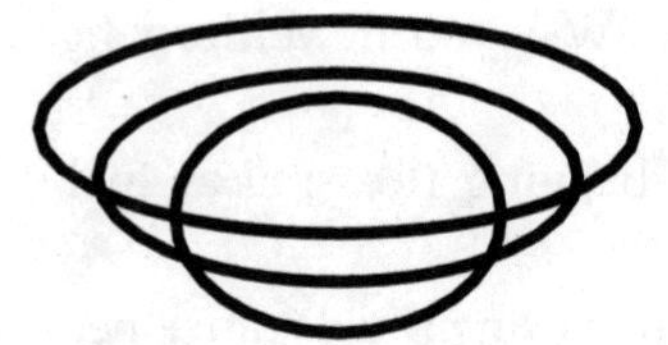

DANTE'S

EDITORS

PETER CROWTHER

Editor of the World Fantasy Award-nominated *Narrow Houses* anthology series for Little, Brown UK, Peter is co-editor of *Heaven Sent* from DAW Books, and *Tombs* from White Wolf. His short stories, articles and reviews appear regularly on both sides of the Atlantic, and the novel *Escardy Gap*, written in collaboration with James Lovegrove, is forthcoming from Tor Books. Peter lives in Harrogate, England with his wife and two sons.

EDWARD E. KRAMER

Ed is a writer and co-editor of *Grails*, nominated for the World Fantasy Award for Best Anthology, *Elric: Tales of the White Wolf*, *Tombs*, the *Dark Destiny* anthology series, and many additional works. His original fiction appears in a number of anthologies as well. Ed's first novel, *Killing Time*, is forthcoming from White Wolf. A graduate of the Emory University School of Medicine, Ed is a clinical and educational consultant in Atlanta.

CONTRIBUTING AUTHORS

James O'Barr created his character *The Crow* in the early '80s as a response to a personal tragedy. A self-taught artist, James credits his distinctive visual style to his study of classical Renaissance sculpture, '40s film noir, and two years of medical school. He lives in Detroit with his wife, Mary, and three cats. He is working on a new graphic novel for Dark Horse Comics entitled *Gothik*, which has been optioned by Jeff Most, one of *The Crow*'s producers; this project has been described as "a car crash between *Bladerunner*, *The Wizard of Oz*, and *Dracula*." He is also the lyricist for Trust Obey, recently signed to Trent Reznor's new label, Nothing Records.

Gene Wolfe has written mainstream and young-adult novels and many magazine articles, but is best known as a science fiction writer, picking up the Nebula Award (for his novella "The Death of Doctor Island"), the Chicago Foundation for Literature Award (for his novel *Peace*) and the Rhysling Award for SF Poetry (for "The Computer Iterates the Greater Trumps") along the way. His most recent full length works, and particularly his exemplary *The Book of the New Sun* series, fall into an entirely different category, merging high technology with an almost Dark Ages environment. Meanwhile, his short fiction continues to prove you never know just what to expect from him.

Harlan Ellison's writing career has spanned over forty years. He has won more awards for his sixty-four books, 1700-plus stories, essays, articles and newspaper columns, two dozen teleplays, and dozen motion pictures than any other living fantasist. He has won the Mystery Writers of America Edgar Allan Poe award twice, the Horror Writers of America Bram Stoker Award and the Nebula Award three times each, the Hugo eight and a half times and received the Silver Pen for Journalism from PEN. Harlan has served as conceptual consultant on the revival of the series *The Twilight Zone* and presently serves as creative consultant for *Babylon 5*. Last year, he was presented with the World Fantasy Lifetime Achievement award and was included in the annual *Best American Short Stories* volume.

Douglas Clegg lives in southern California with his spouse, a black cat, and a border collie mongrel. He was born in Virginia, graduated from Washington & Lee University with a degree in English Lit., and lived throughout the world before settling on the West Coast where he can experience riots, rebellions, earthquakes, fires and flood first-hand. His most recent novel is *Dark of the Eye*. Forthcoming is *The Children's Hour,* to be published by Dell in mid-October 1995. His short fiction appears in various anthologies and magazines, including *Love in Vein, Little Deaths* and *Phobias 2*. In addition to his horror novels, he also writes suspense fiction and contributes time and energy to the AIDS Service Center of Pasadena.

Max Allan Collins is a two-time winner of the "Shamus" Best Novel Award for his historical thrillers *True Detectives* (1983) and *Stolen Away* (1991), both featuring Chicago P.I. Nate Heller. His most recent Heller novel is *Blood and Thunder* (1995). Collins is the author of four other mystery series (Nolan, Quarry, Mallory, and real-life untouchable Eliot Ness) and is one of the top writers of movie tie-in novels (*In the Line of Fire, Maverick, Waterworld*). He scripted the *Dick Tracy* comic strip 1977-1993, and his comic-book credits include *Batman*, his own Ms. *Tree*, and *Mike Danger*, the latter created for Tekno-comix with legendary best-selling mystery writer Mickey Spillane. Max recently completed a screenplay based on "A Wreath for Marley" entitled "Blue Christmas."

Darrell Schweitzer is the editor of *Worlds of Fantasy & Horror* (formerly *Weird Tales*), for which he and George Scithers shared a World Fantasy Award in 1992. He has published about two hundred stories, three story collections and two novels, *The White Isle* and *The Shattered Goddess*. Darrell has also written a lot of nonfiction, reviews, criticism, interviews, and columns. His most recent work is a third novel, *The Mask of the Sorcerer*, published by New English Library. His straight scholarship includes *Lord Dunsany: A Bibliography*, a collaboration with S.T. Joshi.

Ian Watson taught literature in Tanzania and Japan, and futures studies in Birmingham, England, before becoming a full-time writer twenty years ago. He has written over twenty novels of SF, fantasy and horror, most recently the science-fantasy epic *Books of Mana (Lucky's Harvest & The Fallen Moon)* inspired by Finnish mythology. His eighth story collection, *The Coming of Vertumnus*, recently appeared in England, where he lives in a tiny village in the "empty quarter" of Northamptonshire.

Nancy Holder's horror novels include *Making Love* and *Witch-Light* collaborations with Melanie Tem, and *Dead in the Water*, her first solo horror novel. She has also written over fifteen romance and mainstream novels, sixty short stories, and received four Bram Stoker Awards. Nancy's credits also include game fiction, comic books and television commercials.

Brian Herbert is best known for his science fiction novels, including *Sidney's Comet; The Garbage Chronicles; Sudanna, Sudanna; Man of Two Worlds* (written with Frank Herbert); *Prisoners of Arionn* and *The Race for God*. Brian has also published two humor books and has edited three books. Recently Brian has collaborated with his cousin Marie Landis to write the novel *Memorymakers*.

Marie Landis has won numerous literary awards for her science fiction and dark-fantasy stories, including the Amelia Award. She began writing as a news reporter and columnist. Brian and Marie's latest co-authored works include the short stories "The Bone Woman," "The Contract," "Dropoff" and "Blood Month," as well as their dark fantasy novel, *Blood on the Sun*.

James S. Dorr's poetry and fiction have appeared in the previous White Wolf anthologies *Dark Destiny*, *Elric*, *Truth Until Paradox* and *City of Darkness: Unseen*, as well as a number of other publications spanning horror, fantasy, mystery and SF. He also plays Renaissance music with a semi-professional recorder consort and has a large, male Himalayan cat that sometimes answers to the name Fang.

Rick Hautala is the author of eleven novels, including *Twilight Time*, *Ghost Light*, *Cold Whisper* and *Winter Wake*. He has had more than thirty stories published in such antologies as *Stalkers*, *Shock Rock 2*, *Narrow Houses*, *The Ultimate Zombie* and *Nite Visions 9*. He lives in southern Maine with his wife and three children.

Brian Lumley was born on England's northeast coast but currently lives in the southwest in Torquay (of *Fawlty Towers* fame), in Devon. A soldier in the British army for twenty-two years, he first started to write macabre stories while stationed in Berlin. His first books were published in the early '70s by Arkham House and DAW, and upon leaving the army twelve years ago he took up writing full-time. He is the author of more than thirty books, including the *Titus Crow* series, the *Psychomech* trilogy, and the best-selling five-volume *Necroscope* series.

Sean Doolittle lives in Lincoln, Nebraska with his wife, Jessica. His work has appeared, or is forthcoming, in anthologies such as *The Year's Best Horror Stories XXII*, *Northern Frights 2* and *3*, *Young Blood*, and *Darkside: Fiction for the Last Millennium*, as well as in magazines such as *Cavalier*, *Palace Corbie*, *Deathrealm*, and *Kinesis*. He is currently at work on his first novel. Entitled *Holy Man*, it involves lost identity, guns and reservation gambling.

Wayne Allen Sallee lives in Chicago, Illinois. His short stories have appeared in the last ten consecutive volumes of *The Year's Best Horror Stories*, and he is currently the writer for the comic *Dream Wolves*, published by Draemenon Studios. In the coming months, TAL Publications will release his chapbook *Frankenstein 1979*, and the long-awaited short story collection *With Wounds Still Wet* will be published by Silver Salamander Press.

Jody Lynn Nye's first published fiction appeared in a mystery role-play game. She wrote the *Dragonlover's Guide to Pern*, co-authored the *Visual Guide to Xanth*, and collaborated on four novels with Anne McCaffrey, including *The Ship Who Won*. She has also written numerous short stories and seven other fantasy ans SF novels, such as *The Magic Touch* (Warner Aspect) and *The Ship Errant* (Baen Books), both due out in 1996. She lives near Chicago with her husband, Bill Fawcett, and two cats.

Ian McDonald found his literary feet with his first novel, the masterful *Desolation Road*, and then went on to even greater things with a fascinating three-part novel of the world of Faery (*King of Morning, Queen of Day*) and *Necroville*. He lives Belfast, Northern Ireland, with his wife, Trish, in a house built in the gardens of the home where C.S. Lewis grew up.

Gary Gygax has written over a dozen novels and many short stories and is one of the gaming world's most influential figures. Born in Chicago in 1938, he was playing chess at age six and with miniatures by age fifteen. He is the founder of TSR, Inc., co-creator of *Dungeons & Dragons*, and has helped develop nine additional game systems as well. His interests include game-play, reading, travel, bird-watching, fishing, walking, and pyrotechnics.

Rick R. Reed acts as an agent for several Chicago underground bands when not chained behind his typewriter. Currently he is on tour with the Tactile Sluts, known for their grunge arrangements of Billie Holiday standards. He is the author of the Dell Abyss novels *Obsessed* and *Penance* and the story "Tool of Enslavement" which appeared in White Wolf's *Dark Destiny*.

Ray Garton is the author of numerous short stories and novellas as well as twenty-two books, including the upcoming short story collection, *Pieces of Hate*, coming from CD Publications in the fall of 1995, and *Biofire* and another novel tentatively titled *Shackled Innocence* will be coming from Bantam Books in 1996. He lives with his wife in northern California and is currently at work on his next novel.

Alexandra Elizabeth Honigsberg's works appear in *I, Vampire, II*, the first two *Dark Destiny* anthologies, *Angels of Darkness*, *Blood Muse*, *New Altars* and *Sorceries: Magicks Old & New*, as well as *Penthouse* magazine. A violist/conductor, counselor, and religious scholar, she works with author/musician David M. Honigsberg; they live with two cats in Upper Manhattan, land of forests, fjords, and the Unicorn Tapestries.

Robert J. Sawyer is the author of six science fiction novels: *The Terminal Experiment*, *End of an Era*, and *Golden Fleece*, plus the Quintaglio trilogy (*Far-Seer*, *Fossil Hunter*, and *Foreigner*). His work has appeared in *Analog*, *Amazing Stories* and many anthologies. He lives in Toronto, Canada.

Steve Rasnic Tem has published over two hundred short stories to date in such publications as Robert Bloch's *Psycho Paths*, *Isaac Asimov's SF Magazine*, *Year's Best Fantasy & Horror*, *Metahorror*, *The Ultimate Dracula*, *Cutting Edge*, *Best New Horror*, *Love in Vein*, *It Came From The Drive-In*, *Sisters of the Night*, *Tales of the Great Turtle*, *Forbidden Acts* and *Xanadu 3*. He's been nominated for the Bram Stoker Award, the World Fantasy Award, and the Philip K. Dick Award, and is a past winner of the British Fantasy Award. In 1995 he edited *High Fantastic*, an anthology of Colorado fantasy, dark fantasy, and science fiction for Ocean View Books.

James Lovegrove is the author of the novel, *The Hope*, and several short stories. He is currently working on a musical and graphic novel (with artist Adam Brockbank). James has collaborated with Peter Crowther on several short stories plus *Escardy Gap*, a twisted, Bradburyesque study in Ameri-arcana.

Doug Murray began writing at age thirteen for movie-oriented magazines like *Famous Monsters of Filmland*, *The Monster Times*, and *Media Times*. In the mid-eighties, he graduated to comic books as the creator and primary writer on Marvel's *The 'Nam*. Doug has also worked for Comico, DC and Eternity. His short stories appear in numerous anthologies. His forthcoming novel, *Blood Relations*, will be published by White Wolf in 1995.

Storm Constantine is the author of the Wraeththu trilogy, and her more recent books include *Burying the Shadow* and *Calenture*. She has just switched publishers to Penguin and is writing a dark fantasy series of books centered on the legends of the fallen angels, the Grigori. Her own vision of Hell is of course populated by the most seductive of these dark denizens. She lives in the Midlands of England with her husband and eight cats.

Brian Aldiss regaled readers of the innovative British science fiction magazine *New Worlds* with a different slant on writing... a slant which demonstrated a new strength in the field. He has published at least one book every year for forty years. Brian has repeatedly returned to mainstream fiction, embracing the contemporary and the classical with the same consummate ease he displays when dealing with the far reaches of space. His story for this volume, while neither SF nor mainstream (though it could be construed as a perfect blend of the two), is yet another fine example of his story-telling abilities.

Richard Lee Byers worked for over a decade in an emergency psychiatric facility, then left the mental health field to become a writer. He is the author of the novels *On a Darkling Plain*, *Netherworld*, *Caravan of Shadows*, *Dark Fortune*, *Dead Time*, *The Vampire's Apprentice*, *Fright Line*, and *Deathward*, as well as the young-adult books *Joy Ride*, *Warlock Games*, and *Party Till You Drop*. His short fiction has appeared in numerous anthologies, including *Confederacy of the Dead*, *Dark Destiny*, *Fear Itself*, *Grails: Visitations of the Night*, *Freak Show*, *Superheroes*, and *The Ultimate Spider-Man*. He lives in the Tampa Bay area, the setting for much of his fiction.

Michael Bishop has never handled snakes, at least not advertently, and doesn't plan to take up the practice, or any toxic creature with or without scales, in this lifetime. He prefers mammals to either reptiles or amphibians, but would, he admits, rather listen to a chorus of tree frogs than to one of basset hounds or pit bulls. Nonetheless, he is currently at work on a novel about the U-2 spy-plane incident and a boy and his Labrador retriever. By the time this biographical note actually appears, he hopes to have moved on to an altogether new and different project, presumably not pitviper juggling. A story collection, *At the City Limits of Fate*, is forthcoming from Edgewood Press.

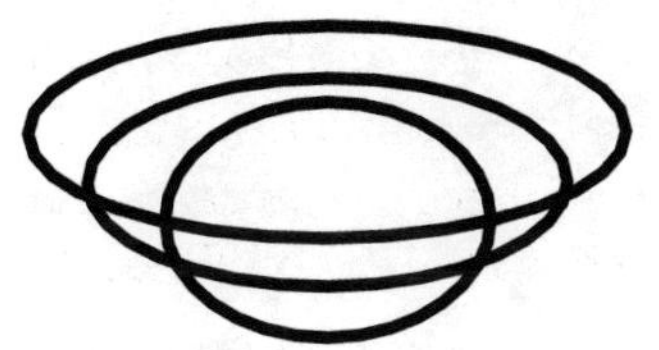

DISCIPLES